I0658662

WINDS OF NIGHTSONG

Borgo Press Books by VICTOR J. BANIS

The Astral: Till the Day I Die * *Avalon: An Historical Novel* * *The C.A.M.P. Cookbook* * *The C.A.M.P. Guide to Astrology* * *Charms, Spells, and Curses for the Millions* * *Color Him Gay: That Man from C.A.M.P.* * *The Curse of Bloodstone: A Gothic Novel of Terror* * *Darkwater: A Gothic Novel of Horror* * *The Daughters of Nightsong: An Historical Novel* (Nightsong Saga #2) * *The Devil's Dance: A Novel of Terror* * *Drag Thing; or, The Strange Tale of Jackle and Hyde* * *The Earth and All It Holds: An Historical Novel* * *A Family Affair: A Novel of Terror* * *Fatal Flowers: A Novel of Horror* * *Fire on the Moon: A Novel of Terror* * *The Gay Dogs: That Man from C.A.M.P.* * *The Gay Haunt* * *The Glass House: A Novel of Terror* * *The Glass Painting: A Gothic Tale of Horror* * *Goodbye, My Lover* * *The Greek Boy* * *The Green Rolling Hills: Writings from West Virginia* (editor) * *Green Willows: A Novel of Terror* * *Kenny's Back* * *Life & Other Passing Moments: A Collection of Short Writings* * *The Lion's Gate: A Novel of Terror* * *Love's Pawn: A Novel of Romance* * *Lucifer's Daughter: A Novel of Horror* * *Moon Garden: A Novel of Terror* * *Nightsong: An Historical Novel* (Nightsong Saga #1) * *The Pot Thickens: Recipes from Writers and Editors* (editor) * *San Antone: An Historical Novel* * *The Scent of Heather: A Novel of Terror* * *The Second House: A Novel of Terror* * *The Second Tijuana Bible Reader* (editor) * *Shadows of Nightsong* (Nightsong Saga #4) * *The Sins of Nightsong: An Historical Novel* (Nightsong Saga #3) * *Spine Intact, Some Creases: Remembrances of a Paperback Writer* * *Stranger at the Door: A Novel of Suspense* * *Sweet Tormented Love: A Novel of Romance* * *The Sword and the Rose: An Historical Novel* * *This Splendid Earth: An Historical Novel* * *The Tijuana Bible Reader* (editor) * *Twisted Flames* * *The WATERCRESS File: That Man from C.A.M.P.* * *A Westward Love: An Historical Romance* * *White Jade: A Novel of Terror* * *The Why Not* * *Winds of Nightsong* (Nightsong Saga #5) * *The Wine of the Heart: A Novel of Romance* * *The Wolves of Craywood: A Novel of Terror*

WINDS OF NIGHTSONG

AN HISTORICAL NOVEL:
THE NIGHTSONG SAGA,
BOOK FIVE

V. J. BANIS

THE BORGO PRESS
MMXIII

WINDS OF NIGHTSONG

Copyright © 1985 by Ben All, Inc.
Originally published under the title, *Winds of Moonsong*.

FIRST BORGO PRESS EDITION

Published by Wildside Press LLC

www.wildsidebooks.com

DEDICATION

I am deeply indebted to my friend, Heather, for all the help she has given me in getting these early works of mine reissued.

And I am grateful as well to Rob Reginald, for all his assistance and support.

CONTENTS

CHAPTER ONE

San Francisco, California—1912

As full as her life had once been, Lydia now felt empty. She reached for her brandy glass and gazed at the amber liquid which had become her friend of late. The delicate etching in the bowl of the Waterford goblet glinted enticingly in the light from the fireplace. She knew she had been drinking far too much these past months; but since Peter's death, brandy seemed to deaden the pain—or did it intensify it?

"Lydia Nightsong," she sighed, resting her head against the back of the chair and swirling the brandy slowly, watching the colors melt and flow. "Nightsong...what a strange name." For a moment she couldn't remember how she'd come by the name. Of course it was no more strange than that of the overbearing Ima Hogg of San Francisco society, nor as insipid and frivolous as Ima's friend Charity Faire.

"Nightsong," she said again. "Oh yes." She closed her eyes and saw the simple little painting some Chinese artist, perhaps centuries ago, had painted on the wall of Peter MacNair's hut in that remote Chinese village. She saw it so clearly. There was a branch of a plum tree, in full blossom, and a bird on the branch singing to a golden crescent moon. Now, as so often before, she felt she had only to listen to hear the nightingale's song and catch the pale flowers' fragrant scent.

"So long ago," Lydia said. She took another sip of the brandy, remembering that night and the little bird singing to the moon, that night she'd so willingly given herself to Peter.

"Peter," she said to the near-empty brandy glass, and the tears came in a rush. Dead. They were all dead, as dead as her own life felt now.

Lydia turned her head when she heard the door to her sitting room open. "Who is it?" she snapped, annoyed by the intrusion.

"Mother? You really shouldn't be sitting here alone in the dark," her son said as he came over to her chair and gently laid a hand on her shoulder.

She shrugged it off. "I prefer to be alone, Leon."

"You're too much alone," he answered sharply. "You are not doing yourself or anyone else any good by locking yourself away and trying to crawl inside that damned brandy bottle. Good God, Mother, what would your tony friends say if they knew?"

"To the devil with those Nob Hill snobs. They never liked me anyway, nor I them. I was only accepted because of my wealth and influence." Angrily she drained the glass and reached for the bottle that sat on the table next to her chair.

Leon took the bottle out of her hand. "I think you've had quite enough."

She glared at him and grabbed it back. "Don't you dare dictate to me, young man."

He smiled. "Young man? Dear heavens, Mother. I'm thirty-eight-years old, which is hardly young."

Lydia splashed more brandy into her glass. "Thirty-eight," she sighed. "Have the years gone by as quickly as that? I feel I've lived two hundred years."

"Only fifty-eight," Leon answered with a grin. "And still an extremely beautiful woman. If you put your mind to it, you'd easily catch another husband."

Lydia sniffed. "I've had my share of those." She reached for his hand. "I have you, darling, and April and my grandchildren. That's enough to satisfy me." She turned her head. "Is April in her room?"

"Yes. She's asleep. I'm worried about her, Mother. Isn't there anything we can do? Perhaps one of those psychiatrists?"

"No," Lydia said firmly. "In her mind your sister is where she wants to be, back in her old world where she was once so happy."

"I was reading in the *Examiner* just the other day about a doctor in Vienna," Leon persisted. "Dr. Sigmund Freud. They say he's performing miracles with people like April, people whose minds have drifted away from reality."

"Reality? You call this reality?" his mother snapped, switching her long, bombazine skirt. "Flying machines and carriages without horses. Unsinkable ocean liners that sink, carrying fifteen hundred people to their graves. And that odious Sun Yat-sen destroying the Manchu dynasty—your dynasty, I might remind you. The world is crumbling around our ears. Better that April retreat to the time and place of her greatest happiness and kindly allow me the same privilege."

"This is 1912, Mother," Leon said patiently. "A time for moving forward, a time for progress."

"Progress? Progressing to what? Machines are taking over the world."

"Everything has its price, Mother, even progress," Leon said softly. "You can't just spend the rest of your life thinking of what was. And from everything you've told me, your past wasn't all that wonderful."

"True, true," Lydia answered with a deep sigh. "But that is when I was most content. It's what I know. I don't want a future. It would be too strange."

"Of course you want a future. It isn't right for you to drink yourself into an early grave. That's what you're doing, you realize?"

"It's my life."

"But what about us? What about your grandchildren and all the people who need you? What about April?"

"Poor April," she said, reflecting. "Forced to pose as my servant when we first came here because the Chinese were so hated and despised. You were fortunate, Leon. You inherited my features and could easily pass as an American, while poor April could never hide what she was—the half-breed daughter of a Manchu prince."

"Nor does she want to hide it even now. April still sees herself as heir to the Chinese throne. She speaks to me of nothing else but the day when we will return to Peking and make claim to our father's royal rights."

"And have your heads cut off by that maniacal Dr. Sun."

"Sun Yat-sen is a republican, not a tyrant like my ancestors."

Lydia chuckled. "Don't let April hear you say that or you will bring on another of her tantrums."

"I'm not proud of my father's heritage, only of yours, Mother."

She patted his hand. "You were always my favorite son, Leon."

"Not Marcus?" he asked, toying with her.

"Dear Marcus. I'm afraid he has too much of Peter MacNair's blood in him. As you know, much as I adored Peter MacNair, he was an overly ambitious and adventurous man. Peter was wild when he was Marcus's age, always taking what he wanted, doing what he wanted, never satisfied. Marcus is like that too."

"Marcus will turn out all right, Mother. He'll marry Amelia and give you dozens of grandchildren to fuss over."

"Perhaps, but I doubt that very much. Oh, I believe Marcus loves Amelia, but he has this racing-machine thing gnawing at him. He will never settle for a quiet life of marriage. That kind of existence is too tame for Marcus. He wants the things his father wanted—excitement, constant change, danger."

When he noticed she was becoming uncomfortable with thoughts of her son by Peter MacNair, Leon changed the subject. "What about Adam?" he asked. "Do you think April will ever get her son back?"

"Adam is Lord Clarendon now, or soon will be. No one in England knows of his true parents. And no one must ever know," she said, narrowing her eyes at him. "Adam seems happy with his life as an English lord; but then why shouldn't he? He never knew anything else. Yet, I think Adam might come back to us one day. When last we spoke, there was a strangeness in him that makes me believe he will never forget that he was born in China to a woman who is a true Manchu princess."

"Has he married that English girl to whom he was engaged?"

"Pamela? No," Lydia said, shaking her head. "In his last letter he said he was still unsure about marriage. He told Pamela the identity of his real mother and father, and she wants Adam to forget them. Poor little Adam, so grown up and yet so torn apart by his loyalties. The Clarendons gave him so much, and yet he now knows he is really not entitled to any of it."

"And Caroline? Is she still gadding about Europe trying to find happiness?"

"Still in Venice with some Italian count."

"I've often wondered why she didn't come back with you when you brought Peter home to be buried."

Lydia frowned. She could never reveal to anyone the reason for Caroline's unhappiness, how miserable and distraught the girl had been after learning that the young man she so desperately loved was in fact her own long-lost brother. Caroline had fled to Italy to try and erase her guilt and shame, but Lydia doubted that was possible.

"Caroline has to find herself," Lydia said simply, dismissing the sordid matter. "And she will...in time."

Leon tightened the pressure of his hand on her shoulder. "I think you should go to bed, Mother. It's past eleven. Shall I call Nellie?"

"No," Lydia said, rising unsteadily to her feet. "I can manage by myself. Don't bother Nellie."

As he helped his mother to her bedroom, she staggered. "Madam, I do believe you are quite inebriated," Leon chided.

"I'm drunk," Lydia admitted. "Inebriated is what proper Nob Hill dowagers become, and I have always been one to call a spade a spade. So I'm drunk, my dear boy, very, very drunk."

"You should be ashamed of yourself," he said with a laugh.

"Well, I'm not. It isn't the first time, you know. Peter and I did so enjoy our champagne...and each other," she added with a lewd wink.

"You're impossible. I always thought that by the time I grew up you'd be a sweet little white-haired lady who knitted constantly and made gingerbread cookies."

"I will never be anything but what I am: a tough old dame who enjoys a good belt every once in a while."

He helped her onto the side of her bed. "Your every once in a while is becoming a habit lately. You know that, of course."

"It's my only comfort, Leon. Please don't lecture me."

"It isn't your only comfort. You're letting Empress Cosmetics go down the drain and you don't even seem to care."

"I don't." She scowled at him. "And if my cosmetics empire is going down the drain, as you say, then you are the one to blame, Leon. You are, after all, in control now. I've left it all for you to run."

"You know I can't manage without your help, Mother. Oh, the company is doing all right, but not as well as it could. The people there need you at the top. They're used to your ways, not mine; and the wholesalers and distributors want to deal with you, not me."

"When I'm dead they'll have to deal with you, so they might as well get used to it now."

"You're not dead yet, nor will you be for a long time unless you kill that liver of yours."

"I'm tired, Leon. Get out of here and let me go to sleep."

He kissed her cheek and bade her good night. "Sleep well, Mother. And tomorrow I want to tell you about a new Nightsong scent I've been developing in the lab."

"There will be no more Nightsong," Lydia said adamantly.

He only grinned. "We'll talk about that tomorrow." He blew her another kiss and quickly left the room before she could say anything more.

Lydia lowered herself back against the pillows and put an arm across her eyes. She hoped, with all her heart, that this night would not be like all the others, filled with those unpleasant memories of her lost love, the nightmare in which Peter's body turned into a skeleton in his coffin. More than anything else she wanted to be in that coffin beside him, holding him in her arms as their bodies decayed together. She pictured the sandy brown hair that spilled carelessly over his forehead, the dark brown eyes that turned a smoldering black when he scowled.

She idly undid the pins that bound up her hair and let it fall in a luxuriant red-gold cascade about her face and shoulders. Gently she touched her fingertips to her cheeks, searching for the wrinkles she knew were there but everyone said she imagined.

"Still a beautiful woman," she remembered Leon saying. She supposed she was, but what did that matter? She had only wanted to be beautiful for Peter, no one else. All she wanted now, she admitted, was to sit here and feel sorry for herself, to wallow in self-pity. It was her right, and that was what she intended to do with the rest of her years.

Sleep came quickly and with it the same old terrible dreams: Lorna MacNair's thin, cruel lips sneered at her as she threw back her head and let out a demonic laugh that brought an agonizing cry from Lydia's mouth.

At last Lorna had what she'd always wanted...her husband safely entombed in a mausoleum where Lydia could never again take him away from her.

Suddenly, Lydia felt the bed, the entire room shaking violently. Lydia imagined the ceiling cracking above her head and the plaster and walls caving in on her.

"Earthquake," she screamed as she opened her eyes wide with terror and stared around her. The room was still. There was no sound except the voice of Nellie, no motion but the housekeeper's gentle shaking of her shoulder.

"You were dreaming again," Nellie said softly. "It's the brandy, Lydia. It makes your mind conjure up dreadful old things."

Lydia became aware of the bright sunlight pouring through the windows, giving the room a new, sparkling look. "Wh-what time is it?"

"Ten o'clock. And look at you. Still in the same clothes you wore last night. Here, let me brace you up. I've brought your coffee and toast. How do you feel?"

Lydia ran her hand across her forehead as if to wipe away the dull ache. "How should I feel?" she snapped. Despite her show of irritation, she couldn't help being thankful that her dreams were gone.

"Evelyn Clary's downstairs having breakfast. She said she will not leave the house until she's talked to you. It's important, she claims."

"Evelyn? Tell her I can't see her."

"She won't leave, Lydia. She made that perfectly plain. She has a briefcase with her, and whenever I see someone carrying a briefcase I know it means trouble."

"Tell Evelyn I will not see her."

"Yes, you will see her," Evelyn said as she came into the room, a black leather case tucked neatly under her arm. Evelyn Clary was not a particularly handsome woman. She had a tailored look about her that clearly proclaimed she was all business. "You've avoided me long enough, Lydia. Now I'm going to have my say and you are going to listen."

"Please go away," Lydia said with a wave of her hand.

"I'm not going anywhere," Evelyn answered as she pulled up a chair next to the bed and sat down. "A long time ago when you first started Empress Cosmetics, you saved me from the streets by giving me a job. You made me a rich and respectable woman, Lydia. I'm not going to sit by and let all we have both worked so hard for be taken away from us."

"No one's taking anything away, Evelyn. I'm sure you and Leon can handle whatever is happening at the office."

"Not this," Evelyn said, unsnapping the briefcase and pulling out a legal document with a blue backing. "A little present for you from Lorna MacNair." She handed the paper to Lydia.

"What does that damned woman want from me now?"

"Everything," Evelyn said. She took a piece of Lydia's toast and began munching it as Lydia scanned the document. "Read."

Lydia saw the worried look that Evelyn was trying to hide. Slowly she read the legal print. As she scanned the sentences she found her fingers tightening on the page. "What in hell?" she breathed.

"As I said, that bitch has decided she wants everything you have."

"Impossible! Lorna is out of her mind."

Evelyn shook her head and leaned forward. "I've checked with our lawyers, of course. She has a case, Lydia." Evelyn's eyes darkened. "Remember when Peter died and left his cosmetics enterprises to you? MacNair Products wasn't much competition for our company, but it's always put out a less expensive line of perfumes and cosmetics and the market for the cheaper stuff is very good these days."

"And now Lorna wants it back."

"Not only MacNair Products, honey. Lorna wants everything. Unfortunately, when you consolidated MacNair Products into Empress Cosmetics you made it one total entity. Lorna obviously figured you would do that—consolidate the two companies—and she just sat like a fat spider waiting for her chance. Now, as you can see by that notification, Lorna has decided to contest her husband's will. If she succeeds in convincing the courts that MacNair Products rightfully belongs to Peter's legal heirs—his wife and children—she will take it away from you. But MacNair Products doesn't exist as such anymore; it's now Empress Cosmetics. So you see, unless you fight it, Lorna will get everything and you and I and your family will be back to square one without the proverbial pot, my dear."

Lydia looked dazed. "Can she do that?"

"She sure as hell is going to try," Evelyn said, pointing to the legal paper.

"Dear God. I just thought of something," Lydia gasped.

"What?"

Lydia thought back. "Do you recall when I first hired you, Evelyn?"

"Sure. You'd met that awful Walter Hanover when you and

April first came here with the dowager empress's personal scent. Walter said it could be duplicated and promised to supply the money to set up Empress Cosmetics."

"And then he skipped out, leaving us with a pile of debts and very little future."

"But we managed to survive rather nicely without Walter," Evelyn said proudly.

Lydia shook her head. "Walter had me sign a paper when we started the company. It was to be a fifty-fifty proposition, which was exactly what I wanted. I had no intention of being beholden to Walter, if you know what I mean."

Evelyn knew. Walter had wanted to bed Lydia and obviously he had, because he wasn't the type of man who gave anything without getting something in return. She nodded.

"Years after Walter skipped out and you and I made a success of our company, he showed up again and laid claim to his fifty percent share. Peter MacNair bought that fifty percent from Walter for an exorbitant price."

"So?"

Lydia ran her hand across her eyes. "Oh, Evelyn, I'd forgotten all about that paper until just now."

"What about it? When Peter died and left you everything in his will, his fifty percent interest in Empress Cosmetics automatically became yours."

"Not exactly," Lydia said hesitantly. "You know how I was after Peter died? I didn't care about much of anything and I wasn't interested in the company. I'd forgotten all about that paper giving Peter half of everything I owned. Fool that I am, I'd never thought to have Peter reassign that half back to me before he died. That claim was in Peter's safe in his private study. I never got it. Lorna obviously found it. All that was mentioned in Peter's will was his bequest to me of MacNair Products. There was no mention of his half interest in Empress Cosmetics. According to the will, the MacNair company went to me and all the other rights and assets in his estate went to Lorna. So Lorna MacNair actually inherited that percentage in our company, Evelyn."

"God in heaven," Evelyn breathed. "That means that in addition to suing for ownership of MacNair Products, Lorna can still claim half of our enterprises."

"And I'm sure she won't settle for just half, my dear. But by God, she isn't going to get anything," Lydia swore, throwing back the coverlet. "I'm getting dressed now, and then you and I are going to pay a visit to our attorneys. That bitch will regret picking a fight with me."

Evelyn clapped her hands. "That's my girl. Welcome back to the living, kiddo."

CHAPTER TWO

Italy was beginning to settle down after the year-long war with the Turks over the rights of Italians in the Turkish colony of Libya in North Africa. Though Libya and the Dodecanese Islands were again under Italian control, there was brewing unrest in the northern parts of Europe. The Balkan Wars had started, the Balkan countries fighting each other for more territory. There were constant rivalries over trade and commerce, everyone battling to control the raw materials, competing for new food sources and new regions to colonize. The German navy was threatening British supremacy on the high seas, and the Russians were hoping to dominate all of the Balkans.

The city of Venice was a fantasy place where Caroline Nightsong tried to forget her unhappiness as she travelled the canals that took the place of streets, visited the museums, churches, and palaces. The city seemed far removed from all turmoil. This peaceful serenity was what kept Carolina rooted to the place. She wanted to think of herself as a woman alone in an enchanted land where the sordidness of her past did not exist. Though only twenty-four and extremely beautiful, she didn't feel beautiful. She always wore her thick black hair as plainly as possible, hid her sparkling green eyes and flawless complexion behind broad-brimmed hats.

Part of her wanted desperately to go back to Nob Hill. But a larger part of her shivered at the thought of returning to the home of her grandmother, who'd only serve as a constant reminder of everything Caroline wanted to forget. Caroline still found it almost impossible to believe that Adam Clarendon was her brother. How could she have had sex with him and not have felt some intuitive warning of their blood-relatedness? He wasn't a full brother, only a half-brother, according to her grandmother. Still, it terrified her to recall the sexual pleasure she'd experienced in the arms of a man forbidden her.

"Dear God, I still love him," Caroline cried aloud, feeling the sting of tears at the back of her eyes. He was several years younger than she, but that didn't matter. He was so sophisticated, so British, with his charming accent and courtly manners. She was sure he loved her as desperately as she loved him. He had to love her.... He had to, she kept telling herself.

She cried into her hands and then began shaking her head. "No, this is madness." She would have to put Adam out of her mind, forget she'd ever even met him.

Of course she'd been telling herself that every day since running away from him that afternoon in London. She still insisted to herself that there was no actual proof that he was Adam MacNair and not the son of Lord and Lady Clarendon. But deep down, she knew the truth.

As Caroline stood on the balcony of the Palicio D'Oro looking through her tears at the bobbing gondolas, she thought she might have made a mistake coming to Venice, land of beauty and romance. A gondolier with his straw hat and fluttering red ribbon was crooning softly to a couple wrapped in each other's arms, oblivious of Caroline standing there, crying softly. The sky was the color of a robin's egg, with clouds as wispy and white as fluttering feathers. It was a clear, perfect day, a day she should be spending happily out-of-doors instead of moping here in her room, wishing for the impossible.

She pushed herself away from the balustrade and went into the sitting room with its high, ornate ceiling and heavy Italian Renaissance furnishings. She'd go into Saint Mark's Square and have some lunch at a little cafe, she decided. The square was one of her favorite spots in Venice, a place where she could sit, almost unnoticed, sipping an aperitif as she watched the constantly changing parade.

She put on a blue dress and wide, floppy hat. Her hair she knotted tightly in a bun at the back of her neck. The mirror told her she looked the way she wanted to look, like a woman alone who wanted to be left alone.

The sun was warm but not hot on her back as she turned along the canal, crossed one of the stone bridges with its wrought-iron railing, and headed toward the square. She'd been warned of the canals' odious smell during the hot summer days, but she noticed nothing objectionable. But then, she thought with a sigh, so many people constantly found fault with perfection. And Venice, to her, was the perfect city.

As always, the moment she stepped into the square something propelled her to its very center. There she stood gazing up at the giant arches, the elaborate carvings, the vaulted windows, the gilt and rich colors, all fused together in one magnificent tapestry so breathtakingly beautiful one could only stare in disbelief. Pigeons fluttered, circling and recircling before alighting as one white mass.

She saw Count Cambruzio sitting alone at one of the small tables under an orange-and-white awning. He was engrossed in his newspaper and didn't look up as she walked toward him. Caroline hesitated, wondering for a moment whether she wanted the company of this handsome young man or would rather sit alone and think about Adam.

Adam is lost to you, a voice inside her chided. She stepped forward and spoke the count's name. "Tonio."

He got to his feet immediately, a brilliant smile showing perfect white teeth. His hair was black and slicked back from his forehead; his eyes were the color of polished onyx.

"How nice to see you," she said, extending her hand.

He bowed over it, touching it with his lips. "My dear Caroline, this is a wonderful surprise meeting you like this."

"I know I should be back at the hotel catching up on my correspondence, but the day was too lovely to waste indoors."

"You did not return my call last evening," he said, sounding hurt.

"I met some American friends who invited me to the opera. I didn't get your message until I'd returned to the hotel and then it was much too late to call you."

"And this morning?"

"I slept late. I was going to call later today."

He shrugged. "It wasn't of any great importance, only that I would have liked to have had dinner with you again." He reached for her hand. "I am afraid I am becoming much too fond of you, Caroline."

Caroline laughed softly and tactfully took back her hand, motioning with it to a passing waiter. "Cinzano, per favore."

"Signore?" the waiter asked Tonio.

"Due," he said curtly, annoyed at the man's failure to address him by his royal title.

Tonio leaned across to her. "And did you enjoy the opera with your American friends?"

"Yes, very much, though Otello is not one of my favorites, I'm afraid."

"Your friends...they didn't, er...make you homesick for your San Francisco?"

Caroline laughed. "No, I have no plans to return to the States for quite some time, Tonio, if that is what you're asking."

He smiled broadly. "Good." He took her hand again, rubbing his finger suggestively over the palm. "You will have dinner with me this evening, yes?"

"If you like."

"I would like very much. There is something I want to ask you."

"Oh?"

He looked around. "It is not a question a man asks of a woman in a public place like this. There must be flowers and music and soft candlelight and wine."

Caroline felt a slight tingling sensation as she withdrew her hand. "Ah, you romantic Italians," she sighed. "I trust your question will not be an indelicate one, Signore," she said with an impish smile and a raised eyebrow.

He continued to smile. "And if it were, would that frighten you away from me?"

Caroline cocked her head as her wineglass was set before her. When the waiter left, she looked him straight in the eye. "No. I'm not easily shocked or frightened, Count Cambruzio."

"Good." He saluted her with his glass. "Wear your most provocative gown. We will go somewhere very smart, and afterward...."

"Afterward?"

"Ah, that you will have to wait and see."

Caroline gave him an encouraging smile.

She had known Count Cambruzio for several months and had seen quite a lot of him during that time. Each month she stayed on in Venice she kept telling herself that she should leave, but Tonio Cambruzio was excellent company and helped her forget Adam. Tonio had not yet tried to take her to bed, and she wondered about that. Italian men, she'd found, were an impetuous lot and not a bit shy about propositioning a lady.

He certainly wasn't homosexual. She knew this merely from the way he looked at her. There was a hunger in his eyes that was unmistakable. Yet, there was something not quite right about him. Behind those dark, smoldering eyes lurked a mystery. Perhaps he was married. That was a distinct possibility, although he'd never mentioned a wife or family in all the times they'd been together.

Now he glanced at his pocket watch. "Forgive me, Caroline, but I have a rather pressing appointment. Had I known I would run into you I would have cancelled it."

"That's all right, Tonio. I have some things I must do. I'll see you this evening."

He kissed her hand. "I will call for you at eight o'clock. I look forward to it with such pleasure." There was that sexual glint in his eyes again, she noticed. If he planned to invite her into his bed, she wouldn't disappoint him, Caroline told herself. She hadn't had a man since Adam, and Adam had been her first.

Now she wanted as many men as it would take to erase him from her mind and heart.

And that might take a great many, she reminded herself as she watched Tonio saunter across the square, one hand thrust deep into his pants pocket, his hat slanted jauntily down over one eye. She liked the way he moved, so masculine and self-assured. She was already looking forward to the evening.

Caroline took a long time finishing her Cinzano. There was no need for her to rush anywhere. She thought of doing the shops, but she had done them all and had little interest in buying anything new. Her trunks were full as it was, which accounted for at least part of her reluctance to leave Venice. The chore of packing everything seemed too bothersome.

She motioned for the bill.

Perhaps she would stop at the goldsmith's and buy that bracelet she'd been admiring. It was expensive, but then money was never a problem. Her grandmother saw to that.

She wasn't paying much attention to anything when she turned down one of the side streets that bordered a narrow canal. There weren't many people about and she quickened her step, wanting to reach the shop before it closed for the afternoon siesta.

"Look out!" a woman yelled as Caroline felt herself being roughly shoved into a doorway. A second later a large slab of masonry crashed down on the very spot where Caroline had been walking.

"Good God," Caroline breathed, looking at the shattered stone. "Where did that come from?"

The woman who'd shoved her was about her own age, no more than twenty-four, with wide serious eyes hiding behind horn-rimmed glasses. "Damn," she swore. "You could have been killed."

Caroline put her hand over her heart to still its pounding. "Thanks to you I wasn't," she said, leaning back against the heavy door as she tried to catch her breath.

The young woman peered upward, scanning the building for

signs of further danger. "It wasn't a part of the cornice," she said, noting that the ornate edging of the building was completely intact. "It must have rolled off the roof, but I don't see how, unless someone pushed it over."

Caroline was still trembling.

To her surprise the woman laughed. "Someone isn't out to kill you, are they?" Her accent was strictly New York, and there was a hardness in her tone that told Caroline the woman was no stranger to danger.

"Kill me?" Caroline gasped. "Good heavens, no. I'm just an American tourist without an enemy in the world."

The woman put out her hand. "I'm Alice Pendergast."

"Caroline Nightsong."

"The San Francisco Nightsongs?"

"Yes. Do you know my family?"

Alice chuckled. "Everyone who reads a newspaper knows the famous Nightsongs."

Caroline looked hurt.

"I'm sorry," Alice said. "I work for a New York paper. Fashions mostly, but I take an interest in anything newsworthy." She stepped out of the doorway and inspected the top of the building again. "I think it looks safe enough. Isn't it odd that no one came out to see what the crash was?"

Caroline let herself be led away. "I can't begin to thank you enough for shoving me into that doorway."

"Forget it, Caroline." She laughed again. "Everyone says I'm the pushy type."

Caroline groaned at the pun. "A newspaper reporter. Sounds exciting."

"As I said, I mostly cover fashions. The newspaper business is still in the Dark Ages when it comes to letting women reporters cover anything but food and clothing. Still, I do a lot of digging on my own and turn the material in to the editor who usually prints it under his own byline. Someday we women will be liberated from this male-oriented world."

"I'm not sure I want to be liberated. It's rather safe to be a woman."

"Safe? You mean like back there when someone tried to knock you on the head with a slab of concrete?"

"I'm certain it was an accident."

Alice shrugged. "I don't believe in accidents like that."

"Please, Alice, let's not talk about it. You'll have me believing that someone really did try to do me in, as they say in the mystery thrillers."

"Sorry. Don't listen to me. I'm always turning everything into a melodrama. I see sinister things everywhere." She frowned. "Still, I would like to know how that piece of masonry found its way from the roof to the cobblestones."

"I'm sure it wasn't intended for me."

"Yes, I'm sure it wasn't," Alice said, trying to sound reassuring. She tugged at Caroline's arm. "Come on, let's go over to Luigi's for a stiff one."

"Luigi's? We can't. They won't let two unescorted ladies in."

"Stick with me, kiddo. I know every back door in Venice. Come on."

Caroline found Alice Pendergast delightful company. She was free and open and said whatever was on her mind. She was pretty enough under her veneer of hardness, which Caroline decided was deliberately applied. Her hair was a soft blonde, her eyes—behind the glasses—were deep, deep blue. She wore no makeup, and her clothes were almost mannish.

"You're April Nightsong's daughter?" Alice said as they settled themselves in Luigi's at a small table separated from the larger front room by a velvet drape.

"Yes."

"But your real name isn't Nightsong. It's something French." She knit her brows, thinking. "Andrieux. Yes, that's right, isn't it?"

"You have an astonishing memory."

"I have a mind like an elephant's." She paused. "Your father was killed last year, I read."

Caroline nodded as she sipped her drink. "He wasn't much of

a father to me. I was raised by my grandmother."

"The Nightsong Chronicles were well publicized. I'd like to meet your grandmother. From what I've read, she's a remarkable woman."

"Very remarkable."

"They never did find your half-brother, did they? Adam? Wasn't that his name?"

Caroline felt uneasy. "Yes. Adam. No, they never found him." She recalled her grandmother's letter telling her about Adam's disastrous reunion with his real mother, at which time it was decided that Adam would keep his identity as the new Lord Clarendon, and that his true origins would be kept secret unless he himself chose to reveal them.

"And you have another brother, a few years younger than you."

"Marcus. He's somewhere in Europe running around in racing machines, I understand."

"Racing machines? How thrilling. I must meet him one day." She sipped her drink. "Your grandmother retired, I understand. Who's running the cosmetics business?"

"Uncle Leon, my mother's brother—until grandmother decides she's tired of doing nothing."

"Ah yes, Leon. I do recall now. His father was heir apparent to the Manchu throne until the republicans took over. You have royal blood then?"

Caroline laughed softly. "Like my Uncle Leon. I do not like to think about it."

"And your mother?"

"My mother is a different matter entirely. She's quite proud of the fact that she's a Chinese princess, and she expects all the privileges accorded to royalty. I'm afraid we don't get along very well."

Alice emptied her glass. "Well, I'm off," she said as she got up and put out her hand. "I hope to see you again, Caroline. I'm staying at the Amalfi. Call me for lunch. I expect to be in Venice for quite a while."

"I'll do that, Alice. And thank you again for the shove back there," Caroline said with a laugh.

"If you like, I'll walk you to your hotel just in case there are more pieces of loose masonry on somebody's roof."

Caroline declined the offer with more thanks. She didn't think the falling stone was anything but an accident. She put it completely out of her mind once she was back in her hotel room and sprawled across the bed for her afternoon nap. However, she couldn't forget that had it not been for Alice Pendergast she might well be dead now.

Being dead might not be so bad, she decided as she began thinking of Adam again. She closed her eyes and punched the pillow. She had to stop thinking of him.

When Caroline opened her eyes again, it was six o'clock. Tonio would be calling for her at eight. Caroline stretched and got up from the bed to start getting dressed.

Tonio was in the hotel lobby when she got off the lift. She thought that in some slight way he reminded her of Adam. Perhaps it was only a case of wishful thinking, though. Tonio was several years older and had neither Adam's features nor complexion, but it was the way he smiled, the way his eyes moved, the motion of his body when he walked that made her think of Adam Clarendon.

"You look ravishing, Caroline," he said, taking her hand.

Caroline had chosen a pale green dinner gown, fully flared in defiance of the hobble skirts that were so much a craze in America. Fashionable or not, she shunned them as she did every-thing else that didn't suit her own tastes. An emerald necklace was draped around her bare throat, and small matching earrings dangled from her lobes. Emeralds were not really her favorite gems, but she knew they brought out the flashing green of her eyes.

"Thank you, Tonio." Her smile seemed to enchant him. "Where have you decided to take me to dinner?"

"Vincente's," he said as he took her arm. He escorted her out of the hotel and into a waiting gondola. "It is a small place, but

I think you will like it. It is very romantic."

"Everything in Venice is romantic," she said. She let him put his arm around her shoulders and pull her against him as the gondolier poled his boat away from the landing steps.

Vincente's was a charming restaurant with dim candlelight and pink damask cloths. Their table was set in a little alcove that looked out over the Grand Canal. Caroline settled herself in the plush velvet-and-gilt chair and gazed out at the gondola lanterns making shimmering shadows on the surface of the water. Through the open windows the soft, lilting voices of the gondoliers' songs drifted through the night air like lovers' murmured sighs.

"This is lovely, Tonio," she said, aware that he was looking at her very seriously.

"You are lovely, my dearest."

"You said you had something to ask me," she ventured.

"There is time. First we eat. You are hungry, yes?"

"Starving."

"Good. I will order. I know the chef. You will not be disappointed."

She wasn't. The food was superb. And by the time she'd finished the several courses, the wine, and the Cassata Napolitana, all she wanted to do was get out of her clothing and relish the feeling of being very stuffed.

"I ate too much," Caroline said, rubbing her middle.

"That is good. I like a woman with flesh on her bones."

Caroline was feeling giddy from the wine and a bit reckless. "It's supposed to curb the more sensual appetites, they say."

Tonio didn't smile. He continued to look deep into her eyes. "I think it is time for me to ask what I have been wanting to ask you for several weeks now."

"And what is that?" She wanted to go to bed with him. She could blame it on the wine, but if she were to be truthful, she knew that she merely wanted the feel of his strong, young, masculine body, powerful and surging; wanted him to take her in his arms and drive himself deep inside her.

"I would like very much, Caroline, if you would become my wife."

Caroline stared. She swallowed hard, unable to believe what she'd just heard. "Your wife?"

"Are you surprised?"

"To be honest, Tonio, yes I am. I'm very surprised."

"Surely you must know that I love you."

"But...."

"I have never loved anyone as much as I love you, Caroline."

"But Tonio, we know nothing about one another."

"What is there to know? I know I love you, and I believe you care for me. You do, no?"

Caroline floundered. "Yes, of course I care for you, Tonio, but.... Well, I never thought.... What I mean is, well, I never thought seriously about marrying anyone."

"Never?"

Caroline was completely flustered. "Someday perhaps, but...."

"You do not want to marry me?" he said, looking devastated.

"Tonio," she pleaded as she touched his hand. "You are a very nice man, an extremely nice man, and I am genuinely fond of you. But marriage? I just don't—"

"Don't say no, Caroline," he broke in, squeezing her hand. "Think about it. I see now that I was lax in not revealing my intentions sooner. I am not acquainted with American customs about such things. Forgive me if I have spoken clumsily."

"I do like you very much, Tonio," Caroline admitted. She still wanted to go to bed with him, but she certainly didn't want to marry him.

"Then you will think about it?"

Adam came back to her mind and she shrugged him away. Perhaps Tonio could remove Adam's memory if she gave him the opportunity. "I promise you I will think about it," she said.

"Good. That is all I ask. Now," he said, motioning for the check, "as long as you have promised to take me seriously I will do as the American men do and prove to you that I will make a good husband."

Caroline didn't understand.

"We will go to my apartment and I will make passionate love to you."

Caroline gasped, feeling the color rise in her cheeks. She didn't know whether she was blushing out of embarrassment or anticipation.

"You do not want me to make love to you?"

For a moment her voice left her. Then she found herself smiling seductively. "I think I would like that very much, Count Cambruzio."

"Good. We will go."

* * * * * * *

Tonio's apartment was not far from the restaurant. They walked the short distance, hand in hand. When he ushered her into the large, airy suite of rooms she had the feeling that the place had been decorated by a woman. Though the overall effect was somewhat masculine, there was something definitely feminine about the curtains, the floral arrangements, the place-ment of furniture and pictures.

Tonio kissed her the moment they were inside the suite. "I do love you, Caroline."

She didn't answer; she simply responded encouragingly to his kisses.

He swooped her up in his arms and carried her into the adjoining bedroom. Here, too, a woman's touch was evident in the color scheme, the coverlet, the fringed canopy of the four-poster. But Caroline was too intent upon the way Tonio was carefully, skillfully removing her clothing to care about anything but the burning need deep inside her. He lowered her to the bed and slowly started to strip himself of his evening clothes. He had a magnificent body, so sleek and muscular, a dark fan of hair covering his well-chiseled chest, trailing down over his abdomen in a thin thread only to bush out into a tangle of black pubic hair that crowned the base of his jutting erection.

He fell down beside her and took her in his arms. Caroline felt a twinge of regret as she realized that she wanted Tonio to make love to her. She was being a traitor to her love for Adam Clarendon, but the erotic feel of Tonio's body swept over her and she found herself oblivious to everything except the way his hands were caressing, stroking her bare skin. His full, sensuous lips scorched her flesh as he kissed her breasts, her stomach, the insides of her thighs, and Caroline found herself surrendering completely to him.

"Make love to me, Tonio," she moaned as he placed his mouth against her seeping wetness.

Tonio pressed his face between her legs and began sucking her greedily until Caroline was moaning with pleasure. He kissed and licked and ran his tongue around inside her.

"Tonio. Tonio."

He raised himself up over her and crushed his mouth to hers. Caroline tasted her own sex on him, pushing her tongue between his lips. She spread her legs as Tonio bent his naked body over hers.

Caroline was quivering with expectancy, waiting to feel the hard contact of him against her. He prolonged it, gently massaging her, taking his time, lowering his lips between her breasts, nuzzling and kissing the pouting nipples until he saw she could not take much more torture. He closed one of her hands around the solid shaft of his penis and whispered hoarsely, "Put it in, darling."

When she hesitated, Tonio said, "Don't you want me to fuck you?"

"Oh yes. Yes, for God's sake, Tonio. I want you. I want all of you."

Tonio smiled and rubbed the head against her. Then with a quick motion he tensed his buttocks and slid in. Caroline moaned and he stopped, poised above her, the head of his erection buried in her warm, wet cavity.

"Not too big?"

She was too aroused to answer. She simply shook her head

frantically.

He tensed his hard, muscled buttocks again and as her hips arched up to meet him he put everything he had into a powerful lunge that sent him plunging deep inside her. Then he lowered his full weight onto her, his muscular chest pressing into her breasts.

Caroline dug her fingernails into his back, pulling him to her with her hands and legs as she worked frantically to match his movements. Her hips tensed and relaxed, squirming and rising to meet his thrusts. Tonio was bringing her to agonizing heights of pleasure with his pounding passion.

Caroline's lips opened to form a passionate whisper that she hardly recognized as her own voice. "Fuck me, Tonio. Oh God, fuck me!"

"Always, my beloved Caroline. I will fuck you until you die."

She smothered another cry as he filled her completely. He was so much larger than Adam, and the feel of his body was smooth as velvet. The hairs on his chest tormented her tender nipples as he drove ever deeper into her. She gave herself up to the ecstasy of her senses, moaning over and over again her terrible need for him.

Tonio was an expert lover, not naive and inexperienced as Adam had been. And with her hands and her lips, Caroline urged him on, meeting his thrusts, arching her hips to give him deeper access.

Something strange was happening to her. As Tonio's passions mounted, all thoughts of Adam left Caroline. The sexual awakening Adam had created dissolved under Tonio's assault. Her passionate fires burst into gigantic towers of flame as the violence of Tonio's thrusts and poundings sent her into oblivion. Little cries of pleasure escaped her lips. Her hands stroked his muscled back, his buttocks. She kissed his face, his neck, his shoulders. She dug her teeth into her own shoulder as her orgasm began to build.

"Tonio," she cried as something wild and wonderful burst into fragments deep inside her. She threw back her head and sacrificed her body to his onslaught. He continued to pound into her until a low, warm flame began to rekindle itself, sending waves of heat coursing through her body.

"Tonio. Oh, Tonio."

Suddenly she felt Tonio tense. A groan came from his throat as he bolted into her, filling her to overflowing.

"Oh, Tonio," she gasped, and exploded again, her mind flashing and sparking as blazing stars whirled around inside her head.

"Love me, Caroline," Tonio whispered. "Marry me," he sighed as the last spasms gripped him and he kissed her lovingly.

"Tonio," she sighed. Something told her that tonight, when she returned to her bed, she would dream of Tonio. She wanted to. She wanted to be free of her love for Adam.

You never will be, an inner voice told her. Never.

CHAPTER THREE

Adam Clarendon felt uncomfortable walking around the familiar grounds of the estate on which he'd been raised. Technically, none of it belonged to him. He wasn't Adam Clarendon at all but Adam MacNair, the son of April Nightsong and David MacNair. It seemed an age since his adoptive father and mother, the Lord and Lady Clarendon, had perished in the fire that destroyed an entire wing of Clarendon Hall. Yet it was no more than a year. What a short and agonizing year, he thought as he glanced at the newly rebuilt wing of the house. He had never before felt like a stranger here, but he did now. Everything had changed so much. Including him.

He thought about Caroline Nightsong. He had fallen in love with his own sister. Or had it been love? She had been the first woman he'd ever gone to bed with and he still wasn't sure whether it was love or lust he'd felt for her.

Adam didn't blame the Clarendons for their part in this nightmare. The lord's letter had tearfully explained how he'd taken Lady Clarendon to specialists in America when she was incapable of giving him the son and heir he so desperately wanted. Their private railroad car had been stopped at the San Francisco station when a poor, bedraggled wretch was found unconscious in one of the third-class coaches. The woman had a small child with her, a boy of about four or five. The woman died before regaining consciousness and the boy was taken to the Clarendons' private car for warmth and comfort. They hadn't known the child had been kidnapped or anything about him, assuming the dead woman to have been his mother. It had all seemed innocent enough until they read in the newspapers about the Nightsong child who'd been taken from his mother in San Francisco. But by then they were almost clear across country and Lady Clarendon was threatening to kill herself unless her husband took the boy as their own.

In his letter to Adam, Lord Clarendon admitted his weakness, admitted having used his influence to adopt the boy, falsify the birth records with the help of a friend (now dead) at the ministry.

No one else knew about Lord Clarendon's posthumous confession to Adam. No one except Lydia Nightsong and Pamela.

Pamela, Adam thought with a sigh as he walked into the house and on through the marble foyer toward the library with its rose-flocked walls and dark woods. He was engaged to Pamela and he'd believed it only right that she read the letter and learn the truth about him, the man she intended to marry. Pamela hadn't wanted him to go to San Francisco to meet with his real mother. She had urged him to forget the letter, to destroy it.

But he'd been determined to go to America. He had to see the woman who'd borne him. It had been a mistake, though. The mother he'd envisioned—the beautiful half-Chinese princess Lydia Nightsong had told him about—turned out to be a dreadful disappointment. Slipping between fantasy and reality, she'd mistaken him for the husband who'd been beheaded in the Forbidden City.

His paternal grandmother, Lorna MacNair, hated him. She saw him as the son she'd lost to the Nightsongs, whom she also despised. The lot of them had frightened him, and he'd run back to England to try to forget the unhappy experience.

But he couldn't forget. In the many long months since his return, he found himself softening toward the poor pathetic woman who was his mother. In his boyish dreams he saw that beautiful Chinese palace with its armored soldiers, its golden lions, its gleaming marble and ivory. He was, after all, a Manchu prince. His mother was a princess. It pleased him to think of himself as her son, despite the unfortunate reunion.

Adam was deep in thought when Pamela came into the library. He didn't know she was there until she put her arms around his waist and hugged him tight.

"You're thinking about your mother again, aren't you?" she asked softly.

He nodded. "I can't help it, Pamela. I really believe it was cruel of me to have run back here without giving her a chance. It was selfish."

"You mustn't talk like that, darling. I do wish you'd put the whole unpleasantness out of your mind and think about the future. You can't go back to something you never knew."

"But I know it now," he argued. "I know I am not Lord Clarendon's son and I'm not really entitled to live in this house or on these grounds. They aren't mine. I'm not Adam Clarendon. It's foolish to think I can live a lie."

"You mustn't talk like that, Adam."

"I'm an impostor and you know it. You read Father's letter."

"See," she said. "You still look upon Lord Clarendon as your father, as you rightly should. He was your father. Oh, perhaps not by blood, but he raised you and cared for you. He loved you, Adam, as did your mother, Lady Clarendon."

"What a bloody mess!"

"Don't swear."

"I'm sorry, Pam. I just can't help it." He ran his fingers through his hair. "I wish Father had never written that letter."

She hugged him again. "So do I."

Adam pounded his fist against the mantelpiece. "I can't help the way I feel. It just isn't right for me to pretend to be something I know I am not."

"We've been over this and over this, darling. Legally, you are Adam Clarendon. There is not a court in the world that can disprove that. You will take your investiture as Lord Clarendon at the beginning of the year and that will be that."

He shook his head. "In all good conscience, Pamela, I can not."

"You must."

He felt her anger. "Please don't be annoyed with me, darling. You know I love you. All I ask is that you look at things from my point of view."

"I'm trying, Adam. Really, I am. I can't see you as anyone but Adam Clarendon, the boy I grew up with. You are not Adam MacNair. You are not American. You're as British as I am. It's the way you were raised and educated. You'd be miserable assuming the role of someone you no longer are."

"I suppose you're right. But still...."

"Of course I'm right." She reached up and kissed him lightly on the mouth. "You and I will marry after your investiture. You will be the new Lord Clarendon and I will be your lady and we will raise dozens of little Clarendons." She laughed but there was no joy in it.

He took her in his arms. "And we'll go to China on our honeymoon."

She stiffened. "China? Good heavens, Adam, why on earth would you want to go to that terrible place? It's in revolution. "

"It's something I've always dreamed of doing ever since I can remember. I've told you this before. You know how intrigued I am by Oriental history. It was in my blood before I knew the truth about myself."

"Will you kindly forget your awful Chinese blood," she said sharply. "You mustn't think about April Nightsong or those people in San Francisco. You don't have Chinese blood, Adam. Forget this Oriental ancestry nonsense you suddenly seem so proud of. Remember, you are a Clarendon and you must never let anyone here know anything about your real mother in America."

He knew she was very annoyed, so he smiled and held her close. "We could always go to San Francisco on our honeymoon," he said with a smile. "It really wasn't such a terrible place. I just didn't give myself the opportunity to enjoy it."

Pamela lost all patience. "Honestly, Adam Clarendon, I wonder if you will ever stop acting and thinking like a little boy.

All this fantasizing about Oriental royalty is infantile. You'll be twenty-one in a few months. I thought you were a man, but I see I was wrong. You'd much prefer to dabble in dreams than to face the truth."

"Damn it, Pamela, I am facing the truth."

"You're not!" she said, stamping her foot. "You're enjoying this idiotic notion about being part royal Chinese. What's wrong with being a lord here in England?"

"A lord," he scoffed. "My mother is a princess. I would be a prince."

"Stuff and nonsense." She turned abruptly. "Enjoy your childish fantasies, Adam. When you decide to grow up, call me. Perhaps I'll be waiting. Perhaps not." She stormed out.

"Pamela!"

The door of the library slammed shut after her.

He stood at the fireplace looking at the door, then turned and bent his head, cradling it on his arm. "Perhaps she's right," he said to the empty room. "Perhaps I never will grow up."

It was true that he didn't want to be responsible for the Clarendon estates. Not yet. Besides, he wasn't a true Clarendon. Still, he wondered if he wasn't using that as an excuse to shirk his responsibilities to the two people who'd raised him.

Caroline hadn't thought of him as a boy, he reminded himself as he glowered at the door through which Pamela had left. Caroline had thought him quite the man despite the almost four years' difference in their ages. But Caroline had acted as young as he and was just as innocent, or so she'd claimed. No, the bloodstains proved it had been the first time for both of them.

Now as before—when he'd first met Caroline—his mind became a confusion. He loved Pamela. He also loved Caroline, or thought he did. He missed her terribly and wondered if she missed him as much. Where she was, he had no idea. Lydia's letter said she was still travelling abroad, which meant she was somewhere on the Continent. Maybe if he found Caroline and talked to her, things would be clearer in his mind.

But what good would that do? he asked himself. Caroline

was, after all, his sister...or half-sister. No matter. What was the difference?

He felt alone and emotionally confused. He wished his father were here. Lord Clarendon had always taken him out riding on Devon Downs when he was upset about something. That's what he'd do, Adam decided. He'd saddle one of the stallions and go for a ride. He had to think.

Pamela kept telling him to grow up and be a man, but he didn't want to. He didn't want to be Lord Clarendon. He wanted to go to China with Princess April, his mother. He'd take her back to the Forbidden City and she would be well again. They would live in a gold-and-ivory palace with dragons and warriors, and everything would be all right again.

CHAPTER FOUR

There was a heavy fog blowing in from the Bay, shrouding San Francisco in a gray, swirling blanket. Not far from the Nightsong mansion on Nob Hill, Lorna MacNair sat alone in the drawing room of her elegant new townhouse staring at the black-framed photograph of her dead husband. Over the past year she had not ventured out of the house, with the exception of her weekly trips to the cemetery. At fifty-five, she felt her life was over.

If it hadn't been for that detestable Lydia Nightsong, Peter would have been the ideal husband. No, that wasn't true, Lorna told herself. Peter had never really loved her; he had loved only her money. But in the beginning he had found her a good outlet for his enormous sex drive. She thought of those early years when the children were born and how she'd clung to Peter's magnificent body, clawing him, lustfully groaning like a common whore, begging him to never stop thrusting into her, degrading her, punishing her. She'd groveled at his feet and would have had him beat her senseless if that would have kept him from loving Lydia.

At least Peter had given her something he'd never given Lydia. Their children were all married now, happy and content with families of their own. That was little comfort, though

Lorna would have preferred the comfort of Peter instead. Her children kept their distance from her. Susan had married Sean Dillon, a rough Irishman from New York, and was living there with him, becoming equally rough. They seldom permitted

Lorna to see her grandchildren. Lorrie was almost fifteen now, David eleven, and Peter nine. Lorna adored her granddaughter, Lorrie, because she was so much like herself, aloof and poised and headstrong. The two boys took after their father and would never amount to anything. She didn't care much for the boys.

Her own son David was dead. Just as well, Lorna thought, leaning her head against the high-backed chair. What kind of a life would that have been, married to Lydia's awful Chinese daughter? And she hadn't much cared for that boy Lydia claimed was David's son. He was no more her grandson than Sherlock Holmes. She hadn't liked his English accent, his typically British effeminate mannerisms. Grandson or no, she wanted nothing to do with him.

And then there was Efrem, her youngest son. He'd married well enough. Ellen Stanton was a charming girl from a decent San Francisco family. She was a little mannish for Lorna's taste, but she was making Efrem into the man he'd never been. And their young daughter, Judith, was a delightful little thing, already showing signs, at one year of age, of being a beauty like all the MacNairs. Efrem had always been Lorna's favorite child but lately his visits, too, had dwindled. At least he had straightened himself out since marrying Ellen and settling down to raise a family. He no longer drank, and he was doing a very good job managing the business, even though—thanks to Peter's foolish will—it was the Nightsongs and not his own family who had control of MacNair Products.

But that wouldn't be true for very long, Lorna vowed as she picked up the legal document resting beside Peter's photograph. The Nightsongs had no claim to Peter's company, and if it was the last thing she did in her life, Lorna would see Lydia Nightsong and the rest of her Chink brood out in the streets or back in that heathen land they came from.

She'd handled her life with Peter very badly. When she'd first discovered that he was being indiscreet with Lydia Nightsong, Lorna thought to arouse his jealousy by committing some indiscretions of her own. She needed a man as much as Peter needed a woman. Why Peter had never been content in her arms she could not understand. What Peter had seen in Lydia, Lorna never knew. Lydia was beautiful, of course, but she did not have Lorna's social graces, her aristocratic bearing, and certainly not her background.

As Lorna looked at Peter's picture, a sudden stirring began deep inside her. She wanted him so badly. She wanted him to take her in his arms, tear the clothes from her body, and ravage her. His lovemaking had thrilled her beyond imagination. She closed her eyes and drew an image of him at the back of her eyes. The sight of him with his long-legged stride and his splendid body, broad of shoulder and boyishly slim at the hips, stirred her. Despite everything, Peter had never failed to satisfy her sexual desires, desires she was often at pains to keep concealed. Too often, they had burned beyond control and she would hate herself afterward for having been weakened by the powerful thrusts of a man. She blushed to think how she'd writhed and clawed and cried aloud, like some animal enslaved by her own sexuality.

Ramsey. The memory of him opened her eyes wide. Ramsey was the only other man who'd made her feel the way Peter had made her feel—lustful and wanton. He too was out of her life now, and in a way she was glad of that. But when she remembered the attentions Ramsey had lavished on her body, she wished with all her might that he would walk through the door and drag her up the stairs and into the bed that she and Peter had once occupied.

Ramsey had been almost a carbon copy of herself, but of a lower class. He had helped her to connive and cheat and plot against Peter and Lydia Nightsong, but all to no avail. In the end, they had been found out and Ramsey was forced to leave San Francisco to avoid facing imprisonment for aiding and abetting in the kidnapping of April's and David's son—something she, Lorna, had paid him to do.

She didn't need Ramsey now; that is, she didn't need his professional services as detective, spy, or conspirator. But there were reasons indeed that she wished Ramsey were here now. She touched the inside of her thigh as thoughts of his powerful naked body flooded her mind. She had used Ramsey when Peter refused to sleep with her. She wondered if she would ever use a man in that way again. And then, as she got up from her chair, turning away from Peter's accusing eyes, she asked herself, Who would want an aging old woman like you? A tear trickled down her cheek.

"Are you all right, Mother MacNair?" Ellen asked as she and Efrem walked into the room. Efrem was carrying their daughter, Judith, a tiny bundle of pink and cream.

Lorna turned sharply and groped for the handkerchief in her sleeve. She touched the comers of her eyes. "I'm sorry, Ellen, dear," she said as she presented a cheek to her daughter-in-law. "I was just feeling sorry for myself, I'm afraid." She smiled at her son and offered him the other cheek. "Efrem, darling."

"Hello, Mother. We were just showing Michael the sights and thought we'd stop and pay our respects."

For the first time Lorna noticed the young man standing in the doorway. She looked at him, frowning, then picked up her steel-rimmed glasses and smiled, putting out her hand.

"Welcome to my home."

"Mother, this is Michael Crane. He's a cousin of Ellen's, visiting from New York."

"How do you do, Mr. Crane. Please come in."

Crane shook her hand. "I'm pleased to meet you, Mrs. MacNair."

Something about the way the young man was looking at her made Lorna feel uncomfortable. She turned and took the child from Efrem's arms. "Here, give me the little darling." She began cooing to the baby. "Oh my, we're getting so big and more beautiful every day." She tickled the child's chin. "And your mama and daddy have been very mean not bringing you to see your old grandmother more often."

"Stop with the 'old grandmother' bit, Mother," Efrem said with a chuckle. "You are still one of the best-looking ladies in

San Francisco."

"I'll second that," Michael Crane said boldly.

"Yes, Mother MacNair," Ellen said, "you really shouldn't keep yourself cooped up in this house. You're as bad as Lydia. The two of you have become hermits."

Lorna frowned. She let a weak smile creep across her mouth. "You know, Ellen, I do not appreciate having that woman's name mentioned in this house."

"Sorry, Mother," Ellen said. "But with Efrem working for the Nightsongs, running the MacNair Products end of the company, I'd think you and Lydia would have patched up your differences long before this."

"We will never patch up our differences, Ellen. And as you know, the Nightsongs will not be controlling MacNair Products for much longer."

"What do you mean?" Efrem asked, surprised.

Lorna merely smiled and glanced at Michael Crane. "Forgive us, Mr. Crane. It's family business, and something that should be discussed only with family. So this is not the time, Efrem," she snapped. "Now," she said, more gently, handing the baby back to her father. "Have you had tea? I'll have some brought in." She pulled the bellcord. "You'll stay for tea, of course, Mr. Crane."

"Thank you," he said sweetly. "I'd like that very much."

Ellen objected. "I'm terribly sorry. Mother, but Judith should be napping. We've had her out too long as it is."

"Nonsense. Have the butler wheel the carriage into the dining room. Little Judith can nap while we have our tea. Besides, I like having a baby in the house again."

Ellen was overruled, the carriage wheeled in, and the tea served. It was an ostentatious display, with too much heavy silver and china and damask as well as an overabundance of food. Efrem looked at it all with undisguised distaste.

"So you're from New York, Mr. Crane?" Lorna asked as she began pouring tea from the Georgian tea service. "Do you know my daughter and her husband?" Before he could answer, she said, "The Dillons. My daughter married a man named Sean Dillon."

"I've heard of him, of course, but I've never met the man."

"You must look them up when you return. Susan married beneath herself, of course, but I understand they live well enough." Her nose crinkled snobbishly.

"Actually I won't be going back East, Mrs. MacNair. I'm planning to settle somewhere here in California."

"Oh? And just what is it you do, Mr. Crane?"

"Not much of anything," he answered with a chuckle.

"You're Ellen's cousin?"

"A very distant cousin. I didn't know I had any relations here in San Francisco until my mother received word of Ellen's father's death a few years ago. Mother was Mr. Stanton's second cousin, so Ellen and I are rather far down the ladder."

"You didn't bring your mother with you?"

"She died last year."

"I'm sorry."

"I inherited some money—not much, but enough to give me a bit of freedom. I never had cared much for life in New York, and then quite by accident I fell into conversation with Efrem when he and Ellen were visiting the city. During our conversation he mentioned that he'd married a Stanton. The name registered and I realized I was talking to the husband of one of my relatives. Your son and daughter-in-law were kind enough to invite me to visit them."

Ellen patted his hand. "I'm glad you took us up on the invitation, Michael. And you're welcome to stay as long as you like."

"Which might not be very long unless I find a job. My meager inheritance won't last long." He looked at Efrem. "Your son suggested he might be able to help me get a job with MacNair Products. I know nothing about manufacturing cosmetics, but I'm sure I could learn. I have a good brain, people tell me."

Efrem said, "I'll speak to Leon about it Monday morning, Michael. I'm sure something can be worked out." He laughed. "We won't let you starve."

"You're so kind," Michael said, looking like a little boy who'd just been given a very expensive present, one he knew he didn't deserve.

Lorna watched Efrem and Michael. Suddenly she was reminded of the sordid business of Efrem's relationship with Leon Nightsong, which had almost become the scandal of San Francisco years and years ago. She had thought Efrem's homosexual proclivities a thing of the past, but there was something in the way her son was smiling at this extraordinarily handsome young man that frightened her.

And Michael Crane was indeed handsome. He had dark blond hair, deep brown eyes, and a quick smile, the features and physique of a Greek statue. Although she guessed him to be no more than twenty-four or five, perhaps younger, his eyes told her that he was much older than that in experience. He smiled too easily, but only with his lips and not his eyes. There was an artificiality about him that bothered her. He reminded her of Ramsey. Far different in looks, of course, but both had the same coldness in their eyes. Suddenly she felt quite uneasy.

"There's time enough," Lorna said, "to be thinking about going to work, Mr. Crane. Enjoy San Francisco. It's a delightful city and very exciting." She smiled. "And it may well be that you will have to come to me for employment at MacNair Products if all goes as planned."

"Family business," Michael said with another smile.

Lorna shrugged. "Being Ellen's cousin, you are more or less family, so I have no objections to discussing my plans in your presence." She was talking to Efrem now.

"You're not going to start in on Lydia again, Mother?"

"Start in again! I have never stopped. And I won't rest until that woman is completely out of our lives."

Efrem said, "If you would just relax and let yourself get to know her, Mother, you'd find that Lydia is a delightful, warm, considerate woman."

"She's a witch, and we all know it."

"Mother MacNair, I think you are being unfair."

"I am not being unfair, Ellen. I know Lydia far better than any of you. She once tried to break up my family. I'll never forgive her for that. And I certainly will not tolerate her taking over the business your father worked so long and hard for."

"But Father willed it to Lydia," Efrem argued.

"That will can be contested, which is exactly what I intend doing."

"Isn't it a little late? Father's been dead for over a year."

"Not quite a year," his mother was quick to remind him. "Besides, when I was going through your father's safe, I found a certain paper that was not mentioned in the bequests he made in his will."

"What paper?"

"It seems your father bought a fifty percent controlling interest in Lydia Nightsong's companies." She felt Michael Crane watching her and turned to him. "I'm sorry, Mr. Crane, this may be boring you."

"Not at all. I'm fascinated."

"Well," Lorna continued, turning back to Efrem and Ellen, "under the terms of your father's will, MacNair Products was bequeathed to Lydia. There was no mention made of Peter's half ownership of Empress Cosmetics. According to my attorney, that fifty percent of Empress falls into the category of 'all other rights, assets, properties and estates,' which your father left to me. I intend laying claim to that half interest in Empress Cosmetics, which has since been consolidated with MacNair Products. That means I now own fifty percent of everything Lydia Nightsong owns." Her eyes were alive. "And before I'm done, I'll have it all."

"Mother," Efrem gasped. "You can't do this. Father would never forgive you."

"Your father is dead. If he is unhappy with me in his grave, so be it. It won't be the first time I've displeased him. I'm only thinking of you and Susan and your families—my grandchildren. I'm doing this for you." She glanced hopefully at Ellen and Efrem.

"Mother," Efrem said, "I think you're making a serious mistake. You mustn't do this."

To everyone's surprise, Michael spoke up. "Why not? I think your mother is right. She should have what rightfully belongs to her. If this woman connived to get MacNair Products away from your family, you certainly should fight her to regain control."

Lorna glowed. "Well, thank heaven there is one young person in this room with some common sense. Thank you for your vote of support, Mr. Crane."

"Michael," he corrected with an endearing smile.

"Michael."

Efrem was annoyed. "You don't know what you're talking about, Mother. MacNair Products has been doing incredibly well since the Nightsongs took over the management. We're making more money now than we ever have. Father was a disaster when he was in the front office."

"Don't speak disrespectfully of the dead." She glanced at Michael as she sipped her tea. "My attorney has already started the necessary proceedings. So whether you like it or not, Efrem, you'd better make up your mind to side with your own family. You have always been much too thick with the Nightsongs, ever since you were a boy."

Knowing she referred to that shameful episode with Leon, Efrem lowered his eyes. "They are very nice people," he insisted. "You just don't know them."

"I know as much as I want to know."

"You don't have to make this into another scandal, Mother," Efrem said. "If you'd talk to Lydia I'm sure she would be more than willing to give you back MacNair Products."

"I don't want only MacNair Products; I want all of it," Lorna said greedily.

"But—"

Lorna slammed her hand flat on the table. "The matter is closed, Efrem. If there is to be another scandal over this, that cannot be helped."

Michael chuckled. "I've read about these Nightsongs. They

seem rather attracted to scandals."

Efrem glowered at him. "You don't know what you're talking about, Michael. Lydia Nightsong and her family are the nicest people I know." He looked at his mother, who caught his meaning only too clearly and tightened her lips, looking hurt.

Michael shrugged. "I only know what I've read about them."

Efrem pushed back his chair and motioned to Ellen. "We should be getting home. Thank you for the tea, Mother." He glanced at the baby sound asleep in the carriage which Ellen had been rocking from time to time.

"Yes, it is getting late," Ellen agreed as she got up. "Michael?"

The young man remained seated. He purposefully picked up his cup and sipped.

"Michael hasn't finished his tea," Lorna said. "Don't rush the young man."

"It's getting late," Efrem insisted.

"Rush, rush, rush," Lorna said. "That's all you young people do these days." She smiled at Michael. "Take another scone, Michael. I'll have Charles drive you over later." She patted his hand. "I know it may be boring, but if you could tolerate the company of an old woman I'd appreciate it. I'd like to hear all about New York. My daughter rarely writes, and when she does she says nothing about the social life, only what the children are doing."

Michael looked at Ellen and Efrem, who were waiting impatiently. "If it's all right with you two, I'd like to visit with your mother for a while longer."

"As you wish," Efrem said, decidedly displeased.

"Splendid," Lorna gushed as she let Efrem and Ellen kiss her on the cheek and say their good-byes. "I'll see that your house guest gets home shortly."

"We'll see you later then, Michael," Ellen said as she wheeled the carriage out into the foyer.

Alone, Lorna leaned back in her chair. "So how are you enjoying San Francisco, Michael?"

"It's a lovely city. I like it very much, Mrs. MacNair."

"I do hope Ellen and Efrem have introduced you to some young ladies. We're quite proud of our girls here."

"I'm afraid I'm not much interested in young ladies, Mrs. MacNair. They all seem so terribly juvenile, always giggling and with nothing very intelligent to say."

Lorna laughed. "The right one will come along someday. You're still very young. You have plenty of time for settling down with the right girl."

"I've always been attracted to older women," he said, giving her a knowing glance and a smile. "My mother always said I was too old for my age."

"And what age is that, if I'm not being too impertinent?"

"Twenty-five."

"My, you make it sound antique. What will you think, I wonder, when you reach my age?"

"You aren't that much older than I, Mrs. MacNair."

She beamed. "Indeed I am."

"Well, you certainly don't look it."

"How galant of you."

"You don't. You're an extremely beautiful woman, if I may say so."

Lorna shifted uncomfortably, pleased by his flattery. It had been a long time since a handsome young man had told her she was beautiful. "You must visit more often, Michael. I have so little company nowadays."

"How about this evening?" he asked boldly.

She stared at him in surprise, then smiled. "Aren't you dining with Efrem and Ellen?"

"I had planned on taking them out for dinner, but Ellen doesn't want to leave Judith with the maid and Efrem never goes anywhere without his wife. So, I was thinking of dining out alone and then perhaps taking in the opera or a concert."

"Do you like opera?"

"Not really. It's just something to do and a place to be among people. I enjoy going to places where people look smart and elegant."

Lorna sighed. "I can't recall when I last went to the theater. I used to like it very much."

"Then how about this evening? I'd be only too happy to take you to dinner and the theater."

"Me?" She laughed nervously. "Oh no, Michael. It's very kind of you, but I seldom go anywhere since my husband died."

"Then it's time you did, Mrs. MacNair. Please say you'll come with me. I'm not at all familiar with your city, and I'd be more than honored to be seen with you."

"You are extremely sweet and most thoughtful, Michael, but I don't think I—"

"Don't think. Just say you'll permit me to call for you at seven this evening."

"You're being impetuous."

"Not at all, Mrs. MacNair. I feel very comfortable with you. I believe we could have a delightful evening together." Sensing her hesitation, he added, "Please."

"Oh, Michael, you can't possibly believe you'd enjoy yourself in the company of an old widow-woman like me."

"You are not an old woman," he said sternly. "You must stop thinking that way. Please say you'll come with me tonight."

Lorna sighed. "Well, if you're sure you want me to."

"I do. I really do."

"Then on one condition. If you call me Lorna, I'll go to dinner with you."

"Marvelous. It's agreed." He took her hand and squeezed it. "We'll have a fine time."

"Until seven o'clock then," Lorna said as she got up, feeling suddenly like a young girl. "Now come along. I'll have my chauffeur take you back." She rang for the servant. "You might just as well have Charles stay at Efrem's and drive you back here later. I won't be needing him for the rest of the afternoon. If you have any errands to run, please feel free to use him. I'll tell him he is to be at your disposal."

"That's very kind. Thank you, Lorna."

She beamed. "Until seven o'clock."

He took her hand and kissed it, making her whole body grow warm.

After Michael left, Lorna found herself humming as she went up to her bedroom. She knew she was acting like a foolish old woman, but she didn't care. It had been so long since anyone had made her feel wanted. Michael Crane was, of course, much too young, but he had admitted that he enjoyed older women. She glanced at herself in the full-length mirror. "Besides," she said to her reflection, "you really aren't all that old-looking, Lorna MacNair."

Meanwhile, in the back seat of the limousine, Michael was feeling smug and complacent. He'd need money if he was to impress Lorna MacNair that evening. He'd have to borrow from Efrem again. Efrem liked him, he knew, and so far had not refused him anything. And soon, if all went according to plan, he would never have to worry about money again. Lorna MacNair had more than she could ever spend. And according to what she'd said about the Nightsongs, she would have still more. He'd help her get it. She was old, but he'd known women older than Lorna who'd been only too happy to pay for his services.

CHAPTER FIVE

Nineteen twelve was a very progressive year for New York City. The new bridges and subway tunnels created a sprawling metropolis of nearly four million people, with Manhattan the most powerful of the boroughs in Greater New York. Business was booming; and Tammany Hall continued to control city politics despite the Boss Tweed scandal of years before. But even though the city was thriving, working conditions were the poorest in the nation and women were still fighting for their right to vote.

It was also a time for terrible tragedies. In March of 1911 a fire broke out at The Triangle Shirtwaist Company on the corner of New York's Washington Place and Greene Street. The building was abominably overcrowded, with row after row of sewing machines crammed into every inch of space. Triangle was typical of the so-called sweatshops, paying girls five dollars for a six-day work week in airless rooms. The narrow passage-ways, the flimsy fire escapes, the single elevator took the lives of 145 workers who had either been burned alive or had jumped to their deaths.

Then, in April of 1912, the luxury liner *Titanic* sank on her maiden voyage from Southampton to New York, and 1,513 people perished.

Susan MacNair Dillon had taken up the plight of the under-privileged years before and was a staunch supporter of women's suffrage. Her husband, Sean, was active in New York politics, and he shared her concern for the poor and belabored. Both were fully aware, however, of the dangers involved in upsetting the powerful men who ran New York.

The Dillon townhouse was on Fifth Avenue near Eighty-second Street, across from Central Park. It was a lovely house, furnished more for comfort than show. This pleased Susan and her husband immensely, but their daughter Lorrie hated the place. Though not yet fifteen, Lorrie was already a full-fledged snob.

"It's so common," she always complained. "I'm ashamed to bring my friends here. Why can't we furnish it as it deserves to be furnished and not with all these old-fashioned, overstuffed horrors."

"You're a little prig," her mother told her. "You're just like your Grandmother. Always wanting to put on airs."

"We can afford a few airs," Lorrie would respond. "Father is certainly rich enough."

"Money isn't everything, Lorrie. You'll learn that one day."

"I want to live in San Francisco with Grandmother."

It was an ongoing argument, one to which Susan and Sean were almost immune.

Thursday was the one day of the week Sean always spent at home alone with his wife. The children were in school and when school wasn't in session, Sean made sure they had somewhere to go so that he and Susan could have the house to themselves, especially the bedroom. After sixteen years of marriage, their lovemaking was both serious and social.

"I love Thursdays," Susan said as she kissed his naked shoulder and let her hand trail down over his abdomen and grip his stiffening penis.

"And I love you, you little minx." Sean rolled over on top of her and began suckling her nipples.

"You don't think we're getting too old for this sort of thing, Sean?"

"Old? Good God, woman. You're not even close to forty."

"I'm beginning to feel old," Susan said as she continued to fondle her husband.

"If you don't stop playing with that thing, you'll have me finished before I start."

"I like playing with your thing," she said, smiling.

"I can think of a better place for it than in your hand."

"Like where?" she teased.

He took his shaft and edged it against the lips of her vagina. "Like here?" he asked, easing himself into her.

"Oh God, Sean, that feels wonderful."

"Tell me about it." He started thrusting slowly in and out of her as she arched up to meet him.

"I wish you'd let me give you more babies," Susan said, savoring the delicious feel of his length and thickness.

"We have enough. Two boys and a girl. Just so long as the Dillon name is secure that's all I care about. Besides, you had too hard a time with little Petie, so let's not push our luck." He felt the heat building up in his loins and slowed down.

"Don't stop."

"I'll never stop. I just want it to last all afternoon." He nibbled at her ear. "I'm hot as a boiler."

"You're always hot."

"It's the Irish in me, love."

"And you'd better not ever take your 'Irish' out of me, Sean Dillon."

"Never. I love you more than my own life."

"And I love you."

He started to move against her again, practiced and even, the kind of lovemaking that's only possible between two people who have enjoyed years of happiness together.

"I adore your body," he moaned. He was getting too hot again and eased out of her. He began making love to her body with his mouth, kissing her breasts, her navel, her abdomen. He placed his face between her thighs and pushed his tongue deep inside her.

"Oh Sean," Susan moaned as she clutched the pillow, tossing her head from side to side.

When Sean felt himself in control again, he moved up over

her and eased himself back into her wetness. He took his time, moving with the graceful precision of an athlete as he brought her to one shattering climax after another.

"Sean, Sean, Sean," Susan murmured, and he drove into her, giving himself up to the flood of release he could no longer hold back.

"I adore you," he breathed as his whole body tensed, his toes curled, his teeth clenched.

Afterward they lay exhausted and content, listening to the pounding of their hearts.

"I think you married me just for my body," Susan said.

Sean propped himself up and reached for a cigarette. "That's right, love. Marrying you keeps me out of the red-light districts. I get you whenever I like and I don't have to pay the tarts."

She grabbed his hair and yanked it hard. They tussled for a moment, laughing and rolling about. Then Susan became serious. "Why did you marry me, Sean?"

He sucked on the cigarette. "To spite your mother, of course. I thought you knew that."

"Oh, be serious." She punched him and pulled his hair again.

He turned and kissed her softly. "I married you, Susan MacNair Dillon, because I happen to have fallen hopelessly in love with you and I wanted you to be the mother of my children."

"I'll accept that," she said, smiling.

"Besides, you're the only high-class lady I ever met who'd have a Mick like me for a husband."

"You're not a Mick."

"I was always a Mick. Low-down, no-lace-curtains Irish. That's me."

"We're very rich, aren't we?"

"Yes. Very. But that doesn't change where I came from. And remember, love, I don't have a very respectable occupation. Owning a distillery may be profitable, but it isn't considered very upstanding in the eyes of New York society. I wish I could give you more."

"You've given me everything I ever wanted, Sean. You know how much I hate those snobs I went to school with. I despised the way Mother made us live."

"Speaking of your mother, I'm going out to the coast next week. I suppose I'll have to stop off and pay my respects or we'll never hear the end of it."

"She'll be just as uncomfortable with you as you'll be with her, if that's any consolation. And if you don't want to see Mother, I won't care."

"Why don't you come with me?"

"As much as I'll miss you, I think I'd rather stay here."

"Maybe I'll take Lorrie. She's always pestering us to send her to her grandmother's."

"I want Lorrie kept away from my mother. Our daughter is enough of a little prig as it is. Mother would only encourage her snobbish tendencies."

"I know what you mean, love, but that girl drives me up the wall. Maybe it would be best for all concerned if we sent her to that school your mother is always raving about."

"I don't know, Sean. I truly believe it will only make Lorrie worse than she is now."

"She can't get any worse. She's unhappy with us, you must admit that. She doesn't approve of you and your suffragettes or factory workers. And I know she's ashamed of what her father does for a living."

"I'll think about it, darling." Susan bit down on her lower lip, knowing he was right. There hadn't been much peace in the house since Lorrie's visit to her grandmother's last year. Lorna had been a terrible influence on the girl. However, perhaps it would be best for everyone if Lorrie were with her own kind, pretentious little brats who thought they were better than everyone else.

"Did you say you're leaving next week?" Susan asked.

Sean stubbed out his cigarette. "Friday, if everything goes according to plan."

Susan was silent for a moment. Then she said, "I've been

thinking about that fire at the shirtwaist company, Sean. You know, the one where all those people died."

He nodded.

"We both agree that working conditions in those places are dreadful. Someone has got to stand up for those poor people who work for peanuts."

"They can't even afford peanuts," he said. "But you know damned well, Susan, the owners will never tolerate even the mention of a union, if that's what you're thinking about."

"I realize that. Yet someone from the outside has got to get on the inside and make the public aware of what conditions there are really like."

"And I suppose you intend to be that 'someone'?"

"I could pass myself off as some poor wretch who needs a job, and once I was working there I could try to get something organized."

"I don't want you getting involved with those sweatshop owners. It's too dangerous."

"Nobody need know who I am."

"I know you, my girl. You'll start instigating trouble the first day on the job. Now I'm giving you an order, wife. You are not to go near those sweatshops. Do I make myself clear?"

She didn't answer.

"Susan," he warned, wagging his finger at her.

"I only want to see what it's like inside one of those places."

"Hell," he breathed. "You'll do what you want, I know." He flopped back on the pillows. "You're a headstrong, spoiled little dickens. Now I'm warning you, love, if you get yourself into any kind of a mess, don't come running to me to get you out of it."

She knew he didn't mean that. She traced the outline of his jaw with the tip of her finger. "Do you mean you wouldn't take me in if I came begging?" Her hand moved over his chest and down across his abdomen to cup his flaccid penis, which immediately started to harden again.

"Stop that."

"No."

He chuckled, giving himself up to her manipulations. "All right, then don't stop."

"I have no intention of doing so." His penis grew harder and longer and thicker as she moved her hand up and down the shaft.

"You're going to kill me, you know that."

"You're good for another hundred years."

"Not if you don't stop torturing me this way."

She lowered her head and took him into her mouth, pulling the shaft deep into her throat. She came off it and said, "You love it and you know it."

"Aye, lass, that I do," he said, then grabbed her and kissed her hard on the mouth. "You're going to get laid again, you know."

"I hope so, you dumb Irish Mick."

* * * * * * *

At dinner that evening, which was always an informal affair—family-style, Sean liked to call it—Lorrie sat pouting, glaring at the bowls of potatoes and vegetables, the platter of meat, the boat of gravy sitting in the middle of the table.

"I simply cannot understand why we can't have the servants wait table," Lorrie said as she sullenly helped herself to a piece of meat. "We dine like peasants."

"We dine very well," her father reminded her.

"Yeah," her younger brother, David, put in. "I don't like all those different knives and forks and having to take whatever is put on my plate."

"You're a cretin."

Petie, who was nine, asked, "What's a cretin?"

"An idiot, a fool," Lorrie sneered.

"That will be enough, Lorrie," Susan said calmly. "We are all hearty and healthy enough to serve ourselves without taxing the help. They work hard enough as it is to keep us comfortable."

"Grandmother would never tolerate this," Lorrie complained as she began picking daintily at her food. "We don't even use salad forks."

"One fork is as good as another," her father reminded her. "It all goes into the same mouth."

"That's revolting."

"And you are becoming a perfect little snoot, Lorrie," Susan said, losing her patience.

Lorrie jutted out her chin. "I want to live with Grandmother. At least she lives like a civilized human being."

Sean decided to tease her. "Your mother and I have been thinking that perhaps you've been associating with the wrong type of friends, Lorrie. After you graduate from school I think I'll find you a job with me at one of my distilleries."

Lorrie was horrified. "Work? In a brewery? I'd rather die."

Sean smiled. "Oh, it wouldn't be very hard work. Perhaps somewhere in the bottling department where all you'd have to do is check to make sure the capping machines are operating correctly."

"Father!" Lorrie gasped. "You wouldn't?"

Sean laughed. "Calm down, girl. I was only having a bit of fun with you. When you're finished with school I'll have you sent to one of those finishing schools you're so anxious to attend."

"Grandmother says there is a very fine one near San Francisco."

Susan frowned. "I do not want you living with your grandmother."

"Why not? She's the only one in this family who truly understands me."

"I understand you," Susan said. "That's why I will not have you spoiled rotten by her."

"Then I'll run away and get married," Lorrie threatened.

Her father turned to his wife in surprise, then frowned at Lorrie. "Get married? To whom, in heaven's name?"

"I'm old enough to marry anyone I please. And there are a lot of boys who would ask me if I encouraged them."

Susan was shocked. "Lorrie, you aren't serious?"

"I'm fifteen. Lots of girls get married before fifteen." She gave her mother a straightforward look. "And they don't have to, either."

Little Petie asked his older brother, "Why would they have to?"

David, who thought himself quite an adult at eleven, whispered, "I'll explain it to you later."

Susan glowered at her daughter. "You are becoming just a little too corporeal, Lorrie. I'm afraid I've been a bit lax about supervising your social life."

"Really, Mother, don't be so primeval. This is 1912, not the Dark Ages."

Susan and Sean exchanged glances.

Later, when he and Susan were alone in the drawing room, Sean said, "Perhaps we should think about my taking Lorrie with me to California. New York may be just a bit too wild for a girl her age. Your mother would be able to communicate with her better than you or I. They speak the same language, and I know your mother is a stickler for propriety. She might be just what Lorrie needs now."

Susan shook her head but didn't choose to tell him about the night she'd walked into Ramsey's rooms and found her mother and Ramsey naked on the bed. "I don't know, Sean. Let me think about it. I must admit, though, that Lorrie is becoming quite a handful."

"If she's even hinting about getting married, then there must be somebody in the background she hasn't told us about. I think we should get her out of New York before she does anything stupid."

"Yes, perhaps you're right."

"The girl's an extremely pretty little thing. I'm sure there are dozens of boys trying to get at her. I'd feel better if she were away from her friends for a while. I just didn't like the way she was talking at dinner tonight. There's something gnawing at her."

"You may be right, Sean. Maybe she should go to Mother's, just for a short while." She put aside the glass of port she'd been sipping, thinking that her mother was older now and still mourning her husband. "Incidentally, what's taking you to California?"

He grinned. "Well, I've been thinking about opening up a new distillery out there. And there's something else: I've had a couple of offers to go in on those new moving pictures."

"Moving pictures? You're not serious?"

"Dead serious. There are an awful lot of people going to the Nickelodeons. They even say that within the next decade they'll be making talking pictures."

"You're crazy," Susan said with a laugh.

"Just getting in on the ground floor. Now don't get all riled. I'm only going to check things out, have a look around. I want to see what kind of money they're bringing in before I invest a penny."

"Moving pictures," Susan said, more to herself than to him. The idea was simply unthinkable. However, Sean had always had a very good eye for profitable business investments.

Susan said, "Take my advice, darling, and don't mention this to Lorrie. The next thing we know she'll be wanting to become one of those moving-picture sirens."

"Fat chance," Sean laughed. "Our Lorrie is too intent upon becoming Queen of England."

CHAPTER SIX

In Paris, Marcus Nightsong sat in a quiet little cafe just off the Rue de la Paix, sipping his morning coffee. Things had become so confused in his mind since he'd gone to San Francisco and learned the truth about his real parents. He'd been happy to hear that Lydia was his mother and Peter MacNair his father. Marcus had never liked his supposed mother, April, and had never really known his supposed father, Raymond Andrieux.

"You're twenty-one now, Marcus," Lydia had told him. "I think you're entitled to know the truth about yourself." And then she'd explained the circumstances of his birth.

Raymond Andrieux was dead now, murdered by Marcus's real father, Peter MacNair. Peter was dead now, too, and Marcus regretted never having known his own father. In fact, he now felt he didn't even know himself any longer. Who am I? he wondered.

"A vagabond," he said to himself. "A nomad who's been living in Paris and dreaming about racing automobiles."

He didn't want to be a vagabond forever, though. He wanted to marry Amelia Wilson, and she wanted to marry him. But Marcus couldn't stop thinking of racing motorcars. He wondered at times if he cared more for the fast machines than he did for Amelia. He knew no one, including Lydia, approved of his love for fast motorcars.

"They're far too dangerous, Marcus," Lydia had warned.

"Racing cars don't kill people, Mother. It's only the drivers who kill other drivers. I'm a good, careful driver. Nothing will happen to me."

She didn't believe him. No one did. Amelia sympathized with him, but he often thought she too was set against his getting behind the wheel of any racing machine.

He had no idea where his sister was but he and Caroline had never been very close. He could understand that now. She wasn't really his sister, not even his half-sister. They were from different parents entirely. Such a mixed-up family, Marcus thought as he finished his coffee. No wonder he felt so mixed up himself.

Marcus looked very much like his father: the same thick sandy hair that spilled carelessly over his forehead, the same dark brown eyes that turned black when he was angry; and he had his father's square, stern chin, along with the ruddy complexion of a true Scotsman, flawless and manly.

Marcus rather liked the idea of being Peter MacNair's son; he doubly liked being his grandmother's son...Lydia's son. It had been easy, strangely enough, to call her "Mother." The transition was quick and natural. Almost immediately he stopped thinking of April as his mother. That, he told himself, was because she had never really been much of a mother to him.

Now that he was of age and free to be the man he chose to be, he was glad to disassociate himself from that half-crazed woman who'd been the first to gloatingly tell him the truth about his birth. He was equally content to have no father to deal with, only a very concerned mother who loved him because he was her son by Peter MacNair.

Yet, now that he was so free and unencumbered, he was anxious to get on with the rest of his life. He wanted to marry Amelia and yet he didn't—not right now at least. He knew it was her sexuality that made him want her. He was more eager to become her lover than her husband. There was too much excitement going on in the world for him to start thinking of settling down and raising a family.

He was terribly in love with Amelia. There wasn't a single doubt of that. And he would marry her, just not for a while. First he had to satisfy all his dreams of speed and adventure. Amelia would understand that, because she was the only girl he'd ever met who truly understood him. She would wait for him, and he would never marry anyone else but her. This solemn promise he made to himself as he paid for his coffee and left the little cafe on the Rue de la Paix.

It would be a sweltering day, Marcus decided as he felt the heat of the late morning sun on his way back to his pension. He hadn't wanted to stay in a hotel, as his mother had insisted he do. He wanted to feel Paris, the real Paris with real Parisians. His French had improved to the point where he could now converse with any of the locals, could ask the most difficult questions and receive complicated answers, could understand and be understood.

When he reached his pension on Rue Voltaire he decided not to go up to his small suite of rooms. Instead, he'd taxi over to Madame Clair's and see if Denise was free for the afternoon. Denise was the whore, crude and crass, whom he'd met on the train the night he first arrived in France. She'd initiated him into the mysteries of sex in his private compartment, and since then he'd been unable to get enough of what she so willingly and expensively offered him.

As he turned from the door of the pension, it opened and the concierge beamed at him. "Good morning, Monsieur Nightsong," she said. "There is a cable for you on the hall table. It came just after you went out."

Marcus looked surprised and a bit upset. He wasn't expecting to hear from anyone, and a cable always meant bad news.

"It is from America," the old woman said as she held the door for him to enter and motioned to the marble table that sat along the wall of the large foyer.

Marcus tore open the flap and read the cablegram:

ARRIVING SOUTHAMPTON ON FRIDAY ABOARD THE LUSITANIA. CAN YOU MEET MY BOAT? AMELIA.

"Good news?" the concierge asked as Marcus folded the cable and put it in his pocket.

"Yes. My fiancée is coming to England. I'll meet her in Southampton."

The old woman kissed her fingertips and threw the kiss into the air. "Ah, *l'amour*. It is what makes life pleasurable. You must bring your young lady here so that I can meet her. I will fix up rooms for her."

"I don't know how long she intends staying, Madame Tourmet. I don't even know why she's coming."

"She is coming because she is in love with my handsome Marcus. Why else?"

"I think it's more than that. Something must be wrong."

"Nothing is wrong when two young people are in love. A young lady would never travel across the ocean just to bring bad news. When does she arrive?"

"Friday. We'll stay in London, I suppose. If she can come here, I'll send you word."

Marcus was worried. It wasn't like Amelia to do anything without a lot of planning. The cable, he'd noticed, had been sent from aboard ship. This was Wednesday, which meant she'd waited until she was almost in Southampton before cabling him. He wondered why.

Of course she hadn't been too pleased when he'd announced his intention to return to Paris to help his mother straighten out the mess left behind after Raymond's death. He was no expert businessman, but Leon had thought it advisable to have a family member in the Paris office to keep things tidy and running the way the Nightsongs wanted them run. Marcus knew he was little more than a figurehead, but he was a Nightsong and the employees and officers of the company gave him every courtesy even though he did nothing more than look at their reports and insist upon seeing receipts and expense and production figures the two or three days he visited the offices each week.

He didn't much like the idea of working as a perfume manufacturer, but it was his father's business as well as his mother's and he felt duty-bound to do what he could for them.

"You and Leon are the only two sons I have," his mother had told him after Peter MacNair's funeral. "Empress Cosmetics and MacNair Products will belong to you when I'm gone. It isn't too soon for you to start learning the trade, Marcus."

But the trade was of no interest to him. Marcus could read a balance sheet and knew how to study a journal and a ledger book. He was quick with figures, but his mind kept wandering away to thoughts of motor acceleration units and pressure gauge readings and numbers of miles per minute. These were the figures that really fascinated him.

Although he felt somewhat guilty about it, he couldn't help resenting Amelia's ill-timed visit. There was a race at Le Mans this weekend, which he'd been planning to attend. Perhaps he could talk her into coming with him, but then he'd be forced to stay on the sidelines instead of mingling with the mechanics and drivers and examine the engines of the newer racing cars, his usual practice. He wanted to get grease on his face and hands, smell the oil and gasoline and the burning of rubber.

He touched the pocket where he'd put Amelia's cablegram. Suddenly he had no interest in going to see Denise. Instead he'd go up to his rooms, change his clothes, and stop in at the Empress Cosmetics offices. There were a lot of things he could do to keep himself busy in Paris until Amelia arrived in Southampton. He didn't have to see Denise. He didn't want to see her.

Back in his rooms, he started to think of Amelia's beautiful face and her perfect, young, exciting body. Maybe he should go to Southampton tomorrow in case her ship docked early. His blood started to race as he considered the possibility that she might even let him make love to her for the first time.

He found himself becoming aroused at the thought of holding Amelia naked in his arms. Denise was nothing but a physical outlet, he admitted to himself. Amelia was the true treasure of whom he knew he would never tire. God, how he wanted her. Denise had introduced him to pleasures he never thought a man could possibly experience. To enjoy those pleasures with

Amelia, a woman he truly loved, would surely be like heaven on earth.

As it happened, the *Lusitania* docked a day late, and Marcus was annoyed at having missed the races at Le Mans. When he saw Amelia stepping down the passageway, however, he felt no emotion except the terrible ache of love. She was carrying a small jewel case and wore a pale blue travelling outfit that set off her dark hair and enchanting blue eyes. She had on a small hat with a long pheasant feather and a tight-fitting, ankle-length skirt that flared slightly at the bottom and clung seductively to the sensual curve of her hips and buttocks.

She ran into his arms the moment she saw him. "Oh my beautiful Marcus," she cried as she flung herself at him, kissing him unashamedly on the mouth. "I've missed you so terribly."

"Amelia." It was all he could say. His heart was so full, his love so great. Everything was forgotten, all his restlessness and indecision. He wanted nothing more than to stay in her arms forever.

Once inside their compartment on the night train to London, his thoughts veered in another direction. He remembered having shared a similar compartment with the whore Denise, who'd taken him into her mouth and brought him to orgasm. He was thinking of that now, looking at the delicate fullness of Amelia's mouth and wondering if she would ever do such a thing. It seemed unlikely, yet he wanted it more than he'd ever wanted anything.

"Darling," he said, drawing her into his arms and kissing her passionately. He moved his hand down slightly and cupped her breast.

"Marcus, behave yourself," she said, blushing and looking at the raised curtains on the door leading to the corridor.

"I can't help myself. I want to touch you all over."

"Marcus," she admonished, adjusting her hat and patting her hair nervously. "Living in Paris has changed you, I see." She smiled seductively. "I'm not sure I approve of the change. You're looking at me quite lewdly, you realize."

His penis was pulsing to erection as he kissed her again. "I feel quite lewd," he murmured.

"Please, Marcus," she whispered, pushing him away gently.

"I want you so badly, Amelia."

She wanted him as badly and damned her righteous upbringing, her sense of propriety, for keeping her from throwing herself into his arms, ripping away his suit, baring herself to him, and letting him ravage her. She saw the lust in his eyes and lowered her eyelids to hide her own desire. She began to tremble as he took her hand and placed it over the erection that was pulsing under his trouser leg.

She let her hand touch it for an instant and then immediately pulled away. The temptation was too great. She couldn't trust herself.

"Don't you want me?"

"Oh yes, darling, I do want you so very much. But can't we wait until things are as they should be?"

"Damn," he swore as he backed up into the corner of the seat and started pouting like a little boy.

"I'm sorry, Marcus. I just don't think we should."

He scowled at her as he felt his erection begin to subside. "You still haven't told me the reason for this sudden visit and why you kept it secret from me until you were almost here," he snapped.

"Please, Marcus, don't be angry with me."

"I'm not angry. I just want to know why you've come." He knew he was acting like a schoolboy, but he couldn't help it. He had grown accustomed to Denise's compliance; she always was so quick to do whatever he wanted, whenever he wanted. He'd expected as much from Amelia. And now he felt a little cheated. Or was he acting spoiled? he asked himself. Whichever, he was aching for sex and she was depriving him of it.

"Well," she said brightly, ignoring his dark mood. "There's quite a to-do going on between your mother and Lorna MacNair."

"What kind of a to-do?"

"There's going to be another lawsuit unless we do something

to avoid it."

"Lawsuit," Marcus groaned. "Good Lord, I had hoped we were finished with the Nightsong-MacNair scandals."

Amelia hurriedly told him how Lydia had invited her to the mansion and explained the whole situation. "Lorna MacNair is instituting a suit against Lydia for control of fifty percent of Empress Cosmetics and all of MacNair Products," Amelia said.

"Mother mentioned something about it in her last letter, but she said it was nothing to worry about." He started to reach for Amelia's hand but decided against it. "At least Mother's back at the helm of the company again. I was worried about her before I left San Francisco. She seemed so terribly determined to stop living after burying Father."

"She's rallied beautifully. You know how Lydia can stiffen her back whenever there's a fight to be had with Lorna MacNair."

"I still don't understand what any of that has to do with your coming here so unexpectedly."

"It was your mother's idea. Lydia didn't want anyone to know what she intends doing to avoid a scandalous lawsuit."

"And what would that be?"

"I'm a sort of emissary. I left San Francisco in quite a cloud of secrecy so Lorna MacNair wouldn't know what was going on. Lydia told me to contact you after I got out to sea and to arrange that we meet in England. We're to communicate with Adam Clarendon."

"Adam? What on earth for?"

"He's Lorna MacNair's grandson, isn't he?"

"So?"

"Lydia wants us to talk Adam into returning to San Francisco, just for a short while. She thinks that Adam might be able to reconcile the MacNairs and the Nightsongs."

"I don't see how."

"You don't realize what Adam means to Mrs. MacNair."

"She scarcely acknowledged him when Mother took him home for Father's funeral."

"Lorna was grief-stricken over Peter's death. You're really

a MacNair too, you know, just as Adam is. Lydia thinks Lorna will have second thoughts when she sees Adam again. After all, it was quite a shock to have him appear out of nowhere, looking so much like her dead son. The way your mother sees it, Adam might be able to fix everything. "

"I still don't understand how."

"You know your mother is more or less immune to scandal, whereas Lorna MacNair will do anything to keep her family skeletons buried. A law suit is one thing but a scandal is another, and Lydia intends to threaten Lorna with a very steamy scandal unless she backs off with this lawsuit business. Oh, Lydia's perfectly willing to give up MacNair Products, but she has no intention of handing Lorna any part of Empress Cosmetics. According to the MacNair lawyers, Lorna is going to try and get all of Empress Cosmetics for herself and make your mother a pauper."

"She'd hardly be that."

"By the time Lorna finishes with her, Lydia will have nothing. Empress Cosmetics, she told me, hasn't been doing all that well since Nightsong can't be reproduced without Raymond Andrieux."

"Leon wrote me that he is working in the laboratory developing Nightsong Two. He said it should be almost exactly like the original Nightsong."

"Almost but not exactly like Nightsong. There's a gamble involved, as you know."

Marcus shook his head. "It's all too confusing. I don't see how Mother can blackmail Lorna MacNair with Adam." He gave her a sharp look. "And that's what she's trying to do: blackmail her by threatening to make a scandal out of all this."

"You aren't aware of the facts, obviously. Lydia told me in the strictest of confidence that it was Lorna and her hired detective, a man by the name of Ramsey, who took Adam away from April that night. Leon found out about it. Lydia is going to expose Lorna's whole kidnapping plot unless she behaves herself."

"Lorna MacNair kidnapped her own grandson?" Marcus

said, astonished.

Amelia nodded. "There's proof."

"Then why doesn't Mother just confront Lorna and be done with it? What does she need Adam for?"

"She wants Adam there as some sort of insurance. Lydia will confront Lorna and, with Adam staying in the Nightsong mansion, apply further pressure by threatening to tell him the whole truth. That would presumably turn Adam completely against his paternal grandmother."

"And Mother thinks Lorna cares enough about Adam for this to work?"

"Lydia is certain of it. It's been over a year since Lorna buried her husband. Since then she's been living alone. Her son seldom comes to see her, and I know for a fact that Susan wants nothing to do with Lorna. So Lorna is completely alone. Lydia thinks she will snap at the chance of having a grandson to dote on."

"And what about me? I'm actually a MacNair, though a bastard."

"Do watch your language, Marcus. Honestly, I don't understand this sudden change in you since you've come to live in France."

"Sorry."

No, Amelia was the one who was sorry. Why had she corrected him? She'd heard the word often enough. Why object to his using it now? Habit, she told herself. Damned habit. She could see that Marcus had grown a little wilder and she wished with all her heart that she'd been with him this whole time so that she too could have had the opportunity to shake off all her inhibitions, get rid of her old Victorian ideals. She wanted to flirt outrageously, pull up her skirt and show her legs, but she couldn't bring herself to do either.

Something shrivelled inside Marcus at Amelia's admonition. It was true, he had changed drastically since making Paris his home. He was accustomed to saying whatever he thought, using whatever words came to him.

He'd forgotten how proper and staid Amelia and the other

young ladies of San Francisco could be. He'd gotten used to the earthy girls of Paris who didn't care a hoot about showing a lot of ankle or swaying their asses or giving a seductive wink. The girls here didn't make such a big deal about going to bed with a man. They were freer, more open and honest, and they didn't live by the double standard. Marriage was something they entered into for security; sex was something they enjoyed simply for the pleasure of it.

Amelia was nothing like the girls he'd recently grown to like. Still, when he looked at Amelia's beautiful face, her radiant purity, all he wanted to do was rip her clothes from her body and make her moan for the need of him.

Amelia sat silent for a moment. "Where can we find Adam?"

Marcus shrugged. "At Clarendon Hall, I suppose. I haven't seen him since Father's funeral. But he's still a Clarendon insofar as anyone over here knows. Mother was very careful to emphasize that nobody here must know Adam's true identity. It would cost him his lordship as well as the Clarendon inheritance."

"Nobody has to know why we wish to see him. It will all be hush-hush. That's one of the reasons Lydia chose me to come rather than a member of the immediate Nightsong family."

"Then I'm not expected to see Adam? I'm a Nightsong, remember."

"It will be alright for you. After all, you met Adam when you were here in London with your mother. Adam will remember you, and you can introduce me so he'll know I'm not some wild woman who came upon him out of the blue."

"Like his real mother," Marcus remarked, almost to himself.

Amelia frowned. "April is much improved, Marcus. She's still a bit dreamy at times, but Lydia says she isn't half as bad as she was. I think Adam had a lot to do with that. She knows now that he's alive, and that has helped her mental state considerably."

"But April thought Adam was her husband when he came to San Francisco."

Amelia shrugged. "Only because Adam looks so much like David. Lydia said there were times when she knew who Adam really was. I spoke with April when I was at your house. She seemed quite rational and very pleasant, though she was rather obsessed with the idea of returning to China. She spoke of nothing else."

"She's still mad as a hatter," Marcus said.

He thought for a moment, then asked, "Won't Mother's threats to Lorna expose Adam for who he is? That kind of scandal would be certain to reach England and then Adam would have to kiss the Clarendon title good-bye."

"I don't think Lorna will let any of it reach the public. She did, after all, arrange for Adam's kidnapping, which is a criminal offense."

"If you ask me, I think they're all crazy."

She frowned at him. "You are so changed, Marcus," Amelia scolded. "I almost don't know you."

He squeezed her hand. "I'm just tired, I guess. All this has come as quite a surprise. I had intended being in Le Mans this weekend for the motorcar races. I guess I'm a little disappointed that I won't be able to take you there."

"You still have your heart set on racing motorcars, I see."

"Of course."

It surprised him when she laughed, then kissed his cheek. "Well, at least that hasn't changed."

"I thought you disapproved."

"Not really. I'm frightened out of my mind that you might hurt yourself, but I find the noise and the speed very exciting."

"You do?"

"I'd so like to go to Le Mans with you, but I don't see how we can. I want to get back home as soon as possible."

"I understand." A sudden fright grabbed him. "I'm not expected to go home with you, am I?"

"Would that displease you?" she asked, looking hurt. "I thought perhaps you'd want to come home with me."

"It isn't that, Amelia. It's just that there is so much that has to be done with the family's business in Paris," he lied.

"You don't have to return home with me," she said flatly. "Just introduce me to Adam, and I'll take it from there. You can go back to your beloved Paris whenever you wish," she finished angrily.

"Amelia," he pleaded, knowing he'd offended her.

"It's all right, Marcus. I really did think you'd be a little bit pleased to see me. But obviously you aren't."

"I am pleased to see you," he said heatedly. He tried to take her in his arms, but she stiffened and eased away.

"I find that hard to believe."

"Come to bed with me and I'll prove it to you," he said boldly.

She wanted that more than anything in the world, but something deep down inside her would not permit it. "You know I can't."

"Why not?" He pressed closer. "We're engaged, aren't we? What's the difference if we do it now or later?"

The nearness of his body, the sweetness of his breath on her cheek were making her weak with desire. "I can't, Marcus. I just can't," she found herself saying.

He slumped in his seat. He suddenly felt like going back to Paris to Madame Claire's and Denise. There, things were so much less complicated and he could be himself.

CHAPTER SEVEN

Michael Crane had become a frequent visitor to the MacNair townhouse on Nob Hill. He and Lorna were seen everywhere together. Basking in his constant attention, Lorna was feeling like a girl again.

Lorna knew there was a callous side to Michael, but she didn't care. Ramsey had had that same quality, and it had excited her. Like Ramsey, Michael Crane made her feel wanted. Peter had never made her feel that way; he'd only wanted her money. Michael created a new feeling in her. She was aware that she was deceiving herself, but that didn't matter. He was giving her something she desperately needed right now—the youth she'd never really known.

It was in this state of mind that Lorna willingly accepted the attentions of Michael Crane. Although she wasn't blind to what he was, nothing but an opportunist, he fed her vanity and gave her something that had been sorely lacking in her life. It would cost her, of course, but she didn't care about that either. He made her feel beautiful, and that was something every woman wanted, no matter the price.

Lorna considered herself in love. Publicly, of course, she would reject the idea, due to Michael's extreme youth, but in her private thoughts she nevertheless looked upon herself as being totally bewitched by him. She could and would deny him nothing. So far he had asked for very little, which made her love him all the more.

Love! A strong word, Lorna told herself as she sat in her

dressing room waiting for Michael to call. He always came at seven-thirty and he was already ten minutes late. A slight twinge of annoyance somewhat dimmed her usual feelings of anticipation.

All the grandeur and comforts of her life seemed so unimportant when Michael was with her. Nothing had any value except him. She'd married too early, Lorna told herself as she sat before her vanity mirror, not particularly pleased by what she saw. She was old, and all of Michael's flattery could not change that fact. She shrugged. She didn't care. The pleasure she took from his company was enough.

"You're a silly woman," she told her reflection. Then she heard the door chimes and smiled. "Time for regrets later." She touched a stray hair and pinned it into place. She stood, sliding her hands down over the tight corset that pinched in her waist. As she left her bedroom she paused and glanced at the large bed that had been hers alone for too long. She wondered idly if she might someday entice Michael into sharing it with her. She had seduced Peter with her money, and Ramsey too; could she have Michael as well? She thought that was a distinct possibility.

Downstairs, the maid had ushered Michael into the drawing room and told him Mrs. MacNair would be down momentarily. He seated himself in one of the large wing chairs that flanked the fireplace and began planning again exactly what he would say to Lorna, how he would broach the subject of his desperate need for money. He'd borrowed too much from Efrem, so much that Efrem was becoming a little wary.

Convinced that Efrem had homosexual tendencies, Michael had made several subtle hints, but all of them seemed to go over Efrem's head—at least he showed no response or interest. Still, Michael wasn't ready to give up. He was positive he'd fathomed Efrem's secret proclivities. It would only take the right moment, the right words.

Michael didn't want to lose Efrem's friendship, but he knew that was inevitable unless he could find a way to repay all he'd borrowed, then move into his own quarters. Michael could think of no one but Lorna to make that possible.

He mustn't make the same mistake with Lorna that he'd made with the others, he reminded himself, crossing his legs and leaning back in the chair. Was it possible he had misinterpreted Lorna's interest in him just as he had Efrem's? Perhaps Lorna was too conventional to go to bed with a man so much younger than herself.

Yet, in spite of all her proper airs, something told him he wasn't wasting his time. For all her coolness, there was a look in her eyes that smoldered with lust. And she never drew away when he touched her; she seemed to welcome his closeness.

Michael looked at the tray sitting on the table against the far wall. He stood up and was just pouring himself a straight scotch when Lorna entered the room.

"Good evening," he said, feigning a look of embarrassment. "I hope you don't mind my helping myself to a drink?"

"Not at all, Michael," she said, smiling broadly. "I could do with one myself. How are you at making martinis?"

"It's one of my special talents."

"Excellent. Very dry, of course."

"Of course."

"You're looking exceptionally gorgeous this evening," he said as he busied himself with the cocktail pitcher, carefully stirring the gin over the ice. He put two ice cubes into the glass and swirled them around, then poured out the ice, filled the glass with liquor, and plunked in an olive. He walked over to Lorna, who was standing near the fireplace, and handed her the cocktail.

Lorna sipped and smiled. "Like everything else about you, Michael, it's perfect."

He toasted her with his glass. "I'm far from perfect, Lorna."

"We all have our little flaws, of course. So far I have not been able to discern any in you."

"I'm afraid I try to keep mine hidden as best I can. I've discovered that once you expose a weakness about yourself, it's the first thing people notice next time they meet you."

Lorna laughed softly. "True. I, too, have found that to be so."

"You have faults?" He sipped his scotch. He wanted to drain the glass, but held himself back. "I can't believe that."

"Perhaps not faults. More like weaknesses."

"Such as."

"Oh no. Now you're trying to trap me into doing the very thing you just warned me about. My weaknesses are my secret," she said, gazing at him flirtatiously. She sat down in the wing chair Michael had occupied earlier. He sat across from her on the brocade divan.

"Rather than going out this evening, Michael, I thought you would enjoy a quiet dinner here at home. I'm feeling just a bit tired."

"Whatever you like," he said, secretly relieved that he wouldn't have to spend any more of his fast-dwindling funds. "I'd welcome an evening alone with you."

"Thank you. That's a sweet compliment."

"It was meant as one."

They both knew they were playing a game, and Lorna was enjoying it immensely. She leaned back, sipping her drink.

"Truthfully, I feel like getting a little tight tonight." She arched her brows. "Does that astonish you, Michael?"

He laughed. "Not at all. I wouldn't mind unbending a bit myself."

"Good." She held up her glass for a refill, and he poured her another martini. "As I mentioned, I'm feeling a little tired," Lorna said. "I had a rather upsetting day, I'm afraid."

"Oh?"

"This Nightsong business has me in a dither."

"How so? I thought everything was going very well for you in that regard."

"Oh, my lawyers are confident that I'll come out on top, but I know Lydia too well. Although she seems to be taking it all very much in stride, I'm afraid she's up to something. It isn't like Lydia to be so calm in the face of impending calamity. I'd expected her to come here blustering and threatening. She hasn't so much as had her attorneys acknowledge the papers I had her served with." She sipped the martini. "She must be up to something. I don't like it."

Michael poured himself another scotch and sat down again. "You seem so far away over there," he said. "Why don't you join me here on the sofa? Then I won't feel like I'm shouting at you."

She smiled demurely and came over to sit beside him.

"Better?"

"Much," he said, moving closer. He wondered if he should take her hand, but decided to merely touch her arm instead. "I've heard something today that might interest you, Lorna."

She leaned toward him. "What is that?"

"Efrem mentioned that Leon Nightsong has perfected a new perfume. They're going to call it Nightsong Two. They think it will excel the original Nightsong in sales and be a lot less expensive to produce."

"I do admit that Nightsong was an extraordinarily lovely perfume. I wear it myself, though I'd never in a million years let Lydia know that." She laughed as she sipped her cocktail. "Why do you think a new Nightsong perfume would be of interest to me, Michael?"

"From all you've told me about your lawsuit against Empress Cosmetics, I suspect you'll have no trouble at all acquiring MacNair Products and fifty percent of Empress Cosmetics. But what of the other fifty percent?"

"I intend getting that too."

"And if you don't? Wouldn't it be to Lydia Nightsong's advantage to hold up production of the new Nightsong until the lawsuit is settled? If they have a new formula, Lydia would be wise to keep it under wraps until the lawsuit is resolved. Then, even if she lost everything, she would only have to turn around and start up a new company, coming out with Nightsong Two. But if we could get her to start producing Nightsong Two now, it would be included in the assets of Empress Cosmetics and thereby become yours if you win the suit."

"True. But how do we get them to produce the new perfume

before the suit is settled?"

"Leave that up to me. Your son, Efrem, and I have gotten to be very good friends," he lied. "He's talked to Leon Nightsong about my working for him. I have every reason to believe that Efrem will urge Leon to take me on." Michael was counting on Efrem's desire to get back a little of the money he'd loaned Michael, something he'd have no chance of doing until Michael was employed. "I expect to be working for the Nightsongs before long."

Lorna looked amused. "You? Working in a cosmetics factory? Frankly, Michael, it doesn't become you."

"It suited your husband and your son," he reminded her.

"My husband was a businessman. You don't impress me as that sort."

"I'm more of a businessman than you think. For the moment, I just want to get inside so I can keep an eye on things for you. I regret to tell you this, Lorna, my dear, but your son is pretty thick with the Nightsongs. If I did get inside the Nightsong company, I believe I'd be your only 'friend in court,' so to speak."

"I must agree with you about Efrem," she said, thinking of his unhealthy boyhood relationship with Leon. "He's very fond of Leon in particular." She was beginning to feel the effects of the two martinis. "There was—" She cut herself off.

Michael's face lit up. He snatched at the straw. "Efrem and Leon?" he asked insinuatingly.

Lorna waved her hand. "It was a long time ago. They were only boys."

So that was it, Michael thought as he drained his glass. He hadn't misinterpreted that look in Efrem's eyes.

Lorna studied his expression. "You're quite the little conniver, Michael, aren't you?"

He shrugged. "I only want to prove to you that I am your friend."

"And just how do I go about repaying you for your loyalty?"

He saw encouragement in her eyes and reached for her hand. "I think we can work something out, Lorna."

"I'm sure we can."

Lorna felt a sudden twinge of conscience and took away her hand. She had schemed and conspired against the Nightsongs with other men, all to no avail and at quite a cost. Would Michael prove to be any different than the others?

She studied his charming smile, his soft, sensuous mouth, and decided to throw caution to the wind. Even if she lost, she would be no further behind than she was now. Why not take what was being offered to her. She wanted to have an affair with Michael Crane, regardless of the outcome, which she was pretty certain would be in his favor. Men always came out on top.

But what did it matter? All she wanted was to feel Michael's shaft driving in and out of her. She wanted to see and touch and taste every inch of his young, magnificent body.

"Are you hungry?" she asked, trying to hide her need.

"Not for food," he answered brazenly. He took her hand again and pressed it to his lips.

"Are you sure you know what you want, Michael?"

"Quite sure."

"Aren't I a little old for you?"

"I told you when we first met, Lorna, that I've always been attracted to older women. I enjoy their experience."

"You don't impress me as someone without experience." She leaned closer.

"I think you could teach me a lot."

"Is it only my body that you want?"

He brushed his lips against her cheek, then searched for her mouth. As she let him kiss her lightly, she felt a delicious trembling run through her whole body.

"I'd gladly pay for it if I thought I could afford it," Michael ventured.

Lorna had been wondering when he'd get around to money. She wasn't offended. She'd anticipated it. A woman her age could not afford to be coy.

"I have plenty of money," she said. "I don't need any more."

He put his arms around her and cupped her breasts. "I wish

I could say the same." Slowly, carefully he began undoing the buttons at the top of her dinner dress.

"Money is never as important as people think."

"Only people with money say that." The buttons undone, he slipped his hand inside her dress and felt the flesh quiver under his touch. He wasn't surprised to find himself getting an erection. Her skin didn't feel old or dry as he had expected. It was smooth and creamy as a girl's. The nipples were already hard as he tickled them with his fingers, pinching them until he saw Lorna wince, grit her teeth, and close her eyes.

"Oh yes," he heard her murmur as his lips covered hers.

"You have beautiful breasts," he whispered. He lowered his lips to the exposed nipple and nipped it lightly with his teeth. "I want to see the rest of you." He put his hand in her lap and dug between her thighs. "I don't want to ruin your lovely gown by tearing it from your body, but I will if I have to."

"It's only a dress."

Emboldened, Michael grasped the neckline and ripped the bodice from her shoulders. He lost no time in disposing of her chemise, revealing her taut, full breasts.

"Michael," she breathed as he suckled her.

Michael pulled up the long skirt until he had it gathered around her waist, and then he began caressing her thighs. He pushed his finger against her core and smiled to himself when he realized she was wearing nothing but a corset. Her vagina was wet. His fingers slipped inside her easily.

With reckless abandon she reached for him, feeling the length and thickness of his erection. She teased it, trailing her fingers up and down the long, hard column. The blood was surging through her veins, blinding her to everything but her own sexual hunger. One by one she undid the buttons of his fly and reached inside.

"God, you're big," she moaned.

"I'm glad you like it," he purred over her mouth.

"I want it inside me."

Michael glanced toward the door. "The servants."

"To hell with the servants," Lorna groaned as his fingers dug deeper and deeper into her wetness.

Michael didn't want a quick, heedless fuck. He wanted her to feel all of him, see all of him, wanted to enslave her with his lovemaking as he had done so often with other older women.

"No. Can we go up to your bedroom?"

She was masturbating him slowly, relishing the hard, hot cock that pulsed and throbbed in her hand.

"Yes," she breathed, hurriedly pulling herself together as best she could. She took his hand and led him up the winding staircase.

Once the bedroom door was closed, she let him rip away the rest of her gown, leaving her panting in his arms.

"You're exquisite," he said as he began undoing the ties of her corset before stripping himself naked.

"So are you." Lorna sank to her knees and began kissing his thighs. "I want to taste you." She pressed her tongue against the underside of his penis and licked it up and down several times. She lapped and sucked the head, flipping the tip of her tongue gently around it.

"You're going to make me come," he groaned.

Lorna was beside herself with lust. She let him help her to her feet and ease her onto the bed. She spread her thighs, feeling wanton and unrestrained. Michael pushed forward. The head sank slowly inside as Lorna moaned and clung to him. Slowly, ever so slowly, Michael pushed it in. He took it slow, boring deeper up into her, savoring the feel of her warmth, her obvious need for him.

Lorna was panting heavily and writhing in a wild spasm of ecstasy as Michael started to pound her savagely. She groaned and bit her lip as she climaxed again and again.

"Michael, Michael," she cried, digging her nails into his back, drawing blood.

"Yes, Lorna. Give it to me. Give me all you've got."

He felt her go limp in his arms and knew he'd brought her to shattering orgasm. He continued to move, feigning his own excitement. Then he stiffened and faked an orgasm, knowing that he had her now. She'd give him anything. He was certain of that.

Lorna lay limp in his arms for a long time, reveling in the sheer ecstasy of her own contentment. It had been too long since she'd had a man inside her, and now that her sexual appetites had been rekindled she never wanted to do without again.

"You're wonderful," Lorna said as she kissed him.

"So are you."

"I feel it only fair to tell you, Michael, that I am an extremely selfish woman and I usually get what I want."

"Regardless of the costs?"

"Regardless of the costs," she answered, smiling. "As I told you, I can afford just about anything."

"Some things are expensive."

"And how expensive are you?" she asked, holding her smile.

"Not too. I don't have overly extravagant tastes. I learned the value of money early in life. Unfortunately, at present, I haven't any."

"You've spent a lot of it entertaining me of late. I must repay you."

He shrugged. "Repay Efrem. He's been loaning me money. He's a very generous man."

"He inherited that quality from his mother," Lorna said. "I also can be very generous...to a point."

"You mean, as long as you receive equal value for your generosity?"

"You understand me exactly." She paused. "Just how indebted to my son are you?"

"About two hundred dollars."

She kissed him lightly and got up. "I have money in a safe in my third-floor sitting room. You can repay Efrem when you see him tomorrow."

He watched her pull on a loose dressing robe while he slipped into his trousers and shirt, leaving the shirt unbuttoned. Then he went with her up the stairs to the top floor. Her sitting room was a cluttered little place with large floor-to-ceiling windows that reminded him of an artist's studio. Lorna went to a picture on the wall, which swung away on hinges to reveal a small round safe. She opened it up and reached inside.

"I'd rather not repay Efrem immediately," Michael said. "He'll wonder where I got the money."

"Tell him you won it gambling. Better still, I'll give you enough to open a sizable bank account and you can tell him your New York bank finally transferred your funds here." She came back and handed him five one-hundred-dollar bills. "Let me know when this begins to run low."

"You're very kind." He reached for her and pulled her into his arms. "Let's go back to bed."

"No," Lorna said. "I think we should go down to dinner. I'm rather hungry."

"Whatever you say, my darling."

"Just remember that," she said giving him a stem look. "I think we had better understand each other right from the start, Michael. Whenever I want you, for whatever reason, you are not to disappoint me."

He didn't like the way she was looking at him, but he'd seen that look before. She owned him now and she knew it. Oh well, he told himself, he had been owned before. And he'd always found it an easy matter to change owners whenever he chose to. Yet suddenly he had the strangest feeling that Lorna MacNair would not be as simple to get rid of as the others.

"Would you like me to stay the night?" he asked as he slipped the five hundred dollars into his trouser pocket.

"I'll decide that later. Right now I think we should have something to eat. Afterward...well, I'll see what kind of a mood I'm in."

"I really should look around for a place of my own if we are to continue seeing each other, Lorna."

"Yes, you should. It wouldn't do for talk to start up about your sleeping here. And if you remain with my son and his family your comings and goings will undoubtedly be questioned. Ellen has already commented on my seeing so much of you." Lorna chuckled. "Poor Ellen is so naive, so innocent. She would never imagine that there is anything but platonic friendship between you and me. I'm sure both she and Efrem believe sexual urges end when a woman reaches thirty-five. To them, it's inconceivable that I would be interested in any man in the physical sense." She put on a new dinner gown. "As for my daughter, Susan, she's a different matter entirely. Unfortunately she is quite a woman of the world and knows I was unfaithful to her father."

"Oh?" He finished dressing himself.

"Susan doesn't come to San Francisco very often. When she does, however, we will have to be extremely cautious." She examined herself in the full-length mirror. Satisfied with what she saw, she held out her hand to Michael. "Come. We'll go down to dinner. And don't worry about the servants. They are very trustworthy. They learned long ago to stay below stairs and mind their own business."

As they went down the long, winding staircase Lorna said, "Tomorrow you will look around for your own flat. Find somewhere quiet but fashionable. It wouldn't do for me to be seen in an unacceptable neighborhood. Spend whatever you like. I'll see that your bank account is always more than full."

"I'll do whatever you say."

"Of course you will, Michael. Of course you will." She squeezed his hand. "And so far as working for those awful Nightsong people, perhaps it would be wise to let Efrem find you that position. I'll insist that he does, much as I'll dislike having to do without you during the daytime."

CHAPTER EIGHT

Sean Dillon and his daughter Lorrie stepped off the train at the Oakland depot looking tired and weary after the long trip from New York. To Lorrie the train ride had been an utter bore. She'd stuck up her nose at the cramped compartments, the food, the service, the discomfort, the people.

"You should have arranged for a private car, Father," she complained.

Sean was not particularly close with his dollars but never spent money needlessly. Lorrie was the only spendthrift in the family. Like him, Susan was sensible about money. She hated everything ostentatious, and she wasn't overly fond of jewelry or expensive clothes. She enjoyed things that were simple and comfortable but of good quality.

They had met in jail, of all places. Susan had been arrested at a demonstration on behalf of the women's suffrage movement. He had been part of the demonstration too—one of the few men involved in it. He'd been surprised to learn that she was one of the wealthy San Francisco MacNairs, dressed as she was in a plain cloth coat and rather shabby shoes and hat.

She had come to his office the following day to thank him for having had his attorney post bail for her and other demonstrators who'd been arrested. He almost hadn't recognized her in the elegant sable coat with matching hat. He'd been attracted to her from the start, but never thought a man like him would stand a chance with such a beautiful woman as Susan MacNair. She was so comfortable to be with, so easy to talk to, that he fell madly in love the first night he took her to dinner.

It was Susan who first brought up the subject of love. "I think I'm falling in love with you, Sean Dillon," she had confessed after they'd been seeing each other off and on for almost a month. "Do I shock you?"

For the first time in his life he knew he was blushing. "No. I know you're trying to, but I've gotten used to being around you liberated types this past year or more."

"You could at least be a gentleman and tell me you like me a little bit."

"I love you. You know that."

"I thought you did. It shows in your eyes. I also thought you might be too shy to tell me."

"I never dreamed you'd be interested in a man like me."

"What's wrong with a man like you?"

"I'm hardly in your league socially."

"Rot. You know I don't believe in all that class nonsense. I ran away from my family in San Francisco so I wouldn't be bound by it."

"Wouldn't your family be scandalized if I proposed to you and you accepted?"

"Most likely. Why don't you do it, and then we'll find out."

He asked her to marry him that night and she accepted on the spot. "Now, if you're man enough, we'll go to San Francisco and tell my mother. I'm dying to see her face when she finds out I'm marrying someone not in the Social Register."

"You aren't marrying me just to spite your mother, are you?"

"You know better than that, Sean Dillon. I'm marrying you because I'm hopelessly and desperately in love with you."

Susan's mother hated Sean on sight, he found. It didn't matter, though. He and Susan were already married by the time he met the formidable Lorna MacNair. He loved Susan all the more for the way she stood up for him on every count, the way she flaunted her adoration of him in front of her mother.

"You're quite a woman, Susan MacNair," he'd said when Lorna left them alone for a few minutes.

"Susan Dillon. Now, my dearest Sean, I think we should go back to New York and start a big family."

Lorrie had been the first born. Sean had been a little disappointed that his oldest child was not a boy, but then David was born, and Peter. Susan had a difficult delivery with little Petie, and Sean promised himself that this third child would be their last. He did not want to place Susan in any unnecessary danger. As much as he wanted a large family, he loved his wife too much to risk losing her.

Every year of their marriage seemed better than the one before. They were extremely happy. Lorrie was the only thorn in their rose garden. Hard as both of them tried, they could not stop their daughter from becoming a complete overbearing snob—just like her grandmother.

Both Sean and Susan had misgivings about taking Lorrie to Grandmother MacNair's house, but for the sake of peace in the family they decided it would be best for all concerned if the girl were turned over to her own kind. Lorrie adored the grandmother for whom she'd been named, and Lorna returned the feeling.

"If she is intent upon being like Mother," Susan had finally said, "we might as well let her. Perhaps after living with Mother for a while, Lorrie will see just how lonely and unloved her grandmother really is."

Now they were in California, and Lorrie was looking around the Oakland station with disdain. "Did you arrange for a car and driver to meet us, Father?" she asked.

He avoided answering. "We will take the ferry across the Bay. There will be taxis on the other side to take us to your grandmother's."

"How terribly common, Father."

He motioned a porter to carry their luggage. "What about my trunk?" Lorrie asked.

"I've already arranged to have it sent on to the house."

Grudgingly, Lorrie followed him toward the ferry. "Do they have motor taxis here in San Francisco?"

"It's very much like New York now. Motorcars are everywhere. I'm afraid in another decade, maybe even sooner, we won't see any horse-drawn vehicles at all."

Sean was surprised to see how large San Francisco had grown since his last visit. There were no reminders at all of the earthquake and fire that had devastated the city just six years earlier. Everything looked new and sparkling as they drove up the long, steep hill and turned into the curved drive in front of the MacNair townhouse. He wasn't looking forward to seeing his mother-in-law. Having Lorrie with him would assure a welcome and make the visit a little less uncomfortable, however.

"My darling, darling Lorrie," Lorna gushed as she ushered them into the drawing room where she'd been sitting with Michael Crane. "Why didn't you let me know you were coming?"

"Didn't you get my telegram?" Sean asked, forcing Lorna to acknowledge his presence.

"Hello Sean," Lorna said flatly. "Telegram? No, I received no telegram." She kissed Lorrie on both cheeks. "But knowing your father, dear, I'm sure he forgot to send it."

Lorrie laughed and embraced her grandmother. "It's so wonderful to be here at last, Grandmother."

"And this time you are going to stay," Lorna said. She looked at Sean. "She is going to stay?"

"For a while. I have to go to Los Angeles on business. Susan and I thought the trip would do Lorrie some good. She's been nagging us for months to let her come."

"Then why didn't you send her before this? You know my darling Lorrie is always more than welcome here."

Sean noticed that her gracious remark hadn't included him... or Susan, for that matter. He glanced at Michael who was standing near the table in the center of the room. Lorna had made no effort to introduce them. "Hello," Sean said, putting out his hand. "I'm Sean Dillon."

"Michael Crane." The two men shook hands.

"Michael," Lorna said coldly, taking charge. "I'd like you to meet my granddaughter, Lorrie. Lorrie, this is Michael Crane, a very good friend of mine."

Sean frowned. It seemed odd for a woman Lorna's age to be entertaining a man so much younger than herself.

"How do you do, Mr. Crane," Lorrie said with her usual imperious smile.

"Miss Dillon." Michael found he couldn't stop looking at her. She was the most stunning creature he had ever seen.

"You must be famished," Lorna said.

"We had lunch just before we arrived at the station," Sean said.

Lorrie sneered. "You could hardly call that lunch, Father." She turned to Lorna. "I haven't had anything decent to eat since we left New York."

"I'll have Cook prepare something special," Lorna said as she rang for the maid. She looked at Sean, studying him with obvious distaste. "Do you intend staying here, Sean?"

"Not if it's inconvenient. Besides, as I said, I'll be leaving for Los Angeles tomorrow."

"I'll have a room made up for you for tonight," she said, but her tone made it clear that he was not really welcome. "Lorrie, you will have your old room, of course. It's still waiting for you, right next to my own."

"Thank you, Grandmother."

The maid came in and Lorna instructed her to prepare tea. Then she settled herself in a large, throne-like chair and motioned for the others to be seated. She looked disapproving when Lorrie sat herself on the divan beside Michael.

"So you are off to Los Angeles, Sean?" Lorna said. "What in heaven's name do you intend doing in that terrible place?"

"I'm opening another distribution center for my business."

"Business? Oh yes, you have something to do with distilleries or some such thing."

"Distilleries is correct, Lorna. I make liquor, in case you've forgotten."

"How could I forget? A disgusting profession, I must say."

"A very profitable one, though. Susan and I live very well."

"How is my daughter? I hardly ever hear from her."

"Busy. She's trying to do something about those terrible sweatshops in Manhattan."

"I'd prefer not to hear about it, Sean. It's humiliating enough to know that my daughter married a distiller."

He glanced at her well-stocked liquor cabinet. "Someone has to supply the needs of the many."

She ignored him and turned to Lorrie. "Michael is from New York, darling."

"Really? Well, we have something in common then," Lorrie said, beaming at him. "Are you staying in San Francisco, Mr. Crane?"

"Yes."

"And what do you do here in San Francisco, Mr. Crane?"

"I'd appreciate it if you'd call me Michael, Miss Dillon. 'Mr. Crane' makes me feel very old." He saw Lorna's immediate frown and cursed himself for his blunder.

"Only on the condition that you call me Lorrie."

"Bargain," he said, smiling as he shook her hand.

Lorna did not like the way Michael and Lorrie were cozying up to one another. She said, "You'll excuse me for being rude, Michael, but perhaps you should leave me with my family. Call me later. What with Lorrie and her father arriving so unexpectedly I'm afraid I will have to cancel our theater date this evening."

"Theater?" Lorrie asked brightly.

Michael said, "We were going to the opening of Camille with Ethel Barrymore. They say she's exceptionally good in the role."

"Camille? How wonderful. It's my most favorite play. I saw Sarah Bernhardt do it in New York a few seasons ago. It was in French, of course."

"Perhaps you'd like to come with me tonight as your grandmother is cancelling?"

"I'd adore it."

"That is out of the question," Lorna fumed. "You've had a long, arduous train trip. You're exhausted. You will spend the evening here at home with me." She gave Michael an icy look. "You are most inconsiderate, Michael. The poor child is in no condition to go out gallivanting her first night in San Francisco."

"I'm hardly a child, Grandmother," Lorrie said defiantly.

Sean sat watching the little scene with quiet amusement. He wondered what was wrong with his mother-in-law. She was obviously upset and annoyed. As he watched Lorna more closely he decided that there was something of the avaricious crocodile in the way she was looking at Michael Crane. There was more to the friendship between Lorna and Michael than met the eye, he told himself. He'd have to speak to Susan about this young fellow. Michael had said he was from New York. Perhaps Susan could find out something about him.

"Of course you're a child," Lorna insisted.

"I'm fifteen. Lots of girls are married by fifteen."

"Yes," Michael said, siding with Lorrie. "I know several. You were quite young, weren't you, Lorna, when you married your husband?"

Lorna glowered at him. "The times have changed since I was a girl."

Michael laughed and winked at Lorrie. "Your grandmother likes to think of herself as being old when anyone can see that she's still no more than a girl."

This time the flattery didn't work. Lorna was annoyed with him. "And now if you'll excuse us, Michael...," Lorna said when the maid entered to announce that tea was ready.

"Of course." Michael got to his feet and bowed over Lorrie's hand. "I trust I will see you soon again."

"I trust you will, Michael. I look forward to it."

Sean thought the man a little pretentious as he kissed Lorrie's hand then turned and kissed Lorna's. "I'll call you later, Lorna."

"Please do."

As Lorna ushered them into the small informal dining room just off the study, Sean said, "He's quite a dashing young man. Lorna. Where did you meet him?"

"He's a distant relation of Ellen's. His mother died not long ago and Michael decided to try to make his fortune here in San Francisco."

"Make his fortune?" Sean chuckled. "What an out-of-date expression. I take it, however, that he's not well fixed."

Lorna was quick to get his meaning. "He's independent to a degree. Efrem has arranged a position for him at Empress Cosmetics."

"Oh yes, the Nightsong conglomerate. According to the Wall Street reports, Lydia Nightsong is becoming less and less active in the business."

"Well, she's planning on coming out with a new perfume," Lorna said as she daintily poured from the Georgian silver teapot. Sean hated teas like this: tiny sandwiches that tasted like cardboard and silly-looking cakes and pastries totally lacking in substance. Already he was missing his hearty meals with Susan and the boys.

"She's been managing the MacNair Products line rather nicely, my brokers tell me," Sean said.

"She won't be managing it for very long. I've instigated a suit to regain my husband's company. It was foolish of Peter to bequeath the company to that woman."

"What would you have done with it if he'd left it to you? You'd only have turned around and sold it."

"What I do with what is rightfully mine is my concern, Sean. The fact of the matter is that Peter should have thought of his wife and family first rather than Lydia Nightsong and her half-breed brood."

"I agree with you, Grandmother," Lorrie said. "Grandfather was most imprudent in what he did."

Lorna gave her a tolerant smile. "When you get older, my dear, you will realize that men are sometimes extremely selfish and foolish."

"There you go again, Grandmother, speaking to me as if I were a six-year-old. I'm quite grown up as you can see."

"A little too grown up," Lorna admonished. "I'm not sure I like that travelling suit. It makes you look too old."

"It's the latest fashion."

"I blame your mother for encouraging you. Susan should not allow you to buy dresses unsuited for your young years."

Lorrie glowered. "I'm going to become quite angry with you, Grandmother, if you persist upon seeing me as a little girl."

Lorna laughed. "All right, my dear. Forgive me. Now tell me. How long has your father decided you may stay with me?"

Sean answered. "Susan and I had a long talk about that, Lorna. If it's all right with you, we thought Lorrie might attend that private girls' school you were so enthused about when we visited last year."

"Wonderful," Lorna said, clapping her hands.

"The truth is, Lorna, we're about at our wits' ends with this young lady," Sean said as he smiled tolerantly at his daughter. "She hates New York and of late she's been associating with young people Susan and I don't even know. Lorrie never brings her friends home. I think she's ashamed of us." He laughed softly.

Lorna said, "I'm sure Lorrie is very select in whom she befriends, Sean."

"I am," Lorrie said. "And the reason I never bring any of them home is because I'm sure none of them would approve of the way we live." She curled her lip.

Sean shrugged. "We live very well and most respectably."

"The only thing respectable is our address."

"That's quite enough, young lady," her father said sternly. "Your mother and I are quite out of patience with you and your highfalutin airs."

"So you are to stay with me," Lorna said, beaming. "How perfectly divine! I'm sure there are a lot of young people your own age whom you'll get to know here."

Lorrie sipped her tea, thinking suddenly of Michael Crane. "How old is Michael, Grandmother?"

Again Sean noted Lorna's flicker of annoyance. "Too old for you to be associating with, dear."

"He doesn't appear to be," Lorrie said.

"Well he is." Lorna's voice was flat and final.

Both Sean and Lorrie were quick to catch her displeasure. Sean wondered why, but decided not to pursue the subject. "By the way, Lorna," he said instead, "have you anyone among your friends and business acquaintances who knows anything about this moving-picture business that is sprouting up in Los Angeles?"

"Moving-picture business?" Lorna said, aghast. "Heaven forbid. A bunch of no-gooders. Drifters, the lot of them. I certainly do not know anyone who would associate with that parcel of derelicts."

"I have it on pretty good authority that it's the up-and-coming thing. There's a lot of money to be made in moving pictures, I've been told."

"Sean Dillon," Lorna said angrily. "Don't tell me you are going to involve yourself with those acting people? Isn't distilling whiskey bad enough?"

He was unmoved by her scorn. "I thought I'd check it out as long as I'm going to be down there."

"Actors," Lorna said with a shudder. "Good Lord."

"Don't be too quick to judge others. I gather that you have never been to a nickelodeon?"

"Of course I have not. Cheap, bawdy trash." Lorna found the subject too distasteful for words. "Tell me about Susan. How is she and what's she doing these days?"

"As I said before, she's very interested in the plight of the sweatshop workers, and of course she's still quite active in the women's suffrage movement." He glanced at his pocket watch. "I promised to call her long distance as soon as we arrived. She worries too much about me, I'm afraid."

"When you speak with her, tell her that I totally disapprove of what she is doing," Lorna said.

"Why don't you tell her yourself?"

Lorna fidgeted. "I don't think Susan wants to speak with me anymore."

It was true, Sean reminded himself. Susan had never told him what had happened just before Peter MacNair died, but mother and daughter had clearly had a big falling out at that time.

Susan had dismissed it as "a distasteful subject" when Sean first inquired about her alienation from Lorna. "I never want to speak of it."

And hard as he'd tried, Sean had never persuaded his wife to tell him about it. He thought again of Michael Crane, and reminded himself to mention the fellow to Susan. There was something about young Mr. Crane that Sean didn't like.

CHAPTER NINE

April Nightsong was sitting in her usual place. The window seat of her bedroom had become her refuge these past years. She sat endlessly dreaming of golden cities, pear gardens, brilliant peacocks, jade, and jewelled thrones. She saw her father's princely house with its marble pillars and yellow silk walls, the silver-breasted sentries who stood guard at the gates and doorways, the hundred servants who prostrated themselves, willing to die for any disservice.

April hated living with her Occidental mother in the cluttered mansion on Nob Hill. She disapproved of everything about America, everything Western. Seldom did April venture out of doors, but on occasion she did visit the Chinese section of San Francisco where she would wander imperiously through the streets and small shops, inhaling the intoxicating aroma and flavor of her beloved China. But mostly April spent her time sitting in the window seat, watching the street, waiting for David.

David was dead, she reminded herself, although a part of her mind often refused to accept that fact. At the moment, that other part of her brain was sleeping and April sat looking out, wondering if her son Adam would ever come home again. She vaguely remembered that he'd been here once before, a long time ago, but it was all muddled up inside her head. Had it been David who'd come that day or had it been Adam? She couldn't remember.

April smoothed the yellow silk of her dress and touched the

jade combs that she'd carefully placed in her hair. She liked wearing her hair loose, flowing down her back. Her mother didn't approve of the dark makeup she used to outline her eyes and exaggerate their Oriental slant, but she wanted everyone to know that she was Chinese, that her father was the great Prince Ke Loo, and that she was the last Manchu princess, the only royal Manchu entitled to sit on the throne of China.

Her father was dead, too, she remembered her brother Leon telling her. "An honorable death," he'd said. Leon never let her speak of their right to the throne.

"That's all in the past, April," Leon always cut her off.

She never understood why he'd changed his name from Li Ahn. She despised him for his disloyalty to his true ancestors.

"We are Americans now," Leon would insist.

How could they be Americans when they had both been born in China and belonged to the royal house of Manchu? Well, if her brother didn't want to acknowledge their birthright, then it would be up to her. She would see to it that she sat on the throne of China one day. It was her inheritance.

She never thought about those unhappy times in China on which her mother constantly dwelled. There had been no unhappy times. David had not been beheaded before her eyes. This was a fabrication of her mother's.

Still, there were those terrible nightmares: April would awaken screaming as the executioner's axe cut off the head of her beautiful husband. She could still see David's dead eyes staring up at her as the head rolled in the dust below the throne where she was sitting with the empress.

Awake and trembling, that other part of her mind would tell her it was just another terrible nightmare. David wasn't dead; he couldn't be. Hadn't he come to see her and then left again to search for Adam, who'd been stolen from them?

She turned her attention to the street when she heard the rattly taxi chug up the hill and turn into the driveway of the mansion. April pulled back the curtain and peered down to see who'd come calling at this hour of the day. She thought she recognized the woman. Yes, it was that strange, quiet girl who was always with Marcus. Amelia Wilson. And there was a young man with her...not Marcus.

April's eyes widened and a gasp caught in her throat when she saw his face as he turned to look up at the house.

"David!" she screamed and threw herself off the window seat, across the room, and out the door. Holding up her long, royal silk robe to keep from tripping on the stairs, she ran down just as Amelia and Adam entered the marble foyer. April stood stock-still staring at him.

"Hello, April," Amelia said. "Look who I've brought home."

"David," April shrieked as she threw herself into his arms.

Adam stood helpless, feeling the weight of her body clinging to him, her tears touching his cheek. "Mother," he said softly.

He was more prepared now than he'd been for the first reunion with his long-lost mother. April had mistaken him for her husband then, just as she was doing now. On that earlier visit her delusion had frightened and appalled him. He had cursed himself afterward for having been so intolerant of the poor woman's state of mind. This time, however, he'd made a solemn vow to be more understanding and not allow himself to be frightened away again.

"It's Adam," Amelia said solicitously.

"Adam?" April looked up at him through her tears. She frowned, turning her head from side to side as she studied him.

"Yes, Mother. I'm Adam." He smiled nervously.

"Of course you are," she said, then hugged and kissed him again. "Your father went to find you. I see he succeeded." Suddenly she started to cry and pressed herself hard against him. "Oh Adam, my dear baby. You have come home to me at last."

He glanced at Amelia, who encouraged him with her eyes. "I've come home," Adam said as he tightened his arms about her and then kissed her on both cheeks, brushing away her tears with the tips of his fingers. "You're looking as beautiful as I remember."

April looked confused. "Am I still beautiful, David?"

"Adam," he corrected gently.

"Yes, yes." She moved away from him slightly and ran her hand across her eyes. "I get so confused sometimes. Adam," she repeated, squeezing shut her eyes and clenching her fists. "I will remember."

"Of course you will," Amelia said. She looked around. "Where's your mother?"

April looked blank.

"Your mother? Lydia?"

April clutched Adam's lapels. "She's been very cruel to me, David. Oh you can't imagine how cruel. She makes me stay here in this awful house. She won't let me go home. I know the empress has written me letters, sent me messages, but Mother won't let me have any of them. She says it is wrong for me to go back to China, that I would be in danger there. But I know that isn't true. My people would never do me harm."

Adam took her in his arms and held her against his chest. "Of course they wouldn't," he assured her.

Amelia shook her head at him, a sign that he was not to encourage her.

Just then Lydia appeared at the top of the stairway. She removed her reading glasses and squinted down. "Amelia? Is that you?" She saw Adam move away from April and smile up at her. "Adam!" Lydia cried as she hurried down the stairs. "Oh my dear, dear boy," she said, hugging him. "How wonderful of you to have come." She turned to Amelia and kissed her cheek. "How lovely, my dear Amelia. You did succeed after all."

"It wasn't all that difficult, surprisingly enough," Amelia answered, returning Lydia's kiss. "Adam was thinking of coming on his own anyway."

"Really?" Lydia stared at Adam questioningly, suddenly thinking of Caroline. "But let's not stand out here in the foyer. Come into the sitting room. I want to hear everything. Where's Marcus? Did he come with you?"

"Marcus is another story," Amelia said, sounding dejected.

She shook her head. "I'm afraid he's decided to stay on in Paris. He said he'd write and explain."

April pulled Lydia away from Adam and took his hand. "He came back to me, not to you," she hissed.

"Of course he did, darling. Of course he did." Lydia glanced helplessly at Adam as the four of them entered the sitting room and settled themselves in a group before the fireplace.

"You're looking extremely well, Adam," Lydia said.

"It's David," April spat.

Lydia shook her head patiently. "It's your son, darling. It's Adam."

April thought this over for a moment and then smiled. "Of course it's Adam," she said. She frowned again at her mother. "Who did you think it was?"

Adam shifted uncomfortably.

April got up from her chair and sat down beside Adam on the couch. "My son and I are going home to China now," she announced. "Aren't we, Adam?"

Adam found himself at a loss. He couldn't answer.

Lydia rescued him. "First things first, dear," she said to April. She turned to Amelia. "Now tell me from the beginning. You contacted Marcus?"

"Yes. I cabled him from the liner. He met my boat in Southampton and we trained to London, where he took me to Clarendon Hall and introduced me to Adam."

Lydia looked at Adam. "Amelia told you of the difficulties I'm having with your Grandmother MacNair?"

Adam fidgeted, then he leaned forward slightly. "Yes," he said, "but I'm afraid I may have to disappoint you on that score, Grandmother. I really don't want to come between you and the MacNair family. It would be very awkward for me. That isn't the reason I decided to return with Amelia. I was coming on my own, you see."

"Oh?"

"You remember Pamela Albright? The girl I was intending to marry?"

"Yes, of course. Are you saying that it is no longer your intent to marry her?"

"We had a rather unpleasant scene, Pamela and I. She is very much against my revealing my true parentage. She doesn't want me to have anything to do with the Nightsongs or the MacNairs. She said she wouldn't marry me if I persisted in renouncing my Clarendon inheritance."

"Renouncing your inheritance?" Lydia said in surprise. "I certainly wouldn't want or expect you to do that. No one in England need know you aren't Lord and Lady Clarendon's son. No one need ever find out."

"But that's the problem, you see," Adam said in his smooth, very British accent. "I can't forget who I really am. Ever since I was a little boy I had dreams of living in a large palace in Peking."

"The Forbidden City," April said, smiling happily and taking his hand. "We did live there, Adam. You haven't forgotten."

"I thought it was a dream, but now I know the truth. Something deep inside me always yearned to make that dream a reality. Knowing now that Oriental blood is in my veins, that my real mother is a Manchu princess, I understand this terrible need I have to go back to China."

"Adam," Lydia said sharply. "You don't mean to tell me you are seriously thinking of going there?"

April stiffened her spine. "Of course we are going. I am a princess, heir to the throne of my homeland. My son is a prince," she said with pride as she laid her hand gently against Adam's cheek. "A prince."

Lydia and Amelia exchanged glances.

Adam said, "I must go, if only to satisfy my curiosity."

"You're being very foolish, Adam," Lydia told him. "China is in a terrible state of revolution, as I'm sure you know."

"I'm not interested in politics. Grandmother. As I said, I only want to see where I was born. It's always been like a magnet drawing me to it. I'll never be content until I go there."

"That would be most unwise, particularly at this time," Lydia insisted.

April jumped up. "We are going home," she said, reaching for Adam's hand. He stood obediently.

"I think you should lie down, April, dear," Lydia said. "Rest yourself before dinner. I would like to speak with Adam for a while longer."

April looked up at him. "She is going to try and stop us, you know. Don't let her, Adam. Don't let her keep us here where we don't belong."

"Grandmother is right, Mother," Adam said, smiling sweetly. "Go have your rest. I'll come up in a little while and we can talk."

April kissed him on the mouth, putting both hands on his cheeks. "My lovely, handsome son. Oh, how I've missed you. I will rest now. Come and wake me soon so we can start planning our trip."

She kissed him again and, letting his hand slip from hers, reluctantly left the room. At the doorway she paused and turned back. She threw him a kiss, then scampered up the stairs humming happily to herself.

"You must not encourage her, Adam," Lydia said when the three of them were settled again.

"I don't mean to, Grandmother. It's difficult for me to explain, but the first time you brought me here I ran away like some frightened little boy. I've had a long time to think about things, and I know I behaved badly toward my mother. I'm more prepared this time to accept her as she is. She is my mother, after all, and I'm not ashamed of her. Actually, I'm rather proud of the fact that my mother is a princess."

Lydia felt deflated. Suddenly she saw her grandson for what he really was: a boy. He was no more than a boy with boyish dreams. Frightened of assuming the responsibilities that went with the title of Lord Clarendon, he had slipped back into the fantasy world of his childhood.

That was why he'd found this excuse to put off the lovely Pamela Albright. He wasn't ready to saddle himself with a title, a wife, a family. He still yearned for adventure and excitement. And knowing his true identity, he was using that as an excuse to escape from his obligations. He didn't want to embroil himself in his grandmother's problems either. He wanted only to be free to chase his dreams.

"When are your investiture ceremonies, Adam?" Lydia asked casually.

"Next February, when I'm twenty-one." He brushed an imaginary piece of lint from his trouser leg. "I'm not certain I want to go back for them, though."

"I see." Lydia decided it would be best not to press him now. "Well, there is time enough to think about that. Personally, I believe it would be a monumental mistake to turn your back on your Clarendon inheritance. Of course, that is for you to decide. I will not try to influence you. You must do what you believe to be right."

"I'm awfully mixed up, Grandmother."

"I can understand that, my boy."

"I didn't want to come here when Amelia and Marcus first approached me. I was going to go directly to China. But something made me want to see my mother again and try to alleviate the hurt I must have caused her by leaving so suddenly the last time I was here. And then, of course, there was my conscience about Caroline."

Lydia shook her head sharply, moving her eyes toward Amelia, who was sitting there listening. Amelia said, "I told Adam that Caroline was still in Italy somewhere. He seemed relieved that she wouldn't be here."

Lydia decided to explain, leaving out the more lurid details. "Unfortunately, Amelia, Adam and Caroline were attracted to one another when they first met. They did not know they were related then. I believe Adam and Caroline would have felt most uncomfortable if they'd met here."

Adam kept his head down, his eyes staring at the flowers in the carpet pattern. He knew his face was burning and did not dare look up.

Lydia said to him, "Caroline has written me that she's received a proposal of marriage from a count she has been seeing. Next time you meet her," she added with a laugh, "she may be a countess."

"A countess," Amelia gushed. "Good for old Caroline."

Lydia didn't look at her; she was watching for Adam's reaction. He showed none, but she could tell that he was noticeably uncomfortable. She said, "You had a boyhood crush on Caroline. It was no more than that, and you shouldn't feel guilty about it, Adam."

He shrugged. "I don't. We just got along extremely well right from the start. I like Caroline even more now that I know we're related," he lied. In all truthfulness, he thought he was still in love with Caroline and, sister or not, he wanted desperately to bed her again. It was unnatural and incestuous, but that didn't seem to matter. She was the only woman he had ever had, and the memory of their lovemaking was the most exciting thing he could think of. He tried to imagine having sex with Pamela, but every time he conjured up a woman, it was Caroline he fantasized about. Caroline's face. Caroline's mouth. Caroline's breasts.

To change the subject Lydia turned to Amelia. "Now tell me about Marcus. What is all this nonsense about his going back to live in Paris?"

"Marcus can think of nothing but motorcar racing," Amelia said. "He claims that your Paris office can't run without him, but I know he's using that as an excuse to pursue his dream of becoming a racer. He told me he knew he would never be able to do it if he came back here, that you'd see to it that he was kept away from the racing tracks."

"And indeed I would. It's a reckless, dangerous pastime. I am completely against his doing anything so utterly foolhardy."

"That's why he's staying in Paris. You really should try to be a little more tolerant of this obsession of his, Lydia."

"How long does he intend to stay abroad?" Lydia wanted to know.

"For always, I guess. He made it rather clear that he wouldn't hold me if I met someone else I wanted to marry." The tears came in a rush before she could stop them. "He's changed so, Lydia. I hardly knew him." She rummaged in her purse for a handkerchief and dabbed at her eyes while Adam and Lydia looked on helplessly.

Lydia got up and went over to her. "Marcus just has to have a little time for his own amusements, Amelia, my dear." She glanced at Adam. "Just like this headstrong young grandson of mine, who has to go gallivanting about trying to live out his boyhood dreams." She patted Amelia affectionately. "If you love someone deeply enough, my dear, you'll wait for him. All men settle down eventually. But first they all seem to have this need to prove themselves—more to themselves than to anyone else. Let Marcus do what he has to do. We can only hope and pray that he doesn't come to any harm. Perhaps I should write him and suggest that if he's really so intent upon killing himself he might as well do it close to home."

"I don't object to his racing motorcars, Lydia. I realize the dangers, but Marcus has always been a careful, sensible man. He isn't reckless. I just wish he hadn't changed in other ways. "

"What other ways?"

Amelia looked embarrassed. "He's become so...so earthy. He was never like that before he went to Europe."

"He's just growing up. He's only a year or so older than Adam here. They're still boys at heart."

Lydia couldn't help noticing that Adam resented the remark, but she had no intention of retracting it. She wanted to make it clear that he was acting like a child.

Amelia said, "I would so appreciate it, Lydia, if you wrote Marcus and let him know that you wouldn't object too strenuously to his racing motorcars. Perhaps then he would think about coming home. At least if he were here I could learn to deal with the changes in him."

"All right, my dear. I will write Marcus." She went back and seated herself across from Adam. "Now, as for you, young man, I do not know what to suggest. You could just stay on here with us for as long as you wish, or perhaps we should think of sending you travelling across the country. America is a glorious place and a marvel to see."

"I want to go to China," Adam said stubbornly.

"You're being very obstinate. You could quite likely get shot over there. You don't know the Chinese. I've lived among them. I know what they are like, and I can tell you from personal experience that they do not take to Occidentals very readily. You saw what happened during the Boxer Rebellion."

"Still, Grandmother, I won't feel that my life has been fulfilled unless I get to see where I came from."

"You're impossible, Adam," Lydia said, losing patience with him. "You're just like your mother."

"Yes, I am," he said evenly. "I'm part Chinese. I can't forget that. I never will."

"Now you're being as foolish and headstrong as your father was."

"David MacNair," Adam said, nodding. "No one has ever told me much about my father. What was he like?"

"David was a carbon copy of his own father. You met Peter before he died. Remember?"

"Very clearly. I liked him. He was the type of man one could look up to."

"He was brash and willful and independent, with no thought for anyone except himself."

"And you were in love with him," Adam said, flashing an engaging smile.

Lydia felt her cheeks flame. "That has nothing to do with anything."

Adam felt suddenly filled with boyish devilment. "I know Marcus is your son, Grandmother. He told me. He also told me that Peter MacNair, my grandfather, is his father." He shook his head. "Quite a family I find myself born into."

Lydia was taken aback by his frankness. She looked at Amelia, who was also smiling at her. "You young people astonish me with your candor. I'm not sure I find it becoming."

Adam was not to be daunted. "If there are any more skeletons in the closet. Grandmother, I'd appreciate it if you'd tell me about them now."

"You're toying with me, I see," she said, noticing the sparkle in his eyes. "Skeletons are put into closets to keep them out of sight, which is as it should be. I have no intention of satisfying your childish urge for gory stories."

"Forgive me. Grandmother. I didn't mean to upset you. It's only—"

"I'm not upset," Lydia broke in. "I just find it rather distasteful to hear you speak so openly of things that were once considered unmentionable in polite society."

"The truth should never be unmentionable," Adam said.

"Sometimes it should. It all depends upon the circumstances." Lydia stood up and said, "I think you are both tired from your long trip. Amelia, you'll of course stay here with us. I won't have you going back to that empty house of yours. I'll go talk to Cook about dinner and see that your rooms are prepared."

"I think I'd like to go up and speak with my mother now," Adam said. He turned to Amelia. "Will you show me the way, please?"

"Of course."

"Let her rest, Adam. There will be plenty of time for talk later. Have a bath and lie down for a while. The cocktail hour is at seven o'clock, and we dine promptly at eight. We seldom dress for dinner here, but since this is your first night home I think we'll make an exception. I've been looking for an excuse to wear my new dinner gown anyway."

As Adam and Amelia started out of the room, Lydia put her hand on Adam's arm. "Darling," she said, "when you do speak with your mother I would appreciate it very much if you didn't support this insane notion of hers about trying to claim title to the Chinese throne. Surely you know that such a thing is not only impossible but deadly. If she did manage to reach Peking, her life would not be worth a penny once her identity was known. You must discourage her from even thinking about going. As for you, if you are so determined to make this junket to the Far East, please boast to no one there about your true identity. I sincerely hope you will forget all about this China nonsense, however. Later, perhaps, when things are less unsettled over there, we might all go back as tourists. It is indeed a beautiful country, though in all honesty it holds only terrible, frightening memories for me."

Adam didn't heed his grandmother's advice when he visited his mother's room. He didn't exactly encourage her, but he was a most receptive audience for her tales about her own experiences in the mysterious Forbidden City of Peking. He loved the stories about the dowager empress's court. The twin-poppy tattoo on his thigh—symbol of the Manchu family, which had originally given his true identity away—was the most important thing in his life. He'd been branded a prince. He couldn't stop studying the tattoo, caressing it fondly as one might caress a lover.

His mother seemed quite calm this evening, more rational than he'd yet seen her. She told him the name she used to call him when he was a little boy: "Yingsuh," she said. "It means 'Poppy,' the royal symbol of the royal house of Manchu."

"Yingsuh," he repeated, liking the sound of it.

"Little Prince Yingsuh," April teased. "That is what I will call you."

During the days that followed, everyone was amazed by the sudden change in April. She and Adam were constantly together, always on some excursion, which neither of them would talk about. Secretly they spent most of their time in the city's Chinese section buying clothes for Adam, silks and velvets which he loved wearing about the house. April was pleased to see that her son was so quick to learn the various Chinese words she taught him.

But then why shouldn't he learn the language so quickly? she asked herself. It was, after all, the first language he'd ever spoken.

The more Adam learned about his true heritage, the more

restless he became. He wanted to go to China and see it all for himself. Then the letter came from Pamela. She wrote about her love and the difficulties she was encountering in trying to manage his affairs without him.

"You should think about going back," Lydia said when Adam showed her Pamela's letter.

"None of it is mine legally," Adam argued. "Let them do what they want with the Clarendon holdings. You are my family."

Lydia didn't argue, knowing she could not get through to him. He was shirking his duties, but there was nothing she could do to change him.

They were seated in the drawing room of the Nightsong mansion. Leon was with them this time but without his wife, Marama, who rarely came to Lydia's house and disapproved of Leon taking their children there. Lydia could understand the girl's feelings. She was, after all, pure Hawaiian and spoke very little English. Without her sarong and loose, flying hair, she felt uncomfortable.

Leon had told Lydia of the difficulties he was having with his wife, who refused to adjust to American customs. They were constantly wrangling about the proper way to raise their children. So far, Leon had willingly deferred to her ideas, but when the children were old enough to go to school he had every intention of sending them, no matter how violently Marama objected.

Leon said, "Lorna MacNair's attorneys haven't contacted us once since your return as head of Empress Cosmetics, Mother. Perhaps she's had a change of heart."

"Not Lorna," Lydia assured him. "She's up to something. I have done my best to keep her from learning about Adam's presence here. I think she knows, however. Surely her spies report everything that goes on in this house."

"You're developing a new perfume, Lydia tells me," Amelia said to Leon.

"Yes. It should be on the market next month. We expect great things of it."

Adam wasn't listening. He was watching his mother, who

was sitting near the window gazing out. He went and sat beside her.

"What do you find so interesting out there, Mother?" Adam inquired.

"I thought your father might be coming home. It's getting so late."

"He most likely got involved and couldn't get away," he said gently. He rather enjoyed humoring her whenever she became melancholy. She was, after all, a royal Chinese princess. He loved to remind himself of that. And he was Prince Yingsuh.

"Come, everyone," Lydia said, rising from her chair when the maid announced that dinner was ready.

They settled themselves in the elegant dining room with its rose velvet walls and crystal chandelier, its shining mahogany table, the chairs upholstered in matching rose velvet.

When the soup was set before them and the maid had left the room, Lydia said, "Adam, I had a letter from Pamela this afternoon."

"Pamela wrote to you? What on earth for?"

"To try and persuade me to have you return to London."

"I have no intention of returning to London. I told her that in my last letter. I've invited her to come here if she wants to."

"She won't do that, and you know it. Both you and Pamela belong in England. It's your home."

"Well, I'm not going back," Adam said, looking to his mother for support.

"Yes you are," Lydia said firmly. "I've already booked your passage on a steamer out of New York for next week. You can catch the train at Oakland tomorrow and be in New York in plenty of time to board the ship."

"I am not going, Grandmother," he insisted hotly.

"And I say that you are. It's time you took up the responsibilities that were left to you."

April slammed down her fork. "You will not run my son's life as you ran mine," she threatened. "Prince Yingsuh and I are going home to China. We have already made our arrangements."

Lydia looked at Adam. "Is that true?"

"We've talked about it," he admitted.

"We are going," April shouted, eyes flashing and fists clenched.

Lydia could see that April was on the verge of one of her tantrums. "Calm yourself, April," she said. "I think it best that Adam return to London. His fiancée wrote and said there were certain complications which only he can solve."

"Who is this fiancée?" April demanded of Adam.

"I told you about Pamela, Mother. We were engaged to marry, but now she says she isn't sure she wants to."

"You see," April accused Lydia. "Prince Yingsuh has no fiancée. You are always trying to make people do your bidding. My son is not going anywhere but to China, and that is that." She pushed back her chair and stormed out of the dining room.

No one looked up. Lydia turned to Adam and said, "Pamela wrote that in view of your upcoming investiture, certain people are checking into your official records. She thinks they might stumble upon something that would reveal the truth about your parents."

"Let them."

"That is not the attitude you should take, Adam. You are being very stupid about this whole matter. You must look ahead. What future do you have here with your mother? Be sensible."

Like his mother, Adam glowered at Lydia. He slammed down his soup spoon, pushed back his chair, and stomped out of the room without a word.

Leon looked at his mother. "Perhaps I should talk to him," he said, getting to his feet.

"No, leave him alone to think things out for himself, Leon. I'm sure he will see the necessity of going back to England. That's where he belongs." She put aside her soup. "He doesn't belong here. He never did."

Oddly enough, that was just what Adam was thinking as he threw himself across the bed in his room: Neither he nor his mother belonged in this house. The more he spoke with April, the more sympathy he felt for her. She had told him all about her difficult life here. Her frequent vacillations between fantasy and reality no longer frightened him as they once had. Now he felt that he loved her, or pitied her...and he pitied himself for not being able to live the kind of life Princess April described in such rhapsodic terms. He wanted desperately to be Prince Yingsuh, the grandson of the great Prince Ke Loo. April had glorified her father to such a degree that in Adam's young, impressionable mind, Prince Ke Loo was now the greatest of heroes.

He knew it would be impossible for him to tolerate his grand-mother's dictatorial ways much longer. He had to get away—back to China. As he pushed himself off the bed and began packing two small suitcases, he considered taking his mother with him. They could sneak out in the dead of night and be gone before anyone missed them.

But no, he decided as he began selecting only the most neces-sary clothes. He would send for April once he got himself estab-lished in Peking. He'd leave her a note, of course, explaining that he hadn't deserted her, that he was only going to prepare the way for her.

He hid the suitcases and pretended to be asleep when Lydia came in to say good night. Adam waited until the house was quiet, then slipped into his travelling suit and carefully sneaked down the service stairs and out the side entrance. He walked down Nob Hill until he found a taxi that would take him to the wharf. He had no idea how long he'd have to wait for passage to China, but at least he was on his way. As the damp salty air of the Bay caressed his face, he leaned back in his seat, relishing the sense of danger and excitement that lay ahead.

He would hole up somewhere until he could find a ship. He'd warned April in his note not to tell anyone where he was bound. He knew she'd keep his secret.

He'd cable his grandmother once he set sail. He'd also cable Pamela. They would both be annoyed, but he couldn't help that. Something was gnawing away at him, something that must be satisfied. China was the only answer.

He thought suddenly of Caroline and wondered if he'd ever see her again.

CHAPTER TEN

The magnificence of Venice never paled for Caroline. She was as much in love with the city as ever, and wished with all her heart that she could say the same about Count Tonio Cambruzio. She thought she loved him, yet every time she considered his marriage proposal, Adam's face blurred her decision. When she was with Tonio, it was easy to forget Adam. Whenever she found herself alone, however, she would daydream about the English countryside with its wide sloping hills and lush greenery and picture the elegant Clarendon Hall with Adam striding across the courtyard in his tight riding britches. During these daydreams she would find herself excited as she visualized the hard, smooth curve of Adam's buttocks, the thick mound of manhood bulging at his crotch.

Then, when she was with Tonio again, all thoughts of Adam would fade and the count would become the most important person in her life.

Her days were Adam's; her nights Tonio's. It seemed right that the one did not belong with the other. Being careful to keep them separate and apart, Caroline was happy with her life in Venice. But she knew she'd have to make a decision eventually.

It had been almost a month since Tonio had proposed, and still she kept him dangling. He didn't seem to mind. By artful manipulation, whenever he pressured her for an answer she would seduce him into bed. Afterward, the question would be forgotten until the next time.

She was surprised, therefore, one late September evening

when Tonio pushed himself up on one elbow and kissed her softly on the mouth. He moved his lips to her breasts and suckled her nipples, crooning like a satisfied child.

"I can never get enough of you, my darling Caroline," he said. "And I have been more than patient with you. You must tell me whether I am wasting my time."

"What do you mean?"

He moved his hand down over the curve of her stomach and pressed his fingers between her thighs. He felt her wetness as he pushed his fingers deep inside her.

"You have yet to say you will marry me."

"I want to, Tonio. Truly I do. It's just that—"

"You do not love me."

"No. That isn't it. I do love you...in my fashion."

"In your fashion? By that I take it you do not love me enough to become Countess Cambruzio."

She could not answer immediately.

Tonio sighed. "Then I must stop seeing you. My family is pressuring me to take a wife. If you will not have me, then I must look for someone else. It will not be easy for me because I love you passionately. My heart is broken, but there is the family to consider. Here in Italy my parents' wishes come before anything else. We have a strict code in that regard."

Caroline suddenly felt frightened. She didn't want to be abandoned with only her memories of Adam to keep her company. "You would leave me?"

"I will have to if you reject my proposal."

"I-I'm not rejecting your proposal," Caroline stammered, stalling for more time. He was driving her wild. She pushed herself against his hand, wanting more and more of him. He was creating such torment inside her that she was blinded to reason. She'd become a slave to his manhood and did not know how she would be able to go on living if she were deprived of it.

"I want you, Tonio," she murmured as he continued to play with her, sending shock waves of such intensity through her that she was certain she would faint away with ecstasy.

"How much do you want me, my darling Caroline?" He kissed her mouth, pushing his tongue between her lips, darting it deep into her mouth.

"Please, Tonio. Don't stop. Don't stop," she moaned as he moved over her, fitting himself between her thighs. Taking her hand, he put it on his throbbing penis. "Take me hard, Tonio. Please. I need you so badly."

"Badly enough to marry me?" he whispered as he moved inside her, grinding his body hard against her softness.

"Yes, oh yes," she said as she responded violently to his thrusts. "Yes, Tonio. Please don't stop."

"Say you will marry me."

"I'll marry you. Oh, Tonio, yes, I'll marry you. More. More. Oh God, I can't stand it."

She didn't see his satisfied smile, the smile of a spoiled little boy who'd outfoxed his betters.

"Darling Caroline," he sighed as he fed hungrily on her mouth. "You have made me very happy."

She didn't hear him. All that was real was the feel of him moving in and out of her, satisfying the terrible itch that ate away at her vulnerability. She wanted his body. God, how she wanted his body. Nothing else mattered at the moment.

* * * * * *

As had become their custom these past weeks, Caroline and Alice Pendergast made a ritual of lunching at Quadri's every day at noon. Then they would stroll Saint Mark's Square, throwing crumbs to the pigeons and lingering over cups of espresso, watching the people, listening to the Campanile bells. Afterward, Caroline and Alice would retire to their respective hotels for their afternoon naps.

Caroline had told Alice very little about her affair with Tonio. Alice knew, of course, that they were dating, but Caroline had made it sound rather casual. Today, however, Caroline was having second thoughts about her acceptance of Tonio's proposal and felt compelled to talk to someone about it.

After joining Caroline at the little table under the brightly colored awning, Alice looked at her friend and said, "Something's wrong."

"I think I did something rather foolish last night, Alice."

"Oh? Who was he?"

Caroline tried to smile, but it didn't work. "You know I've been seeing Tonio Cambruzio."

"Ah yes, the dashing Count of Venice. I know you told me you'd dated him a couple of times. I didn't think you were seeing him on any serious basis."

"Quite a serious basis, I'm afraid."

"Hmm. I sense something foreboding is coming."

Caroline sighed. "I'm not sure I did the right thing, Alice."

"What right thing is that?"

Caroline straightened in her chair and sipped some wine to steel herself before announcing, "I accepted Tonio's proposal of marriage last night."

Alice choked on her drink. "You what?"

"Tonio proposed. I accepted him."

"You're mad."

"Perhaps I was, at the time." She shook her head. "It was just one of those things."

"One of those things that can only happen in the throes of passion, as they say?"

"Something like that."

"And now you are having misgivings?"

Caroline nodded. Of a sudden she brightened. "It isn't that I don't love Tonio. I do."

"But you don't think you want to love him for the rest of your life, is that it?"

Again Caroline nodded.

Alice let out a deep sigh. "I don't know what to tell you, kiddo, except that if you don't want to marry him, for God's sake tell him and get rid of him."

"That's just it. I'm not sure I want to get rid of him."

"You know that old saying about having your cake?"

"I know, I know, Alice. I just don't know what to do."

Alice studied her for a moment. "I assume he has been getting into your virgin panties."

"Not-so-virgin panties, I'm afraid."

"And he got you all heated up and popped the question when you were most vulnerable?"

Caroline sighed and then slowly explained how Tonio had proposed earlier and how she'd kept him waiting for an answer. "He said his parents are pressuring him to marry. Last night he told me that if I rejected his proposal he would be forced to find someone else. I assume his mother and father are being very insistent."

Alice waited until Caroline's eyes met hers. "Tonio Cambruzio has no family," she said evenly.

Caroline frowned. "What do you mean?"

"Just that." She paused, thinking back. "Remember that day I pulled you out from under that piece of falling masonry?"

"What about it?"

"When I walked you back to your hotel you mentioned seeing a bit of Count Cambruzio. The name registered for some reason or other, so when I got back to my newspaper office I checked up on him. I had no idea you were serious about him. He's not for you, Caroline."

"I don't understand."

"First of all, Count Cambruzio is not a count. It's a self-proclaimed title. Oh, there is some Italian royalty way, way back in his bloodline, but it's so remote it hardly exists. Furthermore, he isn't really from Venice. He was born in Sicily. His parents both died about five years ago, and for some reason Antonio decided to come here. There is talk going around that he is connected with the Sicilian Mafia."

Caroline frowned. She'd never heard of the Sicilian Mafia. "What's that?"

"The underworld. The worst kind."

"I don't believe it," she gasped.

Alice shrugged her shoulders. "There's no proof connecting Antonio Cambruzio with the Mafia, but he does have some rather questionable friends."

"I can't believe this," Caroline said, feeling somewhat indignant. "Tonio may not have parents, but that doesn't make him some kind of gangster."

"All I'm saying, Caroline, is that being forewarned is being forearmed. You've heard that expression often enough, I'm sure."

"You must be mistaken, Alice. Tonio can't be involved in anything like that. I'd know."

"How? Do you think he'd tell you? For heaven's sake, Caroline, you must realize that Italian men are very different from American men. Italians look upon a woman as something to possess, to own. Having a wife adds to their respectability, but don't think for a moment that any of them takes marriage seriously. If I were to make a guess, I'd say Tonio needs a wife for some personal or business reason. Try to get him to explain why he's so desperate to get married."

"I couldn't come right out and ask him."

"You could insist on meeting his parents. I guarantee he'll keep finding reasons to put off introducing you to Mama and Papa."

Caroline shook her head. "I'll have to think about it."

Alice picked up her handbag and got up. "Don't think too long, love. Confront him. You'll find that I'm right." She glanced at her lapel watch. "I've got to run. I have an appointment to interview the principessa. She's giving some big party at her palazzo tonight and the paper wants me to find out what the elegant ladies of Venice are wearing this season." She waved and started off across the square.

Caroline sat for a moment trying to figure out what she should do. She could not bring herself to confront Tonio with Alice's accusations. He'd just laugh at her. And if there was even the slightest spark of truth in them, he'd most certainly deny it.

However, as she left the cafe and started back toward her

hotel, she decided that it would do no harm to at least ask Tonio when she might meet his parents.

That evening, as they rode across the canal in a sleek black gondola, a myriad of stars glistening against the velvet sky, Caroline sat deep in thought, her hand trailing in the water.

"You are very pensive this evening, my darling."

"I'm feeling pensive, Tonio." She raised her head from his shoulder and looked into his eyes. "When do I meet your parents?" she asked, her voice a little unsteady.

"I told my mother that you had accepted my proposal," he said. "She and my father are very anxious to meet you."

"When?"

He shrugged. "There will be plenty of time for that. We are engaged, which is all that matters."

"But I would like to meet them."

"And they are most anxious to meet you."

"Can we go there this evening?"

He laughed. She thought she heard a slight note of nervousness in his laugh. "Without giving Mother ample time to prepare for you? Impossible. She would never forgive me for bringing you home unannounced. You must know by now the importance an Italian family places on meeting the only son's future bride for the first time. There are preparations to be made, and everything must be just so. All the relatives will have to be there, of course. Everyone must be wearing their best clothes; the finest linens and dishes and silver must be brought out. It is a very important occasion. This is not America where all is done without ceremony."

He was hedging, she decided. Alice could possibly be right. Perhaps there were no Count and Countess Cambruzio for her to meet. She studied Tonio more closely under the dim light of the full moon. "Where do you live, Tonio?"

"Live? Why on the Piazza Castagno. But you know that. You have been to my apartment often enough."

"No, I meant, where is your family home?"

"They have a large house in Malamocco. You will like it.

It is very beautiful." He eased her head back on his shoulder. Caroline thought he might be finding it hard to meet her eyes and lie at the same time. "We came from Sicily originally," Tonio said.

That much is true, Caroline told herself as she listened to his breathing and the rapid thumping of his heart.

"Now that I think about it," Tonio continued, "my mother mentioned this morning when I spoke with her, that she and my father may have to go to Sicily on some family business. So you see, you will not have to worry about the ordeal of being introduced to them until their return. I think, perhaps, Mother is thinking about having the meeting in Sicily where all the relatives live. It will take time, so you can put it completely out of your head for now. And please do not worry about meeting my parents. They are very charming people, and I know they will adore you as much as I do."

He turned her face up to his and kissed her. "I do adore you, my lovely Caroline." A smile spread across his face. "I will warn you, though, that my mother was not completely thrilled to hear that I am marrying an American. She would have been happier if I were engaged to a Sicilian girl. I told her all about you, of course, and I think she knows I'm desperately in love. She said she only wants what is good for my happiness."

Something was wrong. His words did not have that ring of truth. She needed more time to think things out for herself. She wanted to talk to Alice again. She wanted to see what proof Alice had to back up her allegations.

"Well," Caroline said, trying to sound casual. "If it is to be a while before I meet your relatives, I believe I'll make good use of the time and run up to Paris for a proper trousseau."

"Paris? How long do you think you will be away?"

"Not long, darling. A month, perhaps."

"A month is too long to be without you."

"I just want to make the right impression on your parents. "

"They will love you just as you are." There was a sudden touch of desperation in his words. "I will not have you running away from me."

"It will only be one month, Tonio."

"I want you here in Venice where I can see you every day. There are dressmakers here...good ones. You do not have to go to Paris for clothes."

"I like the Paris fashions. And there is my brother, Marcus, who's living in Paris. I want to see him and tell him about our wedding. He'll want to come, naturally. And of course there is my own family to think about. They must be invited."

"Of course." He sounded disappointed.

Tonio fell silent as the gondola moored on the quay and they stepped ashore. He took her arm and led her down the narrow cobblestone street.

The restaurant was just as she'd expected it to be—all Italian—heavy with drapes and rich colors, trellises dripping strange icy plants, overweight waiters bustling about. She suddenly realized she didn't like any of the exotic dishes that were put before her. She saw the pasta that would make her fat, the wines that would make her want whatever Tonio wanted.

She wasn't Italian. She had no place here except as a tourist. She wanted the clear, clipped sound of the English. She suddenly found Venice, with its exaggerated rococo motifs, its tassels and fringe, a bit distasteful.

As she watched Tonio devour his antipasta with the grace of a starving urchin, she wondered if this was the man she wanted for the rest of her life.

Another glass of wine, another of his devilish smiles, and she knew that Tonio would become irresistible again. She was already feeling a little lightheaded as she drained the last of the Chianti.

Tonio refilled her glass. "You are not eating," he said.

Caroline looked at the pasta with its heavy sauce. "I'll get fat."

"Good. I want you fat. And we will have lots and lots of babies, yes?"

Panic gripped her. She needed time to think. She wanted to

see Adam again. She wanted to hear the sound of her native language and not the smooth, suave lilt of Italian.

But a second later, she looked across at Tonio and wanted to fling herself into his arms, have him rip away her gown and make her forget everything but him.

She was being torn apart by indecision again.

Be careful, an inner voice cautioned, warning her against the carnal impulses that seemed to be ruling her life of late. Go away for a little while. Go away and think clearly without the temptation of this torturously attractive man.

Caroline decided to follow that advice, and the next morning she took the early train to Paris.

CHAPTER ELEVEN

Marcus sat behind the desk studying the papers before him, not the least bit interested in what he was reading. He didn't really care that the sales for the past month were drastically low or that the Paris office of Empress Cosmetics was losing money hand over fist. The perfume business bored him. The company was in worse shape now than when Raymond had been in charge. Lydia's last letter had suggested that he come home and that she send Leon over for a while, but Marcus didn't want to go home.

He had many misgivings about having sent Amelia back alone. He knew he'd hurt her, but even that didn't seem to matter anymore. He thought he was still in love with Amelia but having tasted the erotic pleasures of the Paris women, he found it was difficult to imagine himself settling down to a life of home and family, stability and serenity—all the things Amelia seemed to cherish.

He picked up the letter Leon had enclosed with the first samples of the new Nightsong perfume. Leon wanted him to start a promotion campaign for Nightsong II.

What in hell do I know about advertising campaigns? he asked himself as he tossed the letter aside. He picked up one of the small, fragile flasks of the new scent and held it up to the light. As he looked at it, he wished he were holding a gasket or a sparkplug or a piston ring instead of this silly, feminine thing.

There was another race at Le Mans this weekend. This one he would not miss.

His interoffice telephone rang. "Yes?"

"Your sister is here, Monsieur Marcus."

"Caroline?" he said with surprise. "Send her in."

Caroline walked into the handsome little office with its Louis Quinze furniture and said, "Marcus, you look absolutely ridiculous in this place. I never expected to see you sitting behind a desk."

"What are you doing in Paris?"

"Just larking about, seeing the world, as they say." She picked up the new sample of Nightsong II, uncapped it, and held it to her nose. "Lovely. Is this what Leon has been perfecting?"

"Yes, he wants me to start promoting it over here."

Caroline laughed. "It's just impossible for me to think of you as a businessman. You don't look grown up enough to peddle newspapers."

"Stop poking fun at me, Caroline. I'm uncomfortable enough in this job as it is."

"You hate it, don't you?"

Marcus didn't hesitate. "Despise it."

"Then why don't you go home? Why stay here?"

"I like it here. I'm free to do whatever I like when I'm not sitting in this damned office." He motioned her to a chair. "How long are you planning to stay?"

"Until I decide to leave. I'm thinking about getting married," she announced.

"Married? My God. To whom?"

"An Italian nobleman—Count Antonio Cambruzio. Romantic, isn't it?"

"If you like Italian royalty. Frankly, I can't see you as a countess."

"Neither can I. That's why I came up here. I need time to decide if I'm doing the right thing."

"Countess Caroline," he joked. "It has a nice ring to it, I must admit."

"Yes, it does. I'm not sure I want to be Countess Caroline Cambruzio."

"You're the only one who can decide that."

Caroline fumbled with the strap of her handbag. "What do you hear from the family? And how's that pretty Amelia of yours?"

"Pretty as ever. She was here a few weeks ago. Mother sent her over for some cloak-and-dagger stuff concerning Adam."

"Adam?"

"Your long-lost half-brother."

"Have you seen him?" She felt her insides beginning to quiver.

He told her about taking Amelia to Clarendon Hall to meet Adam. "He and Amelia went back to San Francisco together. As for my engagement to Amelia, I'm afraid it's been postponed for a bit."

"Sorry to hear that," Caroline said offhandedly. She was thinking about Adam. "I like Amelia."

"So do I, but like you, Caroline, I'm not sure I want to settle down just yet."

"I know the feeling." She thought for a moment. "You say Adam went to San Francisco?"

He nodded. "But he didn't stay long. According to Leon's letter, Adam just up and vanished again. He's very good at doing those disappearing acts."

"Vanished?"

"The family woke up one morning and found him gone. They think April knew he was going because she wasn't the least upset when Mother announced his departure. But if she knows anything about it, she isn't talking. Mother assumes that Adam went back to London. She'd received a letter from Adam's fiancée, who said there was some trouble brewing in England over Adam's inheritance. Mother and Adam had a row, and they all think he went home in a huff. They aren't positive, of course, because he hasn't contacted anyone yet."

Caroline considered all this. "I was planning on going over to London myself in a few days. I'll look Adam up and get him to write Lydia if he hasn't done so already."

She felt elated. She finally had a perfect excuse to see Adam Clarendon. It would all be very businesslike, she decided, but she knew she was fooling herself. She wanted to see Adam again and find out the truth about their relationship. If he wasn't her half-brother, as she kept trying to convince herself he was not, then she'd admit her love for him and forget all about Tonio Cambruzio and Venice.

"How about having dinner with me?" Marcus said.

"Lovely. But I don't want to interfere with any plans you may have. I know I've shown up most unexpectedly."

"I haven't any plans." In truth he'd intended to visit Denise as he did almost every night, but there would always be time for that. Denise would be at Madame Claire's whenever he wanted her.

On Friday Marcus told Caroline about the Le Mans races that weekend. "Would you care to come with me?"

"Good heavens no. All that dust and noise and those horrible motorcars. I can't imagine what you find so fascinating in them."

"They're exciting. I'm going to have one of my own someday, or at least drive in one of the races."

"You're an idiot. They're horribly dangerous."

"Only if you don't know what you're doing."

"Lydia will skin you alive," she said.

"Amelia told Mother about my penchant for racing cars. She didn't seem all that upset. In fact she wrote to say if that was why I was staying away from home, I should come back to San Francisco and she'd try to tolerate my hobby, as she put it."

"But what if something happens to you when you're racing?"

"What can happen? I know everything there is to know about the new automobiles. I can tear one apart and put it back together with my eyes closed."

"Promise me, Marcus, that you won't get behind the wheel of one of those contraptions."

"Sorry, No can do. It's all I think about."

"Then don't ask me to come and watch you kill yourself," she said angrily.

"I won't. I'm going to Le Mans tomorrow morning early."

"You'll go without me, be assured."

"Will you be all right here in Paris for the next few days?"

"Of course. I've been on my own practically everywhere else. Paris doesn't frighten me."

"It's a rather wild city."

"I like wild cities. I'll be fine. Don't worry about me."

Marcus appreciated her independent spirit. He was glad he would again be on his own in the world of men and machines. Le Mans was to him the most exciting place imaginable, tucked away in western France on the Sarthe River about 115 miles southwest of Paris. When he wasn't wandering around greasy garages talking to the mechanics and drivers, he loved to sit in the beautiful Cathedral of Saint Julien which dated back to the thirteenth century and was an architectural marvel of Gothic arches and large stained-glass windows. The contrast between the silence of the giant cathedral and the roar of the speed track intoxicated Marcus. It wasn't a particularly lovely city scenically speaking, but there was something about the smell and feel of the place that pulled at his heart, making him feel safe and secure.

As he left the Cathedral of Saint Julien that Sunday morning, he stopped midway down the stone steps to light a cigarette. He looked about and sensed the protecting arms of the city. Nothing, he knew, could ever harm him here.

"Hello," the girl said as she stopped beside him. "I saw you yesterday at the endurance races." She put out her hand. "My name is Claudine Muret."

She was lovely, he noticed, quickly recovering from his initial surprise at her forwardness. She had reddish-gold hair and deep green eyes, the color of forest moss. Her face was an almost perfect oval with the complexion of a flawless peach. She was several inches shorter than he, which made him see her as vulnerable and in need of protection.

"Marcus Andrieux." He'd gotten so accustomed to the only name he'd known until recently, that he never called himself

Marcus Nightsong, especially here in France.

"You don't look French," Claudine said.

"I'm American."

"Ah, but there isn't the slightest trace of an American accent in your speech."

"Thank you." He watched her eyes as they flashed and sparkled in the morning sunlight. "You, of course, are French?"

"But of course. My father is Claude Muret." She laughed. "I was supposed to be a boy and named after him. My father settled upon calling me Claudine, the next best thing to Claude, he decided."

"I'm glad you weren't born a boy. You're very lovely," Marcus said.

"Merci, Monsieur. I like a man who is frank. Americans are always so blunt." She eyed him coyly. "But not good lovers, I think."

"I could argue that point," Marcus said. They started to walk away from the church. "May I buy you some coffee or something?"

"Yes, that would be very nice. I came without breakfast. Something to eat would be most welcome."

As they walked along, Marcus kept glancing at her out of the comer of his eye. "Claude Muret. I know that name but can't seem to place it."

"Muret Manufacturing. My father owns many factories all through Europe."

"Of course. Your father builds railroad locomotives and coaches."

"He is building automobiles too," Claudine told him. "Already he has completed a racing machine."

"Really? How fascinating. Motorcars intrigue me."

"I gathered as much, having seen you more than once here at the race course."

"Do you go often?"

"I adore the fast automobiles. I wish I really were a man so that I could drive one myself."

"I know what you mean. I can't imagine anything more exhilarating than sitting behind the steering wheel going seventy miles an hour."

"Father believes his new Muret engine will go over a hundred miles an hour."

Marcus's eyes widened. "No motorcar can go that fast without blowing up."

"My father is convinced his will." She touched his arm. "Would you care to see it?"

"May I? When?" His heart was pounding.

"After you have taken me to petit dejeuner. I am famished. Then we will go to my apartment and you will prove to me that American men are good lovers."

Claudine laughed at his stunned expression. "You said you could argue the point between the French and the Americans as lovers. I want to find out for myself. Then we will go and I will introduce you to my father."

He was speechless.

"You have been in France long, Marcus?"

"Quite a while," he managed to answer.

"Then you know that we Frenchwomen can be very forward. I think that is because most Frenchmen are so reserved."

The freeness of the Frenchwomen had always astounded Marcus. He loved the ease with which they approached life. Nothing was ever complicated by protocol or ritual. The French girls he'd met all treated everything most openhandedly and with an honesty that would befit a saint.

Claudine slipped her arm in his. "I shock you, no?"

"Yes," Marcus admitted. "But I like it very much."

"Good. We will eat, then we will make love."

Claudine was perhaps a year younger than Marcus, or a year older. Of one thing he was sure: She was no inexperienced virgin.

* * * * * * *

Claudine turned out to be quite expert at pleasing a man. She didn't permit Marcus to undress until she was completely naked and stretched out on the bed. Then she began playing with herself, digging her fingers deep into her wetness while she instructed him to slowly remove his clothing, one article at a time. She led him through the routine as carefully as the most exacting choreographer.

"Now your trousers, Marcus. No, no, slower. One button at a time." After she'd had him strip off his underdrawers she made him stand there, telling him to fondle himself while she admired his body.

"You are magnificent," she breathed. She opened her arms and Marcus fell into them.

Under Denise's tutelage he had learned how to control his passions. Unlike his initial experiences with the whore, he didn't plow into Claudine and thrust and jerk like a rabbit. He kissed every part of her body as she, simultaneously, returned the favors. He'd found his first oral-genital contact slightly degrading. But now he found nothing more exciting, especially with a girl as free as Claudine.

Marcus caressed the smooth, creamy thighs, his fingers fluttering just around the rim of her sex. Then he moved in with his tongue and began licking her with light, feathery strokes.

"Fuck me," Claudine groaned.

Marcus slid up along her body and met her lips with his own, then lowered himself between her wide-spread thighs. He sank deep inside her, her wetness pulling him in with such eagerness that he was certain he'd explode prematurely.

"I can't hold off," he groaned as their bodies slapped together harder and harder. Claudine clung to him, pulling him against her as she twisted under his thrusts.

"Now, now, my beautiful American," she groaned. "Now!" Her head fell back and she gave herself up to the sheer ecstasy of her orgasm. At that exact moment, Marcus stiffened and bolted into her, filling her, grinding himself so deep he thought he'd lose himself inside her magnificent body.

She continued to sway beneath him, arching upward, holding his hard, throbbing shaft captive between her legs. He eased back, then pushed deep into her slithering wetness.

"That's it, Marcus," Claudine breathed, her eyes pinched shut, her head moving from side to side. "Fuck me hard, Marcus. Harder. Harder."

Marcus began to move faster, in and out. Then with a quick, hard thrust, he sank his shaft all the way in to the hilt. Claudine emitted a long, low, sensual moan and her eyelids fluttered open then closed immediately as she locked her legs around Marcus's waist and threw herself up to him.

She groaned as the heat built up in her loins. "Fuck me. Oh *Dieu*, fuck the hell out of me," she cried, becoming wilder and wilder as Marcus's shaft slipped and slid in and out of her.

"Come inside me," Claudine moaned.

Marcus's mind was in flames as he pounded and jabbed and dug deep into her soft, wet, hot body. He'd never had anyone as wild as Claudine. She was draining him of every ounce of his strength and yet he could not stop.

"I'm coming," he groaned, throwing back his head and grinding his teeth together. His fingers dug into her skin as he forced himself deep inside her and blasted out his seed. He shot bolt after bolt of steaming semen up into her.

"Don't stop, Marcus. Don't stop," she moaned. "I'm almost there. I'm coming. Oh God, j'arrive," she cried as she pushed herself hard against his body, impaling herself on the thick, hot, hard, pulsing shaft that was throbbing inside her.

An explosion went off inside her brain as her fluids erupted and the most delicious feeling rushed through her. The flood of wetness that had been dammed up inside her burst forth, a torrent of passion, sapping her strength until she found herself lying limp in his arms.

Afterward, they lay side by side staring up at the ceiling. Claudine kissed his shoulder and said, "You were right, my lovely Marcus. In your case I must admit Americans can indeed be good lovers."

"France has taught me a lot," he admitted.

"Good. Then you will stay here and never go back to wherever you came from. There are so many different ways to make love to a man," Claudine said. "Just as there are many ways a man can make love to a woman. I will show you all of them if you like."

"I'd like that," he said as he took her in his arms and kissed her passionately.

She reached for his penis and felt his erection She slapped him gently. "Enough lessons for today. We go now to meet my father. He expected me an hour ago."

Marcus had been hoping to spend the entire day with Claudine. But as soon as he saw the racing machine that Claude Muret had engineered, all thoughts of sex left his mind.

"It's magnificent," Marcus exclaimed as he studied the intricacies of the working engine with its front-mounted gasoline-powered motor. The most intriguing new invention was the electric starter Monsieur Muret had installed.

"The electric-celled battery drives the cylinders much faster, which is how the speed is accelerated," Claude Muret said.

Claudine's father was a tall, thin man who looked to be no more than thirty-five, though he had to be older, Marcus decided. He liked Claude Muret the moment they were introduced. M. Muret had the same coloration as his daughter but his eyes had a dreamlike quality as though he were always looking into the future without a single thought for the past.

"Would you like to take it for a drive?" the Frenchman asked Marcus.

"Could I?"

"Of course. I am planning on racing it in a few months here at Le Mans. Unfortunately, my eyes are not the keenest or I would drive it myself. I am looking for someone who I think would be able to handle my little pride." He smiled as he glanced from the motorcar to Claudine and then to Marcus.

"I'd be honored, sir."

"Get behind the wheel, my boy. I will ride along with you

and study your style."

The older man instructed him on the delicate turning radius, the pressure of the accelerator, and the braking distances before they started out of the garage and headed toward the dirt track that circled a large field.

"I am calling it the Muret Miracle," the older man said.

Marcus smiled as he felt the power and surge beneath him. For the first time in his life, Marcus Nightsong was desperately in love...with a motorcar.

CHAPTER TWELVE

Sean Dillon's first reaction to Los Angeles was not a favorable one. It was surprisingly hilly but otherwise hot and dry. There was nothing very exciting about the place, unless one could get excited about orange groves and lettuce fields. He'd taken the train down from San Francisco, a bit reluctant to leave Lorrie with her grandmother. However, after seeing the barren desert of Los Angeles, he was glad he hadn't brought her. The place was disheartening enough without having to listen to her complain about it.

One night with Lorna MacNair had reaffirmed his determination to see as little of her as possible. She was a cold, unfeeling woman with a heart and mind as calculating as a factory machine.

He thought again of Michael Crane. Perhaps Lorna wasn't all that cold when it came to men. Sean had telephoned Susan in New York, long distance. Susan had never heard of any family named Crane, but she'd promised to check and see what she could find out. She'd seemed disturbed when Sean voiced his suspicions about Lorna and the young Michael.

"It seems very odd that your mother would take up with a man so much younger than herself, and certainly not her class of man at all," Sean had told his wife.

"Mother has a penchant for taking up with the wrong kind of man."

Sean had wanted to know what she meant, but Susan only repeated her intention to check out this Michael Crane, if there was anything to check out.

There weren't very many expensive hotels in Hollywood, he found when he got off the train at the railroad station in what he later learned was known as downtown Los Angeles. He'd expected Hollywood—where his business contacts were—to be part and parcel of the city itself, not miles away and a complete entity all its own. He'd never seen such a spread-out place. There were shiny little red trolleys connecting the many communities to one another, but the distances were far and Sean found the trolley schedules erratic, despite their reputation for punctuality.

His hotel was on Hollywood Boulevard near the Highland Avenue intersection. Highland Avenue, Sean discovered, wound its way over the Hollywood Hills into the San Fernando Valley and a place called Glendale where Mack Sennett had just opened the Keystone Studio.

The Hollywood Hotel was a sprawling building with lots of gingerbread and large, surprisingly comfortable rooms. It was where all the best people stayed, he'd been told.

The first thing he did after settling in was to call Susan and let her know where he could be reached. She still had no news on Michael Crane to report, but she was very excited about the fact that she had managed to get hired on at one of the shirtwaist factories. She would start work there the following Monday.

"I still wish you would reconsider this idea," Sean said. "It could be dangerous, darling."

"I'm not getting into anything I can't handle, Sean. Now don't you worry about me. Just get your own business taken care of and come home. I miss you terribly. Especially on Thursdays."

"Don't make me think of your beautiful naked body or I'll never get the work done here."

"I want you to think of it every second so you won't stay away long," Susan said.

The people Sean had to meet with about the new distillery and the import liquor business were headquartered in Beverly Hills, a very smart residential community adjacent to Hollywood. Beverly Hills was much more to his liking, he found after hiring a driver and motorcar to take him into its neat, little business district. It reeked of money and progress.

"You'd never get licensed for a distillery here in this town," said a short, balding man in a tight suit, leaning back in a chair that needed a good oiling. An electric fan turned lazily from the sill of an open window. The man was Bram Phillips, and Sean had been directed to him by one of his most reliable New York suppliers.

"Beverly Hills is just a showplace of big houses and palm trees. Zoning restrictions are extremely tight. The town fathers wouldn't let a still within fifty miles of their town." Bram put his hands behind his head, showing sweaty armpits. "Your best location would be down near the harbor in San Pedro. It's fast becoming the busiest harbor outside of San Francisco, and the labor market is groaning for want of new businesses. You'd be able to get good help cheap there, and it's ideal for importing from the Orient. There's going to be a big market for liquor here as soon as the moving-picture business takes off."

"I thought I might check into that too," Sean announced, digging at his collar. He looked at the fan. "Is it always this hot?"

"Not always. We're having what they call the Santa Anas. It's a weather condition that hits us every year at about this time. Strong, hot, dust-bearing winds blow over us from the inland desert regions and travel all the way up the Pacific coastline. They don't last long, but when they come they're murder."

"This moving-picture business," Sean said. "There's a lot of speculating going on in New York about its potential."

"If you want my advice, get in on the ground floor, Mr. Dillon. It is going to be the biggest money-maker in this nation's history. Most of the moviemakers are coming out here because of the long hours of sunlight. They can shoot their pictures out-of-doors without spending a lot on artificial light."

"I wouldn't mind meeting some of these pioneers after I get straightened away with the distillery."

"No problem. I myself sank a few dollars into one of the

newer companies, so I can put you in touch with all the right people. But first things first," he said as he got up from his chair, which screeched in relief as the weight was taken off it. "We'll drive down to San Pedro. I've lined up a few places for you to look at. And there's a fellow I know who's very anxious to take your money and help you establish your import business."

Sean laughed. "There are always a lot of them hanging around."

"This guy is very trustworthy. You'll like him fine. I've been doing business with him since we were caught stealing apples from a pushcart."

"My kind of man," Sean said as he followed Phillips out of the office.

* * * * * * *

Everything was finished up much quicker than Sean had anticipated. Bram Phillips knew his business and his people. It wasn't two weeks before Sean was settled back in Bram's office with a sheaf of rental contracts and business agreements spread out before him. It was agreed to have Bram handle all the management details, though everything would have to clear through Sean's accountants and lawyers in New York.

"I've already alerted one of my best men in New York to move out and run the operation, Bram," Sean said as he checked over the legal documents and saw that they were in perfect order. "It isn't that I don't trust you, but I want someone here who knows my way of running things. You'll do the managing and he'll see to it that everything is done as I want it."

"Perfectly agreeable, Sean."

"I'll read these over at my leisure and ship them to New York," Sean said as he stuffed the documents into his briefcase.

"No rush. I'm not going anywhere and neither is that factory you've leased. When do you anticipate starting operations?"

"The equipment and machinery I need will be ordered immediately if New York gives me the go-ahead. We should be in full swing within a couple of months."

"Fine. I like the way you do business." Bram stood up. "Now, how about relaxing this evening. The little woman and I are having a few people in for a small, intimate dinner. We'd like for you to join us."

"I can't think of anything I'd enjoy more. Thank you. That hotel suite, large as it is, is beginning to feel a bit cramped to me."

"Seven o'clock then. We have a little spread in the Malibu Colony. It's smack on the beach and very comfortable. Bring some swimming togs if you'd care to take a dip in the Pacific. Most of the guests will."

"I'm not that keen on swimming."

"Then don't dress too gussy. We're very casual out here. White ducks and a blazer. Open collar. Bare feet if you want."

Sean laughed. "That's a bit too casual. I'd just as soon wear shoes if you don't think I'll be too out of place."

Bram scribbled the address on the back of his business card. "Your driver won't have any trouble finding the place. It's too big to miss."

It was indeed big. Huge. In fact, it was the largest beach house Sean had ever seen. The property rambled along the oceanfront for acres and had a high pink wall surrounding it on three sides, the fourth being wide open to the sea. There was a tangle of vehicles of all types and descriptions blocking the main entrance to the house; steam-driven motorcars and one or two of the newer gas-engine cars similar to the one Sean had hired. Inside the sprawling mansion (Sean found it difficult to think of this place as a beach house) the hordes of people were as varied as their modes of transportation. What Sean had assumed would be a small, intimate dinner party looked more like a Roman orgy.

The women were particularly surprising to him in their low-cut, revealing dresses. Some weren't even wearing dresses, just form-fitting bathing suits that revealed bare shoulders and lots of leg. Everyone seemed extremely young, suntanned, and healthy-looking.

"Most of them are with the moving-picture business," Bram explained as he began introducing Sean around.

Bram's wife was the biggest surprise of the evening. She was no more than sixteen or seventeen with the figure of a goddess. She wore her silver-blond hair in tiny ringlets all over her head and had the face of a painted China doll, with wide shadowed eyes and a cupid's-bow mouth. She introduced herself as "Crystal Lamour."

"It's her screen name," Bram explained after his dainty little wife left them. He made a sweep of the room with his hand. "They're all actors and actresses, directors, cameramen. And the directors are always looking for backers," he said with a wink.

"I'd like to talk to one. For some reason the idea of making moving pictures intrigues me. Maybe I'm a ham at heart." Sean said with a laugh.

"I think of you more as a man with a good nose for making money."

Bram brought him over to a bespectacled young man with an impish smile. "Mike," Bram said slapping the man on the back. "I want you to meet a friend of mine from New York. Sean Dillon, Mike Sinnott." The man frowned.

"Sorry," Bram said quickly. "I keep forgetting, now that you're a big moviemaker it's Mack Sennett. This is the guy who is going to be the biggest name in the picture industry one day. I used to know him when he was just old Mike Sinnott from Canada. Now that he's pulling in the bucks, he's gone all fancy and decided his real name wasn't dignified enough."

"Shit, Bram, that's not the point at all and you know it. I just wanted to get a lot of my old creditors off my back by spelling my name differently."

"I'm pleased to meet you, Mr. Sennett."

"Mack."

"You used to be with Biograph Studio in New York," Sean commented.

Mack squinted at him. "You're not with Biograph, are you?"

"No, I'm just a distiller who's interested in widening his horizons."

Bram excused himself. "I'll let you two gentlemen talk while I go see how the food's coming along. We'd better get this crowd fed or they'll all be drowning themselves in the ocean."

"Interested in making flickers, huh?" Mack asked as he escorted Sean to the bar that occupied one entire wall of the massive room.

"Interested," Sean admitted. "I read in the newspaper about your building the Keystone Studio out here."

"I saw no percentage in staying at Biograph as a writer and actor when the big money was being made behind the cameras." He eyed Sean quizzically. "You don't want to be an actor, do you?"

"God forbid."

"And no wife or daughter pestering you to get their names up in lights?"

"Nope. Just looking for a source of additional income. However, despite the glowing forecasts I've heard about the business, I find it rather hard to believe that these nickelodeons will ever bring in big profits. It's all too small-change for my tastes."

"The nickelodeons are dead, Mr. Dillon. But there are a lot of real theaters across the country which we'll be adapting for longer films. No more one-reelers. I'm going to concentrate on the comedy angle of filmmaking. The serious, arty stuff I'll leave up to Griffith."

"D. W. Griffith. Yes, I've heard of him."

"You see, in the earlier days of the flicks, the camera was kept in a fixed position, about twelve feet away from the performing area and at a right angle to it. Griffith and I and a few other directors decided to move the camera closer and closer and to use more than one angle. Now we move the camera around the action, and by photographing a single scene from several viewpoints we can mingle long shots with close-ups. There are a lot of new moviemaking techniques being developed. Flicks'll be the biggest thing in entertainment in the next few years. The time will come when people will wonder how they ever lived without moving-picture theaters. And there'll be theaters in every city, town, and borough in the country...no, the world."

"Sounds promising."

"A gold mine, Mr. Dillon. A virtual gold mine, believe me."

"I'm interested. What kind of costs are involved in making a film?"

Mack shrugged. "Depends on the flick. If we can do it without a lot of fancy sets and costumes, naturally the costs come down. Now out here in California the weather is an important factor in keeping expenses to a minimum. We have the perfect climate and, of course, a variety of natural scenery that is ideal for making all types of flicks. There's a desert as well as an ocean, not to mention mountains, cities, and farms. Everything is right here. All we have to do is move the actors and cameras out to the appropriate scenery." He reached into his pocket and handed Sean his business card. "Drive on out to Glendale when you get a chance and I'll show you the layout I've built. I think you'll be impressed."

* * * * * * *

When Sean showed up at Sennett's studio a few days later, he was indeed impressed. Though it all looked rather bizarre, what with actors walking about in strange costumes and cameramen yelling and gesturing without any apparent sense of order, there was something very magical about it too. Sean felt as if he had stepped into a fairyland where troubles did not exist and the real world was some faraway place which everyone knew would not have to be dealt with until the end of the day. In the meantime it was all make-believe, and Sean was as swept up by it as those who were actually creating the fantasies.

"We're a little disorganized, as you can see, Dillon," Mack said, pointing at several carpenters who were trying, unsuccessfully, to stretch a huge painted canvas on a wooden frame. "But then none of us has ever worked together before, so everything is new and experimental."

"It's rather exciting," Sean admitted. "So different from any other kind of business."

"It's different all right, but don't forget for a minute, Dillon, that it is a business. There's plenty of money to be made here. "

"I believe you're right."

"Now where Griffith and the others are planning to concentrate on the big dramatic flicks with lots of plot, I'm sticking to the simple slapstick stuff. I want to make people laugh. I plan on rejecting the logical values of everyday life. My bathing beauties won't fall for the handsome young swain. They'll go for the fat older guy, because fat older guys are the ones who need the fantasies most and will pay to get them. When I film a catastrophe it will be funny and no one will ever get hurt. Cops will never arrest anyone...unless, of course, it's the wrong person."

Sean was laughing.

"See, Dillon, you're amused already and you haven't even seen the pictures."

"The idea is damned good, I must say."

"Of course it's good. I intend making fast, funny pictures with lots of action. Pies in the face, pants falling down, stuff like that."

"As I said before, I'm definitely interested."

Mack raised his eyebrow. "I could always use an angel."

"Angel?"

"In show business, that's what they call the guy who puts up the bucks."

"How much?"

"Let's go into my office and talk about it. I'm sure we can agree on something, Dillon."

Sean was sure they could. Never before had he felt so excited about a new business venture.

CHAPTER THIRTEEN

Susan was completely flabbergasted after her long-distance telephone conversation with Sean. She couldn't believe he was serious about wanting to move the family to Los Angeles.

"You've been drinking," Susan had accused.

"Not a drop, love. Just excited out of my head."

He'd raved on about the Mack Sennett comedies and what a potential gold mine they were. Of course he would keep the distilleries; he'd simply move the head office to California, where he'd continue as head of the company.

Susan thought of Los Angeles as someplace out in the middle of a desert. And she didn't want to leave New York. There was so much to be done there to improve the working conditions of the city's less fortunate citizens. In her mind there weren't any unfortunates in California.

She'd been working long, hard hours at the factory every day for the past few weeks and was finally beginning to make some progress in organizing the garment workers. But too many of them neither spoke nor understood English, and none of them wanted to complain openly about anything. They were afraid they'd be fired or—worse still—beaten up, which had been the fate of several men who'd tried to organize a union. The sweat-shop owners ruled with the help of an army of thugs who kept the slave labor in line with threats and occasional shows of force.

Susan slept restlessly after her talk with Sean. She spent much of the night writing him a long, serious letter, explaining why she was opposed to their leaving New York, reasons which would have been far too costly to go into on the long-distance telephone.

In the morning, however, she decided to wait a bit before posting her letter. She wanted to reread it and take out anything that might upset Sean. They'd never had a major disagreement about anything. This time, however, she wasn't too sure one could be avoided.

She dressed in her usual raggedy work clothes after seeing the boys off to school. Her housekeeper thought her foolish to be bothering with things that were none of her business.

"Someone has to," Susan argued.

"It's dangerous, Mrs. Dillon. You have your family to think about."

She rationalized that the boys were old enough to more or less take care of themselves. Besides, she was dedicated to the cause of helping the underprivileged. Sean had some political connections, as did she. They could be extremely helpful when the time came to approach them with the hard facts about the terrible conditions endured by the poor people who worked in the factories.

"Proof is what we need," the state senator had once told her.

"And proof is what you'll get," she'd promised.

It was a cold, gray morning when she let herself out of the townhouse and hurried toward the subway. People along the avenue looked at her strangely as she went along, clutching her thin coat about her. So far she'd succeeded in keeping her true identity secret from her employers and fellow employees. Even the five cents she spent to ride the subway was never mentioned to anyone. Most of the girls who worked in the garment district walked to work. Five cents for a subway ride both ways each day was a luxury none of them could afford.

The factory was already crowded with workers when Susan arrived. It wasn't that she was late; the others had simply left their cold flats early to take advantage of the warmth of the factory workrooms. Women and children were busy at the sewing machines, cutting tables, and sorting bins. Every worker was paid on a piecework basis. The rooms were dimly lit and poorly ventilated.

Susan's goal was to get laws passed establishing minimum wages, limiting the number of hours women could work, and abolishing child labor completely.

"I want to set up a meeting," Susan said to Mrs. Antolini, the woman who worked at the machine beside hers.

The young Italian shook her head. "No. No meeting, Susan. It is too dangerous."

"But I need you to talk to the other Italians in their own language and explain what I'm trying to do for them. Emma promised to speak to the Polish workers. Unless everyone stands together, nothing will change."

"I cannot get involved, Susan. My husband will need his supper when I get home. And I have children to look after."

"We can meet after work, just for a few minutes."

Susan didn't hear or see the burly supervisor walk up behind her. "Meet after work for what?" the man asked through the cigar stump clenched between his teeth. He was a thick German with meaty hands and narrow, cruel eyes. Mrs. Antolini quickly turned away as Susan fumbled with the shirtwaist she was working on.

"Just a meeting, Mr. Kraus. Woman talk," Susan said.

Helmut Kraus had been attracted to Susan from the first day she'd come to work in his department. There was something about her that was different from the others. She didn't belong here, of that he was sure. Her English was too perfect. She carried herself with too much dignity. He'd followed her when she left the factory one evening and he knew she took a subway...an uptown subway.

"Woman talk," he sneered. He put one of his large hands on her shoulder and caressed it gently. Susan cringed slightly and kept her eyes fixed on her sewing. Helmut leaned close to her ear. "I like you, Susan, so I will tell you something that will help you to stay out of trouble."

Susan didn't look up. She felt his hands move over her

shoulder, closer to her breast.

"The boss man told me to keep my eyes on you," he said. His breath reeked of stale cigar smoke. "You are being watched, little lady, because the big man thinks you are trouble. Now you take my advice and behave yourself. I only warn you because I like you. I like you very, very much."

When his hand touched her breast she stiffened and moved away. "I don't want you touching me," she said angrily.

The big German saw the hatred in her eyes and glared down at her. "It would be a mistake not to be nice to Kraus, Susan," he threatened.

"Leave me alone," she said in a voice loud enough to carry across the entire workroom. The other women were looking at them.

Kraus backed off. He'd been warned several times by his boss about pawing the girls. "You make trouble for Kraus," he growled, "and I will make trouble for you, Miss High-and-Mighty."

After he walked away, Mrs. Antolini leaned close and whispered, "Be careful of Kraus, Susan. He is a very bad man."

"I can take care of myself."

Mrs. Antolini shook her head and bent over her work again. "I pray that you can."

Susan felt unnerved by her exchange with Kraus but forced herself to stay calm. He was indeed a dangerous man, she knew, and could cause a lot of trouble for her. She wasn't ready yet to expose her hand. If she lost her job now, she'd be powerless to do anything for the other workers. She needed more time.

It was a little before four o'clock when Mrs. Antolini suddenly looked up and sniffed the air. Her eyes were wide with alarm. "Smoke," she gasped. "I smell smoke." She turned from Susan to the woman on her other side. "Fumo."

The young Italian woman sniffed the air. "Si, "she gasped, her voice strangled by fear.

The others smelled it at the same moment. They all sat riveted to their stools, staring at the single door that led to the corridor.

Suddenly the door burst open and a little girl of about eight years old raced into the room.

"Fire!" the child screamed. "The floor below is on fire."

Panic broke out as the screaming women rushed toward the door.

"Stay calm, everyone," Susan yelled over the tumult. "Stay calm!"

No one listened to her. Already they could feel the heat beneath their feet, and the smoke was growing thicker and thicker as it drifted up between the cracks in the floorboards.

"Good God," Susan gasped as she heard the distinct sound of crackling flames.

Pandemonium erupted. The women and children dashed for the exit only to be trapped in the narrow passageways to the outer halls. On the narrow, smoke-clogged stairway, bodies toppled over bodies as the terrified workers scratched and clawed their way down the wooden steps. The flames licked their way upward, blistering the floors, buckling the walls. The women pushed into one another in a desperate attempt to open the windows and locked fire doors. Flames crackled at their backs. There was only one elevator in the building that worked, and its capacity was limited to just ten people. Those who were fortunate enough to squeeze into the elevator closed the door, leaving others standing there with no choice but to throw themselves down the shaft onto the top of the descending car. Many died as they fell.

Susan tried to keep her wits. She saw the futility of trying to escape by going downward. She grabbed a young girl who was about to jump out of a window to the ground six floors below. She pulled the child back and carried her, kicking and screaming, toward the far end of the room. Mrs. Antolini was crouched in a corner, her fingers moving rapidly over the rosary beads she clutched in her hand.

"Come with me," Susan ordered, still carrying the hysterical little girl.

Mrs. Antolini didn't move.

Susan grabbed her roughly and pulled her to her feet. "We've got to get up to the roof. It's our only chance," she yelled as she heard the dying screams of the women and children in the passageway.

The door at the opposite end of the room, directly over the fire below, was locked. Susan handed the little girl to Mrs. Antolini, threw her full weight into one of the sewing machines, and rammed it with all her might against the door. The door splintered but stayed shut. Again and again Susan rammed the door, finally wrenching it from its hinges.

"Climb up the ladder," she ordered, then turned back into the room and screamed for others to follow them. She saw the trapped women turn and start to rush toward her, blind desperation moving them forward with every intent of trampling anything and anyone they found in their path. Susan ran through the door and up the already hot metal rungs that led to the roof.

Mrs. Antolini and the little girl had managed to push open the trapdoor that led them out into fresher air. The tar of the roof was already soft from the heat.

Susan pulled those behind her up through the shaft until the billowing smoke clogged her breath and stung her eyes. She staggered back, unable to see.

"The roof! It will collapse under us," Mrs. Antolini screamed, still clutching her rosary to her breast.

"Across to the adjoining building," Susan yelled, pointing to a narrow air shaft that they would have to leap over. "It's not far. Don't be afraid. We can jump it easily," she said encouragingly.

One by one she coaxed them on, jumping the space first to show them how simple it was. When the last of the sixteen hysterical women and children were safely on the opposite roof, she hurried them to the fire escape. She had to stop them from all rushing down at one time. The shirtwaist factory was an inferno. Under the weight of too many fleeing women, its fire escapes had buckled and collapsed, dropping dozens of hysterical workers to the hard, cold cement below.

It wasn't until Susan herself had carefully made her way down the shaky fire ladder and reached the pavement that she found her own hysteria beginning to grow. How she had remained calm and sensible during the holocaust she didn't know. Now she felt the burns on her hands, the blisters of her feet, the scorched patches of skin on her arms and face. The terror she had endured came home to her in such a bone-wracking rush that she put her hands over her face and started to scream. She didn't dare uncover her eyes to look at the mangled dead that littered the ground. The roar of the flames, the shouts of the firemen pounded against her brain.

Silently Susan thanked God that there were no more screams of the dying—the fire's toll had been taken. There would be some who would die in the hospitals. Susan couldn't think of them. She could think only of the injustice of it all. The factory had been a deathtrap, a needless deathtrap, and the money-hungry owners were to blame for this terrible tragedy. These senseless deaths would be on their conscience forever, she told herself.

But no, they would not feel any remorse. There had been other fires, even deadlier ones, and no one had lifted a finger to prevent more of them.

"Murderers!" Susan shouted when she lowered her hands and saw two of the owners sitting safe and snug in their big touring car, watching the flames and chatting calmly. They seemed unfazed, so unruffled by the horror around them that Susan lost all sense of reason. She ran to the automobile and pounded on the hood.

"You killed them all, you bastards," she shrieked. "Killers! I'll see that you pay for this if it's the last thing I do."

One of the fat, smooth-looking men scowled at her. "Who are you? Get the hell away from here."

"I'll go away, but I will go to the authorities with this."

The other man seated farther inside the car leaned toward his partner. "It's the Dillon woman. The one I told you about. She's been trying to stir up trouble among the girls ever since she came to work here."

Susan heard him. "Yes, I'm Susan Dillon. And, believe me, I intend to make more trouble than you've ever had in your rotten lives," she yelled hysterically. "I'll see that you are held responsible for this disaster. Those people would be alive if you'd given them and your crummy factory the slightest bit of attention. But no," she raved, "you were too damned busy making money to care. What does another dumb immigrant's life mean to any of you? Nothing. Well, let me warn you, things are going to be different from now on. I will personally see to that."

Her eyes blazed at them.

"You shut your mouth or you'll be sorry," the fat man warned.

She spat in his face and turned away from the carnage, pulling her thin coat about her. Tears blinded her as she pushed through the staring crowd and ran down the street as fast as she could.

"She's got to be stopped," the fat man said, wiping the spittle from his cheek.

"Kraus can take care of her."

"Good. Do it right away. Don't give her a chance to see or talk to anyone."

"Right."

At the end of the street Susan turned the corner and ran until she could run no more. When she reached the avenue she leaned against the building and tried to calm herself. Deep, wrenching sobs contracted her chest as the hot, thick tears streamed down her face. She was afraid to close her eyes for fear of seeing the terrible nightmare again. She had to get home, far away from the blazing inferno, the blackened dead faces, the crumpled twisted scorched bodies. Somehow she managed to flag down a taxicab and collapsed in the back seat, hugging herself into a comer. She didn't even hear the driver's attempts at conversation. She sat staring out the window seeing nothing, hearing only the heartbreaking shrieks and cries of the dying.

"My God!" she sobbed as her whole body started to shake.

It was the same expression her housekeeper used when Susan

stumbled into the townhouse. "My God! What happened, Mrs. Dillon?"

For a moment Susan couldn't speak. The taste of smoke burned her throat and mouth. "A fire in the factory," she managed.

The housekeeper blessed herself quickly. "Come," she said after a moment, putting her arms around Susan. Slowly she helped her up the staircase and into the bedroom. She sat Susan on the edge of the bed. "Lie back, Mrs. Dillon. I'll see to those burns and call for the doctor."

The minute Susan lay back and put her arm across her eyes the terrible scene came alive again. She screamed and buried her face in the pillows. She felt as if she were suffocating. Then she fainted.

Sometime later, after the doctor had left and Susan had fallen into a laudanum-induced sleep, she opened her eyes to a dark, quiet room. She moved her head and slowly started recognizing the safe, familiar objects that seemed to be standing guard around her. Carefully she eased herself up from the bed. Her head felt heavy and thick, her eyes swollen, her tongue dry. Her legs were wobbly when she tried to stand. She fell back and reached for the carafe of water on the nightstand.

The water refreshed her a little. She hobbled to the window and pushed it open, inhaling the cold, clear night air, sucking it deep into her lungs. The air made her feel better, stronger, and the heaviness inside her head started to lighten.

The housekeeper met her halfway down the staircase. "You mustn't be up, Mrs. Dillon. Go back to bed. I was just coming to see if you felt hungry."

"No, thank you, Annie. I'd just as soon go out and get some fresh air. I'm feeling much better now. A walk will do me more good than anything."

"But the doctor said—"

Susan cut her off with an impatient wave of her hand. "I want to go out for a while. Are the boys in bed?"

"Hours ago. It's too late for you to go strolling about the

streets, Mrs. Dillon."

"I'm all right, Annie. Don't worry about me. I'll only be gone for as long as it takes to walk around the block."

The housekeeper started to protest again, but Susan pushed herself into her heavy coat, wrapped a long scarf around her throat, and pulled on her fur hat. "I won't be long. Fix me some soup and a sandwich. I think I'll feel hungry when I get back."

As she went down the steps and looked across Fifth Avenue at the park, the trees seemed to beckon her. To Susan, their deep, dark shadows represented such a contrast to the angry, brilliant flames of the fire that she wanted to lose herself in them. She wanted to be somewhere where she could hear no sound of traffic, no voices. All she wished to hear was the soft slow sighs of the tree branches swaying in the gentle night breeze.

Head down, hands stuck deep into the pockets of her coat, Susan made her way across the avenue and walked into the park. She had no thought of fear; the fears of the day were already past.

Unnoticed by Susan, Helmut Kraus and another man who could easily pass for his twin in size and stature, slipped out of the shadows and began following her down the dark, winding path that led to the lake.

It wasn't until she was almost at the water's edge that Susan heard the snap of the twig and turned around. Silhouetted against the dim light of the moon she saw the outlines of two men walking purposefully toward her.

"Who are you? What do you want?" she asked harshly. She still felt no fear because all emotion had been drained out of her earlier.

"You shouldn't have said what you did, Mrs. Dillon. The boss didn't like it," Kraus said.

"Kraus? What are you doing here?"

He came closer, the other man right behind him.

"You've got to be taught a lesson, Mrs. Dillon."

"Yeah," the other man chortled. "The last lesson you'll ever learn."

"Shut up," Kraus barked.

Susan backed away until she found herself pressed against a large tree. "Leave me alone, Kraus. You'll regret whatever it is you intend doing."

Kraus grunted. "You ain't going to be around to do anything about it, Mrs. Dillon. Not after we're finished with you." He stood there looking at her lustfully.

"Come on, Kraus. Get it over with. Somebody might come along."

"Not at this hour. Besides, Mrs. Dillon here owes me a favor and I want to collect."

"Favor? What favor?" Susan asked, her voice suddenly tight with fear.

"The favor of that body you won't give me. So if you won't give it to me, then I guess I'll have to take it, won't I?" He stepped closer. "You think you're too grand for the likes of me, huh?" he snarled as he reached out and pulled her into his brawny arms.

Susan opened her mouth to scream, but Kraus put his meaty hand over it and with his other hand tore open her coat.

"Strangle the bitch and let's get the hell out of here like we were told, Kraus."

"Go stand guard up on the path. I'll take care of everything here."

Susan struggled and tried to sink her teeth into his palm, but his grip was too firm. Helplessly she kicked and scratched as he ripped her dress aside and fell with her to the ground. The cold, coarse earth cut into her back as Kraus tore away her undergarments and forced himself between her thighs.

His breath was sour as he brought his face close to hers, and when he took his hand away he strangled her scream with his mouth. He wrapped his arms around her, raising her buttocks for better access, and jammed his swollen penis deep inside her.

Susan screamed under his demanding mouth, only to feel his snaking tongue dart deep down her throat. The taste and smell of him was revolting, but his hard, powerful body held her captive.

Kraus began to pound away, his breath rasping, his hands and fingers digging into the softness of her half-naked body. Then suddenly he gave a strained cry and arched his back, pushing his hard, thick member all the way into her. Again and again he thrust and pushed and ground against her as he growled out the agonizing pleasure of his orgasm.

Susan cried out in pain when his mouth uncovered her. He put his hands around her throat and started to squeeze. Susan kicked and thrashed, trying to tear his hands from her neck. Her eyes bulged in their sockets as she stared up at his leering, evil face.

"Hurry up, for Christ's sake," the other man called. "I think somebody's coming."

The grip around her throat tightened. She found she could not breathe and that her body was growing weaker and weaker. Slowly her eyes closed as the last of her breath passed out of her. Her head lolled to one side. Her lids dropped shut and the pounding inside her head exploded. Somewhere far, far back in the dimmest recesses of her mind, Susan felt Kraus's fingers loosen, but she was too weakened to make the slightest move. Every muscle in her body had died, she thought, and it would only be a matter of seconds before her mind died too and her heart stopped beating.

She didn't know how long she lay there, barely conscious. When she opened her eyes she found she was alone. The trees overhead moved like giant phantoms calling her back among the living.

She wasn't dead. She moved her fingers, then her arms. She rolled over on her side and pulled her tattered clothes around her chilled body. The pain between her thighs burned like smoldering coals. The night was still and cold as she gathered herself together and got to her feet.

They'd left her for dead, she realized as she stumbled and staggered out of the park. She couldn't let them know she was still alive or they'd be back. And the next time they would be sure to finish their job properly.

Susan knew she had to get away, out of New York, as far from the city as possible. She thought suddenly of the letter she had not yet mailed to Sean. She would destroy it the moment she reached home. There was nothing for her to do now but to close down the house, take herself and her two boys, and flee to California and the safety of her husband's arms.

Trying to keep herself alive in New York was useless, she knew.

CHAPTER FOURTEEN

Lorna MacNair looked at the small package she'd purchased at Magnin's that afternoon. She had seen the display for the new Nightsong perfume and been unable to resist buying it, though it galled her to think that her money was going to the woman she hated most in the world.

She undid the fancy wrapping and took out the small phial with its footed base and crescent-moon stopper of crystal. The six ounces had cost a small fortune, but as she held the bottle to her nose and inhaled, she was captivated by its exotic, haunting aroma.

"Damn that woman," Lorna swore as she stared at the bottle. "It's almost superior to the original."

Carefully she applied a drop behind each ear, a touch to the inside of each elbow, and a light streak between her full breasts. It was indeed one of the most beautiful scents she'd ever worn. She knew she should be angry that Lydia had perfected so beautiful a perfume, but Lorna found herself pleased. After all, this new Nightsong would be hers one day soon.

She had taken Michael's advice and done nothing about pressing her lawsuit against Lydia. There'd be plenty of time to go ahead with it after the new Nightsong II perfume was on the market.

Working on the inside of Empress Cosmetics, Michael had learned much about their operations and he reported to Lorna regularly. She would have him continue at his menial job there, at least for a while, she decided. Once she had control of everything Lydia owned, Michael would never have to work another day of his life. She'd see to that.

As she gazed at her reflection she saw the telltale lines of age around her eyes and mouth. She was too old for Michael, but despite the many lectures she'd given herself, she knew she wouldn't send him away. She was in love with the young man and there was nothing she could do but let herself love him. It was totally foolish of her, of course, but she'd always been foolish when it came to men.

Lorrie, however, was a worry. The girl was headstrong and obviously infatuated with Michael. Hard as Lorna had tried to dissuade her granddaughter from pursuing Michael, Lorrie would not be stopped. Threatening Michael had worked to a degree, though Michael insisted he'd never encouraged the girl and was in fact doing everything in his power to discourage her. Deep down Lorna didn't believe that, but she knew Michael would eventually do exactly what she said. First, of course, he'd try to deceive her on the sly. She expected that. What man wouldn't?

"Men are beasts," she said aloud as she adjusted the neckline of her evening dress and slipped on a wide diamond bracelet. But she had to admit it was the beast in men that attracted her. And, after all, the female of the species was always far more dangerous than the male.

Before leaving the bedroom, Lorna picked up the phial of Nightsong II, lifted her long skirt, and smeared a touch on both thighs.

Michael's hair would smell of it before the night was finished, she told herself with a cocky tilt of her head.

Lorrie was sitting in the large wing chair next to the fireplace in the library, feet tucked under her, a thin book in her lap. When Lorna entered, Lorrie eyed her suspiciously. "You look as if you're going out to meet a very important man, Grandmother."

"Why do you say that? I'm only going to the Vernons' for a game of bridge."

"It surprises me that you'd have anything to do with the

Vernons. They're so terribly common."

"I'm only being sociable, my dear. When funds are needed for my various charities, the Vernons never disappoint me."

"Because they're nothing but social climbers."

"Very wealthy social climbers, darling. Of course, they haven't the background to ever go very far in San Francisco society, but their contributions are always generous and we never make any promises in return for that generosity."

Lorrie smiled and let her eyes move slowly over her grandmother's beautiful evening dress. "I'm not sure I like that gown."

Lorna fussed with the neckline and turned away, catching a glimpse of herself in the mirror against the far wall. "What's wrong with it? My dressmaker said it was the latest thing."

"For young ladies," Lorrie said sweetly.

"Perhaps you're right." She glanced at the clock. "Unfortunately it's too late for me to change now." She kissed Lorrie's cheek. "And after all," she added with a sly smile, "I'm not out to impress Mrs. Vernon. She wouldn't know style from a burlap sack."

Lorrie laughed and bade her grandmother good night. She watched suspiciously as Lorna left the room swaying her hips in a manner Lorrie thought most unsuitable for a woman of her age. She was going to meet a man, Lorrie told herself as she listened for the front door to close. Michael, no doubt. They'd had long arguments about Michael. Considering how strenuously her grandmother seemed to disapprove of him, she certainly didn't discourage his telephone calls, always twittering into the mouthpiece like some silly schoolgirl and coming away from the phone slightly flushed.

On impulse, Lorrie got up and went to the telephone. She asked the operator to connect her with the Vernon residence. A maid answered, and Lorrie asked to speak with her grandmother. "I believe she is playing bridge with the Vernons this evening," she explained.

"You must be mistaken, Miss," the maid replied. "The Vernons have been in Europe since the middle of last month.

They aren't expected back for another four weeks."

Lorrie slammed down the receiver. Her grandmother was meeting Michael, she fumed jealously. She'd never seriously entertained the thought of her grandmother as her rival, but she knew now that she was.

"That old bitch!" Lorrie swore as she flounced up the stairs and into her room. She stomped over to the window and pulled back the curtain, staring out at the dark night. Somehow, someway she had to have Michael for herself. How, she didn't know, but she would get him if it was the last thing she ever did.

In all her life, Lorrie had never thought it would be possible to dislike her grandmother. But she disliked her intensely now. What, Lorrie wondered, could Michael possibly see in an old fool of a woman like Lorna? She thought about this for a long time and finally came to the conclusion that her grandmother must have some sort of hold on Michael, something that made him afraid of her and willing to do whatever she demanded of him.

Well, Lorrie reminded herself, she had always gotten what she wanted and no one was going to stand in her way this time either. These past months with Michael had convinced her that he was the only man she'd ever really wanted. Oh, the boys back in New York had just been toys, nothing but trifles to tease and tempt. But Michael was different. He was so mature, so devilishly handsome, and there was a certain coldness in his eyes that absolutely captivated her.

A sudden smile lit up her face as it occurred to her that perhaps she had things wrong. Perhaps Michael was using her grandmother instead of the other way around. She smiled to herself, liking the thought. She and Michael were two of a kind. They were meant for one another and no one, not even her almost senile grandmother, was going to keep them apart.

On impulse she considered going to Michael's apartment and surprising them. But no, better to bide her time and work her wiles on Michael. If it was money he needed, well she had money and could get any amount necessary from her father.

And she was pretty and so much younger than that horrid old biddy of a grandmother.

She'd wait, Lorrie decided, suddenly anxious for her next meeting with Michael so she could begin playing her game. And this game, she vowed, was not one she'd lose.

* * * * * * *

On Saturday morning, Lydia Nightsong decided not to go into her office. She felt lazy and tired after the weekly grind.

During her temporary retirement, she'd forgotten how taxing a long day of work could be. This morning she would luxuriate in a bath, enjoy a large breakfast, and then wander around the stores. She hadn't been shopping in weeks, and there were so many things she wanted to buy.

It was almost eleven-thirty when she came into the gleaming breakfast room with its walls of glass, its green-and-white rattan furniture.

As she put the eggs and sausages down and filled Lydia's coffee cup, Nellie said, "That lawyer friend of yours is here again. I told him to wait in the library."

"Mr. Haskings?"

"That's the one."

"How long has he been there?"

"Not long. Maybe a quarter of an hour. I told him you didn't want to be disturbed, but he insisted upon waiting."

"Ask him to come in, and bring another place setting. He may not have had his breakfast."

Peter Haskings was a tall, good-looking man in his late fifties. He had dark brown hair, silver at the temples. His face was square and pleasant with wide brown eyes that glistened when he smiled. The first time he had come into her office, Lydia had been somewhat taken aback by the strong resemblance between Peter MacNair and Peter Haskings. The fact that both men had the same first name disconcerted her all the more.

"Good morning, Peter," she said now, offering him her hand

without getting up. "Have you had your breakfast?"

He nodded. "I'll have some coffee though."

Nellie filled his cup and left them alone.

"You're looking very serious, Peter."

"I'm afraid I have some rather upsetting news, Lydia. Mrs. MacNair's lawyers have been in touch with me again. They are going to proceed with the lawsuit against your corporations."

"Dear me. I thought she'd decided to drop that. It will just mean dragging out all the old skeletons again. At least that's what the newspapers will do."

"I believe I know why she waited so long before filing against you."

"Oh?" She didn't chance looking at him. It was rather disturbing, this odd sense that she was with Peter MacNair instead of Peter Haskings.

The lawyer sipped the coffee and added two lumps of sugar and a little cream. Lydia noticed. That was the way Peter MacNair had always taken his coffee.

He said, "How is Nightsong Two selling?"

"Extremely well."

"That's what Lorna MacNair was hoping for. Now if she succeeds in taking you over, she'll get the new Nightsong perfume as well."

Lydia remained calm. "Lorna doesn't frighten me, Peter. She may make trouble, but nothing will come of it."

"I'm not so sure about that, Lydia. Lorna has a very good case against you. First of all, she has an excellent chance of getting MacNair Products back."

"She can have it. It's not a very good line anyway, and the profits are marginal."

"Then there's her fifty percent holding your parent company. That's what she's really after."

"Do you really think Lorna can take half of Empress?"

"She may be able to take all of it if we aren't careful. It could get very sticky, Lydia, what with your daughter, April, being Lorna's daughter-in-law. Then there's all the evidence that her husband was your lover." He saw her blush. "I don't mean to be crass, Lydia, but facts are facts. Public sentiment will be with Lorna MacNair. She'll bring out your past, and she'll make it sound as sordid as possible. You'll come out looking like some scheming harlot who inveigled everything you could out of Lorna's vulnerable husband."

"Peter MacNair vulnerable?" Lydia laughed. "Good God."

"She'll make him appear as such, believe me. You're going to be the heavy in this piece, and you know how everyone likes to hiss at the heavy."

Lydia frowned. "What is it you think I should do, Peter?"

"Go to Lorna."

"Never."

"She's not the smartest businesswoman in the world. I think if you can convince her that her husband spoke of no one but her when he lay dying in your arms, she might begin to relent a little."

"She'd never believe that in a million years."

"She might. Humble yourself, Lydia. Tell her that in his last days all he spoke of was going back to the only woman he loved. Lay it on thick. Tell her that MacNair admitted he never really loved you, that he knew he was dying and all he wanted was to be with his wife and the children he loved. Tell her how he longed to go home to them. Tell her he railed at you. Tell her anything you like, but get her to believe that in the end it was she who won Peter MacNair, not you."

Lydia felt a sinking inside her. The only time she had really possessed Peter MacNair was when he lay dying, and now she was being asked to make a lie of that. "I don't think I can do it, Peter."

"Then you may lose everything."

Lydia felt helpless. "She wouldn't believe me, I tell you."

"She would if you handle yourself convincingly. You didn't attend Peter's funeral, and you stayed closed up in this house for months afterward. She most likely thinks it was due to your grief."

"It was."

"Let her think it was due to your rage, that you refused to mourn a man you'd loved all your life who had suddenly declared that he'd never truly loved you at all. Give her MacNair Products and let her know you want nothing whatsoever to do with any of the MacNairs and would appreciate it if she'd return the fifty percent claim her husband so cunningly connived to steal from you."

Lydia shook her head. "I couldn't go through with it."

He reached over and took her hand. "It's the only solution I can think of, Lydia. A court battle would prove extremely costly to everyone concerned, and I'm not just talking money-wise. I know your cash position at Empress, Lydia. You can't afford a long, hard legal fight right now."

The touch of his hand felt so comforting. It had been a long time since she'd allowed a man to touch her. She let her shoulders sag. After all, she thought, what difference did it make what Lorna thought about Peter? The truth was that Peter MacNair had died proclaiming his everlasting love for Lydia Nightsong. No lie she told Lorna would ever change that.

"I'll try," she said finally.

"Good girl."

Peter Haskings stood, holding his hat in one hand, his briefcase in the other. He hesitated a moment, then asked, "Are you free for dinner this evening, Lydia?"

"Dinner?" She looked up in surprise.

Peter stood there awkwardly, feeling like a young teenager asking a girl out for the first time.

"Yes. I thought we could go down to one of those nice little restaurants on the wharf."

She looked up at his face as if seeing him for the first time.

He flushed slightly. "I'm not all law books and legal clauses," he said. "There's an honest-to-goodness flesh-and-blood man under these clothes."

"It's just that—" She cut herself off. She thought for a moment, remembering how she'd enjoyed his touch. "Yes, Peter, I'd like to have dinner with you. Call for me at seven-thirty."

His whole face lit up. For a moment she thought he might jump up and down and click his heels. Instead he remained quite composed. "Seven-thirty," he said, his cheeks flushed slightly.

"I'll look forward to seeing you then."

"So will I."

After Peter left, Lydia found herself humming softly as she finished her breakfast and started back upstairs to dress for her shopping trip. It had been a long time since a man had looked at her the way Peter Haskings had a while ago. He was definitely attractive and well established, highly placed in San Francisco society. But she had to remind herself that she was fifty-eight years old and could never become interested in any man. She was certain there was no room in her heart for anyone but Peter MacNair.

Still, it was rather flattering to be admired by a man like Peter Haskings. Suddenly she realized she knew nothing whatsoever about Peter's private life. Was he married? Did he have children? Surely a man as attractive as he hadn't been a bachelor all his life; and if he had been, then it was unnatural. She couldn't help looking forward to her evening, however, making lists in her head of all the questions she wanted to ask him.

Lydia decided upon the brown afternoon dress with the heavy braid and the smart brown hat with the egret feathers. The chauffeur was waiting when she came down the steps of the mansion.

She hadn't expected to see Lorna MacNair so soon after her discussion with Peter but there she was, standing at the glass counter examining men's shirts and ties with a young man—a very young man, Lydia noticed. Lorna was obviously taking great delight in the shopping expedition, making dozens of selections for him, holding cravats under his chin, scrutinizing his coloration before deciding on a choice. Lydia watched, fascinated and unseen, as Lorna bought a dozen shirts, six ties, and two dozen pairs of hose, paying for them with her own money.

In the suit department Lydia again watched with interest as

Lorna dictated to the tailor how the jackets and trousers were to be cut, closely examining the fabrics and choosing only the most expensive. She bought three complete suits, including vests, one evening jacket, and two hats.

As they were leaving the store, Lydia saw the young man stop in front of the jewelry counter, admiring something in the case. Lorna laughed when he spoke to her, pulling him away. Lydia distinctly heard her say, "I just bought you diamond cuff links for your birthday." Then Lydia saw Lorna turn and smile at the jewelry clerk and remark, "Don't ever spoil a nephew. They get too accustomed to it."

"Nephew?" Lydia asked herself. Lorna MacNair had no nephew.

Lydia hurried to her car without being seen by Lorna. She sat in the back of her Rolls until Lorna and the young man hailed a taxi, then told her chauffeur to follow them at a discreet distance.

The taxi pulled up in front of a smart apartment building on Powell Street. It was a new building and very modern. Lydia stopped her Rolls a short distance back and watched as Lorna and her "nephew" got out. Lorna paid the taxi fare. Once the twosome had disappeared inside the building, Lydia got out of her limousine and walked to the doorway. Inside the small marble foyer, four brass mailboxes were embedded in the wall. Three belonged to married couples. The fourth—the top floor flat—bore the name "Michael Crane."

Lydia walked slowly back to the Rolls Royce, searching her brain in an effort to remember where she'd heard that name before. She kept repeating it and repeating it, and then it came to her. Michael Crane was the young man Efrem MacNair had asked Leon to find a place for in Empress Cosmetics. He was employed there now. If she wasn't mistaken, the man was a distant relative of Efrem's wife, the former Ellen Stanton.

Why was Lorna being so generous with this young man?

Lydia asked herself. She wasn't particularly pleased with the answer that came almost immediately, remembering the stories she'd heard about Lorna's affair with that Mr. Ramsey.

It wasn't possible. Michael Crane was just a boy, no more than in his early twenties. Still, there was something to this relationship that needed checking into. She'd mention it to Peter Haskings when she saw him that evening for dinner.

After a sumptuous meal of sautéed soft-shell crabs and wild rice, preceded by a lobster bisque and cold shrimp, Lydia pushed away her plate. "Not another bite. I'm blowing up like a balloon."

"Never. Your figure is beautiful, Lydia." His eyes grew earnest. "You're beautiful," he murmured.

Lydia laughed self-consciously and touched her hair. "You've had too much wine, Peter. I'm rather old to be called beautiful."

"You're the loveliest woman I have ever met."

She shifted uncomfortably. "You have been drinking too much wine."

"I mean it. I think I fell in love with you the first time I walked into your office."

"Peter, please," she said, her eyes darting about nervously.

"Surely you must have sensed my attraction to you?"

She didn't look at him but rather at her hands folded in her lap. "Truthfully, no. I have never thought of any man except Peter MacNair, if you want me to be perfectly candid."

"Isn't it time you put Peter MacNair in your past where he belongs?"

"No."

"Why don't you try?"

She didn't speak for a moment. She only looked at him, searching his face. "Do you want me to try with you, Peter?"

He shrugged. "It's as good a start as any. I'm a widower, respectable, and I have an excellent practice with a great deal of potential. I'm fifty-nine years old, without many friends and no family. Oh, don't think for a minute that I'm trying to play on your sympathies. I'm reasonably happy with my work and, like you, after Cynthia died I never thought I'd look at another woman, let alone want one. Times change, however. People change. I've changed. I would consider it a great honor, Lydia, if you'd try to think of me as more than just your legal adviser. You are the first woman in a long time to make me feel like a man again." He gave a little laugh. "I find myself rushing through my other work just so I can get to yours. I feel as if I'm with you whenever I'm working on your legal matters."

"You're very sweet, Peter, but I also think you're just a bit tight."

"I'm not. I swear I'm not. I decided yesterday that it was about time I told you how I feel. Somewhere I got the courage. I'm not sorry." He sipped his wine, then winked. "I'm really not a bad catch, you know."

Lydia laughed. "You're an extremely attractive man, Peter Haskings, and I have a feeling that you are well aware of that fact."

"I don't know the meaning of the word conceit."

"Spoken like every other man I have ever known." She cocked her head. "You're obviously well acquainted with the chronicles of my life, so you know I've had quite a few men in my time."

"If you're trying to frighten me off, I don't frighten easily. I don't care how many men you've known. As for me, I'm afraid—with possibly one or two exceptions—that I have never been with anyone except my late wife. You lived your life the way you had to; I lived mine as I had to. That doesn't mean that we couldn't be attracted to one another, even suited for each other."

As he spoke, she saw more and more of Peter MacNair in the way he moved his head, the shape of his mouth, the color of his hair. He had long, heavy fingers with beautifully manicured nails, but not the hands of an attorney. They were more the hands of man who had, at one time, worked very hard for what he achieved.

He leaned closer. "We are both adults, Lydia, so please don't be shocked or offended by what I'm going to say."

She straightened and waited. "I think I know what you're going to say."

"I desperately want to make love to you."

Lydia felt the color rising in her face despite the fact that she'd expected him to say something like that. "Peter!" she hissed, looking around.

"I'm a fighter, Lydia, and I don't like to lose."

"You may lose this time, Peter, dear. I'm just not ready, physically or mentally, to think about that sort of thing."

"I'm also a very patient man. I have no intention of pressuring you. I just wanted you to know how I feel about you. The decision will be yours, of course."

Lydia found herself befuddled. One part of her wanted him, but she wasn't certain it was anything more than her basic need for the fulfillment any normal woman seeks. Yet, as she gazed at him, there was something more. The fact that he looked like her dead lover would make it simple enough to go to bed with him and pretend it was Peter MacNair in her arms and not Peter Haskings. But that would be foolish; she'd only be deluding both of them. She found she couldn't think straight and gave her head a little shake.

"I think we should change the subject, Peter. First, I'd like some more coffee and a brandy. Then I believe we should talk about this young man I saw Lorna MacNair showering with gifts this afternoon."

Peter heaved a sigh and took a cigar out of his silver case. He bit off the end and lighted the tip. "Change the subject all you like, Lydia. I have no intention of letting it drop completely. I'm a difficult man to dissuade once I've set my mind to something."

Lydia avoided his eyes. "The man's name is Michael Crane. He works for one of my companies. Seeing him with Lorna made me think that she arranged through her son, Efrem, to put this young man in my employ so that he could keep an eye on things for her."

"An industrial spy, you mean?"

"Exactly."

"And she's paying him off with gifts, such as those you saw her buy this afternoon."

"I think it's more than that. They were too...cozy, if you know what I mean."

"Then you believe there's a relationship going on between Mrs. MacNair and this young man?"

"It seems unlikely, but it's the only conclusion that comes to mind."

Peter chuckled. "You mean an illicit liaison? They are not as uncommon as you may think in this day and age, Lydia. Rich older women often resort to buying the favors of good-looking younger men."

Lydia frowned. "I'm certainly aware that such arrangements have been a fact of life for a long time, Peter. I'm just surprised that Lorna would resort to one."

"She's a woman with healthy appetites and she can well afford a dalliance or two."

"He's no more than a boy," Lydia protested.

"A boy who is old enough and smart enough to pay compliments where he knows they'll reap the greatest rewards." He puffed his cigar. "You made a note of where this Michael Crane lives?"

"Yes." She rummaged through her bag, handing him the address she'd written down. Peter gave the paper a brief glance, then folded it and put it into his pocket. "I'll check him out," he said. "Perhaps he might be useful in this lawsuit Mrs. MacNair has decided to press."

"What do you mean?"

"You'd be surprised at how easily some people can be convinced that it's in their own best interests to drop a suit."

"Blackmail?"

"That is a very ugly word, Lydia. Certainly not blackmail. I'll merely check up on this fellow and if what you suspect is going on is indeed going on, I'll approach the lady and see if she can't be persuaded to be a bit less greedy in her suit against you." He motioned to the waiter for the check. "But first I've got to establish without a shadow of a doubt that this young man and Lorna MacNair are having an affair. That will mean hiring a detective."

"I don't like it, Peter, but I suppose we must do whatever is necessary. I will not give up everything I've worked for without a fight—dirty or clean."

"I have a feeling it's going to be ditty."

"I'm very accustomed to dirt. I was brought up in it."

When she looked across at him he suddenly seemed an entirely different man than the straitlaced attorney she'd hired. She wondered if perhaps she shouldn't go to bed with him.

She'd have to think about that.

CHAPTER FIFTEEN

When Marcus didn't return to Paris, Caroline became restless. She felt herself torn between returning to Venice and Tonio and going to England and Adam. She was nervous about seeing Adam for obvious reasons, but at least she now had an excuse to go to Clarendon Hall. Hadn't Marcus told her that Adam had disappeared from San Francisco without a word to anyone and that they were all anxious to discover his whereabouts? She rationalized her desire to see him, telling herself that she would be doing everyone a service by getting Adam to communicate with the family, if he hadn't done so already.

Feeling satisfied with her decision, Caroline packed her bags and caught the first train to Calais for the trip across the English Channel. The Channel was rough and cold, and the trip proved most unpleasant for Caroline. Though normally a good sailor, she was nauseous from the moment the ship left port until it docked in Dover. Her mood was dampened all the more as she boarded the train for London. The day was dismal and gray with a heavy wetness that penetrated her bones. An omen, perhaps? She'd been eager to see Adam again, but the weather seemed to be warning her to stay away.

London was wrapped in fog when she arrived. She decided not to stay at Claridge's. She didn't want any reminders of the afternoon her grandmother had found her and Adam naked on the bed. Instead, Caroline chose a small, nondescript hotel across from Kensington Gardens. It wasn't much of a hotel, but she didn't care. With any luck at all, Adam would invite her to stay at Clarendon Hall.

Her first morning in London she arose early, had a small breakfast of tea and hard rolls, and put on her prettiest frock. She took a taxi to Clarendon Hall.

Nothing had changed, she noticed, as she drove along the familiar road that had been cut between the rolling meadows. Stands of trees acted as windbreakers, and the grass was as green and lush as she remembered. But when the taxi turned into the courtyard of the old estate, Caroline's eyes widened in surprise. The left wing had been entirely rebuilt, all new stone and brick. The architect had tried painstakingly to make it look as it once had. But as far as Caroline was concerned, he'd failed miserably. Clarendon Hall looked like two structures—one new and one very old—welded together with a band of masonry that ran from top to bottom in the very center of the building.

"Shall I wait for you?" the driver asked.

"No, I'm sure I'll be able to get a ride back."

When she rang the bell, no one answered. She rang again. Still no one. She lifted the heavy knocker and let it drop with a thundering rumble that seemed to shake the entire house. Then the door creaked open and an old, bent man peered out at her through heavy, steel-rimmed spectacles.

"Is Lord Clarendon at home?" she asked.

"Lord Clarendon is dead, Miss."

Caroline lowered her eyes, embarrassed by her tactless mistake. "I meant Adam Clarendon."

"He's not at home either, Miss."

"Well is there anyone here I may speak with? You see, I dismissed my taxi thinking Adam—I mean, Mr. Clarendon—would be at home."

"There's no one here, Miss. Just the staff, and most of them are away. It's Thursday, you know."

"Of course. I'm sorry. Would it be possible for me to telephone for a taxi to take me back to London?"

The old man stepped aside. "There's a telephone on the desk in the library, Miss. This way please."

Just as Caroline lifted the receiver, she heard the sound of a horse trotting across the courtyard. Her heart leapt, thinking for sure it would be Adam. But when she went to the window and looked out she saw Pamela Albright, dressed in a very smart riding habit. Pamela had dismounted and was hitching the horse to the post by the time Caroline got to the door.

"Well, hello," Pamela said, recognizing her at once. "It's been so very long since we've seen one another, Caroline." She kissed her cheek.

"Too long," Caroline answered. "I meant to see you all before I left for the Continent, but things became rather confused." She looked around at the empty house. "I was told that Adam is not here. Has he gone into London?"

"No," Pamela said, her face tightening visibly. "God only knows where Adam is by now."

"What do you mean?"

Pamela motioned toward the sitting room. "Come. I'll have Roderick bring us some tea and we can talk."

Caroline didn't appreciate the authoritative way Pamela pulled off her riding gloves, tossed her crop on a console table, and strode into the sitting room looking every bit the mistress of the manor.

The sitting room was one of the new rooms that had been added to the house. Pamela stood in its center admiring it. "There was a fire here after you left, you know."

"Grandmother wrote me. I'd forgotten."

"I come over every day to see that everything is as it should be. I'm afraid there was nothing left to salvage in this wing, so I had to start from scratch. All in all, though, it seems to have turned out well enough."

"Very lovely," Caroline said, but she didn't mean it. The room was too fussy, too heavy with furniture that had no real function.

"I tried to remember exactly how it was before, but I'm afraid I didn't succeed. Adam hasn't seen it yet. He'll hate it when he does."

"But I thought Adam came back here after his trip to San Francisco."

"Your brother went to China."

Caroline gaped at her. The word brother stabbed her like a blade. "China?" she managed, trying to hide her hurt.

Pamela wasn't deceived. "You are aware that Adam is your brother?"

"That's what Grandmother claims."

"It isn't just a claim, Caroline. It's the truth. I know because Adam showed me a letter his father—Lord Clarendon, that is—left. It was a letter that was not to be read until Adam reached his twenty-first birthday. Unfortunately, both Lord and Lady Clarendon died before then, so the letter was turned over to Adam as part of his inheritance."

The old man came in carrying a heavy tea service, which he put down on the table in front of the fireplace. After he left, Pamela said, "That letter was intended for Adam's eyes alone. However, he showed it to me because we were engaged to be married and he wanted no secrets between us." She motioned for Caroline to sit across from her and began pouring the tea.

After a long moment Pamela looked straight into Caroline's eyes. "I realize that you were in love with Adam, Caroline. I know you must have felt quite miserable when you learned he was your brother—or half-brother, if you wish."

"I still don't believe he is what Grandmother claims he is."

"He is, believe me. I saw that letter Lord Clarendon wrote." She paused. "It's no secret, Caroline, that I never really liked you very much. Now I feel only pity for you. You've suffered a bitter hurt, a hurt I myself would find difficult to accept."

"I'm sorry that you don't like me, Pamela."

"You came between Adam and me, and I can't forgive you for that. But since you are no longer a threat, I can be perfectly candid now." She leaned forward. "You see, Adam and I had a row just before he went to visit his grandmother in San Francisco. It was about Lord Clarendon's letter."

Slowly, carefully, Pamela told Caroline the whole story of

how Adam had come to be the Clarendons' heir. In conclusion, she explained, "They were going to tell Adam the truth when he came of age so that he could make his own decision as to which family he wanted to belong to. Adam, I'm afraid, can't make up his mind. He's still a little boy caught up in a fantasy of being a young prince born to a Chinese princess."

Caroline could do nothing but sit and stare, ashen-faced.

Pamela noticed her discomfort. The blood had drained from Caroline's face, leaving her looking like someone made of chalk. "You still believe that Adam is not your brother?" Pamela demanded. "Is that why you came here?"

For a moment Caroline couldn't find her voice. She fumbled for a handkerchief and kept twisting it between her fingers as she tried to think. "Yes. No. I don't know...."

"I understand, Caroline. You're still in love with Adam and you don't want to believe the facts. But I assure you, dear, they are the facts and you must accept them. Along with his letter Lord Clarendon included a newspaper clipping that described the kidnapped child and mentioned a twin-poppy tattoo engraved on his thigh. It's there. I've seen it."

Seeing Caroline's eyes widen, Pamela smiled demurely. "It isn't what you think." She quickly explained how Adam had once been shot in the leg and how she'd discovered the tattoo after ripping open his trouser leg to bind the wound.

Caroline had seen that tattoo also—under rather different circumstances.

"Adam is your brother," Pamela insisted. "Nothing will change that." She paused again, sipping her tea. "I really shouldn't be saying all this here because someone might be listening. If word of his true parentage ever got out, Adam's rightful Clarendon inheritance would be taken away from him. I intend on doing everything I can to prevent that by convincing Adam he must return and swear to keep his secret. He was brought up to be Lord Clarendon's sole heir. He can't just throw all that away."

"I understand," Caroline said, feeling as if all her life's blood had suddenly been drained out of her. "You may be assured of my discretion, Pamela."

"I thank you for that, Caroline." She leaned back and sipped her tea again.

"You say Adam went to China? My brother Marcus told me that he'd vanished from San Francisco without a trace."

"Your family more than likely has had word from him by now. He cabled me from aboard a ship bound for Shanghai. He should be there by now. I only hope and pray he'll be safe."

"Why did he go to China?"

"As I said earlier, Adam is still a little boy with grand notions of being the son of a royal princess. He's been overly imaginative and adventurous ever since we were children growing up together. After reading his cable, I had the impression that his real mother had something to do with his decision to make the trip."

"Mother? What did Adam say about her?"

Pamela shook her head. "Nothing. Just that he was going to China to discover his roots."

"Dear God," Caroline breathed. "There's a revolution going on over there. Surely he knew that."

Pamela shrugged. "I don't think that Adam cares about revolutions. He's only thinking about his claim to a Manchu throne. I'm certain it's all his mother's idea. After he came back from his first trip to America, he told me that he'd found her quite unstable. Still, in subsequent letters during his second trip there, he wrote more flatteringly of her—how royal she was, how grand and regal, and how she was the last living relation to Prince somebody-or-other, the direct heir to the Manchu throne. He said that it was his right and duty to try and claim his mother's heritage."

"Adam is mad!"

"Adam and I are the same age, Caroline, but Adam has yet to grow up. He's deluded himself with all kinds of fantasies. His head was always filled with knights and damsels in distress and he was always intrigued by Oriental history. We all thought it rather strange back then, but now I realize that even as a small boy he must have had some sense of his origins. And now that he knows he was born in China, he wants to be there."

"How utterly foolish."

"I agree. But I love him very much and I will not stand in his way. He must find himself and then, with the grace of God, he'll come to realize that this is where he really belongs."

"Yes, I think you are right," Caroline said after a moment. "After all, he was raised and educated here. It's the only home he knows. He will never be happy anywhere else."

"You must try to convince him of that, Caroline."

Caroline looked up sharply, her eyes staring. "Me? Oh no, Pamela. I could never talk with Adam now that I know the whole story. In fact, I never want to see him again."

Pamela reached over and patted her hand. "I can imagine how you must feel, knowing what you do, my dear. My only advice would be for you to forget your brother. Look around. You are an extremely beautiful woman. You should have no trouble at all finding a suitable husband."

Caroline expelled a sigh of defeat. "I've already found such a man. He's Italian. A count," she said, trying to smile. "He has asked me to marry him."

"Then you should marry him if you love him."

"I'm not sure that I do. I'm just not sure...."

Pamela filled in what Caroline didn't say. "You're not sure you love him because you're still in love with your brother."

"Don't say that," Caroline cried as the tears welled up in her eyes.

Pamela quickly got up and sat down beside Caroline, putting an arm around her shoulders. "It must be faced, Caroline. Believe me, I'm not trying to be cruel, I only say what I must for your own good. Marry this Italian count, or at least go back to him until you are truly convinced you can never have Adam." She patted Caroline's shoulder and stood up. "If you wish, I'll show you Lord Clarendon's letter and the newspaper clipping that was enclosed. I had wanted Adam to destroy them, but he wouldn't. He keeps them here in the house."

Caroline dabbed her eyes and shook her head. "No, please. I don't want to see them. I really must go now."

"Walk back with me to my place. I'll borrow the car and drive you into London to your hotel."

"That is very kind of you, Pamela, but I can telephone for a taxi to fetch me. I'd like to be alone, if you don't mind."

"I can understand that, my dear."

* * * * * * *

It seemed an eternity before the London taxi arrived to carry Caroline away from Clarendon Hall, a place she hoped never to see again. She had made love to her own brother! Disgust welled up inside her like the spillage of a cesspool. Her skin crawled as she remembered the way he'd touched her, the way she'd touched him. Her lips burned from the memories of their kisses. She felt infested with the most horrible disease. Nothing, she decided, would ever make her feel clean again. Nothing... no one.

There was only one hope left, Caroline told herself as the taxi deposited her at the entrance of her hotel. She would go back to Italy, back to Venice, back to Count Cambruzio. Perhaps with his help and patience she might become a whole woman again. Perhaps he would be able to rekindle some sense of decency in her and rid her forever of this horrible guilt.

Yes, Tonio was her only hope. She would marry him, if he still wanted her, and she would push Adam completely out of her life. She would have to if she were to survive, she told herself as she ran into her room and threw herself across the bed. When she closed her eyes Adam's face materialized again, but this time it was made of wax that began to drip and melt until it was but a distorted ugly mass. A scream caught in her throat, stifled by her fist, and she gave herself up to tears.

CHAPTER SIXTEEN

Lydia replaced the receiver and stood with one finger resting against her cheek. She wasn't sure she had done the right thing in accepting an invitation to dine at Peter Haskings's apartment. He had said, however, that he wanted to talk to her somewhere private, someplace where they couldn't possibly be overheard. It was of the utmost importance, he'd whispered ominously, and it had to do with Michael Crane.

Still, dinner in Peter's apartment meant only one thing to Lydia: he would try to seduce her. A pleased smile crept across her lips. Perhaps she'd let him. He did remind her of the Peter she'd loved so desperately, yet that wasn't his total attraction. Peter Haskings had a warmth about him that Peter MacNair had lacked. There was a deep glow of sincerity in Peter Haskings's eyes, whereas Peter MacNair's sincerities shifted like drifting sands, sometimes there, sometimes washed away.

She'd go, she decided after debating with her conscience. As she went upstairs and started to dress, she found herself looking forward to the evening.

"Going out?" April asked as she came into Lydia's bedroom and stood watching her mother sift through her dinner gowns.

"Yes, dear. I'm meeting Mr. Haskings. Business affairs he claims are most urgent."

"I had another letter from Adam this afternoon," April said.

Lydia hesitated and turned to look at her. "Where is he? How is he?"

"He's reached Shanghai, and he's starting out for the legation in Peking tomorrow."

"Oh, April, how foolish he's being. Can't you communicate with him and tell him to come home? It's too dangerous there. "

"He is home. He's where he belongs. And I intend to join him there as soon as possible."

"You mustn't, April. It's madness to go to China now." Lydia flung her dinner dress across the bed and frowned at her daughter. "Adam shouldn't be there either. It was you who put the insane notion into his head in the first place. I know it was, and I'm furious with you for doing it."

April looked pleased with herself. "It's where he wanted to go, where we both belong."

"Stop it, April. Why don't you bury the past? It was cruel of Adam to leave without a word and heartless of him to send a bare cablegram announcing his destination. I was certain he'd gone back to England."

"He doesn't belong in England. He was born in China. That is his homeland."

"Foolishness," Lydia snapped. "And if you are seriously entertaining any ridiculous notions about joining him, I'll have you locked in your room and post guards at all the doors."

April laughed. "I wouldn't put it past you, Mother. It wouldn't be the first time you made me a prisoner in my own home."

Lydia went to her daughter and put a loving arm around her waist. "I was only making idle threats, April, darling. You know I'd never interfere in anything you really wanted to do, but surely you must see the dangers involved in going to China."

"I don't belong here. I never did." April turned, shrugging off her mother's arm, and left the room.

Lydia stared helplessly at the empty doorway, then heaved a weary sigh and picked up the dinner dress. She knew that one day April would slip away just as Adam had, and there was nothing she could do about it.

Well, she told herself as she slipped into the long yellow silk gown that revealed a good deal of cleavage, the future would just have to take care of itself.

She hung a three-strand pearl necklace around her neck and added matching eardrops. She liked the billowing effect of the skirt and the narrow, cinched waist—thank heavens Paul Poiret, the Paris designer, had finally liberated women from the restricting corset. She was tempted to twist a rope of pearls through her red-gold hair but decided against it, choosing two pearl combs instead. Because of the chilly night she took her Bolivian chinchilla from the armoire and draped it over her shoulders.

Her Rolls Royce and chauffeur were waiting at the curb when she left the mansion. She relaxed back into the sable-covered seat, looking out at the fog that swirled up the hill from the Bay.

When Peter showed her into his expansive drawing room, Lydia was pleasantly surprised. The room was very tastefully decorated in a masculine style of browns and tans with accents of orange and green. The walls were lined with bookshelves, all filled to capacity. A massive fireplace of beige marble dominated one wall.

"I'm afraid the den became so overcrowded with my books that I had to move many of them in here," Peter apologized as he guided her toward a chair by the fire. "A cocktail before dinner, Lydia?"

"Please. martini."

"A woman after my own heart," he said as he went to the cellaret and began mixing the cocktails.

"Now what did you find out about this Michael Crane?" Lydia asked when he handed her the tall stemmed glass that had been carefully frosted.

"He's quite a bad little boy, I'm afraid."

"Oh?" She sipped her martini and raised an appreciative eyebrow. "Excellent." She took a deeper sip. "Just how bad is he?"

"I think before I tell you about our friend Michael Crane, we should enjoy our drinks and dinner. I'm rather a good cook, if I say so myself. I, Madame, am your chef for the evening. I hope you like duck. I've prepared it in a cherry sauce—one of my specialties."

"Are there no limits to your talents?"

"None," he said as he sat down beside her and leaned close. "I wish with all my heart that you'll allow me to demonstrate one of my more highly developed talents before the night is over."

"You have that look in your eye, Peter," she admonished with a grin.

"Do I see the same look in yours?"

She lowered her eyes. "Surely you don't think me so naïve as to come to a gentleman's apartment without some idea of his intentions?"

"My intentions, dear Lydia, are completely dishonorable."

"I assumed as much." When he put his hand on hers she did not pull away. "I like honest men. The devious ones always disconcert me."

"Was Peter MacNair disconcerting?"

"Oh yes," she said, thinking back. "I never really knew when he was telling me the truth or lying through his teeth. Yet, toward the end I knew. Or at least I thought I knew."

"You must have loved him very much."

Lydia looked wistful. "I loved him. I hated him. But then there are those who say that love and hate are really the same thing." She sipped her cocktail, emptying the glass, and held it out to him. "Let's make a bargain. We won't speak of Peter MacNair this evening. I'd like to try and forget him for at least one night."

"Bargains should be sealed with a kiss," he said, leaning closer.

Lydia closed her eyes and touched her lips to his. A strange sensation ran down her spine as she let him put his arms around her and draw her close to his chest. The kiss grew more passionate as Lydia felt herself melting in his arms.

Then he released her and smiled. "I'll fix you another drink. We can continue where we left off after dinner."

Lydia never thought she could feel so bold. She'd downed the first cocktail much too fast and it was already having its effect on her. "Then forget the second cocktail and take me into dinner."

Peter laughed and reached for her hand. "The table awaits, madame."

The dinner was excellent. And it was delightful to be alone with a man like Peter who never seemed to be at a loss for something to say. He knew how to make her laugh, poking fun at the staunchest members of San Francisco society. His jokes were hilarious, always just a bit risqué but never bawdy. He was obviously well read and most knowledgeable about music.

And while they were having their brandy and coffee in the drawing room, he put a plastic disc on something he called a Victrola, an upright cabinet with a huge horn atop it looking like a giant morning glory. To her astonishment, music began to pour from the morning glory. He insisted on teaching her the latest ragtime and jazz steps. Lydia was having an uproarious time. Of course the two bottles of wine with dinner had helped.

When Peter went to replace the record, Lydia put a hand to her heart and collapsed on the divan. "No more, Peter. I must remind you that I am an old woman who is not used to such strenuous exercise."

Laughing, he fell down beside her, breathing as hard as she. "I keep forgetting that about myself." He turned toward her, his eyes serious. "But when I'm with you, Lydia, I feel like a kid."

"Thank you," she answered, laying her hand on his cheek. "You are a very sweet, dear man, Peter Haskings."

He took her hand and kissed it. "It took you long enough to recognize that fact," he said with a smile. He looked deep into her eyes. "You know I love you very much."

She couldn't answer. She leaned her face close to his and sought his mouth. His arms went around her and their bodies crushed together in a passionate embrace.

"I think I'd better take you to bed," Peter whispered, his hands fondling her breasts.

"I'm feeling very vulnerable," Lydia said.

"It was the food," he joked. "I put a special aphrodisiac in it."

"It's working."

She hadn't been sure she would be able to respond to his caresses, but once they were undressed and lying close, Lydia's body came alive with a need she had kept smothered for too long. When his fingers and lips touched her nipples she moaned with pleasure and wrapped her arms around him, urging him on.

He was an expert lover, knowing just where and when to touch her. He took his time arousing her and made no move to enter her until he knew she was ready for him. His entry was painstakingly slow and gentle, but once she started moving under him he became almost savage in his thrusts. He was large and thick and hard and Lydia almost swooned for the want of his sex.

"Peter. Peter," she moaned, "I never—"

He hushed her with an ardent kiss, deep and fulfilling. "I adore you, Lydia. I want to be with you always."

She could only concentrate on the delicious feeling that burned inside her. He moved with the grace and strength of a stallion. She clung to him, wanting this moment never to end. And when she cried, "Peter," again, she wasn't thinking of Peter MacNair; she found herself trying to make the name sound different, new, almost a stranger's name.

Lydia felt him moving faster, more urgently, and she arched up to meet his climax. He pressed his mouth to hers and held her tight in his arms as every nerve in his body grew tense and finally snapped, forcing a groan from deep inside him.

For Lydia, time had stopped. Her heart pounded in her breast as she felt the outpouring of her passions. She moaned and thrashed against him, then fell limp in his arms as she gave herself up to her orgasm.

Peter kissed her tenderly and smiled down at her. "I'll be good for another round in about half an hour," he said, grinning. "I guess I'm getting old. It used to take me only a few minutes."

"We're both getting old, Peter. But you've made me feel sixteen again."

"You look sixteen."

"Spoken like a true gentleman."

"Through and through," he said, still grinning. Then he kissed her breasts, nipping the still taut nipples. Lydia groaned and smoothed his hair, crooning contentedly.

"Can you stay the night?" he asked.

"Heaven forbid. What would my children say?"

"To hell with your children. Surely they know men still desire you. You're an extremely beautiful woman, Lydia."

"I'm a grandmother, and that's how my children see me. I'd scandalize them if I spent an illicit night with you or any other man."

"Then marry me."

Her eyes widened. "You're not serious."

"I mean it, Lydia. I never thought I'd ever want to marry again. But then I met you, and now I can't think of anything else except having you as my wife."

"You're very sweet, Peter, but marriage for me is out of the question."

"Why?"

She had no answer to that.

He kissed her again and then began fondling her breasts. His hands slid down over her abdomen and between her damp thighs.

"You said half an hour." She smiled as she felt him becoming aroused again.

"I think you've stripped thirty years from my age."

She'd almost forgotten how wonderful it was to hold a naked man in her arms. Peter's body was a marvel for a man his age. The skin was smooth and warm and the graying hairs on his chest tickled her breasts when he gathered her into his arms.

"You're lovely," he whispered, kissing her tenderly.

"I know I should be ashamed for making it so obvious that I want you, Peter," she said as she started to masturbate him slowly.

"You're driving me wild."

"Good." She continued to play with him.

"We're both too mature to pretend we don't need sex. You know," he said as he tried to control the heat that was bubbling up inside him. "I rather like getting old. Making love like this is so pleasant, not hurried and frantic." He eased himself away from her hand to suck on her nipples, then ran his tongue between her breasts.

He worked his way down, licking and kissing her navel, her stomach, then retraced his path to find her mouth again.

"I'm getting fat," Lydia said as she felt his hands smooth over her waist.

"God no. You're perfect. I wouldn't want you any other way."

"Make love to me again, Peter."

He took her hand and placed it on his throbbing erection so she could draw him inside. "Oh God, that feels good," she moaned as he entered her slowly. She arched up and pushed herself against him, taking him all the way. Slowly she rotated her hips as he slipped in and out, sending tingling waves of passion shooting through her body.

"I love to feel you inside me."

"You're going to make me come too soon if you're not careful." The way she was sucking his tongue, moving under him, was driving him wild with lust.

"Let's not be careful, Peter. I want you so damned bad I think I'm going to explode."

He began to move faster, pounding against her with renewed force.

"Oh God, Peter, that feels so wonderful."

He was breathing hard as he pushed himself against her with such force that he knew he couldn't hold back much longer. "I'm going to come," he whispered roughly in her ear.

"Peter. Oh, Peter," she moaned. She began to writhe more frantically, throwing herself up to him with abandon. At last the shock waves of her orgasm burst over her and she lost herself in it.

"Christ," he gasped, throwing back his head as ribbons of his hot streaming seed bolted up into her voluptuous body.

* * * * * * *

Later, when they were dressed and sitting in his drawing room, Lydia set aside the balloon glass of brandy he'd handed her and said, "You've almost made me forget why you invited me here. Tell me what you found out about Michael Crane."

"As I said, a very bad apple. Rotten to the core."

"Tell me."

"I did some checking, as I promised you. He's from New York, that much is true. And he is a very distant relative of Efrem MacNair's wife, Ellen. But the connection is very distant," he emphasized. "Almost nonexistent." He sipped his brandy. "The young man is a no-good wastrel and a very clever opportunist. His mother is still alive, living in a tenement on the Lower East Side. She's poor as dirt and has no idea of her son Michael's whereabouts. It seems he was arrested several years ago and then disappeared after serving a short jail term."

"Arrested? For what?"

"He was only seventeen at the time and you wouldn't believe the charges on which he was convicted."

"Try me."

"They are rather shocking, especially considering his age at the time."

"I'm not easily shocked, Peter."

"When he was fourteen he was arrested for burglary, which isn't the shocking part. He served time in a center for boys. After he got out, he moved in with an older man who fenced stolen property. Do you know what a fence is?"

Lydia nodded.

"He lived with this man for two years. Then at seventeen he moved in with a woman who ran a house of ill repute."

"At seventeen?"

"The boy was rather big for his age, if you get my meaning."

Lydia flushed slightly and nodded again.

"Then he met another woman of rather questionable morals, a Mrs. Gloria Marlock, but she had enough money to safeguard her reputation while indulging her appetite for young men...very young men. She had almost a dozen boys living in her town-house uptown, some of them no more than twelve or thirteen years old."

"Good heavens."

"The New York police knew what was going on in the Marlock house, but the lady had a lot of influence so nothing was ever done about it." Peter shrugged. "They figured she was at least keeping the boys off the streets and closed their eyes to it."

He sipped his brandy before continuing: "According to my investigators, Michael stayed with Mrs. Marlock for almost five years. By then he was getting a little old for the lady, so she told him he would have to leave. Michael became enraged, beat her rather savagely, stole a lot of money and some very expensive jewelry, and ran. But he got caught and was sent to jail. With the help of the fence he'd lived with years before, he managed to escape. He had obviously hidden the money and jewels he'd stolen, and when he was free he set himself up in a rather expensive hotel, selling his body to anyone who'd pay his price—man or woman, he wasn't particular. But he knew the police were closing in on him, and he started making plans to get out of New York. Then, by chance, he ran into Efrem MacNair in the downstairs bar of the Astor Hotel and struck up a conversation with him. MacNair invited him to meet his wife, for reasons unknown. Michael Crane found out she was a Stanton and mentioned that his grandmother was also a Stanton. The young man must have the charm of a cobra. The MacNairs invited him to San Francisco, and Michael grabbed the chance to leave New York. End of story."

"He's a monster."

"A very clever one."

Lydia sat aghast. Finally she said, "I've got to warn Lorna."

"Do you think for one moment she'll believe you?"

"You have your investigative report? I'll show her that."

"Knowing how Lorna MacNair feels about you, my dear lady, I'm convinced she'd tear it up and throw it in your face."

"But the man is a thief and a woman-beater and obviously wanted by the police. God only knows what he's capable of doing." She thought for a moment. "Couldn't we alert the San Francisco police and tell them where to find him?"

"There's a little thing called extradition that has to be considered. Michael can only be arrested in New York."

"He could do Lorna harm."

"That's Lorna's worry."

"I disagree. She must be told, regardless of her reaction."

"Look, Lydia. Remember what we talked about the other day...about your going to Lorna with the story of how her husband wanted only to be with her and his family when he was dying? If you tell her this business about Michael it will turn her completely against you. Even if she believes it, which I don't think she will, she'll hate you more than ever. She'll never let you set foot inside her house again."

Lydia thought for a moment, the said, "Couldn't we communicate with this Mrs. Marlock and tell her where Michael is?"

"Mrs. Marlock's methods, Lydia, would be the hard-muscle kind. She'd have him killed, I'm sure of that. You wouldn't want to be responsible for his murder, would you?"

"No, of course not. But something must be done."

"My advice is to let things take their natural course."

"And possibly have Lorna's death on our hands."

Peter shook his head. "I'm sure it will never come to that. The boy might rough her up when she gets tired of him, or vice versa, but nothing more serious."

Lydia stood up. "Regardless, Peter. I intend paying Lorna a visit first thing in the morning."

"I think you're making a mistake."

* * * * * *

When Lydia showed up at the MacNair mansion early the next day Lorna flatly refused to see her. Lorrie received Lydia in the morning room, studying her with frosty eyes.

"Mrs. Nightsong," Lorrie said haughtily, not bothering to extend her hand. "I'm afraid my grandmother has nothing to say to you."

"You've grown to be a very striking young lady, Lorrie," Lydia said cordially. "The last time your mother brought you to see me you were just a tiny little thing."

"I'm sure you did not come here to talk about my degree of maturity, Mrs. Nightsong."

"No, I have a rather personal matter to discuss with your grandmother."

"If it concerns Grandmother's lawsuit, kindly speak with her attorneys."

"It's not about the lawsuit, Lorrie. It's important and extremely personal."

"I doubt there is anything personal between you and Grandmother."

"Please, Lorrie," Lydia said patiently. "I must speak with your grandmother. It's urgent."

"Tell me."

"I can't do that. It's something I can discuss only with her."

"Then you will have to excuse me, Mrs. Nightsong. Grandmother will not receive you, and if you refuse to tell me your business I am afraid I will have to ask you to leave."

Lydia turned when she heard footsteps behind her.

"Good morning," Michael Crane said, showing a dazzling smile. "Lorrie, aren't you going to introduce me to your charming guest?"

Lorrie stiffened, folding her hands in front of her. "This is Mrs. Nightsong, Michael. She was just leaving."

Michael extended his hand. "Michael Crane," he said, bending over Lydia's hand to kiss it. The touch of his lips against her skin made her cringe. It felt like the kiss of death.

"How do you do," Lydia managed.

"At last I get to meet my lovely employer. They told me you were beautiful, but I never imagined how beautiful." As his eyes slowly moved over her, Lydia trembled nervously. "Efrem MacNair was kind enough to find me a position with a division of your enterprise."

Lorrie didn't like the way Michael was looking at the older woman. "Mrs. Nightsong," she said, "you will have to excuse us. We were just going out. Good morning."

Michael took Lydia's hand again and kissed it, letting his lips linger and the tip of his tongue touch the soft skin. Lydia pulled it away. "Good morning, Mr. Crane," she said, trying to keep her face expressionless.

"I trust we will meet again, Mrs. Nightsong."

Lydia gave a curt little nod and. holding her back straight, walked out of the room.

Once outside she took a deep breath and let it out slowly. She knew, instinctively, that everything Peter Haskings had said about this young man was true. Somehow Lorna had to be warned. Then a more disconcerting thought occurred to her. Lorrie had said, '"We were just going out." Perhaps she should warn Lorrie as well.

CHAPTER SEVENTEEN

Marcus hurried through his letter to Amelia. There was nothing to say except that he was spending all his free time at Le Mans. Naturally he didn't mention his affair with Claudine Muret, nor did he choose to tell Amelia that he was going to drive the Muret Miracle in the upcoming twenty-four-hour endurance race. He knew she'd worry.

He wasn't in love with Claudine. He liked her very much but it was all physical, nothing more. Claudine was the most inventive sex partner he'd ever known. She taught him things that would have mortified the most hardened French prostitute, but Marcus found her so stimulating that he couldn't get enough. Although he knew his body was ruling his mind, he was powerless to control himself. Claudine and the other girls he'd met in France had corrupted him utterly, he admitted. He knew Amelia would never be able to satisfy him in the way he had grown to crave. When he wasn't with Claudine he was spending his nights at Madame Claire's. He lived for women and what they had to offer. His sexual appetites were becoming more and more demanding.

Marcus reread his letter to Amelia, then quickly sealed it, knowing he'd written nothing she wanted to read. Perhaps she would find some solace in the fact that he had signed off with "All my love." He did love her, but in a way he could not explain even to himself. What he hoped was that Amelia could change just as he had changed, though he realized that wasn't very likely.

It was almost five o'clock when he posted the letter in the corner drop and headed back to his rooms at the pension on Rue Voltaire.

He had a quick meal at a comfortable little restaurant nearby, then hurried home to pack for the trip to Le Mans. The trains would be crowded, being that it was Friday and the twenty-four-hour endurance race had been well advertised. A large crowd was expected.

Claudine was waiting on the platform when his train pulled into the Le Mans depot. The minute he stepped from the coach she rushed into his arms and kissed him hard, pushing her tongue deep into his mouth. The feel of her soft, full body aroused him immediately. The kiss was long and passionate, and when he eased her away Marcus glanced self-consciously around and was reassured to see that no one was paying the slightest attention to them. Ah, how he loved the French.

"You will stay at my apartment, of course," Claudine said.

"What will your father think?"

She laughed. "You are still so American. Do you imagine for a moment that Father does not know what is going on between us? Every weekend you come to Le Mans and every weekend we are together. He is not blind. And, besides, he likes you very much. He knows we are lovers. I have admitted that already to him."

Marcus stared at her. "And he doesn't mind?"

"What is to mind? My father is a very understanding man. He knows that if I were not sleeping with you—a man he knows and respects—I would be sleeping with someone else, someone he might not like so well."

Marcus shook his head in disbelief. "If we were living in America, your father would have me drawn and quartered."

"What does that mean, 'drawn and quartered'?" Claudine asked.

"Executed."

"But why? Do American fathers not want their daughters to be happy and content?"

"Not in the way you define happiness and contentment, love."

"I do not think I would like living in America then."

"Why do you think I stay here in France?" Marcus asked with a laugh.

She snuggled close to him. "We will go to the apartment and make love. Then we will go again to see my father. He wants you to look at the new parts he had installed in the Muret Miracle."

"He telephoned me about them during the week. I'm anxious to see what modifications he's made."

"Sometimes I think you are more in love with that car than you are with me."

He leaned down and pecked her cheek without answering. He only smiled and put an arm around her waist.

Marcus was fascinated by Monsieur Muret's modifications to the new racing machine. Where two seats had been—one for driver and one for passenger—only one remained; the passenger seat had been removed. The steering wheel and drive shaft were now placed dead center of the chassis. Fenders had been stripped off and the front and rear axles elongated.

"The longer axles will give you better balance and keep you from turning over on the curves," Muret explained. "And the engine is much smaller, you see. The car is lighter and will thus be faster."

Marcus was impressed.

Monsieur Muret pointed to the solid rubber tires. "Notice the deep tread. They will stand up under the worst kind of punishment. I had them cast especially for this car...at quite a cost, I might add."

"Marvelous. Simply marvelous, Monsieur Muret. I think you have a winner here."

"I know I do, unless you do something foolish like running into a fence."

Marcus laughed. "You can rely on me, Monsieur. No fence is going to stop me from winning the race for you."

The older man clapped him on the back. "That's my boy. We will have the fastest racing machine in the world and everybody will try to copy my designs."

The Muret Miracle machine did create quite a stir when it was pushed to the starting line the following morning. The field of entrants was rather impressive. All the new manufacturers were there with their models. Ray Harroun was driving the Marmon Wasp in which he'd won the Indianapolis 500 the year before with an average speed of almost seventy-five miles an hour. There was a new Peugeot, a Delage, a Renault, a Mercedes, The National, and several Italian models like the Fiat and other unknowns without names or insignia. As Marcus studied the field, he was confident that the Muret Miracle would easily outrun all the others.

When the signal was given for the drivers to crank up their engines, everyone turned to stare at Marcus, who sat smiling behind the steering wheel, pulling his goggles down over his eyes.

"Crank it up, Marc," Ray Harroun yelled to him.

Marcus waved and grinned and pressed the electric starter button. The Muret Miracle roared to life. The entire row of racers gawked at him.

"How'd you do that?" Ray asked after he'd finally gotten his engine primed, chugging and sputtering.

"An electric starter," Marcus yelled back. "Something new Monsieur Muret learned from an inventor in Ohio."

"I'll be damned. Hope it don't electrocute you."

"Just stay out of my way, Ray, and hope you don't choke in my dust."

"Fat chance."

He liked Ray, had liked him since that first race in Indianapolis, a race Ray had won. Ray had taught Marcus a lot about racing machines, and as Marcus revved his motor, he found himself remembering everything he was supposed to remember.

It was a raw, steely morning with a sharp wind that would interfere with every racer's speed. Wind resistance was a major factor, and they were all praying it would let up once the sun came out. The route was a circuitous one, curving and twisting through the town and surrounding countryside, up and down steep hills. There'd be no pavement, only dry hard dirt with ruts sometimes as deep as half a wheel. Twenty-four hours was a long time to race, and they were all anxious to begin. As for Marcus, he wanted it to start and never stop.

This is what I was born to do, Marcus told himself as he waited impatiently for the starter to raise the green flag. The cars were all jockeying into position, engines gunning, smoke billowing out of rear and side exhausts.

The green flag swooped down and the cars shot forward. Right at the outset a Peugeot swerved too far to the left and sideswiped one of the Italian cars. There was a crunch of metal, but the cars kept tearing along down the straightaway.

After the first thirty minutes Marcus began to relax behind the wheel. The Muret Miracle was humming along as if it hadn't a care in the world. He wasn't trying yet to overtake any of the three or four motorcars ahead of him. There would be plenty of time for strategy later on. For the moment, he would concentrate on maintaining his position and a steady pace. The speedometer needle was wavering between fifty-five and sixty miles per hour. He kept a steady eye on the fuel-consumption gauge. Too many stops for refueling could be costly. Keeping down his speed would conserve fuel, but it might also make him lose position.

The steely-gray sky began to darken late in the afternoon. Marcus had been forced to make two refueling stops, and each time the gasoline tank was filled, the car became heavier and harder to maneuver. He kept his position in fourth place until the rain started to come down in light, stinging slashes. Between the now steady rain and the dwindling light of the dreary day, visibility was greatly reduced. Yet Marcus was still exhilarated, thrilled by the power beneath him and the speed at which he was travelling.

He found that by increasing his speed each time the gasoline tank started getting low, he was able to move up one position before each refueling. By the end of the tenth hour he was right behind the lead car, a Peugeot, and the Marmon Wasp was directly behind the Muret Miracle.

Now the rain was coming down in sheets, turning the hard dirt roads into slushy, sloppy mud tracks. Steering became more difficult, but thanks to the wide axles front and back, and the thick, solid rubber tires, Marcus found himself gaining on the Peugeot.

There was a narrow grade ahead, which led over a steep hill and then down into a smooth valley that twisted and turned around burly oak trees and clumps of thick shrubbery. Marcus yawned and pushed up his driving goggles in order to see more clearly as he crept closer to the lead car. He wished suddenly that he had not stayed with Claudine the night before. They had slept intermittently, wanting sex more than they'd wanted rest. Now he regretted that. His bones were aching, his legs felt as if they were being jabbed by thousands of tiny pins. His right foot was too heavy on the accelerator pedal, but he wasn't aware of that. And he was concentrating too hard on catching up with the Peugeot to remember that he hadn't had anything to eat since the enormous breakfast Claudine and her father had insisted he eat before the start of the race. Suddenly his stomach began to growl and his head felt a little too light. His bladder was full, as were his bowels.

Marcus pressed down, unthinking, on the accelerator and pulled up next to the French driver in the lead car. He wanted to get a good distance ahead so that he could make a rest stop, albeit a very brief one. He saw the driver turn and glare at him. Marcus lifted his hand from the steering wheel and waved happily as he raced past.

His bravado obviously annoyed the Frenchman because the Peugeot pulled out, racing neck-and-neck with the Muret Miracle. The two cars had mounted the steep grade of the hill, dipped down over the ridge, and were heading for the twisting curves of the valley road below. Both engines were puffing and steaming in the cold sleety rain. Marcus glanced at the gasoline gauge and noticed that it was almost empty: only about five gallons remained. But he had two reserve canisters of gasoline wedged behind the seat. As soon as he had achieved a safe lead, he'd refill the tank and relieve himself. With any luck he'd still be able to retain the lead.

His heart was pounding as he roared down the slope with the Frenchman directly beside him. Up ahead was a sharp turn. He knew he'd have to overtake the Frenchman quickly if he intended gaining the first-car position because the road ahead was so narrow and curved that there would be no possibility of passing his rival for many miles to come.

But the Frenchman was just as determined as Marcus. The Peugeot kept even with him, both cars recklessly speeding toward the sharp, narrow curve. Marcus pulled ahead just slightly, while the Peugeot started to fall back. Marcus gave a hoot and jammed his foot down hard on the accelerator, pressing it flat against the floor boards. He was inching ahead, the Peugeot now almost completely behind him. Marcus turned his head and saw the Frenchman swerve to make the turn. Still farther back the Marmon Wasp was just reaching the bottom of the hill.

How it happened or when, Marcus never really knew. One moment he was just clear of the Peugeot and the next moment something was dragging him back. He turned and looked behind him. The wide axle of the rear wheel had somehow locked with the front wheel of the Frenchman's car. The Peugeot driver tried to wrench free by twisting and yanking at his steering wheel. The French racer bucked against the Muret Miracle just as Marcus rounded the curve. Marcus's car pitched sideways, hit a deep muddy rut, and flew onto its side as the Peugeot raced by.

Marcus sat dazed in the confining front seat, unaware of the smoke billowing out the back of his machine. When the flames burst from the almost empty tank Marcus tried to scramble free of the overturned racer. But his right leg was caught somehow and he couldn't get out. He pulled with all his might as the flames began licking around the two reserve tanks of gasoline stored behind his seat. Marcus screamed as the flames crept closer and closer. The heat was scorching his face and hands as he tried in vain to free himself. He heard the Marmon Wasp screech to a stop, sending mud and water splattering everywhere.

"Ray!" Marcus yelled.

He felt hands under his arms trying to yank him to safety. Then the gasoline exploded and the entire world seemed to blow up in his face.

* * * * * *

Marcus was certain he was dead when he opened his eyes. Everything was so white and still and colorless. His mind was numb, his body felt weightless, as if it were drifting through space. This was what death must be like, he decided as he slowly moved his eyes across the icy white ceiling of the hospital room. Death was a stark nothingness with shivery shadows, like dead birds' wings fluttering helplessly across an empty expanse.

"Marcus?"

He tried to focus in the direction of the strange voice.

"Marcus?"

His eyes moved slowly, reluctant to encounter the first face he was meant to see in death. Would it be some angel? his dead father? the face of God? He couldn't remember ever having been this frightened.

"Marcus, it's me. Claudine."

He remembered that name from somewhere, but it was from some other time. He couldn't think. His mind refused to function. He tried to repeat it, but he had no voice. Now he knew why dead people didn't communicate with the living: they couldn't speak.

"Look at me, Marcus," Claudine said, her voice slightly demanding.

Marcus blinked. It hurt to open his eyes. Something strange began to happen. The whiteness suddenly looked less stark and the shadows less ominous. As if looking up from the bottom of a cloudy lake, he discerned the outline of a face looming over him. He stared hard, trying to bring it into focus. The film over his eyes gradually subsided, and he realized for the first time that he wasn't dead after all. It was a familiar face he saw, a living face of flesh and blood.

"Claudine," he managed in a choked voice.

"Don't talk, Marcus. You've been badly hurt. But you are going to be all right. It will take time. Just rest and try not to think about anything except getting well. I'll come again tomorrow."

As she spoke, the pain began. It started in his legs, then gradually moved up over his abdomen and into his chest, his neck, his head, until it became so unbearable that he wanted to scream out, but couldn't. A blackness enveloped him and swept him back to that same terrible void where he'd been before.

Whether Claudine came the next day he didn't know. But ever so gradually he became conscious of the passing of time between those moments when he had his eyes open and when they were closed. Most of the time he spent in the vacuum of blackness, and it hurt him to look at the white hospital ceiling. Faces came and went. He didn't remember any of them. He heard voices, some familiar, some strange. He was never aware of anything definite except the excruciating pain that wracked his body.

It must have been night when he first became fully cognizant that he was lying in a hospital room. He tried to move his arms but couldn't. Instead, someone—a nurse, he decided—touched him gently and told him to remain still.

"The bandages won't come off for some time, monsieur," she said softly. "But you will be all right in time."

Time, he thought. How long had he been in that bed? He couldn't remember anything except the terrible heat and the immense ball of flame that had wrapped itself around him. He closed his eyes with effort and sank back into the darkness.

"Well, how are you feeling this morning?" a strange voice asked.

Marcus looked up into the face of a sad little man with steel-rimmed glasses and a gray goatee. Wisps of gray hair fringed an otherwise hairless head. The stranger smiled as he fumbled with a gadget of tubes and dials that was sitting beside Marcus's bed.

"How long—?" Marcus tried, but his voice broke and he started to cough. The pain was horrible.

"Don't talk. You've been here almost three weeks now. You were badly burned, my boy, but in time you will heal. Lucky for you, your face and the front of your body were buried in the mud when the explosion occurred. We have you in a sling, which is why you feel suspended."

"But my legs," Marcus choked. "I feel—"

"Rest and don't worry," the doctor broke in softly. "You will be all right in time."

With every passing day Marcus became more and more aware that something was dreadfully wrong, but no one would tell him what. Claudine never came to see him, although he asked for her each time a nurse or doctor came into his room. No one else came, and on the first day he was able to move his arms and feel his body he knew why they had all abandoned him. His body was intact, he felt, fumbling his bandaged hands over his chest and stomach and genitals. He tried to wiggle the toes of his left leg and felt the terrible pain. He could deal with that. But an agonized scream tore from his throat when he realized to his horror that his right leg was missing from the knee down. And then he kept screaming and screaming and screaming.

CHAPTER EIGHTEEN

Lydia opened Caroline's letter and read it carefully. It was filled with hurt and shame, but at least Caroline was finally willing to admit that Adam Clarendon was her brother. Her meeting with Pamela must have been an ordeal, Lydia thought, but she had to smile at Caroline's courage in owning up to the truth.

"I'm going back to Venice," Caroline wrote. "If Tonio still wants to marry me, I think I'll go ahead with it. Naturally, I'll write you again and give you all the details. I've begun to put Adam out of my life completely (except as the brother he is), and I think I'll be happy married to Count Cambruzio."

She'd signed off breezily enough with the promise to write again as soon as she was resettled in Venice.

"A letter?" April asked as she walked into the study and saw Lydia folding Caroline's letter back into its envelope.

"From Caroline. She's been to England to see Adam."

"Adam? He isn't in England," April said. Her lips were drawn back tight against her teeth as though she were angry about something.

"No, he wasn't there when Caroline arrived."

"You read Adam's cablegram. He's in China where he belongs."

"I know that darling, but Caroline didn't know until Pamela told her."

"Pamela?"

"The girl Adam intends to marry."

April bristled. "Adam does not intend to marry any

Englishwoman."

Lydia skirted the argument by smiling. "You should be resting, darling," she said gently. "Remember that Leon and his family are coming for dinner tonight. The children can be tiring, as we both know."

"I was just going to my room," April said haughtily. She turned and strode out of the room, her yellow skirt slithering around her.

Lydia was, of course, concerned about Adam's safety in China. She had spent many a sleepless night thinking about the dangers that lurked over there. She also found herself frustrated and helpless in the matter of Michael Crane and Lorna. Repeatedly she'd tried to reach Lorna, and repeatedly she'd been refused. She'd tried talking again to Lorrie, but she too was unwilling to grant Lydia an audience. Peter Haskings had told Lydia to try to forget it and let things take their natural course, but she couldn't bring herself to do that. There was a deep foreboding smoldering inside her: she knew something dreadful was going to happen unless she intervened.

By chance she happened to stroll to the windows overlooking the street just in time to see Lorna's motorcar pass the house and pull up in front of the MacNair mansion one street farther on.

"At least I know she'll be at home," Lydia said as she hurried out of the study and pulled on her hat, coat, and gloves. She patted her hair carefully and marched out of the house and up the steep block to Lorna's house.

When the maid opened the door, Lorna was just going up the long flight of stairs that led to the second floor. Lydia pushed herself in and called Lorna's name.

"What do you want?" Lorna said impatiently as she turned around sharply. "I would appreciate it, Lydia, if you would kindly leave me alone. I have nothing whatever to say to you." She continued up the stairs and turned down the corridor toward her room.

"It's about Michael Crane," Lydia yelled, not bothering about decorum or the maid, who was staring at her. She waited, confident that Lorna would reappear. "You have got to listen to me," she said a moment later when Lorna reappeared at the top of the stairs. "It is of the utmost importance that I speak to you about that young man."

Lorna frowned and her mouth turned down. She hesitated, wondering what evil gossip Lydia intended to circulate, and how she even knew there was anything going on between Michael and herself.

"Michael Crane?" Lorna asked as if trying to place the name. "What about him?"

Lydia glanced at the maid. "I don't think we should have to shout at one another about this, Lorna. I'd like to speak with you privately, please."

Again Lorna hesitated, glancing at the maid, who was standing beside Lydia. "Show Mrs. Nightsong into the solarium, Martha." To Lydia she said, "I'll be down in a moment." Her voice was like icicles.

"This way, please," the maid said, leading Lydia into the sunlit room with its lush greenery. The solarium had a wall of windows that overlooked a beautiful sculptured garden just beyond the terrace.

Lydia wandered idly about the room admiring the plants, then stopped abruptly when she glanced out of the windows and saw Lorrie and Michael Crane seated in the little lattice gazebo that dominated the center of the garden. Lydia's hand clutched at her throat as Michael took Lorrie into his arms and kissed her passionately, the young girl's body arched hard against his. For a moment Lydia could do nothing but stare at them. She watched as Michael took Lorrie by the hand and led her down a path and behind a high box hedge.

"Well?" Lorna said as she placed herself just inside the door of the solarium. "What is it you want to say to me, Lydia?"

Lydia turned and carefully positioned herself to block out Lorna's view of the garden. "I think you'd better close the door, Lorna. What I have to say is for your ears alone."

Lorna reluctantly shut the double doors and turned back to

Lydia, folding her hands in front of her and stiffening her back. "If this is some filthy gossip, Lydia, I won't listen to it."

Lydia sighed and tried not to think of what she'd just seen in the garden. "It isn't gossip, Lorna. I've discovered something about Michael Crane that I think you should know."

"Discovered? Dear God, Lydia, don't tell me you've stooped to spying?" She smirked. "But then of course you have. You'd stoop to anything to hurt me."

Lydia tried to remain calm. "What I have to tell you has nothing to do with our business matters. It has to do with your personal safety, Lorna, and I feel it's my duty to warn you."

"Warn me? About what?"

"Not 'what,' but 'who.'"

"I assume you mean Michael."

"Precisely. Unfortunately I was in Magnin's a while back when I saw you and Mr. Crane together."

She saw Lorna's face flush slightly but Lorna kept her regal stance, not moving a muscle. "Unlike you, Lydia, I do not sneak about because I have nothing to hide. My relationship with Michael Crane is none of your business, nor is it anyone else's. We are friends, if you must know. Nothing more, no matter what that evil mind of yours may have imagined."

"The nature of your relationship with the young man is, as you say, no concern of mine. I don't want to know anything about it, Lorna. All I want to do is warn you of something you may not know about the man's background."

"I don't need you to tell me about Mr. Crane's background."

"I would advise you to check it out, Lorna. I honestly don't think you know anything whatsoever about him. I had no trouble at all finding out about the young man with the help of an experienced investigator."

"Investigator?" Lorna cried indignantly. "How dare you!"

"To be perfectly frank, I thought the gentleman in question had something to do with industrial espionage, insofar as he is working for one of my companies."

"He's working for MacNair Products, which technically is

my company, need I remind you?"

"That's neither here nor there," Lydia said, waving the remark aside. "I will gladly give you MacNair Products."

"You know I want more than MacNair Products."

"Please, Lorna, that is for our lawyers to straighten out. But I must warn you about Michael Crane."

"I won't listen to anything you have to say about him, Lydia. Now kindly leave my house."

"Michael Crane is wanted by the police in New York," Lydia blurted out.

"The police?" Lorna gasped.

"There was some trouble. He was living with an older woman, whom he abused rather brutally before stealing a great deal of money and jewelry from her."

Lorna put her hands over her ears. "I will not listen to this. You are an evil, malicious woman. Leave my house at once."

Lydia went over to Lorna and pulled her hands away from her ears. "You've got to listen."

They both turned when Lorrie and Michael walked in from the garden. Lorrie asked, "Listen to what, Mrs. Nightsong?" Her eyes were blazing.

"This vile woman," Lorna said as she turned aside and pulled open the door, "is trying to cause trouble again. Lydia, I want you out of here this instant."

"Lorrie," Lydia said, turning to the girl. She looked at Michael, who was smiling at her. "I've only come to tell your grandmother something I think you both should know."

Lorna straightened her back and glared at Lydia. "Mrs. Nightsong has come," she said to Lorrie, "to try and discredit Michael."

"Discredit me?" Michael asked, looking surprised but still smiling. Lydia stared at him closely, watching for signs of nervousness or fear. She saw nothing but his innocent, smiling face, which now looked just a little bit hurt. "Why would a beautiful woman like you interest herself in a poor little waif like me?" he said to Lydia. To Lorrie he said, "But I'm not too knowledgeable about the ways of San Francisco society." He turned his fixed smile to Lydia. "If you have any interest in me, Mrs. Nightsong—which I gather you have—it would be a simple matter to have dinner with me one evening, at which time I would be more than happy to tell you all about myself."

"I doubt that very much, Mr. Crane," Lydia snapped.

Lorrie fumed. "She's jealous, Grandmother."

Lydia scoffed. "Don't be ridiculous, child. I only—"

But Lorrie wouldn't be put off. "From everything you've told me, Grandmother, Mrs. Nightsong has always resented anyone you've befriended. She's even managed to steal away the affections of my own mother and Uncle Efrem. She hates you, as you well know. She'll say or do anything to make you miserable. Tell her to leave."

"Lorna," Lydia pleaded. "You must listen to me."

"Get out!" Lorna ordered. "Get out this instant or I'll have you thrown out."

Lydia knew it was hopeless. Michael was still smiling that smug intolerable smile, but his eyes were so cold and evil that Lydia actually shuddered. Her blood chilled as she found herself unable to look at him.

"Come," Michael said, reaching for Lydia's arm. "I'll walk you to the door."

Lydia shrugged his hand away, snapping, "Don't touch me." But as she turned and walked out of the room, she could feel an icy hand tightening around her heart.

* * * * * * *

Lydia was in a rather sour mood when she returned home and found her son, Leon, sitting in the drawing room with his wife and children. Lydia had almost forgotten she'd invited them to dinner, and after her run-in with Lorna she was sorry she had. She would have much preferred to spend the evening alone.

Her good intentions had all been in vain. She tried to tell herself that she'd at least warned Lorna, which was all she could do. The rest would be up to Lorna herself. But this was of little solace. Nothing good would come out of Lorna and Michael's liaison. At the very least, there'd be a confrontation between grandmother and granddaughter. That was inevitable, she knew. Michael Crane was a danger which should be avoided. But hard as Lydia tried, she could not think of any way to rid the MacNairs of that danger.

Oh well, it was their business, not hers. She should have taken Peter Haskings's advice and kept completely out of it.

"You look upset, Mother," Leon said when Lydia entered the drawing room.

She took off her hat and put it on the table beside the door. "Just another rather uncomfortable conversation with Lorna MacNair."

"You went to see her?"

"It wasn't about the lawsuit, Leon. It was something personal. I'd rather not talk about it now." She turned to Leon's wife, who was sitting quietly near the window with her three children huddled against her knees. "How are you, Marama, dear." Lydia kissed the girl's cheek.

Lydia had never warmed up to this beautiful Hawaiian woman Leon had chosen for his wife. She was so reserved and obviously unhappy to be living away from her family on the Islands. From all Leon had told her, Lydia knew that Marama was dreadfully homesick and hated San Francisco. More than once he'd mentioned the possibility of sending her back, but she would not leave without the children and Leon would not let her take them with her. Thus, they were stalemated while Marama smoldered inside like the rumbling of an overdue volcano.

"And how wonderful you all look," Lydia said, embracing the children. The two boys smiled pleasantly and let themselves be hugged and kissed. But the little girl was as dark and shy as her mother and drew back when Lydia reached out to her.

"Where's April?" Lydia asked Leon. "Hasn't she been down to greet you?"

"I went up earlier to let her know we were here," Leon said.

"She didn't answer my knock, so I supposed she didn't want to be disturbed."

"She has been acting even stranger than usual lately. She's unusually secretive and she smiles constantly as if she's hiding a wonderful surprise from the rest of us."

"Adam was a fool to go to China," Leon said.

Marama looked up with dark, sad eyes. "It is where he wanted to go. I see nothing foolish about that."

Leon smiled patiently and put his hand gently on her shoulder. "We'll go to see your family very soon, Marama. I promise you. As soon as the work at the factory is running smoothly I'll take you back for a visit."

"I do not want to visit. I want to stay there. It is where I belong, Leon."

"You belong here with your husband," he reminded her sternly. "I want my children educated here where they will learn about the modem world."

Marama scowled and lowered her eyes. She knew it was useless to argue with him. There had been too many arguments of late.

Lydia looked uncomfortable and changed the subject. "I'll go and see about dinner. Why don't you fix yourself a cocktail, Leon. I know Marama doesn't imbibe, but there are some soda-waters in the kitchen and I asked Nellie to fix a fresh pitcher of lemonade for the children." She paused in the doorway. "Incidentally, I saw the recent sales figures on the new Nightsong perfume. They are very encouraging."

"I think we have another winner, Mother. It's doing very well. I wish I could say the same about Marcus, though. He's not doing anything at all to promote it in Europe. He doesn't even answer my letters."

"I'll write to him. Marcus never did have much of a head for business. Perhaps it might be wise for you to go to Paris yourself." Seeing Marama's disapproving look, Lydia quickly added, "After you've spent some time in Hawaii, that is." She smiled sweetly. "I might even come to Hawaii with you. I've never seen the Islands. I'd like to." She turned and walked toward the kitchen.

Nellie was supervising the cook, who wasn't taking the supervision very gracefully. Lydia listened to them argue for a moment and was tempted to walk away. It seemed the entire household was at odds with itself.

"Is April lying down, Nellie?"

The housekeeper looked up from the sauce she was tasting. "She went out," she said simply.

"Out? Out where? When?"

"Just after you left the house earlier."

"Didn't she tell you where she was going?"

Nellie shrugged. "I just saw her getting into a taxi."

"A taxi? But April never goes out."

"Well, she went out this afternoon. That's all I know."

"Alone?"

"From what I could see she was alone. All wrapped up in a long cloak with a hood."

"How very odd. I can't imagine where she'd be going."

"To Chinatown no doubt. She sneaks off and goes there every once in a while when you're at the office."

Lydia sighed. "I suppose she'll be back in time for dinner. How long will it be?"

"You go up and change. Everything will be on the table in about half an hour."

April didn't return in time for dinner. Nor was she home when Leon and his family left. Lydia was worried but didn't want to say anything to Leon. She had become irritated with him and his whole family. Her nerves felt frayed and she wanted to be alone. But by the time the clock in the hall sounded ten, Lydia was completely at her wits' end. She went to the telephone and called Peter Haskings.

"I wonder if you could come over, Peter?" she began. "April went out this afternoon and hasn't come home." She hurriedly told him that she thought April might have gone to Chinatown, and considering the lateness of the hour it wasn't the safest place for her to be.

"I'll be there in twenty minutes," he said.

When Peter arrived fifteen minutes later Lydia met him at the door. Seeing how upset she was, he took her in his arms. "Don't worry about April, darling. I'm sure she's quite safe."

"I want you to take me to Chinatown. There's no guessing what she's gotten herself into."

"Where would you suggest we look once we get there? The shops and everything will be closed by this time."

"We can drive around. She might just be wandering about."

When they were seated in the back of Lydia's car, Peter took her hand and felt how cold it was. "Something else is troubling you," he said. "It isn't just April."

She hesitated a moment and then told him about her disastrous meeting with Lorna and about seeing Lorrie and Michael kissing in the garden. "I tried to talk to Lorna, but she wouldn't listen. We had a very ugly scene."

"You shouldn't have gone there. I tried to tell you."

"I know, I know, Peter. But I had to do something."

He sighed. "At least you told her. That's all you can do. You mustn't feel responsible if anything does happen, which I doubt it will."

Lydia wasn't so sure about that. She stared out the window at the dark, silent streets of Chinatown. Peter had been right. There wasn't a shop open and very few lights. They drove up and down the narrow streets and alleys without seeing any trace of April. By the time they had completely scoured the area with no success, Lydia was beside herself.

"Perhaps she's home by now," Peter suggested.

But when they reached the Nob Hill mansion, April still wasn't home. Peter tried to make light of the situation. "She's a grown woman, Lydia. Perhaps she met some old friend and got to talking."

"She has no old friends that I know of."

"She may have some you don't know about. You've told me how she keeps to herself."

Nellie came in, pulling her night robe around her and looking very upset. "I'm sorry to bother you, Lydia, but there's something you should know."

Lydia's eyes widened.

"I went up to Miss April's room to turn down the bed, and I noticed that some of her things are gone. So is her reticule."

"Oh no," Lydia gasped.

"She must have packed on the sly. There's no note or anything. But she's gone, Lydia." The old woman's eyes brimmed with tears. "I didn't see her carrying a suitcase or anything. I just saw her getting into the taxi. I would have tried to stop her if I'd seen anything suspicious."

Peter frowned. "Where would she go?" he asked Lydia.

Lydia put her hands over her eyes and started to weep. "I think I know," she sobbed. "Oh, that foolish, foolish girl."

"Where?" Peter asked.

"Where else?" Lydia said as she let her shoulders droop. "I have a feeling that if we checked the sailings, we'd find a ship leaving for China earlier today—and April is sure to be on it."

Peter hurried to the telephone and asked the operator to connect him with someone Lydia had never heard of. He put his hand over the mouthpiece and said, "This is a friend of mine who's connected with the maritime. He'll know if any ships left for China today."

He spoke into the receiver, apologizing for the late hour. Lydia saw him nod and then hang up. When he turned to her his face was drawn. "Nine o'clock. The *Rising Star*. It's a steamer bound for Shanghai."

"Dear God," Lydia breathed.

"There's no way we can verify that April is aboard," Peter said. "At least not tonight. I'll check first thing tomorrow."

He saw Lydia start to crumble.

"There is nothing whatsoever anyone can do about it now, Lydia. If April is aboard that ship, she's gone and we can't get her back." He turned to Nellie. "See that Lydia gets into bed and give her something to make her sleep." To Lydia he said, "I'll telephone you the very first thing tomorrow, as soon as I can check the passenger list on the *Rising Star*."

* * * * * * *

Lydia knew before he telephoned the following morning what he would tell her.

"I'm sorry, Lydia. Yes, there was a passenger listed as April Nightsong. The ship docks in Shanghai in eleven days."

Lydia started to cry.

CHAPTER NINETEEN

As soon as April set foot on Chinese soil she knew she would never leave it again. Everything tinkled like wind-chimes on a soft summer morning. The junks with their ribbed sails and bamboo hulls swayed to the ancient rhythms of China. April closed her eyes to the squalor of the wharf and rode a rickshaw into the old section. Here was the native land she remembered so clearly. Once she was sitting on the throne she would have to become accustomed to seeing the newer part of Shanghai with its smoky factories and high buildings, but for now she wanted only to see the China of her dreams.

Yet even here in the old town, things had changed. The people held themselves more erect and some had the audacity to look straight into April's face when she passed. That would all change, and it would again be as the dowager empress had ordered it to be, April promised herself. She kept her veil lowered, her eyes straight forward, and stared into the middle distance. In her mind's eye she saw nothing but the golden throne room and her subjects prostrate at her feet.

She chose not to linger in Shanghai. The changes there were too disturbing. Peking was where she would begin her struggle to restore China to its former glory. Lydia had thought her daughter deaf to the warnings she'd given about the situation here today. April had listened to every word, pretending not to hear, preferring not to hear—but listening. She knew only too well about the revolution and the odious Sun Yat-sen. He would be her starting place, she decided. The people had voted him the temporary president of the new Chinese Republic.

"Temporary," she kept reminding herself. Her people would reject him when they learned that the true heir to the throne had returned. They would want the China of old, not this bustling commercial monstrosity.

April made herself as inconspicuous as possible when she arranged for transportation to Peking. She listened intently to everything that was said, always pretending not to hear. The younger Chinese boasted about the new regime and China's entrance into the modem world. These boasts disturbed her.

Yet there were those who whispered their discontent, and that encouraged her. She had no concrete plan as to how she would achieve her goal. Adam would help her with that, she thought as she started out on the long trek to Peking. Adam would be at the legation compound there. She'd find him, she knew.

* * * * * * *

To her delight, Peking was little changed. The new arrogance of the peasants was present, of course, but that could easily be quashed once she was established in the Forbidden City. She was careful to keep her true identity hidden when she entered the compound and rented a suite of rooms under her married name: April Andrieux, tourist.

The small diplomatic community was the same. She chose the Peking Hotel in the legation rather than the American Embassy because she felt it would give her more maneuverability. She noted that even though the foreign compound was occupied by foreigners, all of the servants were Chinese, as were many of the lesser clerks in the diplomatic offices. The palace of Prince Su was just down the street from the Peking Hotel. He was long since dead, but it was still a popular place for banquets and dinners, hosted by the republicans who lived there now.

Surely even here within the compound walls, among so many Chinese, however loyal they might consider themselves to the new republic, there must be some, perhaps many, who would be willing to carry out the commands of their true empress, April told herself.

After settling in her rooms, April went back down to the registration desk. "Do you have a Mr. Adam Clarendon registered?" she asked in Chinese.

The clerk, an old Chinaman, looked up in surprise. He stared at her for a moment then looked down at the register. "Adam Clarendon? Ah yes, he is staying here."

April's heart leapt.

"He occupies a suite on the second floor across the hall from yours, Mrs. Andrieux." He smiled a toothless smile. "You speak with the Manchu dialect. Quite perfect."

"I used to live here," April said.

"Peking is much changed."

April could not resist. "Perhaps it will change again."

The man shrugged. "There will always be change."

"President Sun Yat-sen?" April asked. "I knew him when he was a lowly doctor here. Has he established his headquarters in Peking?"

The man nodded, eyeing her suspiciously. "Yes, in the new town." He gave her directions. "You will have no trouble finding his offices. Just follow the soldiers."

"Mother!" Adam called when he came down the stairs and saw April standing at the registration desk.

She whirled around and threw herself into his arms. "Adam. Oh, my lovely Adam. My beautiful boy. How wonderful you look." Tears stung her eyes.

"When did you arrive?"

"Just half an hour ago."

He hugged her tight and whispered, "We have a lot to talk about. I've been to see President Sun."

She took his hand and hurried him into a remote corner of the reception room. "What have you found out?" she asked the minute they were seated out of earshot of any passersby. "You didn't tell him why you were here or that I was coming?"

"No, I said nothing about our plans. I did everything you told me to do before I left San Francisco. The progress has been slow but steady. There is a great deal of unrest among the peasants, which I know will work to our advantage."

"Good. Good. Tell me everything."

"I merely paid a courtesy call on President Sun Yat-sen, introducing myself as Lord Clarendon, an Englishman who wanted to express his country's support of the president. I think he believed me. He was most cordial. His position here is quite tenuous, so he is grabbing whatever support he can from whoever offers it. His most powerful adversary is a man named Yuan Shih-k'ai."

"Yuan Shih-k'ai," April said with glee. "I know the man. He was head of the Manchu armies when I lived in the palace with the empress."

"There is talk that General Yuan intends to wage a revolt against Sun Yat-sen and restore China to Manchu rule."

April clapped her hands. "Such wonderful news. We must communicate with General Yuan immediately and let him know that I am here."

"Your cousin was deposed," Adam told her. "He no longer sits on the throne."

April scoffed. "Of course. He was only six years old, nothing more than a puppet. When I left the Forbidden City and the empress was deposed, there was no one directly in line to succeed her, so they put the silly child there for political purposes. But now the people will recognize me as their true empress."

"There is talk that General Yuan wants the throne for himself."

"He has no royal blood. The people are aware of that. They will want a royal Manchu and not an interloper. Come," she said, rising. "We will go and pay our respects to General Yuan and let him know that the true claimant to the Manchu throne has returned to Peking."

* * * * * * *

General Yuan Shih-k'ai was a tall, thick man with deep-set eyes, a bull neck, and a pudgy face the color of dried lemons. He had the sandpaper cough of a man who enjoyed smoking and wore a splendid uniform of gold and silver that fit snugly around his corpulent stomach. When April entered his office, the general stood respectfully as a man might do for any woman. However, when April threw back her veil and stood imperiously before him, General Yuan stiffened for an instant, recognizing her, and made a low, subservient bow.

"Princess," he said with a faint smile that revealed wide-spaced yellow teeth. "You do me great honor." His eyes moved to the young man standing behind her.

"My son," April said, making it an imperial command.

The general bowed to Adam. "You are most welcome." He motioned to chairs and remained standing until April and Adam were seated, then took his place behind his massive hand-carved desk.

April turned slightly and regarded the two soldiers who stood guard just inside the door. "I will speak with your master alone," she told them. The two soldiers looked at Yuan, who nodded slowly, and then left.

"Now, my princess, tell me how I may serve you."

April straightened herself. "I am pleased that you recognize me, General Yuan. It has been many years since last we met."

"It would be difficult not to recognize the beautiful princess. You have your father's eyes and mouth. The great Prince Ke Loo was well known to me, of course. We spent many hours together. His passing was regrettable."

"You know then that my father is dead?"

Yuan nodded. "I was informed."

"Then you also are aware that it is I who am the rightful heir to the Manchu throne?"

Again he nodded. "The young emperor, your cousin, sits on it no longer."

"This I have learned. I have also learned that you intend opposing this pretender, this President Sun Yat-sen."

"I have always remained loyal to your family, Princess. China must be reestablished as a Manchu empire."

"Good. That is why I have returned. You will amass an army to oppose these republican upstarts. I will, of course, remain in Peking until this is accomplished."

"If I may suggest, Princess," Yuan said. "It might not be wise for you to reveal yourself just yet. The armies are already being mobilized. We are very strong in number. Sun Yat-sen is well aware of the threat I pose. We have discussed the future of China. I believe the man will see reason when confronted with our strength. He has already hinted that he might step down and I would become president in his place."

April gave him a stony look. "President?"

Yuan smiled viciously. "It is only one steppingstone toward my ultimate goal."

"To seat yourself on the throne?" April asked, reading his mind.

"No, no, Princess. The people would never accept me as their emperor once they learn that a royal Manchu princess is here to govern them." His eyes slid away for a second and then returned to hers. "The throne is rightfully yours. I will see that you occupy it. It is your right."

"Your loyalty pleases me, General Yuan. My son and I are presently residing at the Peking Hotel. You will receive orders from me from time to time and I expect to be kept closely informed of your progress against Sun Yat-sen." She got to her feet. Adam rose immediately.

Yuan lumbered out of his chair and bowed again, this time lower than before. "I am your servant, Princess," he said.

April turned and swept out of the room with Adam in her wake.

The minute Yuan was alone he signaled for his aides. When they were gathered in the large room, Yuan glowered at the door through which April had vanished.

"That woman must be destroyed," he growled.

"She is but a woman," one of his aides said.

"She is the dowager empress's closest relation and the daughter of Prince Ke Loo. We have enough to contend with without some royal bitch showing up to cause trouble. Get rid of her."

"And the son?"

Yuan shrugged. "He may pose some threat, but I doubt it. However, just to be safe, perhaps they both should be removed."

The aides bowed.

"And do it soon. I do not want the princess and her bastard learning of my pact with Sun and his followers. If she discovers that I want the throne for myself she will stir up the Manchus, who might, out of loyalty and respect to their ancestors, decide the princess should rightfully rule China. Old customs die slowly, you realize, so it is imperative that the princess cause no unnecessary conflict among the people."

"We understand, General Yuan."

"Then see to it...and quickly."

Alone, General Yuan leaned back in his chair and lit a cigarette. "Stupid woman," he said to the empty room. The princess would pose no problem now, he told himself. The young emperor had already been deposed and the only living heir to the Manchu throne would soon be annihilated, leaving clear his path to the throne room in the Forbidden City. There would, he reminded himself, be trouble with the republicans once it was announced that President Sun Yat-sen had stepped aside in favor of Yuan. Sun's republicans would rise up against him, but their revolt would be squelched quickly and easily enough. He, Yuan Shih-k'ai, would be the emperor of China before the year was finished, and there wouldn't be a single member of the royal Manchu family lurking in the shadows to oppose and threaten him.

* * * * * * *

Adam took his mother's hand as they made their way back to the hotel. "I don't trust that man," Adam said.

April was too involved with her dreams of the future to allow anything to disturb them. "Yuan has always been loyal. He can be trusted." She smiled and touched Adam's cheek. "You will be a prince, my son, and one day emperor of China."

"Emperor of China," Adam sighed.

"China is ours. China is ours."

Adam gave no thought to ruling China. He was too intrigued by the thought of his royal blood. He knew nothing about government, but he could easily envision the grandeur of his future, the pomp and ceremony. People would bow to him. An entire nation would be his servant. He would have anything he wanted and everything. He would live in palaces with harems of lovely girls, and soldiers to protect him from the outside world.

Like two small children, April and Adam bubbled with enthusiasm, chatting endlessly about what lay in store for them. April rhapsodized about the beauty of the Forbidden City, its untold wealth and riches. She spoke of the clothes she would wear, the jewels. She told him about the ivory and jade palaces scattered throughout the country, all of which would belong to them. Adam's dreams involved stables of fine horses, trips to foreign lands where he would be treated like the emperor he would soon become.

"We will do whatever we like, my son," April said. "This is what we both were born for."

Adam leaned anxiously toward her. "You will teach me to rule one day."

"Rule?" April laughed. "We will have hundreds of advisers to carry out our commands. I will only have to tell them what I want and it will be done. The people will obey without question. That is what the great Dragon Empress did, and you and I will follow her example."

Neither of them mentioned the present unrest in China. They were both too childlike in their fantasies to even consider such mundane things as laws and government. They would have lackies attend to such things, leaving their own time free for idle pursuits of pleasure.

"I will have Arabian stallions," Adam said as they sat watching the twilight darken.

"You will have whatever your heart desires, my prince."

"It will be wonderful, won't it. Mother?"

"Like all our dreams come true," she said wistfully. "Now come. We must dress for dinner. Afterward I will take you into the Forbidden City and show you your inheritance."

"The Forbidden City? We must not reveal ourselves, Mother. Remember what General Yuan said."

"I know ways into the city that no one else knows exist. I want to show you your mother's palace, your home for the rest of your life."

Adam's eyes sparkled with boyish excitement. "Do you think we dare?"

"It is our home. Who is there to deprive us?"

"But—" He wanted to remind her again of Yuan's warning.

"There is nothing to fear, my prince," she interrupted. "Those who dwell inside the Forbidden City seldom leave it. I know many there who will recognize me and be overcome with joy to learn that I have returned to claim the throne. No one will betray us. Come," she said. "We will dress for dinner. Then we will wait until dark and venture inside our new world. I want to be the first to show you what you were born to possess."

Adam was suddenly too inquisitive, too awed to resist her. All his life he had read about the city of gold, the city of the Dragon Empress and her magnificent court. Reckless as it was, he wanted to see it all and he wanted to see it tonight with his mother's royal hand in his.

Their dinner was a hurried affair, neither of them concentrating much on what they ate, both absorbed in their forthcoming adventure. Adam, though, thought it rather odd that his mother wore a matronly black dress with high collar and white lace cuffs, so unlike her usual yellow silks with the rich embroidery and flowing sleeves.

"You finish your coffee, my son," April said as she got up from the table. "I want to change before going into the Forbidden

City."

When April returned a short while later she was wearing a long black cloak with a hood and veil, which she lowered as soon as they left the hotel.

"This way," she said, pointing.

A crescent moon suspended in the black sky gave a mysterious glow to the night. Adam's heart pounded against his ribs as he followed his mother out of the compound and into the narrow, crooked streets of Peking. They didn't speak until they reached the walls of the dowager's sacred city. The gates were guarded by soldiers. April pulled Adam into the shadow of a building and took his hand. They inched their way along the building until they came to an alleyway that led them deeper into the darkness.

"There is a passage through the wall hidden by a long hedge," April whispered. "It was always guarded when I lived inside. But they were the empress's guards, not foolish revolutionaries like this lot," she said, moving her eyes through the dark to the soldiers lounging before the main gate. "I'm certain these fools know nothing about the secret ways in and out of the city. How could they?" she sneered. "They are nothing but peasants."

They worked their way through the shadows until April stopped and motioned toward a clump of shrubbery that had outgrown its once sculptured contours. "They are allowing the topiaries to grow wild," she complained. "Come."

She had no trouble finding the low planked door with its iron reinforcements and latch. As she'd suspected, it was unlocked, an inexcusable oversight which she would certainly rectify once she was empress. She pushed down on the rusting latch and leaned her full weight against the heavy door. It moved an inch or two with a stubborn groan. Adam put his shoulder to the door and moved it enough so they both could squeeze through.

"This way," April said softly, gazing about the courtyard. "We can go in through the plum garden."

It was through this very garden that she'd been allowed to make her escape so many years ago. And now she was returning home by the very same route. It seemed only right somehow, as if by retracing her exact steps she could erase all the years of her absence.

There were oil lamps burning in the corridors, throwing ghostly shadows against the walls and ceilings. But there was no one to be seen, they found, as April moved toward the golden throne room.

"Surely it should be guarded," Adam said, noticing how empty the entire place was, hearing no sound but their soft footsteps padding lightly over the marble floors.

"I suppose the republicans want no reminder of royal rule and are letting the entire city fall to ruin."

Adam turned abruptly, thinking he'd heard voices coming from somewhere behind them. They both stood quite still, straining to listen, but heard nothing but dead silence.

"A bird perhaps," April said as she pressed forward. "There are many birds, especially parrots. The Dowager Empress loved parrots." She pointed toward the two solid-gold doors that rose at the end of the wide corridor. "There," she said as her eyes suddenly took on a brilliant gleam and her smile broadened to reveal her perfect white teeth. She stood for a moment as if mesmerized by the doors. "The royal throne room," she said with awe. "My throne room."

She threw back her hood and let the cloak fall to the floor. Adam saw that she was wearing the flowing, yellow silk robes of a princess. Her hair was entwined with pearls. April moved toward the doors, as if she were walking through the gates to heaven. Her eyes stared straight ahead. When she reached the doors she placed one palm flat on each panel and pushed. The doors swung open with a sigh, like the opening of heavy flower petals kissed by the first warm rays of the sun.

Adam had never seen a room so vast or so beautiful. Oil lamps and torches burned in gold and silver cages set atop intricately carved pillars of ivory and jade. The floor was a mosaic of marble embedded with precious stones, the ceiling a canopy of shimmering gold garnished with topaz, lapis lazuli, moonstones, sapphires, and amethysts. The walls were of damask and silk with huge bronze and gold lions and polished cabinets of rosewood and ebony. Directly in front of them was a raised dais of solid gold with yellow gossamer trappings and elaborate tapestries; it was dominated by a heavy throne encrusted with rubies, diamonds, and emeralds.

"There I will rule," April said as she slowly walked toward the dais, mounted the steps and turned, smiling to her invisible subjects. As if in a trance she raised her arms for silence before lowering herself onto the priceless seat. "Yes, here I will command."

"And here you will die, Princess," a voice boomed from the open doorway. Adam turned sharply just as the hiss of an arrow was released from its crossbow. He heard his mother give a sharp little cry, more of surprise than pain, and when he looked at her, horror-struck, she was clutching her breast and blood was oozing from between her fingers. She stayed erect staring down at him, then fell back against the throne, her eyes still open, a faint smile curling her lips. Then her head fell forward and her arms slumped to her sides.

"And now you, Bastard Prince," the voice roared.

Adam turned in time to see the archer raise the crossbow again. He stared in terror as the man pulled back the drawstring. In an instant, Adam threw himself to the floor and rolled to one side. The first arrow whistled over his body. Again he rolled and rolled until he found himself against a wall, deep in darkness.

"You won't escape, Bastard Prince," the assassin warned as he reloaded the crossbow and sent another deadly arrow in Adam's direction.

The arrow struck the wall just over Adam's head, making a sound like that of shivering harp strings. He had to get out of there but didn't know which way to go. He lay there frozen, staring in disbelief at his dead mother, who was still sitting on her royal throne, as if she'd simply fallen asleep in front of a boring audience of ministers and advisers.

The next arrow came closer. Adam clamped a hand over

his mouth to stifle a cry of panic and crawled on hands and knees toward the darkest end of the wall. His hands groped the darkness, his eyes strained to see some way of escape. As he huddled against one of the deep, heavy cabinets, he felt the sweat pouring out of him. His face was dripping with it, and his entire body was shaking.

Carefully he moved his hand up the wall and found what he recognized as a window ledge. He reached higher and touched latticework of ivory, hard and cold as death. Gently he pushed against the lattice. It didn't move. He groped for a latch, all the while watching the assassin as he came deeper into the throne room, peering through the shadows.

Adam found the hook that undid the window. He pushed it up with trembling fingers and eased open the casement. The darkness stayed in his favor as he hoisted himself up onto the ledge and dropped through the window just as another arrow whistled over his head.

He emerged into a long, dark corridor with a maze of turns and doorways. He ran through the first unlocked door he found and ran headlong through the room, stumbling over low tables and banging his shins against heavy furniture. He was oblivious of the pain, oblivious of everything but his desperate need to escape the killer stalking him. He tried to think, but his mind was numb. He staggered along through the empty rooms and hallways in search of someplace safe to hide.

He had to rest and plan what to do next. How long the Forbidden City would protect him he did not know. From all his mother had told him, the place was a labyrinth of hidden rooms and secret passageways. With luck he would be able to elude his pursuers. But for how long? He didn't want to think of that. He couldn't think. Every time he closed his eyes he saw his mother sitting so regally on her throne with an arrow in her heart.

CHAPTER TWENTY

Venice had been cold and rainy ever since Caroline's return several days ago. She hadn't told Tonio she was back. She wanted some time to herself to think things out clearly before seeing him. Even though she was now certain that Adam was indeed her brother, she was equally certain that she still loved him, incest or no. Hard as she tried to convince herself of the wrong of it all, she could not. Adam had been the first man to take away her innocence. She would never forget that—what woman would?—and in her weaker, more desperate moments, she yearned to have him again in her arms, naked and hard and demanding.

She must forget Adam, she kept telling herself. She must. The tears came all too frequently of late, and she was crying into her pillow when the telephone beside her bed jangled.

Caroline looked at it as if it were some strange, frightening object in a museum. She had told no one she was back in Venice and had no idea who could possibly be calling her.

She recognized Alice Pendergast's voice immediately.

"Hiya, kiddo," Alice said brightly. "I bet you thought you could sneak into town without anyone knowing."

"Alice," Caroline said, sniffing back her tears and trying to sound as if she'd been asleep. "How on earth did you know I was here?"

"I have my spies. But relax, kiddo. Tonio doesn't know. No one does but me, and that's only because I happened to see you getting off the train when I was at the station seeing off an old friend. You looked as if you didn't want to be recognized, all buried in furs and hat, so I didn't call out. How was Paris?"

"Oh, fine," Caroline said vaguely.

"How about lunch? I'm dripping with gossip which I think will interest you."

"Lunch? Oh yes, I suppose so." Her days of isolation and hiding were over, she decided. She'd have to face Tonio sometime. She couldn't stay in her hotel room forever, and she didn't think she should run away from him again. He did, after all, offer the only possible solution to her dilemma.

"We'll lunch at your hotel," Alice said. "Twelve o'clock."

"Twelve o'clock," Caroline agreed.

* * * * * * *

At noon Caroline found Alice sitting at a table by the window overlooking the canal. They kissed each other's cheeks.

"You look terrible, kiddo. I hope you haven't had another narrow escape from a piece of falling masonry?"

"No, nothing like that. I need a drink," Caroline said as she motioned to a waiter.

"You may need two," Alice retorted. "As I said, I dug up some rather juicy gossip you should know about."

"Oh?"

"Not gossip actually. Facts."

"Like what?"

"Sip your drink first. This is going to throw you for a loop."

Caroline sipped the straight gin she'd ordered and gave Alice a quizzical look. "What's this all about?"

"Tonio Cambruzio."

Caroline felt a sudden tightening around her chest. "What about him?"

"He's married, kiddo."

Caroline choked on her drink, splashing some on the tablecloth. "Married? He can't be."

Alice shrugged. "Sorry, love, but it's true. I checked it out very carefully. He's been married for four years."

"That's impossible. He proposed to me. I'm to meet his family."

"What family? I told you before you left that Tonio is a fraud. He has no family. Just a wife."

"I don't believe you," Caroline said.

"After finding out that he isn't really a count and having some time on my hands while you were away," Alice said, "I did some more checking. I dug deeper. He married a Sicilian girl named Lucia Bregetti. It wasn't a very good match. But you know divorce is impossible in Italy, so legally they are still very much married...regardless of his proposal."

"I won't listen to this, Alice. It can't possibly be true." Whether he was a count or not didn't matter. Nor did she care a fig for his family. Tonio was her only hope for forgetting Adam.

Alice shrugged again as she sipped her drink. "Find out for yourself, kiddo. I just thought I should warn you about the kind of man you're involved with."

"I think you're jumping to conclusions," Caroline protested. "Perhaps this wife you found out about died or something."

"Could be," Alice admitted. "I didn't check the death records. I'd think, however, that a man would mention a thing like that to his future bride."

"Unless it's too painful," Caroline said, snatching at straws.

"I just thought you should know, kiddo. As a friend I thought you had a right to know."

"Thank you, Alice, but I'm sure Tonio will tell me the truth if I ask him."

"Ask him," Alice urged. "Just ask him."

* * * * * *

Caroline mulled over everything Alice had said before calling Tonio to announce her return to Venice. They made a date for dinner that evening.

As soon as Caroline saw Tonio, she was convinced that Alice

was merely trying to cause trouble. Caroline couldn't bring herself to come right out and ask Tonio about this wife Alice had dug up. Sitting across the table from him, gazing at his handsome, innocent smile, all Caroline wanted was to throw herself into his aims where she'd be safe from the threat of Adam Clarendon.

"No more wine," Tonio said as he took the glass from her hand. "We will celebrate your return to Venice properly in my apartment. After you telephoned me, I chilled two bottles of very fine champagne. They are waiting for us just as impatiently as I waited for you, my darling."

"I'd like that very much," Caroline said as he kissed her fingertips and ran his tongue over the palm, sending a delicious thrill rushing through her.

The champagne was forgotten the moment they stepped into Tonio's apartment. She looked up into his face and was immediately lost in his eyes. He was so beautiful. Caroline reached up and kissed him.

"No champagne?"

She shook her head. "Later."

Her lips parted as he took her in his arms. The kiss was demanding and urgent with a hunger only deprivation can create. She tasted his tongue, the warm wetness of his mouth. Caroline kept telling herself that this was Tonio's mouth, not Adam's. These were Tonio's lips, and it was Tonio's body pressed so hard and commandingly against her own.

His hands moved upward, cupping her breasts. He fondled them lovingly, rubbing the flat of his thumbs against the hardening nipples.

"I adore you," he breathed.

She moaned softly under his mouth, wrapping her arms tighter about his strong body.

A moment later they were in his bed, entwined in a passionate embrace.

"You are the most ravishing woman I have ever known," Tonio murmured. They kissed ardently as he caressed her naked flesh. She found herself tormented by a desperate desire to be possessed by him, and she pushed her body tight against his. A gasp escaped her lips.

"I want you," Caroline murmured, shivering with wanton desire, as he worked his lips over every part of her. Boldly her hands explored his body, memorizing each muscle, each curve. A craving obsessed her as her impatient hands moved involuntarily over him, pulling, feeling, urging, teasing the throbbing power of his manhood.

"Caroline," he moaned as he felt her hands tighten around his shaft and draw him toward her.

She felt oddly in control as she manipulated his passions from one peak to the next. Easing herself onto her back, she moved so he could fit himself between her thighs.

It was all going too quickly. Caroline didn't want it to end so soon. She knew that once her passions were satisfied, thoughts of Adam would creep back into her heart and the pain would return. Here, safe in Tonio's arms, she knew Adam would not dare intrude.

She arched her back as Tonio moved slowly, deliberately into her. After gaining his advantage he held himself motionless, allowing her to adjust to the length and fullness of him. Then he began to move, slowly at first, then more urgently, more forcefully.

"Yes, yes, yes," Caroline moaned as her body was lifted higher and higher into some vast beautiful world alive with color and brilliance. She moved mindlessly matching him pace for pace, rhythm for rhythm, desperately trying to hold back the flood. She was lost in this world of lust.

"I love you," Tonio whispered as he pushed himself deeper and deeper into her body. "Marry me soon, my darling."

Caroline's eyes suddenly opened as Alice's voice came back to her. "He's married already." But the feel of his hard, thick shaft driving relentlessly in and out of her obliterated all reason.

Caroline screamed in total ecstasy as the juices flowed out of her and she felt Tonio's seed spill into her. Their bodies strained together as they clutched each other tightly.

And then it was finished and they fell limp and exhausted into the softness of the bed. After a long moment Tonio sighed and fumbled for a cigarette. Caroline saw him glance at the wall clock and frown.

Jokingly she said, "Are you worried about the time?"

She thought he looked frightened for an instant.

"Why do you ask me that?" Tonio said.

She took the cigarette he handed her and inhaled, then coughed and handed it back to him. "I saw you look at the clock. Am I to be sent home early?"

"No-no," he stammered as he turned away from her. "You returned to Venice so unexpectedly. I had to cancel an appointment."

"Another woman?"

He lay back down beside her and propped himself up on his elbow, touching his lips to hers. "There will never be another woman for me."

She didn't know where her courage came from, but the words just popped out of her mouth: "You don't have a wife tucked away somewhere, do you?"

Again she saw the flicker of fright pass across his face. He laughed, but it was forced and hard. He took her in his arms once more and began stroking her breasts. "I want you again, my darling," he murmured, avoiding her question.

As he moved over her, urging her thighs apart with his knees, Caroline took his face in her hands and kissed his eyes. She felt his hardness against her leg and reached for him as her own passions began to build again.

Suddenly the door burst open.

Caroline screamed and sat up when she saw two men scurry to the foot of the bed. A second later there was an explosion of burning magnesium powder, producing a flash of light and a billow of smoke. A heavy camera on a tripod clicked. A moment later the two men were gone, leaving behind the pungent odor of magnesium.

Caroline could only stare, her eyes blinking from the instant flash of light. She screamed again and clutched Tonio.

He cradled her to him. "It's all right, my darling. It's all right."

When she looked at him she was astonished by his total calm. If she wasn't mistaken he looked pleased, almost happy. "Tonio," she gasped.

"It is nothing. I am sorry. If I had told you what was going to happen you might not have gone along with my little plan."

"Plan?"

He kissed her softly. "I should have told you when I first fell in love with you, cara."

She blinked. "Told me what?"

He took a deep breath and let it out slowly. "I am a married man," Tonio said.

She could only stare at him. Alice had been right. "Oh, my God."

He held her tight. "It was cruel of me not to mention it, but I have not seen my wife for almost four years. She left me soon after we were married. She lives in Sicily. It was a mistake from the beginning. I did not love her. The marriage was arranged when we were both very small children. Under Italian law divorce is impossible unless...." He hesitated.

Caroline had heard of the law. "Unless adultery is proven," she finished.

"Yes."

"Oh, Tonio."

"It was unforgivable of me to put you through this frightening experience. I would understand if you hated me, never wanted to see me again."

All Caroline could think of was that he hadn't deceived her. He had told her the truth.

"Do you hate me, darling?"

She shook her head. "No, Tonio. I don't hate you." She found she was still trembling from the scare. "It's just...." Her voice trailed off.

"I know. You are frightened. I can feel you shaking."

"You should have told me."

"And would you have continued to see me? I do not think so."

He was right. She wouldn't have. Now, of course, it was different. Alice's warning had been unnecessary. Tonio had revealed the truth himself. Her respect for him soared. Suddenly Tonio seemed such a noble figure and Alice a mere gossip-monger.

"And do not worry about the scandal, Caroline. There will be none."

She hadn't yet given a thought to what repercussions the photographs would produce when made public. "I'm not afraid of a little scandal, Tonio."

"But I promise you, there will be none. My wife, Lucia, is aware of what I had planned. In fact, it was she who suggested it. I only regret that you had to be involved." He traced a fingertip across her lips. "But then I could not go to bed with any other woman. It is not in my nature. I fear, my dearest, that you will be marrying a very old-fashioned man. I do not bed women for the pleasure of it. Only out of love, and I love no one but you, Caroline."

"Darling Tonio. I do love you very much."

She meant it at the time. But afterward, alone in her room, she began to waver again. By agreeing to go along with Tonio's plan, she had committed herself to him completely. There would be a delay, of course, which made her feel slightly better. Yet, once the divorce decree was granted, she would have no other recourse but to marry Tonio Cambruzio and that would be that. A part of her welcomed the impending delay. Another part wanted the divorce to be finalized immediately so that she could concentrate on being Tonio's wife and erase Adam Clarendon from her mind forever.

Caroline wore a smug smile when she met Alice for lunch the next day. As she slipped into the chair across from her friend she smoothed the napkin on her lap and rested her elbows on the table, studying Alice.

"You look like the proverbial cat," Alice said, noticing the self-satisfied grin.

"He told me he was married."

"He told you? You didn't ask him?"

"No. He volunteered the information." Caroline motioned to the waiter for an aperitif.

"Well, I'll be damned," Alice breathed. "Frankly, kiddo, I took Tonio Cambruzio for a first-class heel. Obviously he is more reputable than I gave him credit for being." She thought for a moment. "But if he's admitted having a wife already, how does he explain his proposal of marriage to you?"

Caroline waited until her drink arrived before leaning closer to tell Alice what had happened in Tonio's bedroom. "It was all prearranged. His wife's idea. Tonio said she is as anxious to be rid of him as he is of her. He said there is a young man in Sicily she wants to many and this is the only solution to both their problems."

"I'll be damned," Alice said again, astonished. "So you are going to go through with the wedding?"

"Of course. You know the Nightsongs' reputation. We aren't afraid of a little publicity."

"I'd still think twice about this if I were you," Alice warned.

Caroline saw again the mischievous, almost malicious gleam in Alice's eyes. "Now what have you dug up?"

"Nothing really," Alice answered noncommittally. "Just rumors."

Caroline was getting exasperated. "More rumors. Don't you ever tire of besmirching people's good names?"

Alice shrugged. "I have an inquisitive nature. It's a prerequisite to being a newswoman."

"You seem to have taken a rather perverse interest in my involvement with Count Cambruzio."

"I told you. He isn't a count."

"What of that? I don't care if he's a street beggar."

"How do you feel about criminals? Would you care if he were one of those?"

"Criminals? Really, Alice, aren't you carrying this a bit too far? There's nothing criminal about Tonio."

"According to my sources, your Tonio Cambruzio is rather closely involved with the criminal element here in Venice."

Caroline put her hand down hard on the table, making the glasses jiggle. "Enough of this, Alice. You're overstepping yourself. I won't hear another word against Tonio."

Alice was not intimidated. "What does he do for a living? Have you asked him that? He lives in a rather exclusive neighborhood, wears expensive clothes, spends money like mad. Where does it all come from?"

Caroline was genuinely annoyed. "It really doesn't matter to me where any of it comes from, Alice. Perhaps he inherited it. Maybe he stole it. I really don't care." She stood up, almost knocking her chair over backwards. "I suddenly have no appetite for you or for food, Alice. Good afternoon."

"Think about it, kiddo," Alice called after her. "Just think about it."

CHAPTER TWENTY-ONE

To Marcus, Paris had lost all of its appeal. The city was in ruins as far as he was concerned, and so was his life. The long stay in the hospital had depressed him to the extent that he would rather have died than be released with only one leg and the stump of another.

It was over...all over. He saw no reason on earth to go on living. Claudine's father had been kind and considerate. Or had he merely been trying to exorcise his guilt for what had happened? It was, after all, the wide axle on the rear wheels that had caused the racing machine to overturn and burst into flame.

Marcus told himself a thousand times that it was Monsieur Muret's fault and not his own. He'd driven skillfully and should have won the damned race. It was the machine's design that had caused the catastrophe.

But did it really matter who or what was to blame, he asked himself as the tears welled up and streamed down his cheeks? He was a cripple—that was the bottom line; he would hobble through the rest of his life.

"Why didn't I die?" he wailed as he buried his face in the pillow and pounded the mattress.

Claudine had never come back to the hospital after the amputation. Her father came and reassured Marcus that there was nothing to worry about concerning expenses: the hospital bills had been paid and he had arranged for a full-time nurse to see to Marcus's needs.

Now that Marcus was back in Paris, Claudine and her father

had vanished from his life, except for the monthly checks that came from the Muret Company, which Marcus promptly returned uncashed. He didn't want their pity and certainly not their guilt-money. It wasn't long before the checks stopped coming.

What girl would want him now? Who could love a one-legged man? Amelia's letters still came, filled with her love for him and begging him to write her. He could never bring himself to saddle Amelia with a cripple. It sickened him to think that he would have to lean on someone until he died. Why not die now and get it over with? He'd entertained that idea until it had become an obsession.

Yet he was too cowardly to cut his wrists. He couldn't string up a hangman's rope. And there was no way in hell he could obtain the drugs that would let him sleep forever; the nurse saw to it that all these were carefully kept out of his reach. She'd nursed amputees before. That was obvious.

Nurse Bonnand was a hard-faced, florid woman with huge breasts and a wrestler's arms. She picked him up as if he were an infant and treated him like one. Her patience and solicitude made Marcus cringe. Just looking at her was a reminder of his total helplessness. He knew, however, that he could not do without her, or someone similar.

"Another letter from America," Madam Bonnard announced as she came into the bedroom, her long white apron and skirt rustling from too much starch. She sniffed the envelope. "The beautiful young lady of yours."

Marcus kept his face hidden in the pillow. "Send it back. Mark it: 'Deceased,' 'Moved,' 'Unknown,' I don't care."

"Now, now, Monsieur Marcus. You cannot do that. Think of your lovely girlfriend. It would hurt her terribly." She held the scented letter out to him.

"I don't want it," he stormed. "Go away and leave me alone."

"I will not go away and I will not leave you alone." She folded her arms across her bosom and planted herself solidly beside the bed. "If you are any kind of man you will at least answer the poor girl. You owe her that much. She writes you several times a week and you never write back. All you want to do is lie in that bed and feel sorry for yourself."

"Go away."

"No. You have lost part of one leg. You are still a man in every other sense. There is nothing you can do that will grow your leg back, and now you must be manly enough to accept that fact."

"You rotten woman. Get the hell out of here."

"Rotten woman, am I? Because I tell you the truth I am rotten? What are you intending to do for the rest of your life, Monsieur? Lie in that bed and cry into your pillow all day and night? If you want me to get out and leave you to yourself, that can be arranged," she said threateningly. "Crawl around on your hands and knees, if that is what you want. It means nothing to me. And when you are finished feeling so sorry for yourself you will find that there are people who truly care for you. Your family—"

He sprang up at her. "Don't you dare mention this to my family. If you so much as hint to anyone of what happened to me, I'll...."

"You will what? Kill me?" She shook her head, her heavy jowls quivering. "You cannot keep your affliction a secret forever. Your office calls every day. How long can you go on telling them you are not feeling well? You must face reality, monsieur, and accept help from those who love you."

"I don't want anyone's help, nor anyone's pity."

"You will get pity whether you want it or not." She was trying to make him angry enough to do something to help himself. "You will also get help, understanding, love, and care. You cannot lose yourself in a world of strangers. You must be with your family and friends, people who want you, not with someone like me who is well paid to put up with your tantrums."

"Go away."

She held out Amelia's letter. "Read it. Write to your young lady. Even if you want to make yourself miserable, there's no reason to make her miserable too with your silence." She put the letter on the pillow and walked out of the room.

Marcus curled himself into a ball and blinked back his tears. He lay there for a long time cursing the day he was born and all the days that lay ahead. As he rolled over, Amelia's letter crinkled under his head. He reached for it and stared at her familiar handwriting. He started to crumple the envelope in his hand, but something stopped him. Instead he tore it open and took out the neatly written letter. "Darling Marcus," he read:

> I haven't heard from you in so long and I am worried sick. You haven't written your mother either. Everyone is concerned, though your secretary wrote Leon to say that you were well but laid up with a torn ligament. Your silence makes me think it is more than that, and I am terribly distressed. Please, please write and let me know that you are well. Even if you've met someone else and don't love me anymore, I would rather live with that than the fear that there is something terribly wrong with you. I won't tell you how much I love you because it may upset you if you no longer feel the same. Just write, Marcus. Please write—if not to me, at least to your mother.

He read the signature then reread Amelia's letter. "Even if you've met someone else and don't love me anymore...."

He loved her. Oh, how he loved her, and yet he could never go back to her as he was now. He had to cut her out of his life even if it meant hurting her terribly. It was only right that she be rid of him. He wasn't worthy of her love. He wasn't worthy of anyone's love.

He stiffened his courage and rang the little silver bell which Nurse Bonnard always answered so promptly.

"I'd like pen and paper," he said when she came in. She saw the letter in his hand. "Good." A moment later she returned with a portable writing desk, which she placed across his lap after propping him up against the pillows.

"My dear Amelia," he wrote, carefully choosing his words:

> You must think me a beast not to have written before this, and after you read my letter you will know that I really am the worst beast in the world. I didn't want to hurt you because I care so much for you. Still, it isn't being fair to either of us to withhold the truth from you.

His hand stopped. He could picture in his mind Amelia's face when she read those words. He could see the hurt, the anxiety, and for a moment he was tempted to tear up the letter and not write at all. But he forced himself to continue:

> I'm sorry, Amelia, but you are right. I have met someone else. We couldn't help falling in love. It just happened. I won't write about her because it would pain you only more. You are the last person in the world I want to hurt, but I think it only right and gentlemanly of me to tell you we intend marrying soon.

Oh my God, he thought. How miserable she will be when she reads that. Still, the only noble thing was to give her freedom. The hurt would go away in time, he felt. She would meet someone else. Her life wasn't over, as his was.

I know how much this must hurt you. Hate me for what I'm doing, Amelia. I deserve it. Put me out of your life forever. I only pray that you will meet a man who will be worthy of your love. I am not that man.

He read over the letter then signed it simply, "Marcus" and pushed it away from him.

For a long time he sat there on the brink of indecision. It seemed heartless to send such a letter, and yet in the long run it would be a kindness to Amelia. He had to let her go, despite the anguish it would cause her.

Marcus took an envelope and addressed it, then hurriedly folded the letter, slipped it into the envelope, and rang for Nurse Bonnard. "Post this for me, please," he said.

"Of course."

He wondered if she'd look so pleased if she knew what was in the letter. When she left the room, Marcus turned his face into the pillow and started to cry again.

* * * * * * *

"No! Oh dear God, no!" Amelia wailed when she read Marcus's letter. "You can't. You're lying. You aren't marrying someone else." She threw herself down on the couch, crumpling the letter in her hand, and began to sob bitterly. The pain of her father's death hadn't been as bad as this. She remembered Marcus holding her, blocking out the hurt of that death as her father was lowered into his grave. She doubted that she could have gotten through that terrible time had it not been for Marcus's strength. But now she had lost them both. She wanted to crawl into her father's grave and die.

"Marcus. Marcus," she cried as her heart burst into a million fragments.

Somewhere deep inside the house she heard the telephone ringing. Amelia didn't want to talk to anyone. She wanted only to be left alone with her broken heart but the telephone kept ringing, ringing, as if determined to intrude upon her grief. The shrill sound started to anger her and she pushed herself off the couch, sniffed back her tears, and yanked up the receiver.

"Yes?" Her voice was choked with misery.

"Amelia?" Lydia asked. "You sound odd. Is something wrong?"

Amelia couldn't hold back her anguish. "Oh, Lydia," was all she could get out before she broke into uncontrollable sobs.

"Amelia! Dear God, what's the matter?"

"Marcus," Amelia managed. "Marcus," she said again, her throat tightening on his name.

"I'll be right over," Lydia said, sure that something dreadful had happened. She didn't want bad news coming over some mechanical device.

When Lydia arrived ten minutes later, Amelia was still lying on the couch, her head cradled in her arms, tears running unchecked down her face. As Lydia walked into the little parlor, Amelia looked up through her tears, then flung herself into the older woman's arms. "What am I going to do?" she wailed.

Leon had insisted upon coming with his mother, knowing that Amelia had some upsetting news about Marcus. Now he put his hand on Amelia's shoulder as Lydia tried to console her. "What's happened, Amelia?" he asked.

Amelia continued to cry against Lydia's breast. With one hand she pointed to the crumpled letter lying on the cushion of the couch. "He wrote...." Again the terrible sobbing caught her breath and she couldn't say any more.

Leon walked over and picked up the letter. He read it slowly, then looked at his mother with a great sadness in his eyes. "Marcus is getting married."

"Married? To whom?"

"He didn't say," Leon replied, handing her the letter.

"Does it matter?" Amelia cried.

Lydia read the letter and looked up, frowning. "It isn't like Marcus to be so cruel, so unfeeling. He may be headstrong, but this...," she said, brandishing the letter. "This doesn't sound like him at all." She bit down on her lower lip. "Something is wrong. I can't believe what he's written."

Leon said, "Do you think I should go over and talk with him, Mother?"

Lydia didn't hesitate. "Yes, I think you should. I'd go myself, but what with this legal suit of Lorna's I'm rather stuck here."

"I'll leave as soon as possible. Marama will be upset, but that can't be helped. I agree with you, Mother, something is definitely amiss."

Leon hugged Amelia. "It's going to be all right, Amelia. I'll talk with Marcus. I'll make him come to his senses if I have to thrash him."

"I want to come with you," Amelia said.

"No, I'd better go alone. If what Marcus wrote is true, it will only be more painful for both of you. He's always listened to me. I should be able to reason with him about this."

CHAPTER TWENTY-TWO

Susan MacNair Dillon never ventured outside the townhouse after her rape by Kraus. She stayed safely indoors, arranging for the closing down of the house. But the children could not be taken out of school until midterm, which caused a long delay and made it all the more difficult for Susan to stay safely out of reach of the thugs she knew would kill her if they found her still alive and capable of reporting, first-hand, the deplorable way the sweatshops were being run.

She was too frightened to contact any of her important friends, people who should be told about conditions in the sweatshops. They would only expose the fact that she was still alive, which would place her life in further jeopardy. She talked to her husband by telephone almost every night and kept telling him—without ever mentioning anything about her nightmare in the park—how eager she was to join him in California.

When the train finally pulled out of Grand Central with Susan and the two boys safely closeted inside their compartment, Susan breathed a sigh of relief. She calmly watched the platform disappear as the train dove deep into the dark tunnel and emerged again into the dwindling light of day, heading west to safety.

It was a long, monotonous trip for Susan, but an adventure for the boys. The monotony was bearable only when Susan reminded herself that she was finally free of Kraus's threats and that once she was reunited with Sean she'd be able to tell him what had really happened...all of it.

Or would she? How would he react to the story of her rape? Perhaps she shouldn't tell him. The debate inside her head occupied her for most of the journey. When they finally reached Oakland, they took the ferry across the Bay to San Francisco. Sean had suggested that she and the boys stay with Lorna for a while until he had a house ready for them in Los Angeles, and Susan had agreed.

Once inside her mother's house, Susan was tempted to ask Lorna's advice about what to tell Sean, or whether to tell anyone. As usual, however, the moment Susan found herself alone with her mother, she also found herself at odds with her. Lorna was not the woman to give any sensible advice, Susan thought, noting the radical change in her mother.

The last time she'd seen her. Lorna had been a drab, aging woman always dressed in black and looking twice her age. Now she bubbled and fussed and seemed resentful of the reminder that she had growing grandchildren.

Susan didn't understand the change until the evening Michael Crane came to dinner. At first Susan thought he was Lorrie's new friend, but as the evening progressed she saw that young Michael paid more attention to Lorna, who simpered like a silly girl of fifteen while Lorrie, a true teenager, sullenly adopted the airs of a woman her grandmother's age. There was an obvious rivalry going on between Lorrie and her grandmother.

Tensions mounted after dinner when the boys were excused and put to bed and Susan, Lorrie, Lorna, and Michael Crane settled down over coffee in the drawing room. Everything Lorna said to Michael, Lorrie contradicted. Everything Lorrie said to Michael, Lorna put down as girlish immaturity.

Michael was thoroughly enjoying himself, Susan noticed. And as if to intensify the competition between Lorna and Lorrie, he made a point of being overly attentive to Susan.

Susan didn't like Michael Crane. He was obviously deriving some sadistic pleasure out of pitting grandmother against granddaughter, urging them on by openly flirting with Susan. He was an expert at his craft, she had to admit.

Susan finished her coffee and declined an after-dinner drink. She noticed that it was Michael who offered her the brandy. He was very much at home in this house, it was plain to see. "I should make sure the boys are asleep, and I'm rather tired myself." She turned to her daughter. "Lorrie. How about coming up with me? We haven't had a private chat since I arrived."

"I'm really not ready for bed yet, Mother."

Lorna said, "It's getting late, Lorrie. Go along with your mother. It's time all you children were in bed." She glanced at Michael. "Besides, there's something I want to discuss with Michael."

What it could be, Susan didn't have a clue. There was such a disparity between their ages, she found it impossible to imagine anything they might have in common. Yet Michael continued to look complacent as he stood politely and bid Susan and Lorrie good night. Out of the comer of her eye, Susan noticed that when he sat back down it was beside Lorna on the divan.

So this was the man Sean had asked her about. She hadn't done any research on him, but now she wished she had.

Susan linked her arm through her daughter's as they started up the stairs. "Who is he?" Susan asked.

"Michael? You heard Grandmother when she introduced him. He's a relation of Ellen's."

"I know that, but who is he really? I mean, it's rather odd that your grandmother and he are so...close. He's quite at home here, I noticed."

"Michael is only being kind to Grandmother. Actually," she said a bit defensively, "he comes here to see me, if you must know."

Susan chuckled. "He seems a bit old for you...and far too young for your grandmother."

"I am hardly a child, Mother, I do wish you would stop thinking of me as one."

"I don't think of you as a child, Lorrie. It's just that I don't believe this Michael Crane is anyone you should become serious about."

Lorrie bristled. "I happen to be in love with him."

"In love with him?" Susan said, amused. "Well. When did all this happen?"

"When I first met him. Michael wants to marry me. He's only cozying up to Grandmother to get her to like him."

"Oh, I don't think you have to worry about your grandmother liking him. From what I've seen, I'd say she likes him a little too much."

"You're being horrid," Lorrie said, breaking free of her mother's arm. "Michael can't stand that old woman."

"Lorrie! That is a very mean way to speak of your grandmother."

"Well, she is an old woman. Every time Michael comes here, she starts acting like she owns him. She'll never approve of my marrying Michael."

"Don't you think your father and I have something to say about that?"

"I'll marry whomsoever I please, Mother. And if you or Father or Grandmother don't like it, then that's just too bad. Michael and I will elope."

Susan wasn't amused anymore. "You will do nothing of the kind, young lady," she said, angrily pulling her daughter into her bedroom and closing the door. "Now you listen to me, Lorrie, and listen good. There is something about that young man that isn't right. He impresses me as an opportunist. I don't like him, and I don't trust him. You are to break off whatever relationship you've established with him. Do I make myself quite clear?"

"I will not stop seeing Michael," Lorrie said, her eyes flashing. "You can do whatever you like to try and stop me, but I intend to marry Michael and there is nothing you or anyone else can do about it."

Susan gripped her daughter's shoulders and shook her. "You have always been a very foolish, stubborn, willful girl, but if I have to lock you in your room until it is time for us to join your father, that is precisely what I'll do."

"Like everyone else, you're jealous," Lorrie spat. "You want

Michael for yourself."

"Lorrie, stop it. You're vain and spiteful and sometimes I think you haven't a brain in your head. I am going to call your father early tomorrow morning, and you are coming with me and your brothers to Los Angeles on the first available train."

"I am not leaving here. I'll kill myself if you separate me from Michael."

Susan could see that her daughter was bordering on one of her hysterical rages. "Listen to me, Lorrie," she said, trying to keep calm. "You're undergoing a girlish infatuation. Nothing more."

"It is not an infatuation."

"Then prove it. Come to Los Angeles with me and the boys. Spend some time away from Michael. If he truly loves you as much as you claim, he'll follow you."

"No. I won't go."

Susan attacked. "Then you know deep down that he won't follow you. You aren't sure he really does love you."

"He loves me. I know he loves me."

"Make him prove it. Come to Los Angeles." She could see a flicker of doubt in her daughter's eye. "Think about it, Lorrie. If he wants you as desperately as you think, he won't be able to stay away from you for very long."

She gave Lorrie a hug and steered her toward the door. "Just think it over. And don't do anything foolish like trying to run off with him. You're only fifteen, remember. I'll have you stopped legally if I have to."

There was hatred in her daughter's eyes as she left the room. Once alone, Susan leaned against the door and breathed a sigh. Tomorrow she would get Lorrie away from Michael if she had to drag her away.

However, Susan was in no condition to travel the next morning. She awoke feeling well enough, but suddenly a terrible attack of nausea gripped her. She stayed in the bathroom for a long time throwing up, feeling quite sick. At first she assumed she'd simply eaten something that didn't agree with her.

But as she made her way back to bed and lay down, the nausea returned accompanied by a terrible fear. It couldn't be morning sickness, she told herself. Sean and she had been apart for almost four months. A sickening thought occurred to her when she remembered Kraus's brutal attack in the park.

"God no," she breathed as she felt the queaziness in her stomach, the throbbing in her head. "Please God, let it not be that."

Too ill to travel, she claimed a splitting headache and stayed in bed all day. The following morning she felt a little better, but not much. The nausea started to go away around noontime and then she was able to keep some solid food in her stomach.

By midafternoon she was feeling like her old self again and romped with the boys in the park down the street. But that evening she felt sick again and went to bed early. Lorrie, she found, was staying close to the house, and Susan was satisfied to think that she was at least mulling over her comments about Michael.

Sean called every day, eager to come to San Francisco to be with her and the children. Susan put him off, saying it was silly for him to leave his business and that she was feeling better. He wasn't to worry, Susan insisted; she, Lorrie, and the boys would join him within a day or two.

Actually, she knew from past experiences that she was indeed pregnant even though the doctor in New York had told her she was unlikely to conceive again after her difficult delivery of Petie. Unlikely or not, she was pregnant now—and not by Sean. She would have to stay in San Francisco for a little while longer, at least until she decided what to tell her husband. In the end, however, she knew she would have no other recourse but to tell him the truth. What to do about the baby would be something for them both to decide. It couldn't be her decision alone.

At around midnight that Saturday evening, Susan awoke feeling very fit and very hungry. She didn't want to bother the servants and decided to go down to the kitchen and make herself a sandwich. First she went to Petie and David's room and saw that they were sound asleep. She tucked the blanket around Petie, smoothed his hair and kissed his cool brow.

"Mom?" David said, his eyes hardly open.

"Go back to sleep, love. I just came in to check on you two."

"Are you feeling okay?"

"Fine, sweetheart. I think we'll be able to join your father in a day or two."

"I'd like that, Mom. I don't much like it here."

She kissed him and pulled his blanket up around his chin. "I don't much like it here either, love. Go back to sleep. We'll check the train schedule tomorrow."

She let herself out of the boys' room and started down the back stairs. She fixed herself a cold turkey sandwich with lots of Russian dressing and onions and a dish of ice cream. She was pregnant all right, she told herself. No doubt about it.

As she started to put the fixings back into the icebox she thought she heard voices coming from somewhere downstairs. She listened for a moment, trying to place the speakers. Without trying to be too quiet, she pushed open the kitchen door and began following the sounds. In the foyer she decided they were coming from the library. The sliding double doors were closed. Susan stood there, straining to identify the voices. One was unmistakably Michael Crane's. The other was a woman's, but she wasn't exactly speaking—the sounds she made were more like moans and sighs and low, guttural gasps.

"You love it when I take you rough like this, don't you?" Susan heard Michael say.

"Yes. Oh God, yes, Michael. Don't stop. Don't stop."

Susan clutched her throat. It was her mother's voice. It was Lorna.

It was as if Susan had opened a book and was rereading something she'd read before, something familiar and frightening and unforgettable. She didn't have to slide open the library doors to know what was happening on the other side. She remembered that awful night years ago when she and Leon Nightsong had gone to the house of Mr. Ramsey, and found him and Lorna moaning and thrashing naked on the bed.

Now the disgust and horror of it was happening all over again, sickening Susan. She could never forget seeing her mother in the arms of that gross, hairy man as he shoved himself ruthlessly into her. She didn't want to see anything like it ever again, but she knew that if she looked inside the library that's exactly what she would see.

She backed away from the doors, then turned and raced up the carpeted steps to her room where she was violently ill again. This time it wasn't due to her pregnancy, though.

In the morning Susan felt better. She didn't want to think about the previous night's discovery, but wondered if she should confront her mother with it. That wouldn't do any good at all, she told herself. Lorna would treat it as casually and callously as she had once before. Another scene would only alienate them all the further.

No, Susan decided. She would take her children and leave this dreadful house, never to return. As for Lorrie, she wasn't sure what to tell the girl, if anything. Needless to say, Lorrie must never see Michael Crane again.

Sean would tell her what to do, she thought. "Dear Sean," Susan said aloud. "I'm coming to you with an awful lot of problems."

Susan was surprised that Lorrie didn't make too much of a fuss about leaving Michael and San Francisco. The girl came along rather quietly, looking smug and secure. Susan wondered what could be going on in that silly head of hers.

"Michael will come for me," Lorrie said confidently. "I told him you were forcing us apart, and he promised me that no one could ever separate us."

It was as if she had already won a battle against her mother and was content to sit quietly and wait for the fruits of her victory. Susan was content too to let her feel victorious. It would mean peace for at least a little while, until Lorrie found that Michael wasn't coming for her, that he would never come.

* * * * * * *

It was odd to see flowers and so much greenery and sunshine during winter months, Susan thought as she looked out the train window.

"When does it snow?" Petie wanted to know.

"It only snows up in the mountains," Lorrie said. "Everyone knows that."

Petie put a protective arm around his little brother's shoulder. "I wish you had stayed with Grandmother, Lorrie," he said.

"So do I," Lorrie answered without looking up from her book.

"Then why didn't you?"

"Ask Mother. She's the one who dictates what we all must do."

Susan turned from the window. "That will be enough, Lorrie."

"Yes, Mama," Lorrie said obediently. "Whatever you say."

Susan gave her an irritated look and snapped open the newspaper. The news from New York was good. The garment workers had called a strike in both New York and Boston, demanding higher wages and shorter hours. From all accounts, their efforts would succeed. And the suffragettes were now demonstrating in London. The women's movement was spreading, which pleased Susan greatly.

Still, she hadn't taken part in the last-ditch efforts of the garment workers and she felt she'd let them down. She also felt cheated. She sighed. At least, she thought, she'd done what she could. Her family had taken priority. Or had she run away for more selfish reasons?

On the other side of the ledger was the bad news. The Sixteenth Amendment to the Constitution was destined to pass into law and everyone would have to begin paying taxes on their income. Sean wouldn't like that at all, Susan knew. And there was more bad news, she read. Congress had passed the Webb-Kenyon Act, which forbade the shipment of liquor from a wet state to a dry state. That would hurt Sean's distilling business. He'd be in a sour mood when she arrived with her heavy load of problems.

When they stepped off the train in Los Angeles and Susan saw Sean standing on the platform grinning and waving, she thought it was just a façade he'd put on. She was proven wrong. Sean was overjoyed to see her and his family and was happier than she'd seen him in a long time.

"I read about that Webb-Kenyon Act in the papers," Susan said after they'd settled themselves in the large touring car Sean had insisted upon driving himself.

"Oh that," he said, dismissing it with a wave of his hand. "It doesn't matter."

"Won't it slice into your business?"

"I'm thinking of getting out of the liquor business, darling. Oh, I'll keep control of the companies I already have, but I've found something much more entertaining and far more lucrative money wise."

"This moving-picture business you've been telling me about?"

"Moving pictures will be the nation's biggest money-maker one of these days." He started to glow, his face lighting up as hot and bright as the sun overhead as he told her his plans for the future. "I'm certainly not interested in making the pictures, just distributing them and building my own theaters all across the country. 'First Runs,' I'm going to call them."

"Isn't it rather risky?"

"Everything is a risk, darling. People want to get out of their humdrum lives for an hour or so. They're already flocking to the few theaters that are showing movies, as they call them here. Projecting new movies, first-time-out films, will draw huge crowds. I'm going to build movie houses that can seat hundreds and hundreds of people. We'll make more money than you ever dreamed about," he boasted.

Petie was looking at the passing scenery. "Where are the cowboys and Indians?"

His father laughed. "They're all on the movie lots. You'll see plenty of them, son."

"He means real ones. Dad," David clarified.

"There's some of them still around too." He glanced in the mirror at Lorrie, who had said nothing more than a cool "Hello, Father."

"You're extremely quiet, Lorrie," he said. "Cat got your tongue?"

"Father, really. Must you be so prosaic?"

He started to say something, but saw Susan's warning look and thought better of it.

The sprawling Spanish-style house he'd rented and furnished was on a palm-lined street in Beverly Hills. It had a magnificent front lawn and—to the boys' amazement and delight—a swimming pool in the backyard.

"It's lovely, Sean," Susan said as she took his arm and hugged him. "But can we afford it?"

"It's only rented, darling. I'm planning to build a bigger place up on the hill," he said, pointing. "And to answer your question, yes, we can afford it. We can afford just about anything you want. Your old man is making bucks by the truckload." He puffed out his chest as he surveyed the sculptured grounds with the pink-and-white marble fountain, the lily pond, the topiaries, and the small shuttered cabanas at the far end of the pool. There was a huge barbeque pit and an outside bar and dining area. "Not bad for a poor old Mick like me, huh?"

"Very impressive," Susan said, then reached up and kissed him. "I never had any doubts about that poor old Mick I fell in love with and married."

He winked. "You didn't meet some slick playboy in New York who turned your head?"

"Not a chance. How about you? No beautiful actresses lurking about?"

He moved his hand to her breast. "It isn't Thursday, but if you'd care to have me dispel any notions you might have about me and some beautiful actress, how about coming up to the bedroom and I'll make up for all those Thursday afternoons I've missed so terribly."

She shivered with desire as he took her hand and led her into the house. "The children," she murmured, hesitating.

"To hell with the kids. They can play their own kind of games. We're going to play ours."

Their lovemaking was as beautiful, romantic, and passionate as she remembered. Sean was a fantastic lover, the only one she ever wanted. At first he was anxious and hurried, as was Susan. The second time they were both a little more in control but still finished too quickly. The third time Sean entered her he moved slowly enough to satisfy both their cravings.

"I love you, Susan," he whispered as he gathered her into his arms again and kissed her breasts, her mouth, her navel.

"I adore you."

Almost mindlessly they started to make love again, then burst out laughing when both realized they couldn't summon up the strength.

"I'm wearing out," Sean said, grinning.

She felt for him and fondled his semi-erection. "Never. It's all those actresses you've been having," she teased.

He slapped her buttocks, making her yelp, and they began wrestling on the bed, laughing and tickling and kissing. A tap on the door broke them apart, and Susan pulled a sheet up over them.

The Mexican woman Sean had employed came in looking a little embarrassed. "I'm sorry, Señor Dillon. I was wondering what time you would want dinner. It is already six o'clock."

"Good Lord," Sean said as he checked the time. "We'll eat at seven-thirty, Rosa."

When they were alone again, Sean said, "I'll leave the running of the house to you, of course. You might have a little trouble getting used to the way people do things out here. It's very relaxed and informal, usually."

"I'll manage."

"Now what's with Lorrie? Trouble?"

"Just what I started to tell you about on the telephone," Susan said and brought him up to date on the situation between Lorrie and Michael Crane.

"And you don't believe her young man will come storming the castle walls?"

"I doubt it." She fidgeted. "I found out her young man has other interests."

"Oh?"

Susan raised her eyebrows. "Mother."

Sean stared at her. "Your mother?"

"Mother and Michael Crane are having an affair. I heard them going at it in the library the other night."

"Saints alive!" He scowled. "That sonofabitch."

"Michael Crane is the least of our problems right now, darling," she said hesitantly. "There's something else." When she looked at him, something inside her crumbled. One moment she was sitting there calmly, bravely preparing herself to tell him about that night in Central Park, and a moment later she was hanging on to him for dear life and weeping bitterly against his chest. Finally, she blurted out the whole horrible story.

Sean went into a rage. "I'm going back to New York and kill that fuckin' bastard." He flung back the sheet and got out of bed.

"No, Sean. That won't accomplish anything. Besides, it would only be my word against his, and Kraus has a lot of important friends."

"Why in hell didn't you tell me about this when it happened?"

"I knew you'd say exactly what you just said. I know that Irish temper of yours. It just wouldn't have helped anything and you might have wound up getting yourself killed. I wasn't physically hurt in any way."

"You were raped for Christ's sake."

Susan took a deep breath and folded her hands in her lap. She lowered her eyes. "There's more," she said softly. "I'm pregnant."

The room was so quiet she thought for a moment that he wasn't there. Slowly she raised her eyes and found him standing naked, staring at her.

"You're what?"

"There isn't any doubt about it, Sean. I'm sorry. I'm going to have another baby." All her courage left her. She let herself slump down on the bed and buried her face in the pillows as she started to cry hysterically.

Sean rushed to her and took her in his arms, smoothing her hair, kissing her eyes, her temples, her mouth. "Hush, hush, darling. We'll work it out. Just try to stay calm."

"But it isn't yours, Sean. It will never be yours," she wailed. "I don't want it."

"It's yours, isn't it? So if it's yours it will be mine," he said, trying to comfort her. But she saw the deadness in his eyes. She'd never seen him look so sick at heart.

"I'm sorry, Sean. I'm so sorry," she sobbed, clinging to him.

"It wasn't your fault, love. Calm yourself now. Just calm yourself."

"What are we going to do?"

"Do?" he asked as he tilted her face up to his and kissed away the tears. "Why we're going to have a baby, that's what we're going to do."

CHAPTER TWENTY-THREE

Caroline had expected something to appear in the Italian tabloids, but her indiscretion with Tonio was apparently being kept from the public.

"It's just something for the family's lawyers," Tonio had told her. "The photograph will never be published, only used as proof for the divorce."

For the first time in a long time, Caroline felt content. Tonio had crowded Adam out of her mind. For how long, she could not say. She hoped forever. She wanted to marry Tonio as quickly as possible, and he'd assured her there would be very little delay. He had connections in high places, religious as well as political, who would expedite things.

"Lucia wants to remarry as quickly as I," he assured Caroline.

Alice Pendergast was off somewhere on an assignment, so Caroline was being spared her friend's reproachful looks. And as Caroline stood on the arched bridge, feeling the threat of rain, she realized suddenly that with the exception of Alice and Tonio, she didn't have a single friend in Venice. When she wasn't with Tonio or Alice, she was usually alone.

What would it be like after she and Tonio were married? There would be his friends, of course, but oddly enough, Tonio had never introduced her to any of them.

She shrugged. She was beginning to think like Alice. There was nothing shady about Tonio. He was an honorable, respectable man who loved her, and she loved him. Yet, she couldn't help but wonder why he was constantly disappearing, sometimes staying away for days. Why had he suddenly cancelled their dinner date last night? And where was he now? She'd rung up his flat and gotten no answer.

Caroline felt the first heavy drops of rain and glanced at her watch. She was quite near Tonio's apartment; he might be home by now, she decided as she ran off the bridge and turned the comer onto his street.

The hall porter had just finished mopping the tile floor when Caroline dashed in out of the downpour.

"Signorina," he greeted her with a bright smile and elegant bow.

Caroline brushed the raindrops from her forehead. "I was wondering if Count Cambruzio had returned, Giovanni."

"I have not seen him at all today, Signorina."

"Perhaps he came in while you were out. Would it be all right if I went up and checked for myself?"

"Of course, of course, Signorina," the porter said, holding open the ornate grill of the tiny elevator cab.

Tonio's apartment occupied the entire top floor of the building, and the elevator emptied out into a broad foyer. Caroline didn't care much for the overdecorated rococo flat and hoped that after they were married they could either redo the place or move somewhere else.

She walked into the drawing room, softly calling his name. No one answered. She stood looking around, satisfied that he wasn't there. Outside the windows the rain was coming down more heavily. She would wait until the rain stopped, she decided as she listened to it beating against the copper roof. She might even nap and surprise him by being in bed when he got back. Caroline took off her hat and gloves and started toward the bedroom.

As she opened the bedroom door and walked in, her eyes were drawn to the bed. "Tonio!" she cried, more shocked than angry at the sight of him making wild, passionate love to a beautiful young girl barely out of her teens.

The two on the bed sat up, the girl clutching a sheet around her breasts.

"What are you doing here?" the girl demanded.

Caroline stared at Tonio. "What...what is this?"

He gaped at her. "C-Caroline," he stammered.

The girl threw a pillow at Caroline. "Get out of here or I will call the police."

"Who is this girl?" Caroline asked.

The girl bristled. "Rather, who are you? What right have you to invade the privacy of a man and his wife?"

"Wife?" Caroline frowned. "But I thought—"

"I can explain," Tonio broke in.

His wife pulled at his arm. "Who is this woman, Tonio?" Her eyes sparked with anger. "Tell her to get out of here."

"Be quiet, Lucia," he said, pulling away from her.

"I will not be quiet. I want to know what right this woman has to come barging into your apartment like this."

"Be still."

Caroline noticed his voice was getting desperate. Tonio started to pull on his robe.

Caroline shook her head at him. "Your wife?" Caroline asked again, totally confused.

"Of course his wife," Lucia said with a defiant thrust of her chin.

"But...but you're divorcing him to marry another man," Caroline said.

"Divorcing Tonio? Are you insane? Why would I divorce my husband, even if I could? I love him. He loves me. You are a madwoman," Lucia ranted. "I will call the police," she said, reaching for the telephone.

Tonio grabbed the telephone away from her, barking out something in rapid Sicilian which Caroline didn't understand. There was a quick, staccato exchange before the girl shrugged and turned away from him.

Caroline said, "You were lying to me about the divorce, weren't you, Tonio?"

"It is all very involved," he said. "I will explain it to you this evening, Caroline."

The girl turned and glowered at him. Speaking an Italian dialect Caroline understood, she said, "You told this woman you and I were to be divorced?"

"Please, Lucia. Just be quiet for now."

"Signora Cambruzio?" Caroline said, stiffening her spine.

The girl tilted back her head. "Countessa Cambruzio," she corrected.

"Your husband told me that you wanted to divorce him in favor of another man. Is this true?"

"I told you before. Of course I cannot divorce my husband, nor do I want to." She shrugged. "You misunderstood him, I think."

Caroline's eyes moved from one to the other. Slowly she nodded. "Yes, perhaps you're right, Countessa. Perhaps I misunderstood him." She turned slowly and walked down the corridor toward the elevator in the foyer.

"Caroline!"

Behind her she heard another wild exchange of Sicilian, then Lucia shrieking her husband's name followed by what sounded like threats as Tonio caught up with Caroline in the foyer.

"You must listen to me, Caroline."

The hurt was rushing through her like a fire out of control. She didn't understand any of it, but she knew that the haven she thought she'd found in Tonio Cambruzio's arms was suddenly gone.

"Listen to what, Tonio?" she asked evenly.

He stammered, trying to choose the right words.

"Tell me one thing, Tonio. Did you intend divorcing that girl?"

"Of course," he said quickly. "It's only—"

"Why did you lie to me about the divorce being your wife's idea?"

He hit his head with the palm of his hand, trying to dislodge a reason. When nothing came he said, "I can explain. I...."

The elevator door opened.

"I'm waiting, Tonio."

"Have dinner with me tonight, Caroline. Please, my darling. I will explain everything tonight."

"I want to know now, Tonio."

He was in torture, she saw. "It is so confusing. It will take time to tell it all to you."

"Tonio!" Lucia yelled. "I am waiting."

"This is not the place nor time, Caroline. Tonight. I will call for you at eight o'clock."

Caroline hid behind the terrible pain she felt in her heart. She stepped into the elevator. "No, I don't think so. Good-bye, Tonio."

"Not good-bye, Caroline," he called as the elevator cab started down. "I will explain. You must let me explain."

She ran through the rain all the way back to her hotel, crying bitterly over her loss. Why had he lied to her about his wife? Why had he gone to such great pains to take incriminating pictures so that he could divorce a woman who obviously had no intention of divorcing him?

Tonio had used her for some reason, Caroline told herself. It didn't matter what that reason was; he'd used her, and it made her feel cheap and unwanted. She'd have nothing more to do with him. Suddenly she began wondering if everything Alice had said about him might not be true after all.

A little before eight o'clock Caroline heard a tapping on her door and ignored it until she heard Alice's voice calling her name. "I know you're in there, Caroline. It's urgent that I speak with you."

"Go away, Alice. Leave me alone."

"I can't. The police....," Alice whispered harshly through the door.

Caroline froze, frowning at the bolted door. Then she went over and undid the latch. Alice pushed her way in.

"You can't marry, Tonio," she announced, slamming the door shut. "I've got to talk to you."

"What's this about the police?"

"I need a drink." Alice went over to the cabinet and poured herself a straight bourbon. She took a sip, letting it singe the back of her throat, then gulped down the rest in one swallow.

"What's going on?" Caroline asked.

"I found out some more about your boyfriend. You've got to listen to me."

"He isn't my boyfriend any longer."

Alice saw her tears and said gently, "What happened?"

"Everything."

"You're not marrying him?"

"No," Caroline said, dabbing at her eyes. "He's a bastard and a liar."

Alice sighed and poured herself another bourbon. "Good, that makes it all the easier."

"Makes what easier?"

"Turning you against Tonio. I know you've been more or less avoiding me lately because of what I've been saying about him. I don't know what happened between you two, but whatever it was, happened for the best. Tonio Cambruzio is going to be arrested."

"Arrested? For what?"

Alice swallowed almost half her bourbon. "You know how I'm always sticking my nose into things that don't concern me," she said. "Well, after our little tiff that day at lunch I decided I had to prove to you that marrying Tonio Cambruzio would be a mistake." She paused. "So I went to Rome to speak with a friend of mine at police headquarters there. It's all true, Caroline. Tonio is being investigated by the police in connection with a smuggling operation."

"Alice, please. Tonio may be a bastard and a liar, but he is no smuggler."

"He is. And I can prove it."

Caroline saw she was deadly serious. "How?"

"I told my friend about Tonio's proposal to you. They had already heard about it. In fact, someone is being sent here to question you. It seems they have been onto Tonio for some months now, but didn't have sufficient evidence to arrest him. Last night they found a body floating in one of the canals. It was a man who was closely associated with Tonio. They think he was murdered by some rivals of his and Tonio's, a Sicilian family that was also involved with smuggling drags and artwork in and out of Italy. The police found very incriminating papers on the body, papers that proved Tonio's connection with a smuggling ring."

"This is madness."

"The papers were obviously planted on the corpse by Tonio's enemies. But the Italian police don't care about that. All they care about is that the papers give them enough evidence to arrest and convict Tonio."

"I don't understand any of this, Alice. What does it all have to do with me? Why would the police be coming here?"

"To alert you to the fact that Tonio only wants to marry you so he can get the hell out of Italy before his rivals kill him or the police arrest him, whichever comes first."

"I still don't get it."

"If Tonio married an American citizen, he'd be eligible for American citizenship and become untouchable by the Italian authorities. He's been trying to reach America for years so he can join up with some Sicilian gang that's already established there. Unfortunately, the authorities here have so far been able to keep him from leaving Italy. But once he's out of the country, neither the police nor his enemies will be able to touch him."

Caroline just stood there shaking her head.

"Hasn't Tonio ever mentioned anything about moving to America after you're married?"

"No."

"That surprises me. But then I bet he was planning to go there on your honeymoon and never come back."

"No marriage, no honeymoon. Not now," Caroline said as fresh tears burst from her eyes and ran down her face.

"Good God," Alice breathed as she witnessed Caroline's misery. "You still love that louse."

In spite of everything, Caroline had to admit that she thought she did. Or was it just that Tonio had seemed the sturdy crutch she so desperately needed to help her forget Adam? "I still love him," Caroline said.

Alice sighed. "That's what the police are afraid of, my friend told me. He also told me that Tonio will most likely make one last dash out of Venice—taking you with him—as soon as he finds out about this corpse that was dragged from the canal. In order to keep him preoccupied and away from his contacts, it was arranged that his wife arrive unexpectedly from Sicily. She was to be brought here yesterday afternoon."

"She arrived safe and sound," Caroline answered.

"Oh?"

There was a sharp rap on the door. Alice and Caroline exchanged looks. Caroline hesitated.

"Official business," a gruff voice said.

The man wore no official uniform. His papers identified him as Inspector Franco Pardino, Ufficio Roma.

When they'd settled themselves, the inspector said, "You have accepted a proposal of marriage offered by a man named Tonio Cambruzio, *Signorina*?"

"Yes," Caroline said. "But there will be no marriage. He already has a wife who apparently has no intention of freeing him."

"Yes, we know that," the inspector said. "But you are wrong if you think he has no intention of marrying you, *Signorina*. He does intend to marry you, though his wife is not aware of that fact."

"Knowing what I do," Caroline said, "I doubt if I would ever consider marrying Tonio now."

"Ah-ha, you see," the inspector said, smiling broadly. "You 'doubt' but you are not 'positive.' *Si*?"

Caroline floundered. "What I meant to say—"

"What you meant to say, *Signorina*, is that if *Signor* Cambruzio came to you again with a plausible story, it is probable that you would want to believe him. He is an extremely handsome young man. I can understand how irresistible he must be to a woman."

"It isn't that," Caroline objected. "It's—"

The inspector held up his hand. When she fell quiet he said, "I understand that there was a certain photograph taken of you and Tonio Cambruzio...one of a rather indelicate nature."

Caroline blushed to the roots of her hair.

"Not a very flattering likeness of you, *Signorina*," the inspector said as Caroline's face turned crimson.

"He told you that the photograph was necessary in order to prove his wife's suit for divorce, *si*?"

Caroline kept her head bowed. "Yes."

He looked at Alice and then back at Caroline. "Haven't either of you ever thought it odd that whenever Miss Pendergast here found out something questionable about *Signor* Cambruzio, very soon thereafter he had a perfectly logical explanation?"

Alice and Caroline frowned at one another.

"You are not as clever as you believe yourself to be, Miss Pendergast. In fact, I am very much annoyed with your insistence on putting your nose into things that are not your concern. More than once you almost cost us our prey."

Alice gasped. "Me?"

"Tonio Cambruzio is very aware that you have been checking up on him and reporting back to the Signorina here. He has friends in high places, who have enabled him, so far, to slip out of our hands." He grinned. "Naturally, being married to the daughter of a member of the president's cabinet makes him somewhat untouchable."

"His wife is...?"

The inspector nodded gravely. "I am surprised that you did not find that out when you were doing your investigating, Miss Pendergast. It only proves to me that you are more of a meddler than a help." His twinkling eyes were suddenly dark and cold.

He turned to Caroline. "That photograph was taken because Cambruzio was told that you'd learned he already had a wife. To keep you interested in him, Tonio invented that whole masquerade." He chuckled. "Knowing Lucia Cambruzio, I think she would see him dead before she'd let him leave her for another woman's bed. Her Latin blood runs hotter than most men's." He shook his head at Caroline. "You would be no match for Lucia Cambruzio, believe me."

Caroline was growing annoyed with him. "You just said that Tonio still intends marrying me...or at least wants to."

The inspector nodded. "Oh yes. He will try to contact you and will tell you some more lies. He will ask you to run away with him. Perhaps you will believe him and do as he says, perhaps you will not. Whichever, we can take no chances on a feminine whim."

Again Caroline and Alice looked at one another and waited.

"We are going to make an arrest as soon as certain things can be substantiated. During that time we want to be sure that Tonio Cambruzio neither gets away nor learns of our plans. So, Signorinas, I came here tonight on behalf of my government to politely ask that you leave Venice on the next train, which is at ten o'clock tomorrow morning."

Alice started to object.

"Be assured, *Signorina* Pendergast, your employers will be informed. The head of your New York office already knows that we are asking you to leave."

"You've gotten me fired!" Alice cried.

"I doubt it. But if that does happen, then you will have only yourself to blame for snooping into things that do not concern you. You are not aware of this, *Signorina* Pendergast, but your life was endangered more than once by your digging into sensitive files and records. Fortunately you were not intelligent enough to know the value of the material you were sifting through."

The inspector stood up and smiled tolerantly at Caroline. "I know how affairs of the heart can sometimes get mixed up with common sense. It would be most unwise for you to see Tonio again. To prevent any weakness on your part, you will be carefully watched until you leave Venice. Tonio is a very handsome fellow and quite convincing when he wants to be, especially when he is desperate and a beautiful woman such as yourself is involved. You are his one chance to slip away from us. He won't be given that chance, believe me, *Signorina*."

Caroline said nothing. She lowered her eyes and folded her hands in her lap.

"The train leaves at ten o'clock," he said again. "You will both be on it." Then he bowed and clicked his heels. "Buona notte."

Alice swirled the bourbon around in her glass, waiting for the door to close. "Well, I suppose we've been kicked out of better places," she said, trying to be flippant.

Caroline got up and fixed herself a drink. "Just for damned spite I'm tempted to contact Tonio."

"I wouldn't suggest that, Caroline. The Italians adore their women, but they can get pretty rough if one crosses them. You might end up in prison with Tonio."

"Would that be so bad?" Caroline said as she gulped her drink.

"Nobody loves a man that much," Alice said, squeezing Caroline's waist. "Don't do anything stupid, kiddo. Get yourself packed. I'm going to pick up my shadow and go back to my hotel and do exactly what that inspector told me to do. I want no trouble with the Italian authorities. I'm going to be very nice-nice until I get safely back to the States...and then watch out 'cause I'll be going on the warpath."

The following morning just before ten o'clock, Caroline and Alice boarded the train leaving Venice for Zurich and then on to Paris. Caroline hadn't slept all night, intermittently packing and reaching for the telephone to call Tonio. In the end her common sense prevailed and she resigned herself to returning home to America and trying to forget everyone she ever knew in Europe.

As the train pulled out and Caroline watched the domes of Saint Mark's disappear, she knew there was one person she might not be able to forget. She wondered if she would ever see Adam Clarendon again.

CHAPTER TWENTY-FOUR

"Adam!" Lydia cried when he walked into her study. She threw her arms around him. "Adam, my dear, dear boy. Thank God you're home." She held him at arm's length and looked him up and down. "You look dreadful." She glanced behind him. "Isn't your mother with you?"

"I think you'd better sit down, Grandmother," Adam said with sad eyes. "There's a lot I must tell you."

"Where's April? Where's your mother?"

"Sit down, Grandmother. Mother didn't come with me. I'm afraid she isn't ever coming home."

Lydia saw his tears and moved numbly toward the divan. Adam kept hold of her hand and sat beside her. "I have very bad news, Grandmother. My mother is dead."

Lydia took in a sharp breath that stuck somewhere inside her. "Dead?" she gasped.

Adam nodded gravely. "I'm afraid she died as she had always hoped to die...sitting on the throne of China."

"I don't understand," Lydia managed, fighting to keep calm as her tears threatened to overwhelm her.

Adam proceeded to explain what had happened to him and his mother in China. "I barely escaped with my life," he ended, lowering his head. For the first time since his long, arduous escape from the Orient he began to cry openly.

"You poor child," Lydia sobbed, holding him tight.

"I stayed in the Forbidden City for several days. It was easy enough to hide there, what with all those strange rooms and passageways. I knew I couldn't risk going back to the hotel in the legation compound, so I remained in the palace until I figured out a way to get out of China undiscovered. My desperation made a thief out of me, I'm afraid," he admitted.

"Thief?"

"I had no money, just a few dollars that I had put into my billfold. I realized that my only chance would be through bribery, so I took some gold pieces from the palace and gouged out several large jewels from the throne. I put everything in a sack and changed into some peasant clothes I found in one of the work sheds. I managed to slip out of Peking without any trouble and made my way to Hong Kong. There I pawned everything I'd stolen and bought myself some decent clothes and passage on a steamer. I never thought I was capable of doing what I did. But the need to stay alive makes a man do the unnatural, I suppose."

"Adam," Lydia cried as she leaned against him. "My poor, darling April." Her tears soaked into his suit jacket.

"She died happy, Grandmother. There's some consolation in that. I'll always remember her sitting on that throne. I won't remember the arrow, just my beautiful mother in her royal yellow silk, sitting there so regally, so much at home, so happy."

Lydia looked up at him and sniffed back her tears. "It would be wise for you to put all of this out of your mind now, Adam. Forget your Chinese blood and go back where you really belong. There is nothing for you here. Go to England and claim the Clarendon inheritance."

He shook his head. "I really don't want to go back, Grandmother."

"You must. It's only right that you do."

"I want to stay here for a while and try to straighten things out in my head."

"You can stay as long as you please, of course, but in the end you must return to England."

"I just don't know."

* * * * * * *

The days dragged sadly on as the household mourned April's death. Lydia did not let herself think about what had become of April's body. Her only consolation was that the China segment of her life was at last ended. As for the painting of the little bird sitting on the branch singing to the moon—her Nightsong painting—she would always cherish it as a romantic souvenir not of China but of her love for Peter MacNair.

Adam was gradually recuperating from his perilous escape, but Lydia was distressed to see that he seemed no more interested in returning to England than ever. She spoke to him often about it, but he was deaf to everything she said.

The telephone call from Caroline changed things. Lydia was sitting behind her desk at Empress Cosmetics, talking with Evelyn Clary, when the long-distance call came.

"Caroline," Lydia cried. "How marvelous to hear from you. Where are you?"

"In New York, Grandmother. I thought I'd let you know that I'll be home as soon as I can get a train out of here. I'm so anxious to see you."

"Are you alone or are you coming home a countess?"

"Sorry, Grandmother. Regretfully, that didn't work out."

"Oh well, everything happens for the best, they say." She started to mention Adam's presence in San Francisco, but something stopped her. "Hurry home, darling. I've missed you terribly."

"I'm bringing a friend, Grandmother. A girl friend. I invited her to stay with us if that's all right."

"Of course, Caroline. She's more than welcome. Now don't let anything keep you in New York. Come home immediately."

"Alice is trying to get reservations on the train right now. If she does, we'll be on our way tomorrow."

"Marvelous. See you soon, darling."

"I can't wait."

Lydia replaced the receiver.

"Caroline?" Evelyn asked, raising one eyebrow.

Lydia nodded, frowning.

Evelyn cocked her head. "You didn't tell her that Adam was here." There had never been any secrets between Lydia and her oldest and closest friend, not even dark personal secrets.

"I thought it might scare her off," Lydia said.

"Perhaps it will scare Adam off."

"That's what I'm hoping."

Evelyn watched her expression. "You have that crafty look in your eyes, Lydia. What are you up to?"

"A couple of little white lies, that's all."

She wouldn't actually lie to Adam; she'd just refrain from telling him the whole truth. By the time she got home later that afternoon she knew exactly what she'd say to him.

Adam was reading the afternoon newspaper when Lydia walked into the sitting room. After a few moments of idle conversation, she said, "Incidentally, Caroline telephoned from New York."

She watched the color drain out of his face. "Caroline?"

"Yes. They're leaving for San Francisco tomorrow."

"They?"

Lydia fixed her eyes on him. "She is not alone, Adam."

He felt a stab of pain. "Then she married her Italian count."

"No. I think she wants to be married here among her family and friends."

"I see."

"I hope it won't be too upsetting for you, Adam. I know how much you care for Caroline."

"She's my sister," he said, trying to hide his hurt.

"She's more than that to you and we both know it. But I hope you will remember that she is your sister when she arrives."

Adam was afraid he was going to burst into tears. He got up and started out of the room. "I don't think I'll be here when they arrive."

"Adam," Lydia said, stopping him. "I know that emotions can sometimes get in the way of things. But you must face reality. You aren't happy here and you are only going to be more miserable when Caroline marries. I don't want you to do anything that might change things for her. What happened between you two was an unfortunate mistake. You must not compound that mistake. Go home where you belong, Adam. I say that only because I love you and want you to be happy. Marry Pamela and become Lord Clarendon. Forget everything that happened and start being the man your parents raised you to be. You are Lord and Lady Clarendon's son, not my daughter's. They did a fine job in raising you, my boy; don't make all their love and efforts a waste. It would be a terrible unkindness on your part. You've had your adventure, now forget it and assume your responsibilities."

He stood there, his head bowed, tears brimming in his eyes. "Yes, I suppose you're right, Grandmother." He sighed as a sob caught in his throat. "I do wish things had worked out differently, though."

"They worked out as they were supposed to work out, Adam." She got up and embraced him. "I will always love you, darling. Now make me proud of you by doing what you know you must."

He hugged her, letting the tears roll down his cheeks. "I will, Grandmother. At least I'll try."

"And you'll succeed. Remember, there's Nightsong and MacNair blood in your veins, my boy. That's a pretty powerful combination. Both have always been fighters. We never lose."

* * * * * * *

Lydia waved good-bye as the locomotive started on its trek to New York and to a ship that would carry Adam far away. She wondered if she would ever see her grandson again. She thought of Caroline and knew that Adam would never come back. Never.

CHAPTER TWENTY-FIVE

Leon found Paris beautiful but confusing. All the way from San Francisco he'd worried about the temper tantrum Marama had thrown when he'd told her he was going to Europe on family business instead of taking her and the children back to Hawaii as planned.

"When I get back," he'd promised.

"I will not be here when you get back."

At the time, he'd believed it to be an idle threat—Marama was always threatening—but the more he thought about it now, the more he began to think she might indeed be serious.

It had been foolish of him to think that Marama would change once he got her away from her family. She would never change. He knew that now. If she were gone when he got home, he knew he would miss her terribly; but, on the other hand, it might mean happiness—or at least contentment—for both of them.

It was their children he was most concerned about. He didn't want them brought up as Marama had been raised. He wanted his sons and daughter to live a normal, civilized life without all that claptrap about vengeful gods and hocus-pocus magic.

True, they were direct descendants of King Kamehameha, but he too was of royal birth, Leon reminded himself, and it meant absolutely nothing.

* * * * * *

Leon didn't like what he saw on the Continent. Everywhere

there was unrest, even talk of war. Secret pacts were being made between nations, and it seemed clear that the shaky peace of Europe was at the mercy of an accident. No one knew that that accident would occur when Gavrilo Princip shot Archduke Ferdinand in Sarajeva the following year. France and Germany had the most powerful armies, and Leon was sure that they would be the first to be at each other's throats. He wanted to find Marcus and get him out of this mess as soon as possible. If Marcus was so intent upon marrying a French girl, then he should bring her to America where they could live in safety.

After settling into his hotel, Leon started out in search of Marcus. Marcus was no longer at the address Amelia had given him. The Paris office of Empress Cosmetics was surprised when Leon showed up asking to see Marcus.

"But he has gone home to America," the secretary told him. "He left Paris weeks and weeks ago, monsieur."

Leon knew that wasn't true and his concern for Marcus grew. Something was terribly wrong.

"Marcus wrote saying that he intended to get married here," Leon told the secretary.

"Monsieur Marcus married?" She giggled. "That is rather difficult to believe. Monsieur Marcus is not the marrying kind. We all know that. He is too busy having many women to concentrate on only one."

"Has anyone seen him lately?"

The girl shrugged. "As I said, he told us he was going home to America. He didn't even come into the office to take away his personal things. He just telephoned and said he would not be coming to the office anymore, and that was that."

"How very odd," Leon said, frowning.

Leon went back to the last address he had for Marcus and asked to speak to the concierge. When he inquired about Marcus, the woman shook her head. "No, I do not know where the young American went. After he returned from the hospital he stayed in his rooms and never came out."

"Hospital?"

"*Oui*, Monsieur. He had an accident. Surely he wrote to you about it."

"No," Leon said. "What kind of accident?"

"Something happened to the motorcar he was racing at Le Mans. He came home from the hospital in a wheelchair with a nurse. The next thing I know, both he and the nurse are gone." She heaved her bosom. "Americans? Who can figure them."

"Didn't you speak with him before he vacated his rooms?"

"There was only a note saying he was leaving some money to pay for any inconvenience he may have caused me. He was very generous."

"A nurse, you say. Do you remember her name?"

The old woman thought for a moment, laying a finger alongside her nose. "Bonnard. Madame Bonnard, yes, that was it."

"Bonnard," Leon repeated, fixing it firmly in his mind.

He went back to his suite at the George Cinq and began telephoning the hospitals, asking for a nurse named Bonnard. He made dozens of calls, but came up with nothing. No one knew or had a listing for a Nurse Bonnard.

Leon was at a loss as to what to do next when an idea occurred to him. The concierge had mentioned a motor accident in Le Mans. Perhaps it was the Le Mans hospital that Marcus had been in. He picked up the telephone and asked the operator to place calls to all the hospitals in Le Mans. There were only two, and the second one proved rewarding.

"Yes, we have a Madame Bonnard on our registry," a man's voice said. He gave Leon a telephone number where the nurse could be reached.

Madame Bonnard told Leon the devastating news. "The leg was amputated just below the knee."

"Oh my God," Leon gasped. When he'd composed himself somewhat, he asked, "Is he still in your care in Le Mans, Madame?"

"No. The young gentleman wanted no help from me. I was a constant reminder that he was a cripple, and so he dismissed me."

"Do you know who is caring for him now? He must have gotten someone to move him out of his rooms."

"A young girl came often to see him. Mademoiselle Denise," the nurse said with an audible sneer. "He preferred her to me, obviously. A disgusting little thing. She will only use him and make him even more miserable than he is now."

"This girl, do you know where I might find her?"

"If what I suspect is true, all you need do is visit every brothel in Paris. You will find her."

"Brothel?" Leon asked, thinking he had not heard her correctly.

"Brothel, Monsieur."

"Surely not. Marcus wouldn't...."

She chortled. "Monsieur Marcus is not a nice young man, Monsieur. You will see that for yourself when and if you find him."

Leon rang off feeling dazed and more confused than ever. He had no idea where to start looking. He considered telling his mother and Amelia what he'd discovered, but decided not to. There was no point in upsetting them with such terrible news. He would have to find Marcus and see for himself what should be done. If Marcus wanted to hide himself away from everyone, then Leon would have to respect his decision. It was Marcus's life, and he had a right to do as he chose with it.

As luck would have it, Leon happened upon a taxi driver who said he thought there was a girl named Denise working at Madame Claire's.

And when Leon went to Madame Claire's she said, "Denise is not available."

"I only want to talk with her, Madame. I am looking for a relation, a man named Marcus Nightsong. Have you ever heard of him?"

"Marcus Nightsong?" She shook her head.

"Perhaps you might know him as Marcus Andrieux."

He saw the instant glimmer of recognition before her eyes became wary under their fleshy hoods. "I am sorry, Monsieur.

I cannot help you."

Leon knew she was lying. He also knew he would get nothing out of this painted, plump woman. But perhaps the other girls in her establishment would be able to tell him something.

He smiled sweetly and looked toward the red and gold salon just beyond the beaded curtains. "As long as I am here, Madame, perhaps I could have the pleasure of the company of one of your lovely girls. I have only been in Paris less than a week, and Marcus told me of your fine establishment in the most glowing terms."

He took out a fat roll of francs and watched Madame Claire eye it with greed.

"Of course, Monsieur," she said, taking the money and tucking it securely between her breasts. "Come with me."

It had been quite a while since Leon had visited a brothel. He tried to remember the last time. It must have been the night he took Efrem MacNair to see the singsong girls in Chinatown. That had been the night he and Efrem had wound up in the same bed, he remembered uneasily. They had only been boys at the time, but it still disconcerted him to think of it.

As he looked around at the young girls—and some not so young—lounging about in various stages of undress, he decided that no matter what comer of the globe you were in, all brothels were the same. There was an unmistakable smell to the place that could only be associated with sex.

Madame Claire introduced Leon to a lovely little blond creature with eyes as wide and innocent as a child's. Her skin was flawless but had that dull finish of someone who rarely ventured out into the daylight.

"This is Yvette. I think she will suit you, yes?"

"Very nicely," Leon said. "Thank you."

Yvette smiled seductively and asked if he would buy her a glass of champagne. When they settled themselves on the velvet settee, Leon said, "I was here once before. Is Denise still working for Madame Claire?"

"Denise?" He saw the girl's beautiful eyes move toward a

pretty little thing sitting almost naked near the heavily draped windows. "Denise is over there. But she is getting old now. Surely you do not prefer her to me?"

"Oh no, no. I only want to renew old acquaintances," Leon lied. "I'll just say hello and be right back." The girl gave him a petulant look, but when he asked the cruising waiter to bring her a full bottle of champagne and told Yvette to wait for him, she settled herself with a smile, pulling her sheer negligee across her lovely breasts.

Leon went over to Denise and said, "May I speak with you for a moment?" Up close he saw that she was far from old, with dark flashing eyes and a full mouth that seemed to be curved in a perpetual smile.

"Of course," Denise said, making room for him beside her. "But Yvette may scratch my eyes out."

Leon smiled. "I only want to ask you about Marcus."

The smile quickly disappeared. "Marcus? What about him?"

"I am a very close friend of his. I just wanted to know how he is and whether or not I could see him before I leave Paris."

"You were sent by his family?"

"No, nothing like that," Leon lied. "I know about Marcus's accident. I just wanted to make sure he's comfortable and in need of nothing."

"He is well. Depressed, of course, but I see to his needs," she said.

"Does he need money?"

"You can give him money?"

"If he needs it, yes."

Denise thought for a moment, pulling down her lip with one finger.

"And I could see to it that some money is sent him every month," Leon said, pressuring her.

Denise cocked her head. "How much?"

"Just name a figure and I will arrange to have it sent to him."

"Five hundred francs."

It was a large sum. Leon nodded. "If Marcus agrees, I'll see that he gets five hundred francs every month. But he must first agree to it."

Denise moved her eyes toward the ceiling. "He is upstairs on the third floor. Madame Claire has furnished rooms for us. But do not send the money here. Madame will only keep it for herself."

Leon stood up. "I'll arrange things with Marcus when I speak with him." He bowed over her hand and went back to Yvette.

When Yvette led him upstairs to her room on the second floor, Leon followed somewhat reluctantly. He feared he would have difficulty concentrating on sex, knowing that Marcus was so close by.

He needn't have worried. Yvette was expert at arousing him to a length and firmness he didn't think possible. He'd heard about French girls and their skillful mouths, but never imagined any woman capable of doing what Yvette did to him. She drew him completely into her throat, at the same time laving him with her tongue until every nerve in his body vibrated. He came into her mouth almost immediately and tried not to notice the look of disappointment on her face.

"You will rest for a while and we will do it again, *oui*?"

Leon was trying to catch his breath. "I'm afraid I'm out of commission for a while, little one. You are too good at your trade."

Yvette shrugged. "Then you must leave so that I can get back downstairs."

Leon dressed hurriedly and slipped out of the room while Yvette was busy with her bidet. Why she was using it he couldn't imagine, but he supposed it was force of habit. He wondered idly if the girls gargled afterward.

He had no trouble finding the back stairs that led up to the top floor. Marcus was lying on a chaise, sound asleep.

Leon touched his shoulder and shook him gently. "Marcus."

Marcus opened his eyes and sat bolt upright. "Leon?" His surprise turned immediately to anger. He yanked the lap robe over the stump of his leg and twisted himself, hiding his face in shadow. "What in hell are you doing here? How did you find me?"

"I know what happened to you," Leon said, ignoring Marcus's outburst. "I want to help."

"No one can help, for God's sake. Get out of here and leave me alone, Leon."

"You know I can't do that, Marcus."

"Damn it, Leon, get out of here."

Leon sat down on the edge of the chaise, trying not to look at the dip in the lap robe that marked the missing leg. "You hurt Amelia very deeply with your letter," he said.

"And what in hell would you have done in my situation? I don't want her pity any more than I want yours."

"Amelia loves you, Marcus."

"I'm not the Marcus she thinks she loves. I'm a different man altogether: a fucking cripple and a whoremonger. Do you think I'd dump myself on a wife who'd only pity me for the rest of my life?"

Marcus's eyes filled with tears as he grabbed Leon's arm, squeezing it until Leon felt pain. "Please, Leon. I've never asked a favor in my life, but I'm asking one now. Please, I beg you. Don't tell Amelia. Promise me that. Just leave me alone. I'm all right here. Denise takes care of me." He released his grip and threw himself back against the chaise.

"You can't stay hidden away up here forever."

"I can stay until I decide what I want to do."

"I want to help you. Come home with me, Marcus."

"Never."

"It's where you belong. This is no place for you."

"It's the only place I want to be."

"You can't mean that."

"I do mean it, Leon. Now kindly leave me alone and forget you ever saw me. So help me, I'll kill myself if you breathe a word of this to Amelia. I swear to God I will."

"All right," Leon said after a moment. "I'll go, and I give you my word that I won't say anything to Amelia about this."

He purposely put his hand on the thigh of the stump and felt Marcus cringe. "It isn't the end of the world, Marcus. You're still a man. They have prosthetic devices you could be fitted with. You mustn't give up. You mustn't."

"Please go away, Leon. Just go away. I'll be all right. Don't worry about me." He forced a smile. "Actually, I rather like it here. I get everything I want, all the sex I can handle." He closed his eyes. "If you want the truth, Leon, I don't think I'd be happy with an ordinary woman like Amelia. I've gotten too used to more unorthodox sex, things Amelia would find down-right disgusting. I'd never make her happy, so it's best we go our separate ways. Now leave, Leon. If I ever do need your help, I promise I'll write you."

"All right. Just remember, you have a family who cares about you very much." He put his hand on Marcus's head and ruffled his hair. "Take care of yourself, Marcus."

As he left the brothel, Leon realized that Marcus needed more time to think things through for himself. He was, after all, the only one who could decide his own future.

Leon had no reason now to linger in Paris. Of course he could stick around and see about introducing Nightsong II perfume to the Continent, but business was the furthest thing from his mind right now. He could only think about Marcus and his terrible invalidity.

Leon wrestled with his conscience for another day or two trying to decide whether staying near Marcus, acting as a constant prod, might accomplish anything. It wouldn't, he told himself as he started to repack his suitcases. Marcus would have to face his incapacitation on his own with no pressure from anyone.

* * * * * * *

Leon returned to San Francisco to find that he had troubles of his own. Marama had carried out her threat and left San Francisco, taking the three children with her. Lydia greeted

Leon with the bad news when he showed up at the Nob Hill mansion after finding his own house empty.

"Marama just came and said she was leaving," Lydia told him. "I gave her a long talking to, urging her to at least wait until you got home. I thought she was listening to me. But obviously she wasn't, because when I went to see her a few days later the maid told me she had discharged all the other servants and sailed for Hawaii with the children."

"I'll have to go after her, naturally," Leon said.

"Darling, you look so very tired. Did you speak to Marcus?"

Leon nodded gravely. "Something's happened, Mother. I don't think you should count on seeing Marcus for a while."

Lydia stared at him. "What are you saying? What happened?"

Leon lowered himself into a chair and put his head in his hands. "Something dreadful, I'm afraid. Marcus doesn't want anyone to know, especially Amelia. I gave him my word that I wouldn't tell her, but I didn't say I wouldn't tell you." He thought for a moment. "Oddly enough, Marcus didn't ask me not to tell you. Perhaps on some subconscious level he wanted you to know."

"Know what?" Lydia demanded impatiently.

Leon looked up at her, shaking his head from side to side. "He was in a racing-car accident in Le Mans many months ago."

"Accident? Dear God. How bad?"

Leon sighed as he rubbed his hand across the back of his neck. "He lost part of his leg, Mother."

"What?" She couldn't stand. The floor was suddenly heaving under her feet. She groped for support and lowered herself into a chair across from Leon. "Lost a leg?"

"Only part. From the knee down."

"Oh my dear, sweet boy," she wailed as she cried into her hands. "I knew it. I knew it," she moaned. "I knew something dreadful had happened. I knew Marcus wouldn't really marry anyone but Amelia." She sat sobbing, letting the ugly news seep in. After a while she asked, "How is he otherwise, Leon? No internal damage? His face?"

"No, nothing but the leg. The right one. He's in a very deep state of depression, as you can imagine."

"Poor Marcus. To think I'll never see him running and jumping about again."

"Mother, please," Leon said sharply. "Don't you start feeling sorry for him. Marcus is doing a good enough job of that all by himself. He doesn't need our pity. He needs our help."

"Of course, of course." She sighed.

Leon slammed his fist into his palm and started to pace. "We've got to think of getting him home." He hurried on, telling his mother how and where he'd come to find Marcus. "The girl will continue to care for him as long as we continue sending money. Actually, I think she may even be in love with him. But a girl like that...." He didn't finish the sentence.

Lydia finished it for him. "A girl like that might easily find Marcus getting in her way, especially if his care takes up too much of her time and infringes upon her 'career.' I don't think we should send money to Marcus. It might force him out from under the girl's protection." She paused. "You think she's in love with him, you say?"

He shrugged. "Who knows. Maybe Marcus is paying her. There's one thing I do know, however, Mother: Marcus is still in love with Amelia. You should have seen how upset he got when he thought I might tell her."

Amelia chose that inopportune moment to walk in. "Tell me what?" she asked. "Leon, you've talked to Marcus. What did he say?" She saw Leon's face. "What's wrong? What happened?"

Leon turned away from her.

Lydia said, "Amelia has a right to know, Leon."

"Please, Mother. I gave a solemn promise."

"You may have given him a promise, but I didn't."

Amelia felt an icy cold creep up from her feet, over her thighs, her stomach, until it tightened around her heart. "Tell me, for God's sake. What's the matter? I demand to know."

Lydia was looking at Leon. "Amelia is right, Leon. She does have a right to know."

"Marcus will never speak to any of us again," he warned.

"Why?" Amelia cried. "What's happened?"

Lydia took the frightened girl's hand and led her over to the divan. "There's been an accident, Amelia. It isn't all that serious, but it is something you must face and accept."

"Mother, please," Leon said. "Don't do this. You'll drive him away forever."

"I'm sorry, Leon, I must." She squeezed Amelia's hands. "Marcus lost his right leg in a racing accident."

It was as if a terrible explosion had rocked the room, to be followed by the deadly quiet of billowing dust silently settling to the floor. Amelia stared at Lydia. The only thought in her mind was that Marcus wasn't going to marry someone else. It had all been a misguided lie to keep her from knowing the painful truth. But what did it matter if he lost a leg? Nothing mattered except the knowledge that he must still love her or he would never have concocted such a dreadful lie.

"He's not marrying someone else?" she managed, as if Lydia's words had meant nothing at all.

"No," Leon answered. "He just wanted you to be free of him."

"Free of him? I'll never be free of Marcus. I love him more than my own life. I don't care if he's lost both his legs and both his arms. I love him. I love him, not his legs or his hands or his eyes."

Lydia patted her hand and tried to smile. "Marcus didn't want you to know, Amelia."

"Of course he didn't want me to know. He doesn't want anyone to know. Oh, my dear, sweet Marcus. How miserable he must be. I've got to go to him," she said abruptly, jumping to her feet.

"No," Leon shouted. "It's the last thing Marcus wants."

"What do you know about it? Marcus doesn't know himself what he wants. And why shouldn't I go to him?" Amelia said, her eyes brilliant, her smile radiant. "Do you think I'm going to pity him? Never. It's the last thing I'll ever do. All I want is to tell him that I still love him regardless of what has happened. And

I want him to tell me to my face that he doesn't love me, that he never wants to see me again. I don't think he'll do that. We've always had a special kind of love, the kind that will endure."

Leon touched her arm. "It isn't only the loss of his leg, Amelia. There's something else."

She noticed his face getting red. "Just tell me where he's living, Marcus. My last letter came back marked 'Moved.' "When he didn't answer, she asked, "Is he living with a woman?"

Leon avoided the question. "He's a different man, Amelia. He's changed in his attitude about things."

"You didn't answer my question, Leon. Where is Marcus living?"

He stared at the carpet. In a low, embarrassed voice he said, "In a brothel."

To Lydia's and Leon's surprise, Amelia laughed. "Good. He'll be well taken care of there until I can get him away."

"You can't go to Paris," Leon insisted.

"But I am going to Paris, Leon." She found herself feeling braver and stronger and unconcerned about everything but the fact that Marcus might still love her. She looked at Leon. "You spoke with him, Leon. Tell me truthfully. In your opinion, do you think Marcus is still in love with me?"

Leon couldn't answer. After a moment he nodded his head.

"That's all that matters then." She started toward the door.

"You are only going to be hurt, Amelia," Leon said.

She turned. "You don't have to tell me how Marcus has changed, Leon. I saw that when I was with him in England. He wants physical love, the type he can find so easily with the loose women he's met in France. He hinted as much to me, and I turned him away. I won't do that again. No matter how shocking you may think me, I'll give myself to him naked in the street if that will make him happy. Marcus is my life. I have no other. I'll kiss his feet, if he wants me to." She grinned suddenly. "I suppose I should have said 'foot.'"

She turned sharply and started out of the room, ignoring the flush on Leon's cheeks, Lydia's lowered eyes.

Leon said, "Amelia, please, you can't go."

"And who is going to stop me?"

Leon and Lydia exchanged glances. Lydia got up and went to Amelia. "I'll come with you, dear."

"No," Amelia said emphatically. "I'm going alone. If I have to fight for Marcus I want the sides to be even. I don't want him to feel overwhelmed."

"But think," Leon argued. "Even if you do reconcile with Marcus, there's trouble brewing over there in Europe. Amelia. I know. I just got back and, believe me, the entire place could erupt in war at any time."

"Oh, I'll reconcile with Marcus all right. And what do I care about a war? If I'm killed, at least I'll be with the only man I've ever loved, even if I have to live in a brothel and take the place of the prostitute who's caring for him now."

She stiffened her back and ran out of the room, leaving Lydia and Leon staring after her.

CHAPTER TWENTY-SIX

Michael Crane was pleased with the way things were turning out. He knew he shouldn't have stopped for those drinks at the bar, but they made him feel good. Also he was beginning to miss the excitement of picking up people in bars, the way he had in New York. He missed the danger, the adventure of it all, but he knew he couldn't afford to go back to those ways just yet. He needed more security first.

Unfortunately, the two MacNair women had made life here in San Francisco rather complicated. Lorrie was young and innocent, and while he certainly wasn't in love with her, he did want to make love to her. It suited his vanity to think how easily he'd be able to take away her virginity if he chose to do so. The temptation was terribly great.

But Lorna represented immediate security. She could give him everything he ever wanted in the material sense. Making love to Lorna, however, was becoming a chore. She repulsed him physically, although he prided himself on his acting abilities. He always performed better than he thought himself capable.

Sex with Lorna was like masturbation; it left him feeling empty, unsatisfied, and restless. There were dozens of other women he knew who would give him sex, but he didn't dare chance it now, what with Lorna's constant demands for his attention. She was always showing up at his flat when he least expected her. If she found him there with another woman he'd be finished. Lorna MacNair had a temper equal to his own, and she was no stranger to violence, he suspected.

She was beginning to bore him with her repeated demands, and more than once she'd flown at him over one trifle or another. She treated him like a chattel, something she owned completely, like an expensive Dresden figurine she could smash at her own whim. Unlike the other older women he'd known, Lorna never gave him any time of his own.

He sat fidgeting in the drawing room of the MacNair townhouse, waiting for Lorna to decide to come down and join him. Lately, she seemed to take a perverse pleasure in inconveniencing him. He started to get annoyed, and to calm himself he mixed another drink, a drink he didn't need. He was already feeling a little lightheaded from all the drinks he'd had at the bar.

Michael knew Lorna liked making him wait on her, but she was paying for that pleasure, he reminded himself angrily as he stirred the martini and poured it into a chilled glass.

He turned when he heard someone come into the room, expecting to see Lorna; instead, Efrem walked in.

"Michael. I didn't expect to find you here," he said, a look of surprise on his face. "Where's Mother?"

"Upstairs getting dressed to go out for dinner. She asked me to join her." He held up his glass. "Drink?"

"Yes, thank you." Efrem sat down and watched Michael mix the cocktail. "You and my mother have become quite chummy of late, I understand."

"Oh? Where did you hear that?"

"Here and there," Efrem said noncommittally.

Michael shrugged and handed Efrem the cocktail. "Your mother and I enjoy each other's company. I see nothing wrong with that."

"Ellen said it was Lorrie you were interested in."

"Your wife is imagining things. Lorrie's just a kid."

"She's all grown up, according to Ellen. I'm sorry I was away on business while she was here. I understand my sister was also here and not feeling very well."

"She left to join her husband in Los Angeles. She asked about you, naturally."

"You met Susan?"

"I had that pleasure." Michael sipped his martini. "A beautiful woman."

Efrem smiled. "She always was. I haven't seen her in quite a while. I'm afraid I was never very close to my family."

"I find that odd, especially knowing how very close you've always been with the Nightsong family. Leon in particular."

Efrem blushed. "Leon and I more or less grew up together." His hands were trembling slightly and he set his glass down.

"So I heard," Michael said pointedly. "You and Leon were quite close according to what your mother told me."

"Like brothers."

"Just brothers?" Michael said insinuatingly.

"What else?" Efrem found he couldn't look him in the eye.

"Leon Nightsong is an extremely handsome man, as are you." Michael noted Efrem's discomfort with a sly smile.

"What are you trying to say, Michael?"

"Say? Nothing. Your mother likes to talk when she's had a couple of drinks. There was a slight...indiscretion, I understand, concerning you and Leon. At least that's what she implied."

"I have no idea what you're talking about," Efrem said, fighting to keep his hands still.

"I see nothing to be embarrassed about, Efrem. I've been guilty of the same kind of indiscretion myself. There's nothing wrong with it."

Efrem forced himself to pick up his glass and swallow some gin. He didn't like the way Michael was looking at him.

"How old are you, Efrem?"

"Thirty-seven. Why?"

"I hope I look as good as you when I'm thirty-seven."

"Thank you."

Michael leaned forward, putting his elbows on his knees and cradling his glass between his hands, turning it slowly back and forth. All the while he kept his eyes fixed on Efrem. "Do you ever think about making love to a man, Efrem?"

"Good Lord," Efrem breathed, trying not to look guilty or self-conscious.

"I've tried it on a number of occasions. Is it wicked of me to admit that?"

Efrem saw now that Michael was slightly drunk. Michael had raised his glass and some of the cocktail was sloshing down over his vest, unnoticed.

"I'm no judge. Do whatever you like."

"I'm embarrassing you, I see." Michael leaned back and smiled rather suggestively as he crossed his legs. "My apologies."

"Just what are you leading up to, Michael?" Efrem frowned at him. "Why are you talking to me this way?"

Why indeed? Michael asked himself as he looked at Efrem. He guessed it was because he needed to have a hold on everyone he came in contact with. It gave him a feeling of power to be able to manipulate people. He enjoyed preying on a person's weaknesses. If he could lure Efrem into bed it would be like having extra insurance on his unstable life. Even if Lorna tired of him and Lorrie's parents refused to accept him, he'd have Efrem to fall back on, at least until something better and more profitable turned up.

"I'm making a pass at you, Efrem," Michael said evenly.

Efrem rubbed his sweaty palms on his trouser legs. He started to reach for his glass again, but didn't trust himself not to knock it over. "Good God," he gasped.

"Aren't you just a little bit tempted?" Michael asked.

Of course he was tempted. Efrem had been attracted to Michael since the day they'd met at the Astor Bar in New York. He didn't like to think that he frequented that particular bar because he'd heard it catered to a rather discreet sprinkling of homosexual men.

He'd never given in to his secret urges since his marriage to Ellen, tempted though he had been. Now he was being openly propositioned by one of the most attractive men he'd ever seen and it frightened him.

Efrem said, "I'm a very happily married man, Michael."

"You didn't answer my question. Aren't you just a little bit tempted?"

Efrem swallowed the lump in his throat. "Not even a little bit," he managed. The words came out with an effort.

"Ah, that's too bad." Michael smiled again and got up to fix himself another drink. "But I must warn you, Efrem, I don't intend giving up on you. You're quite a good-looking man. Very sexy," he slurred.

"Cut it out, Michael."

Michael swayed slightly. "I bet nobody ever told you that you had a terrific ass."

"Shut up!"

Neither of them saw Lorna standing at the half-opened door. They didn't know she was there until she greeted them. "Good evening, Michael," she said, glowering at him. One look and Michael knew she'd been listening. "Efrem," she said, kissing his cheek. "This is a surprise. When did you get back from Chicago?"

Efrem was completely unnerved. "This afternoon," he stammered. "I thought I'd come over and catch up on the latest news. Susan was here with her family, I understand. I hope you don't mind that I let myself in with my old house key."

"No, no. This is your home. The servants are off this evening."

"Susan wasn't feeling well, Ellen told me."

"She wasn't, but then she up and left very abruptly. I tried to get her to stay on, but she wouldn't think of it. She seemed to be rather angry with me about something. I never did understand your sister."

"You never understood me either, Mother."

"True. You were always a source of great concern, but you never wanted anyone's help, especially mine or your father's."

Efrem slapped his thighs and got up. "Well, I won't keep you from your guest," he said, glancing at Michael.

"Stay, darling. We were planning on going out for dinner, but we can at least have a cocktail together. I haven't seen you in weeks."

"Sorry, Mother, but I promised Ellen I'd be right home. I just wanted to find out what was happening with your lawsuit against Lydia."

"The lawyers tell me she's fighting it, of course. I'm not concerned. I'll get what I want, which is everything she owns."

"Your spitefulness is going to be your undoing one of these days, Mother."

Michael spoke up. "I think your mother is right to take everything she can get from Lydia Nightsong. As I understand it, it was your father who got Mrs. Nightsong started in the first place."

"No one helped Lydia," Efrem argued. "She did it all by herself, and I'll stand against you on this, Mother," he threatened.

"You always did prefer the Nightsongs to me, especially Leon," she snapped.

Efrem found himself blushing again. "Leon is the only friend I ever had, except for Ellen. And I would appreciate it, Mother, if you would not gossip about me behind my back." Again he glanced at Michael. "Ever since I can remember, you've been saying the most malicious things about Lydia Nightsong. I see now that you'll say awful things about anybody, even your own son." He pushed past her and walked out of the room, slamming the door behind him.

Lorna turned on Michael. "What in God's name are you up to, Michael?"

"Up to? What do you mean?" He looked as innocent as a babe.

"You know goddamn well what I mean. I heard what you were saying to Efrem. Christ, Michael, have you no morals at all?"

He grinned. "Would you be attracted to me if I had?"

She waved his remark away. "You're a monster. I didn't mind your playing up to Lorrie so much. At least she was female, though far too young for you to take seriously. But another man!"

she gasped. "That's fiendish. You're some kind of animal."

Michael saw her disgust and tried to placate her. "I was only toying with Efrem, Lorna."

"You were more than toying with him. You were deliberately trying to seduce him. And don't tell me that you wouldn't have gone through with it if my son had weakened. Thank God he proved himself a man, which is more than I can say for you, Michael."

"Now wait just one damned minute, Lorna. I'm as much a man as any you've ever met."

"You call yourself a man when you're capable of going to bed with other men? That isn't a man by my definition." She felt herself losing control. The specter of Efrem's indiscretion with Leon Nightsong so long ago kept coming back to haunt her. She found that type of physical coupling degrading and disgusting; it utterly offended her sense of decency.

"It's filthy and loathsome and I really think I'm finally seeing you for what you are, Michael. I want nothing more to do with you. I will not have you in this house, knowing that you represent a perverse threat to my son's morals."

"You're blowing this all out of proportion, Lorna," he protested. "You heard what Efrem said. He'll have nothing to do with me."

"And I heard what you said. You won't stop trying until you get whatever it is you want out of Efrem. I know my son, Michael. He's weak. I'm sure you are also aware of that fact. He'll succumb to you eventually; you won't let him alone until he does. Well, I have no intention of allowing that to happen in my own home." She twisted the handkerchief in her hands. "I should have known better than to trust you, to let you get me drunk enough to say things I'd regret later." She put back her head and shut her eyes. "I've always been weak when it came to men I wanted to possess and be possessed by. Efrem is right. I'd destroy anyone to get what I want." She scowled at him. "But I am not weak now and I am not blind. I want you to leave this house, Michael, and never come back. And if I ever see you even speaking with Efrem, I'll have steps taken against you."

Michael was frightened, but he forced himself to stay calm. He smiled at her. When he reached for her, she pulled away. "Just what kind of steps could you take?" he asked smoothly.

"You forget that Lydia Nightsong came here to warn me about you. Perhaps I'll do a little investigating on my own into your past. If what Lydia told me is true, I'm sure it will be a simple matter to take care of you through the proper authorities."

"Don't do this, Lorna."

"I saw what hell Efrem went through after his unfortunate experience with Leon Nightsong. He tried to kill himself with drink. His conscience tore at his heart and mind every hour of every day. I will not allow Efrem to go through that misery again, no matter what it costs me. You won't destroy the only son I have left. I won't let you."

"You can't get rid of me so easily, Lorna," Michael said.

"Can't I? Just watch and see."

"It might prove rather difficult getting rid of a son-in-law...or more exactly, a grandson-in-law."

Lorna glowered at him. "What are you trying to say, Michael?"

He smiled sweetly. "Lorrie wants to marry me. I doubt if anyone will change her mind once I run to her, as I have promised to do."

Lorna dropped her handkerchief and tightened her hands into fists. "Don't you dare touch Lorrie."

He grinned maliciously. "I'm afraid you're a little late with that warning, Lorna. Lorrie has already fallen in love with me. She wants me to come to Los Angeles so that we can elope."

"What kind of insanity is this? Do you think that after I've telephoned Lorrie's parents they'll let you within a foot of her?"

"You know I'll manage it somehow," Michael said. He paused. "But there is a much more civilized way of handling all of this, Lorna."

Lorna straightened her back and folded her hands in front of her. "Such as?"

"You want me out of your life and away from your family. The only way I can possibly manage that, Lorna, is with your help. I'll need money. Lots of money."

She laughed in his face. "What audacity you have, Michael. Do you think for a moment that I'll pay to be rid of you when I hold all the aces in my hand? I'm sure Lydia meant well when she came here to warn me about you. Knowing her, she wasn't bringing idle gossip. I misjudged that woman on many occasions in the past. And I'm afraid I did so again when she came to see me the last time." She pointed to the door. "Get out of here, Michael. Leave this house and never come back."

He stood glaring at her from under his heavy brows. "I have nowhere to go without your help."

"That isn't any concern of mine. You've shown yourself for what you are, and I want no part of a pervert like you. You are obviously capable of anything, so long as it keeps you in creature comforts."

He nodded. "Yes, you're right. Lorna. I'm capable of just about anything." He took a threatening step toward her.

"Don't touch me, Michael."

He grabbed her wrist before she knew what was happening. He twisted it hard, almost breaking it. Lorna groaned in pain as she doubled over. Michael clutched the emerald necklace from around her neck and ripped it off. He pushed it into his pocket and said, "You have money in your third-floor study safe. I want what's there."

"Michael, you're hurting me."

"I'll do more than hurt you, Lorna. Now come with me and no tricks. And so help me, if you try to scream it will be your last. Upstairs," he ordered, shoving her roughly toward the foyer.

Lorna winced with pain as he propelled her to the door and up the stairs. She cursed herself for having sent the help away so she and Michael could have the house to themselves after dinner. She tried to think.

All of a sudden she remembered the gun she kept with her valuables in the safe. It wasn't loaded, but Michael wouldn't know that and she could threaten him with it. The idea calmed her as Michael rudely pushed her up the last flight of stairs and into the small study.

"Open it," he demanded. "And hurry up. I don't want any funny business."

Lorna stumbled toward the picture. She swung it back on its hinges, and for a moment she found she couldn't remember the combination. Tightening her nerves, she began twisting the dial. She retained enough presence of mind to remember to keep herself between the safe and Michael's eyes. The steel door opened quietly. The small Derringer was lying on top of a stack of bills. She saw Michael move to grab the money. Quickly she shoved her hand into the safe and took the gun in her hand.

She spun around, pointing the muzzle at his heart. "Just one more step, Michael, and so help me God I'll put a bullet in you. I'm an excellent shot, in case you're interested." She kept her voice low and menacing and fought to keep her hand steady.

"You fool." He took a step closer.

"Stay back," she warned. "Just turn around and walk out of this house and never come back. We'll forget all this. But if you ever try to contact Efrem or Lorrie, I'll see that you're put behind bars."

"Okay, okay," he said, holding up his hands. He started to back away. On top of a long, low cabinet just inside the door was a collection of bric-a-brac, pictures in heavy frames, an ornate gold clock, and other dust collectors. He moved slowly, facing her all the while.

"This is very stupid of you, Lorna. You wouldn't dare shoot me. You haven't the nerve."

"Try me," she said, still brandishing the Derringer.

He bumped into the cabinet. His hand groped behind him until he touched the heavy gold clock. He put his fingers around it. "We could talk this out, if you like, Lorna."

"We have nothing to talk about. All I want to do is forget the day I met you. Now get out, Michael, and don't show your face anywhere in San Francisco again." She took a few steps toward him. "I could forgive you almost anything, Michael, because I suspected what you were and I admit I have a weakness for men like you. But what you tried with Efrem is beyond forgiving."

He had a good hold on the clock, and kept it hidden behind his back. "It surprises me that a woman with your lack of morals is suddenly so righteous."

"My morals may be base, but at least they are within the confines of normalcy. It disgusts me to know you're capable of going to bed with another man. You'd destroy Efrem if I gave you the chance. But I have no intention of giving you that chance. Now get out, Michael."

He threw the clock, striking her hard on the shoulder. Lorna cried out in pain and toppled backward. In an instant, Michael was on her, wrenching the Derringer from her hand. He was blinded with rage. He aimed the gun at her head and pulled the trigger.

"You bitch," he growled when the gun didn't go off. He started to slap her face, hitting her again and again as he pulled her to her feet. Lorna clawed at his face, and this time he hit her hard enough to send her stumbling against a table, knocking it over. Then Michael grabbed her by the hair of her head and knuckled her alongside the jaw. He held her with one hand and kept slapping, punching her with the other, while Lorna tried desperately to cover her face.

He put his two hands on her shoulders and pulled her face close to his. "I always thought you were an ugly, disgusting old bitch. Now get the hell away from me. I'll take what I want and leave. And don't worry. I won't be back. I won't have to come back, from what I see in that safe of yours. The money and jewelry should get me far away from a dirty old hag like you."

He gave her a hard shove, and Lorna toppled backward. She tripped over a footstool and was propelled headlong toward the high, multipaned windows. There was nothing to stop her from smashing against the fragile glass she'd had installed to give her an unobstructed view of the Bay, the view that had so intrigued her husband with its distant horizons.

She hit the window full force, the weight of her body shattering the delicate window frames as easily as her own pain of unfulfilled passion was shattered.

She screamed Peter's name, and knew she would soon be reunited with the only man she had ever loved. As in their lives together, Lorna realized that even in death she was again being forced to follow him. She screamed again as she fell through the window, groping for something to break her fall. Nothing did. The casement collapsed and she fell through the glass and down three stories to the hard, cold concrete driveway below.

A dead, deafening silence followed. Michael stood staring at the empty window. He ran to it and looked down. Lorna's lifeless body was lying on the cement in a pool of blood. He knew she was dead.

Hurriedly he raced to the safe and began stuffing money and jewelry into his pockets. When he ran out of the house he didn't even glance at the body lying dead in the drive. He didn't look at anything. He would never look back again, he told himself. He never had. He'd get the hell out of San Francisco tonight and nobody would ever find him.

As he hurried down the steep slope of Nob Hill, he started planning where he should go. New York or anywhere on the East Coast was out of the question. There were too many people looking for him there...and once Lorna's body was found, there would be more people looking for him here.

The only place he could go was to the west. But where?

Hawaii! He'd never been there, but he'd heard about it. Why no, he asked himself as he patted his pockets? He had enough now to make good his escape and live in comfort while waiting for the next pigeon to come along.

"Yes, Hawaii," he said, quickening his steps as he headed for his apartment. He had no intention of leaving all his expensive clothes and gifts behind.

CHAPTER TWENTY-SEVEN

Lydia did not attend Lorna's funeral. She didn't think it fitting. People might misinterpret her presence there and assume she'd come to gloat over the death of an enemy. Already some vicious gossips in Lorna's circle of friends were hinting that Lydia had somehow been behind the murder.

And it was murder. The police didn't doubt that. The safe had been found empty and there'd clearly been a scuffle. Efrem had confirmed Michael Crane's presence in the house that night; the Derringer was found with Michael's fingerprints on it; and now, Michael Crane was nowhere to be found.

Lydia's world seemed to be growing narrower each day. Leon had gone to Hawaii to try and bring back his children and Marama, if she'd come. Caroline was too quiet and remote to be very much company; she spent most of her time moping about and showed no interest in anything. Even Alice Pendergast's offer to help Caroline get a newspaper job in Los Angeles hadn't raised a spark of interest. Amelia had already gone to Paris, and Lydia feared Marcus might never come home again.

The letter she'd received from Adam had been somewhat encouraging. He was going ahead with his marriage to Pamela and he was to be officially proclaimed Lord Adam Clarendon. But he did not invite any of them to his investiture or wedding.

Caroline had taken the news well enough, but Lydia knew she was very unhappy about it.

Caroline's mind was all twisted around. If Adam was Lord Clarendon, then he wasn't any relation at all. She dwelled on the idea for a long time and even considered the possibility of their meeting again—as strangers, so to speak. She didn't want to think about facts. She only wanted Adam, and she retreated into her fantasy that he was a Clarendon and she a Nightsong, with no family connection whatsoever.

His plan to marry Pamela had come as a blow even though she'd known that was one of the reasons he'd returned to England. Still, she hadn't really believed he'd go through with it.

* * * * * * *

Lydia and Caroline were in the upstairs sitting room one day when Nellie announced that Peter Haskings had come to see Lydia.

"I've shown him into the drawing room," Nellie said.

"Thank you, Nellie. Tell him I'll be right down."

Caroline looked up from the sweater she was knitting. "He's becoming a regular fixture around here. Anything about you two that you haven't told me, Grandmother?"

"Peter is just a good friend and my attorney, of course. With the MacNair lawsuit, we've had a lot to talk about."

"You aren't fooling anyone, Grandmother. You're interested in that man. And it's not hard to see by the look in his eye that he's interested in you—and not just as a client."

Lydia felt herself blushing. "You have too romantic a nature, Caroline."

Caroline bent over her knitting. "Yes, I suppose I have," she said, thinking again about Adam. "You know, Grandmother, I wish I could be more like you."

"In what way?"

"Strong and positive about everything. You see the right and wrong of things so clearly. There are no gray areas for you." She shook her head. "I'm not that way. I get everything so confused."

"That's because you are still very young, my dear. Once you get to be as old as I am, you'll have no trouble recognizing what's right and what's wrong. You're letting your heart rule your head. It must be the other way around."

Caroline knew Lydia was referring to Adam and was sorry she'd said anything. "You mustn't keep Peter waiting. Give him my regards."

"I will."

Lydia liked Peter Haskings more than she cared to admit. She always looked forward to seeing him, but not with the old urgent impatience she'd once felt toward Peter MacNair. Peter Haskings exuded a comforting aura which made Lydia forget all her problems the moment he smiled at her. He was still a handsome man, lean and athletic with bright, cheerful eyes and a mouth so sensual it made her heart race.

She didn't love him as she'd loved Peter MacNair. Still, she loved him in a different way. This love was mature and comfortable without all the foolishness that went with youthful passion.

He was impeccably dressed this afternoon in a black suit and black tie. Despite the somber attire, Lydia thought he reeked with sexuality. And when he smiled at her she wanted only to have him hold her and tell her everything would be all right.

"Darling," he said, taking her hand and drawing her against his chest. He touched his lips to hers in a lingering kiss. Lydia trembled at his touch.

"I didn't expect you, Peter."

"I heard from Lorna's attorneys. It seems the children have decided not to go ahead with her suit against you."

"Poor Lorna. She'd be miserable if she knew." She sighed. "We were never friends, you know, but I feel so sorry that she had to leave the world in such a horrible way."

Peter lowered his head. "Yes. It was tragic." After a pause he said, "You didn't go to her funeral."

"I told you I didn't intend going. I thought my being there might be misconstrued."

"You're probably right. But the MacNair children bear no grudge against you, Lydia. I've spoken to Susan and Efrem. They are genuinely fond of you."

"As I am of them. I was going to go over and pay my respects in a little while. After the crowds thin out."

"I'll go with you if you'd like."

"Thank you, Peter, but I really think I want to go alone. I'll take Caroline. With you standing beside me, it might look as if we'd come there for business reasons."

"As you wish, my dear. Then perhaps I can take you to dinner this evening. You haven't been out of this house since Lorna's death."

"I'd like that, Peter. Thank you. I can't help taking death rather hard—even Lorna's. I suppose it's because anyone's passing is a reminder that we all must die."

"You'll never die, Lydia. I won't permit it." He kissed her again. As he eased her away he asked, "You haven't been questioned by the police, have you?"

"The police? Why would they want to question me?"

"They approached me with some rather vague questions. I think they were just covering all the bases to make sure you had nothing whatsoever to do with Lorna's murder."

"Lorna may not have been murdered, Peter. It could have been an accident."

"That's unlikely."

"Michael Crane, as we found out, was a cruel man, but he was no murderer."

"It's that report we obtained on Crane that the police found most interesting. They heard that you'd hired detectives through me to investigate him and thought there might be a connection between you two."

"I hope you explained the reason for my interest in Michael."

"I did. They seemed satisfied, but I thought they might have been to see you themselves."

"No." She sighed. "Of course, I couldn't blame them for being suspicious of me. I had every reason to want Lorna dead."

She shook her head hard. "I don't want to think of how she died. I want to remember her as she always was—strong and willful and determined. She was a lot like me in that she fought for what she wanted. Actually, I admired her in a way.

As for her weakness concerning men.... Well, we all have our share of weaknesses. She must have been a very lonely woman, thanks to me. I never wanted us to be enemies. It's just that we happened to fall in love with the same man." She blinked back her tears. "They are both gone now. I pray that Lorna and Peter are together somewhere."

Peter Haskings saw her sadness and tried to make light of it. "They'll be together until you show up on the scene. Then the trouble will start all over again."

Lydia had to smile. "Yes, I suppose you're right. However, I don't intend joining them for a long, long time."

"That's my girl," he said, taking her in his arms and kissing her lovingly. "If you're sure you don't want me to go to the MacNairs' with you, I'll run along, Lydia. There are some things I should attend to. I'll call for you at seven-thirty."

"Fine. And Peter," she said, "see to it that MacNair Products is given back to Efrem and Susan. If they want it, that is. "

"I've already spoken to them about that. Efrem's content to let things stay as they are. MacNair Products has never been so profitable. He'd like to continue as its president, of course, but is satisfied to have the company remain a satellite of Empress Cosmetics."

"Whatever he wants he'll have. Assure him of that."

"Why not tell him yourself when you pay your respects."

"I will."

She walked him to the door and kissed him again. "What a dear, sweet man you are, Peter Haskings."

"I'm never going to let you forget that, Lydia. Just keep remembering that I love you very much. Nothing would make me happier than your becoming my wife."

She drew back a little.

"I could make you happy, Lydia. I know I could."

"Yes, perhaps you could, Peter. I just need a little more time to think about it."

"Please don't take too long. I want to be a husband to you while we are both still young enough to enjoy it."

She kissed him again. "I'll expect you at seven-thirty."

"I'll be here."

Lydia closed the door and started back to the upstairs sitting room where she spent the next hour considering Peter's proposal. She knew it was time to start making a life for herself. Caroline would be going off again somewhere soon; she was already showing signs of restlessness. Leon was in Hawaii, and there was no telling when he'd be back, or if he'd be back at all. If Marama refused to give up the children, she knew Leon would stay—if only for his sons' and daughter's sakes. And Marcus? She shook her head sadly. She had no idea how any of that would turn out. During those last few days before Amelia left for Paris, Lydia had seen a side of Amelia she'd never noticed before. That quiet, lovely young girl had changed into a determined woman who had no intention of letting anyone or anything stand in her way. Nothing could intimidate her, not the threat of a war nor Leon's warning that Marcus might refuse to see her.

"He'll see me," Amelia had stormed, "if I have to tear down the door to get to him. And once I do, I will drag him out of there by the hair of his head if necessary. By God," she ranted, "he won't run away from me this time. Cruel as it may sound, he has only got one leg where I have two. I am going to remind him of that, and if he's hurt by it, then that's just too bad. He'll have to live with it, just as I will have to live with it. I am going to pull out all the stops. This is a win or lose situation, and I definitely do not intend to lose."

How it would end, Lydia couldn't guess, but seeing the fire in Amelia's eyes, she was betting on the girl.

Lydia wished she felt as sure about Peter Haskings as Amelia did about Marcus. She decided to stop worrying about it all for now and went in search of Caroline. She found her lying across her bed daydreaming again.

"I want you to come with me to the MacNairs', Caroline. It's time we both paid our respects."

Caroline sat up and said, "Yes, we should have gone before this. I'll change my dress."

Only the immediate MacNair family was gathered in the drawing room when Lydia and Caroline were ushered in by the maid. Efrem was the first to greet them. Lydia hugged him and offered her condolences.

"I'm so very, very sorry, Efrem."

"I know you are, Lydia. It's too bad Mother never allowed herself to become your friend. I tried to get her to come around, but you know how stubborn Mother could be."

"Susan, my dear," Lydia said as she kissed her cheeks. "Why must we always meet under unhappy circumstances?"

"I had intended to come to see you when I was here last, Lydia, but unfortunately I wasn't feeling all that well." She patted her stomach. "I'm expecting again."

Lydia hugged her tight. "How marvelous for you." She smiled at Sean. "How are you Sean? My heartiest congratulations to the new father-to-be."

"Thank you, Lydia."

Lydia looked around. "Where are the children?" she asked as she accepted Sean's hug.

"The boys are napping," Sean said. "Lorrie's upstairs. She should be down in a moment."

"And your wife and daughter, Efrem. They're well?"

"The baby has a slight fever, so Ellen thought it best to keep her at home."

While Lydia was making her condolences, Caroline was following in turn. Caroline said to Susan, "I'm so pleased about your new baby. When is it due?"

"Oh, I have another four months, but as you can see I'm already as big as a house so I guess it's going to be a regular little bruiser."

"Like his father," Caroline said, smiling at Sean. She thought she saw a strange flicker in his eye, but he returned her smile.

Sean said to his wife, "You're jumping the gun, darling. It might turn out to be another girl, you know."

"Whichever," Susan said. "It will be ours, Sean. That's all that's important."

Sean put a protective arm around her. "That it will, love. Ours and nobody else's."

"Sit down, Lydia, Caroline," Efrem said, motioning to the divan. "I know this is going to sound unfeeling of me, but I want to say it nonetheless. Now that Mother is gone, I do hope we can all become closer friends."

"I'll insist upon it," Lydia said. "After all, I was almost your stepmother, remember. I want you to come to me whenever you like. And if you don't visit me very often, I will be quite annoyed."

Susan laughed. "She's sounding like a member of the family already."

Lydia turned to Efrem. "Peter Haskings told me you don't want MacNair Products separated from the parent company."

"That's true, I don't. I think it only sensible to continue on as we are. As for the fifty percent divested interest Father had in Empress Cosmetics, we intend forgetting all about that. We know he would have willed it to you if he'd thought about it, and we want you to have it."

"No. I have something else in mind concerning that fifty percent of your father's. I'm having my attorney get together with your mother's estate lawyer. I want you and Leon to be partners, Efrem. I'll remain as the figurehead, but the conglomerate will be yours and Leon's. My son and Peter's son. It's what your father and I wanted from the beginning."

Caroline leaned forward. "What about Marcus, Grandmother?"

Lydia knew what she meant. If anyone was entitled to control both Empress Cosmetics and MacNair Products it was Peter and Lydia's son.

"Marcus never had an interest in the cosmetics business, as you well know. Don't worry, he'll be more than amply provided for. He'll be able to build all the racing cars he wants, which is all he's ever wanted to do anyway."

She wasn't ready to tell the MacNairs about Marcus yet. That was an unfinished story, and no story is worth being told until it has some kind of an ending, happy or sad. Marcus's tale would resolve itself in time. But for now, it remained incomplete.

Lydia turned to Sean. "I'm hearing brilliant things about you, Sean. The moving-picture business! How very exciting."

"I never thought I'd become interested in anything like that, Lydia; but, believe me, it's where the money's to be made. Naturally I'm keeping a tight hold on the distilleries just in case the flicks turn sour, but I doubt they will."

"And you've moved to Los Angeles."

"We're building the most beautiful house," Susan gushed. "You must come and visit."

"Indeed I will."

"You too, Caroline," Susan insisted. "Once you see Hollywood you'll never want to leave. It's the loveliest place on earth...all sunshine and excitement."

"I may take you up on that," Caroline said.

Suddenly Susan had a great idea. "What exactly are you doing now, Caroline?" She asked. "Is there anything holding you here in San Francisco?"

Caroline glanced at her grandmother. "No, not really. Why?"

"Why don't you come back with us when we leave? The children are such a handful, what with my expecting again. You'd be wonderful company for me. It would be just like when we were girls in school together." She laughed. "Remember how I used to have to sneak out of the house to meet you for fear Mother would find out I was friendly with a Nightsong?"

Sean saw Caroline hesitate. "There's a tremendous lot of very handsome young men down there, Caroline. They'll dance you off your feet. You'll like it, I'm sure."

"Well...."

Lydia pressed her hand. "I think it's a marvelous idea. Since you got here, you have been doing nothing but moping around and making me feel twice my age. I insist you go."

"Do come, Caroline," Susan pleaded. "We'll show you the time of your life, and there's scads of room. I'll be starting with the inside decorations when I get back, and you'd be such a help.

Please say you'll come."

Caroline really wanted to go to England, which she knew was the last place she should go. Perhaps a visit with Susan might help settle her mind. She and Susan had always been able to talk openly about everything. "Sure," she said. "Why not. I have been a bit restless here of late. And my friend, Alice Pendergast, is down there. She's asked me if I'd be interested in working with her." She looked at Lydia questioningly. "But I don't want to leave you alone, Grandmother."

"I won't be alone, Caroline. I have Efrem and his family now, and Leon will be coming back soon. Besides, since when have you started worrying about me?"

"That isn't fair. I've always worried about you."

"Then stop worrying about me. I have always been quite capable of taking care of myself. I insist you go and lead your own life, just as I've always led mine. It's only natural. Besides, I may not be completely alone for too much longer," she said, thinking of Peter Haskings.

Caroline winked at Susan. "Grandmother has a new beau."

"Caroline!" Lydia admonished, feeling herself blush.

With an impish little giggle Caroline said, "Peter Haskings. He's mad about her."

Lydia switched at her skirts. "Stop this, Caroline. You're embarrassing me."

Efrem turned to his sister and Sean. "Peter Haskings is the most eligible bachelor in San Francisco," he explained. "Quite a dashing devil. He's perfect for you, Lydia."

Lydia's face was flaming now. "You're as bad as Caroline, Efrem. Kindly stop trying to pair me off like some ugly maiden aunt."

They were all teasing her and in high good humor when Lorrie walked into the room. The young girl glowered at them, letting her eyes come to rest on Lydia. Her brows curled into a hideous frown. "This is supposed to be a time for mourning," she stormed. "It sounds more like a New Year's Eve party."

Susan said, "We were only trying to forget our grief for a

moment, Lorrie. Sit down, dear. Lydia and Caroline came to pay their respects."

"We don't need your sympathy, Mrs. Nightsong," Lorrie said.

"Lorrie," Sean warned. "Watch your manners."

Lorrie stood her ground. "How can you all be so nice to this terrible woman? She's the cause of everything that's happened, and here you sit treating her like some dear, dear friend."

"She is a dear friend," Efrem said harshly. "More of a friend than you'll ever know."

"She's a monster who was responsible for Grandmother's death," Lorrie charged. "Grandmother would be alive today if it hadn't been for her."

Lydia stood up and started toward Lorrie. "You're upset, child. I was only trying to warn your grandmother about Michael Crane. I wish to God she had listened to me."

"Don't you dare even mention Michael's name," Lorrie cried. "You are not fit to speak of him."

Lydia looked at Susan and Sean. "I learned some unpleasant things about Mr. Crane's past and thought your mother should know about them. I came to tell her what I'd found out. Unfortunately, Lorna wouldn't listen."

"Lies. All lies," Lorrie shouted. "You always wanted to make Grandmother unhappy. Everything she had you wanted. You were jealous of Grandmother's friendship with Michael."

"Lorrie," Lydia said smoothly, "you know that isn't true."

"It is true."

"Stop it, Lorrie," her father said firmly. "You're acting like the child you are."

"Lydia Nightsong wanted Michael for herself," Lorrie cried.

Lydia placed herself directly in front of the girl and pointed an accusing finger. "I happen to have seen you and Michael together in the garden the day I came here to speak with your grandmother. I'm sure Lorna had no idea what was going on between you two, but as God is my witness, Lorrie, I would have moved heaven and earth to get that evil man out of your lives."

Lorrie's hands tightened into fists. "Don't you say another word against Michael. I love him and I intend marrying him."

Sean jumped up. "Lorrie! Stop it. How can you even think such a thing after all that's happened?"

"And just what did happen, Father?" Lorrie said, jutting out her chin. "Grandmother was forcing Michael to sleep with her. He told me." She saw their astonished looks. "You all still think of me as a baby. Michael was the only person in the world who treated me like a grown woman. He told me the hold Grandmother had over him. She was forcing him to find out things for her that would be helpful in her lawsuit against Mrs. Nightsong."

Efrem bristled. "You don't know what you're saying."

"Oh, don't I? I know more than you think. Michael's written me everything."

"Written you?" Sean said, staring at his daughter. "When? Where?"

"I called him on the telephone when mother forced me to leave here. I told Michael where to come for me. We were going to elope. We still intend to do so, in case you're interested."

"Like hell," her father yelled.

Lorrie remained unfazed. "And who is going to stop us?"

"I'm warning you, Lorrie. Show a little more respect or I'll put you over my knee and tan you good."

"Threaten all you like. Father. I happen to know where Michael is and I intend going to him."

"You know where he is?" Efrem said, aghast. "Where?"

"Someplace where you'll never find him. What happened to Grandmother was an accident. He wrote me about it." She saw her mother's questioning look. "Don't worry, Mother, his letters didn't come to the house. He told me he'd write in care of General Delivery at the post office. We've since made other arrangements, now that he has a permanent address in—" She stopped abruptly.

"In where?" Efrem urged.

Lorrie stuck her tongue out at him. "Do you really think me

so stupid as to tell you? Never." She turned back to her parents. "Grandmother tripped and fell out that window. Michael had nothing to do with it. As for the money and stuff, Grandmother gave it to him. Michael told her he was going to marry me, and she wanted him to have something to see us through until he could get situated."

"Good God, Lorrie," her father said. "Do you actually believe all that rot?"

"It's the truth. You're all against Michael. I know that and Michael knows it too. He won't come back because he knows none of you will even listen to his side of the story. My marrying him should help convince at least a few people that he didn't do anything criminal."

"Regardless of what you say," Sean said evenly, "you will never marry that man."

"You can't watch me night and day, Father. Oh, I'll marry Michael, you can count on that. And," she said angrily, turning to Lydia, "if you think Grandmother was a formidable enemy, just wait until you find yourself up against Michael and me. I don't know how, Mrs. Nightsong, but I'm going to get back everything you took away from my grandparents." Lorrie turned around and stomped out of the room. Lydia had been sure that the rift between Lorna MacNair and herself had finally been closed. Now she knew it would be opened even wider by Lorna's granddaughter.

"I'm sorry about that, Lydia," Sean said as he glowered at the door through which Lorrie had disappeared.

"I'm afraid," Susan said, "that we have always been too lenient with Lorrie."

Sean started for the door, his knuckles white with fury. "I intend to start rectifying that right now if I have to beat some sense into that little hellion."

Lydia grabbed his arms. "She's only a child, Sean. Leave her be. Just make certain she has nothing to do with Michael Crane, if for no one else's sake than her own."

"You can count on that," Sean swore.

Remembering the look of determination and defiance in Lorrie's eyes, Lydia doubted that anyone would be able to control the girl.

CHAPTER TWENTY-EIGHT

For the first time in her life Amelia discovered that she had a spine. All the way across the country and during the stormy voyage over the rough Atlantic, she thought of nothing but how she would get Marcus to come home. She decided that if he refused to return to America, she would go with him wherever he wanted to go. Just being with him was all that mattered. From the time she'd first met him so many years ago, she'd known that Marcus was the only man she would ever love, could ever marry.

She'd been a fool not to have given herself to him the last time she was here. Why had she refused him? Marcus was the one she wanted as her first—and last—lover. And afterward, if he deserted her, at least she would have the memory of a perfect love.

This was the beginning of 1914. The Victorian Age was finished, Amelia reminded herself. It was time she became as modem as the year. Having nearly lost Marcus because of her prudish pride, she was ready to adopt a whole new set of values. No longer would she be the quiet, demure Amelia Wilson. She would change, just as Marcus had obviously changed. If he wanted a slut in his bed, she would be that slut. If he wanted to throw himself naked into a public fountain, she'd have her clothes off before he'd unlaced a shoe. To think of life without him was the most terrible thing she could imagine. She thought often of his having only one good leg and, perverse as it seemed, found herself loving that deformity. She wanted to fondle it, to kiss it, to make love to it, just to prove how unimportant it was to her, just to prove she loved his half leg as much as she loved and adored the rest of him.

Paris was cold and snowy when she checked into the Hotel Marjorie, a quiet, inexpensive place just around the corner from the Sorbonne. She'd chosen it with the thought that if Marcus did agree to leave that brothel with her, he wouldn't want to be taken someplace where people would gawk at him sitting helplessly in a wheelchair, or hobbling about on crutches. The one problem she hadn't solved was how to get into the brothel to see Marcus. Leon had given her the address and told her of the madam who was obviously being paid to protect Marcus from any and all outsiders. And what of this Denise Leon had mentioned?

"Well, the women are the least of my problems," Amelia told herself as she hurriedly unpacked. "How to convince Marcus to come away with me is going to be the toughest part."

It didn't take her long to unpack the few dresses and underthings she'd brought with her. She slid the single suitcase under the bed and lay down. Every time she closed her eyes she could feel again the sickening roll of the steamer and hear the icy waves pounding against the hull. She'd originally planned to go directly to Madame Claire's, but now she reconsidered. It was night and the brothel would be too active. Amelia decided to wait until morning when things would be quieter and the house asleep.

She got up and forced herself to eat dinner at the little restaurant adjacent to the hotel. Whether the food was good or bad, she didn't notice. Several men openly flirted with her. Two were bold enough to ask if they could join her. She told them both that she was waiting for her husband. Secretly she was pleased that they'd found her attractive. It helped restore her flagging confidence. She was still beautiful. She'd make sure Marcus noticed that.

* * * * * * *

At ten o'clock the following morning she had croissants and coffee in her room, dressed carefully in her most expensive street dress, and hailed a taxi. She gave the driver Madame Claire's address. She noticed his raised eyebrows and wondered if he was reacting to the address or her fluent French with its American accent.

The brothel's façade was innocuous enough. There were no red lights burning over the door, no gold cupids. That's how Amelia had pictured it in her mind, and she was a little disappointed by the rather austere reality.

A thick-necked, tough-looking man with bulging muscles under a dirty undershirt answered her second ring. "What do you want?" he asked angrily. "We're closed." He started to shut the door.

"No, wait, Monsieur. I would like to speak with Madame Claire."

"She's still in bed."

"It's very important," Amelia urged. "I've come such a long way. Couldn't I wait for her?"

His eyes moved over her body. "You looking for a job?"

She jumped at the excuse she'd been searching for. "Yes. I have nowhere else to go," she lied. "Please, Monsieur. Permit me to wait until Madame is up."

He hesitated again, then swung open the door. "Very well. Come this way," he said after she'd stepped into the large entry hall. He moved toward a small sitting room.

The inside of the house didn't disappoint her. It was everything she'd imagined a brothel would look like. There were red carpets and gold cherubs and ostentatious chandeliers of tinkling crystal prisms...and mirrors, mirrors, mirrors. Pink ball fringe edged the heavy draperies that kept out even the most insistent sunbeams.

The room reeked of stale liquor and dead cigars, only slightly diluted by the telltale aroma of women's bodies drenched in cheap perfume and seldom-laundered clothes. The atmosphere of the place was sickening, but Amelia closed her eyes to everything except her reason for being here. Somewhere up those stairs Marcus was lying, perhaps asleep, perhaps trying to move about. It took a tremendous effort on her part to hold on to the bottom of the chair in which she was sitting. She wanted to race up the stairs and fling open every door until she found her love.

She wasn't too surprised when Madame Claire finally came into the room. She looked exactly like Amelia's fantasy of a whore. Madame Claire was a large woman who at one time must have been extremely beautiful. But now her skin was sagging and her waist had long since thickened. She was pulling on a loose pink dressing gown with feathery hem and collar as she walked over to Amelia and frowned down at her.

"Well? Turk told me you were looking for work."

Amelia stood, feeling a bit unsteady. "Yes. I've had a rather unfortunate experience and I find myself somewhat stranded."

"American?"

Amelia nodded. "I came to Europe a few months ago," Amelia lied. "I thought my companion was a gentleman." She lowered her eyes. "He was not."

Madame Claire laughed. "None of them are, honey." She sat down in a flurry of pink feathers and rested a fleshy arm on the back of an ornate divan. She let the dressing gown fall open, and Amelia couldn't help noticing that she wasn't wearing anything underneath.

Madame Claire eyed Amelia closely. "So your boyfriend walked out and left you unprovided for."

Amelia nodded, trying hard to look lost and forsaken.

"You're dressed pretty classy," Madame Claire noted. "The guy must have been rich."

"Very rich and very generous...at first."

"Yes, they all eventually get tired of the same old hole. Men are like kids on a carousel, always wanting a different saddle to ride." She kept studying Amelia. "You don't strike me as any ordinary whore."

Amelia couldn't help herself. She felt her face get hot and knew she was the color of the red carpet on the floor. She stiffened her spine and boldly met Madame Claire's accusing eyes.

"I am not a whore, Madame. I happen to have come from a very distinguished family in New York. I have only been with a few men and I personally chose them. I have always been rather select."

"You got class all right, pretty one." She leaned toward Amelia, spreading her legs apart. "But you won't be doing much choosing if you work for me, I can tell you that right now. You'll go with whoever I tell you."

Amelia lowered her eyes again. "Unfortunately, Madame, I am in no position to dictate any terms of my own. I need somewhere to stay, somewhere to work until I can afford to pay my passage back to New York."

"Seventy-thirty," Madame Claire said, slapping her thigh and leaning back. "It's the best split you'll find in Paris. I treat my girls right—feed them, clothe them if necessary, and give them a roof over their heads. I run a good, clean business here, and I don't take any crap from anyone, not customers, not employees. What I say goes. I am not a greedy woman. I'll see to it that you get enough work to salt away money for your passage back." She laughed. "Maybe after you see how good I treat my girls you won't want to leave."

Amelia forced a smile. "That's a possibility, of course, Madame."

"Good. It's agreed. When do you want to move in?"

Amelia shrugged. "I have nowhere to go and no money. If it is all right, I would like to start work now."

Again the fat old madam laughed. "You're in quite a hurry. Ain't been laid since the old boy left you high and dry, huh?" She lumbered up off the divan. "Nobody works during the daytime unless under special circumstances. I'll have Turk show you up to a room." She looked around. "Don't even have a suitcase, I see. He sure did leave you without a pot to piss in, didn't he? Must have been real anxious to get rid of you." She squinted at Amelia. "You ain't one of those troublemakers, are you?"

"No. It was nothing like that. I'm afraid I got a little too friendly with a business associate of his and found myself locked out of the hotel suite."

"Well, I guess we can fix you up with whatever you'll need. Borrow an evening gown from one of the girls upstairs. They won't mind. Later on you'll have enough to buy your own things. I let the girls out every other afternoon to do their shopping and personal stuff. Work starts at five o'clock, and I don't tolerate anybody being late."

Amelia nodded. "I understand, Madame. And thank you."

Madame Claire stood eyeing her. "Yeah, you got class all right. The boys are going to love that. And I don't have to tell you to go out of your way to cozy up to the rest of my girls. They always resent a newcomer. But you're one of the family now, and I expect everybody in my family to get along."

"You'll get no trouble out of me, Madame."

"Let's hope you're right."

As she followed Turk up the long flight of stairs to the second floor, Amelia looked around for the stairway Leon had mentioned, the one that led to the third level where Marcus was living. She saw no sign of it.

"From the outside," she said casually to Turk, "I noticed that the house has three floors."

"The top one ain't never used except for storage and stuff."

"Madame Claire said I might find some things I need. I'm afraid I came here with just what I have on my back. Would there be any dresses in the storage upstairs?"

"Don't know. Never go up there."

"Could I check and see?"

He shrugged. "I suppose. The stairs are at the far end of the hall. But I'd ask the old lady's permission before going up if I was you."

"Yes, I'll do that," Amelia said, but of course she knew she wouldn't.

"I suppose the girls are all still asleep?" Amelia said to Turk when he showed her into the drab, sparsely outfitted little room. It had a single bed with an iron headstead, a washstand, bidet, and toilet. A sagging bureau rested heavily against the far wall, and there was a large oval picture of three horses' heads over it.

"They don't usually get up until around noontime."

"Then I think I'll sleep awhile myself," Amelia said as she yawned and started to remove her hat and gloves.

When the door closed behind him, Amelia hurried to it and pressed her ear against the panel. She smiled as she heard his footsteps receding down the corridor. Quickly she undid the hooks and eyes at the back of her dress, let it fall to the floor, and stepped out of it. Studying herself in the full-length mirror just inside the door, she started to tremble. What she'd planned might not work, but at least she had to try, she told herself.

She was wearing the undergarments she'd bought so many months ago for her honeymoon. They were sheer and provocative and extremely sexy, she thought as she smoothed the fabric over her hips and admired the fullness of her breasts. The top of the corselet held her breasts high and full, just barely covering the brown nipples.

No one would give her a glance if she met them walking the halls wearing only her scanties. She took the small bottle of Nightsong perfume from her handbag and dabbed it generously behind her ears, the insides of her knees, and along the creamy flesh of her thighs. She'd worn shoes with high heels, totally inappropriate for daytime wear but the long hem of her street dress had hidden them. Without the skirt, the shoes made her legs long and sleekly curved. Amelia knew exactly what she looked like: a wicked, provocative female set upon seducing the man she adored.

Before she left the mirror she took out her hairpins and let down her long, lush, raven hair. She pinched color into her cheeks and smiled at herself. Her sparkling blue eyes glinted with sexual desire. She licked her lips the way she'd seen French prostitutes do just before approaching a prospective customer.

Satisfied with what she saw reflected in the glass, she left the room and stole along the corridor until she found the back stairs that led up to the top floor.

The door was ajar, and when she pushed it open she was astonished by the contrast between this room and the rest of the house. A huge skylight allowed the bright sunshine to cascade in. It was an overcrowded room, stuffed with castoffs, odd bits and pieces of furniture, fringed lamps, ornate tables, even a battered upright piano that had obviously seen many nights of long, hard use.

Marcus was lying on the chaise, propped up on his elbow and staring out the window at the street below. He didn't hear her walk in, and the expression on his face made her think he was miles away from everything, lost in his own dreams.

"Marcus." She spoke his name as if it were a prayer.

He turned slowly and his eyes widened when he saw her standing there. His whole face lit up, but as he tried to get off the chaise he was reminded of the fact that he couldn't stand without help. The reminder angered him, and his expression turned to one of dark fury.

"What in hell are you doing here?" he demanded. "And what in hell are you wearing?" Her half-naked body was the most beautiful thing he'd ever seen. He forced his eyes to hers. "I'll kill that goddamn Leon," he swore.

"Leon didn't tell me where you were. Your mother did."

"Get out of here, Amelia," he said, turning his face away.

She went over to him and sat down on the edge of the chaise. "Look at me, Marcus." And when he refused to turn, she grabbed his shoulder. "Look at me, damn it."

He sensed something very different in her, but when he turned around he was still scowling and seething with rage.

Amelia slowly lowered her face to his and kissed him gently on the lips. Marcus pulled away and ran the back of his hand across his mouth. "You're wasting your time," he snarled.

"I don't think I am. I love you, Marcus. I'll never love anyone but you."

"Then you're going to lead a very lonely life because I don't love you. So just get the hell out of here."

Amelia refused to believe him. "Why don't you love me

anymore, Marcus? Because I don't do things like this to you?" she asked in a low seductive voice as she let her hand slide over his hip and between the opening of his lounging robe. Her fingers cupped his genitals.

Marcus flinched, pushing her hand roughly away. "What the hell are you doing?"

It was the first time she'd ever touched him there, and she found the feel of him so exciting that she started to tremble. Amelia kept the purr in her voice. "I'm going to do everything you want me to do." She reached for him again, this time letting her hands play over his naked chest, pushing aside the robe until his torso was exposed. She toyed with the nipples on his chest and bent to kiss them with her full, wet lips.

Again he shoved her away. "You're crazy. Get out of here."

"I'm not going anywhere until you've fucked me. Is that the word you like to hear from your other women, Marcus? Fuck?"

"Stop it, Amelia. You're disgusting."

"That's the way you want me to be, isn't it?"

"No."

"I don't believe you. Look, Marcus," she murmured as she slipped down the top of her corselet and exposed her creamy breasts. "They're really quite beautiful, don't you think? Wouldn't you like to touch them? Here," she said as she took his hand. "Feel my breasts, Marcus."

He pulled his hand away. "Have you gone completely insane? Put some clothes on, for Christ's sake."

Amelia noticed, however, that he couldn't stop looking at her full, ripe breasts.

"I want you, Marcus. I'm not leaving here until I have you inside me. And you can't run away this time," she whispered as she put her lips close to his ear and let her tongue snake out, teasingly. She had to shock him, make him very angry. "Where would you run on only one leg?"

She saw the tears suddenly bubble up in his eyes. "Damn you, Amelia, get the hell out of my life and never come back."

"No." She took the lap robe that covered the stump and threw it aside. Marcus grabbed her arm and tried to push her away, but she hurled herself down beside him and ran her hand over the stump.

"Jesus Christ," he cried as the tears rolled down his cheeks. "Don't, Amelia. Please don't."

Amelia would not be put off. She lowered her head to his lap, moved the dressing gown aside and kissed his thigh, running her tongue up and down its length, lavishing kisses on the red, ugly scars of the stump.

Marcus grabbed her by the hair of her head and pulled as hard as he could. A strangled cry of pain caught in her throat as he brought her face up to his. He was white with rage.

"I want you out of here right now, Amelia. I don't want your fuckin' pity. I don't want you acting like some goddamn whore. If I want a fucking whore I can get a dozen of them without leaving this goddamn bed. So get the hell out. Now!"

"I'm not going, Marcus, regardless of what you do or say. I love you and you love me. I can see it in your eyes. You do love me, don't you?"

He let her go and turned away again. "No."

"Liar." She pressed her cheek against his chest and touched his face. "I can make you happy, Marcus. Please let me. What happened to you doesn't matter. I don't want to marry you out of pity. I want to marry you because I can never marry anyone else. No one will ever take your place in my heart, Marcus. I want your children. So what if you've lost several inches of a leg. What's that? I didn't fall in love with part of your leg. I fell in love with you—your soul, your mind, your voice, your dreams. I want to be a part of all of that again if only you'll let me."

She felt him heave a heavy sigh and relax back against the chaise. Idly he toyed with her long, silky hair. "I couldn't saddle you with a man like me now, Amelia."

"Saddle me? You haven't changed so much. I was blind not to see what you needed of me when I was with you last. I wanted to go to bed with you then, but my stupid antiquated principles wouldn't permit it." She took his hand and placed it on her exposed breasts. This time he didn't pull away.

"Feel my nipples. See how hard and erect they are just from your touch. Take me, Marcus. Make love to me. I want to feel you all over, kiss you all over," she said as she cupped his genitals again. "I never felt a man's testicles before. And your penis is so thick and long." She worked back the foreskin and saw the shaft begin to harden and lengthen in her hand.

She moved her head down and kissed the glans.

"Don't, Amelia. I don't want you to do that."

"Of course you do. Besides, I want to. I've heard that this is what makes French girls so in demand." She took him into her mouth. "It's very nice...so smooth and hard and big. I won't be very good at first, Marcus, so you must tell me if I'm doing anything wrong."

He was so aroused he couldn't answer. Tears were still blinding him, but all he could concentrate on was the feel of her wet, hot mouth moving up and down on his throbbing shaft.

"Ejaculate in my mouth, Marcus. I want to taste you."

Amelia continued to suck him hungrily. She noticed the thick salty taste on her tongue and, knowing nothing about ejaculation, she looked up at him and asked, "Did you ejaculate?"

Marcus had his eyes closed but there was a grin on his face now. "Damn you, Amelia, if you want to act like a goddamn whore you'd better learn to talk like one. If you mean, 'Did you come?' the answer is no. I always leak like that when I get too hot."

Amelia snuggled into his arms. "Then I've made you hot?"

"You have indeed, you little prick-tease."

"I'm not teasing. I want you to make love to me. Throw me out afterward if you like, I don't care. Right now I only want to have you take away my virginity. If you won't, no man ever will. You wouldn't want me to die a virgin, would you?"

She eased one leg across his lap and sat up. Reaching back she took his turgid, rock-hard penis in her hand and placed the head of it against the lips of her vagina. She settled down on the shaft, forcing the wide, mushroom head deep inside her. It met with a resistance and Amelia pushed down harder. Suddenly, something tore, causing a splitting pain to course up and down her back. She groaned and felt a trickle of blood ooze out of her. But she would not stop. She sat on him for a moment, her head down, her eyes closed to the pain. A short while later she felt the ache subside and she began to move up and down on him.

"Damn it, Amelia," he swore. "You're treating me like a fucking cripple." He grabbed her and rolled her onto her back, fitting himself between her yawning thighs. "This is the way I intend fucking you," he snarled.

"Yes, Marcus. Please. Take me anyway you want," she moaned as she kissed his mouth, his eyes, his cheeks, his neck. The feel of him driving in and out of her was the most delicious sensation she'd ever experienced. At last she felt fulfilled.

Marcus drove into her with such force that her teeth rattled. She clawed at his muscled back and wrapped her legs around his waist, throwing herself up to him, meeting his powerful thrusts. United completely for the first time with her lover, Amelia swore that nothing would ever separate them.

"Come in me," Amelia moaned. "Oh, Marcus, something's happening. I feel like I'm going to explode. Don't stop. For God's sake, don't stop." Brilliant flashes of color streamed across the back of her eyes, setting her brain on fire. Her whole body was alive with a tingling sensation, as if it were being scorched by tiny tongues of fire.

She felt his body stiffen as a groan tore from his throat. "Oh Christ, I love you, Amelia," he cried.

"I adore you, Marcus," she groaned as the explosion rocked her brain and every nerve in her body came alive with pleasure.

Marcus wrapped his arms around her and kissed her passionately. Amelia tried to roll him onto his side but moved the wrong way and they both toppled off the chaise and onto the floor.

They lay there laughing and hanging desperately on to one another. But when Marcus tried to help Amelia back onto the chaise he was again confronted by the rude reminder of his deformity. He fell back and put his arm across his eyes.

"Oh damn, Amelia. Why did I let you do this to me?"

Amelia knew what he meant and laughed. "Do what? I really think you have it the other way around, friend. It was you who did it to me." She kissed his mouth.

"It can't be, Amelia. You know that as well as I."

"We did it, didn't we?"

"Not that," he said irritably. "I can't have you spending the rest of your life helping me in and out of chairs and beds."

"I don't intend to," she said with a shrug. "You'll just have to learn to do those things all by yourself. I don't want to marry you so I can play nursemaid all my life. I want to marry you because I happen to be desperately in love with you. You'll learn to cope with your little loss. Actually," she said as she ran her hand along the stump and lowered her head to kiss it again, "I find it rather sexy, like an oversized penis."

"You're impossible."

"Impossibly in love with you, my darling." She slapped his belly. "Now that you know what a good lay I am, do you truthfully believe you'll be able to find anyone better?"

"Lay? Where in hell did you learn that expression?" He was smiling.

"I went to a very proper girls' school, remember. You'd be surprised to know what girls talk about when they're alone. All the niceties, that strict propriety, is just for show. Down deep, we're just as hot and earthy and coarse as any man."

"I don't believe you," he said as he turned and looked lovingly into her eyes.

"Believe me." She stood up. "Now, just this once, I'll help you to your feet, or should I say foot." She giggled.

"I can do it myself." He raised up and eased himself onto the chaise.

"See, you're making progress already, thanks to me. I'm damned good for you whether you want to admit that or not, Mr. Nightsong."

Marcus sat on the side of the chaise, his elbows resting on his knees. It was the first time, he realized, that he'd let anyone see him naked with his thick stump exposed.

Amelia saw him staring at the stump and said, "If I recall, Marcus, you had a very oversized big toe on that foot. I noticed it once when we went swimming together. I'm glad you had the sense to get rid of it."

Marcus couldn't help but laugh. "You truly are amazing. Amelia," he said as he put his arms around her waist and pulled her down beside him.

"I'm glad you finally discovered that. And remember, this was only our first time together. How did I do on my first try?"

"Magnificently."

"I'm going to get better."

"You don't have to get better."

"Oh, yes I do. I want you to show me exactly what you like. Whatever it is, I know I'll get as much pleasure out of it as you. I know one thing now, Marcus," she said seriously.

"What's that?"

"There can never be anything disgusting or wrong when two people who love one another make love."

He looked at her, seeing her completely for the first time since she'd walked into the room. "Where the devil did you get that outfit?"

"I was saving it for our honeymoon. Not too sexy for you, is it?"

"I'd like to strip you completely naked and start all over again."

"Be my guest, but you're going to have to go out and buy me another just like it."

"That's a deal," he said as he grabbed the top of the corselet and ripped it down, exposing her completely. "My God, you're beautiful," he sighed, feasting his eyes on her.

"In case you don't know," Amelia said as she reached for his penis, "so are you."

They made love again, this time more slowly but with loving passion. He did things to her with his mouth that made her flail and thrash about like a rag doll being deliciously tortured by a teasing child. In turn, she kissed every inch of him, places she never thought herself capable of kissing, but it was Marcus's body and there was nothing that didn't tempt her tongue or her lips.

The third time they started to make love Amelia asked, "Shall we try it Greek fashion?"

Marcus laughed. "Greek fashion? Don't tell me you learned about that in your proper little girls' school."

"Greek, French, Italian, and the English Rub," she said, grinning at him. She frowned for a minute. "I never did learn the subtle difference between the Greek and the Italian."

"And I don't intend showing you. It doesn't interest me. Too messy for my taste."

"Ah, but we have to try everything," Amelia insisted.

"Not today, love. If you like we'll experiment later."

She brightened. "When?"

She watched his expression fade. "I don't know," he murmured as he hid his eyes under his arm again and lay back.

"Listen to me, Marcus Nightsong or Andrieux or whatever you've been calling yourself here. If you don't intend moving out of this damned whorehouse, then I'm moving in."

He took away his arm and stared at her.

"I mean that with all my heart. I've already told Madame Claire that I came here looking for work. I'm supposed to start entertaining the gentlemen clients this evening."

"Like hell you are."

"And just how are you going to stop me?"

"Christ, Amelia, you can't be serious."

"Just as serious as you are about hiding yourself up here for the rest of your life. I mean what I say, Marcus. Either we both leave this place together or we both stay here together. I'm not budging unless you do."

"I can't—"

"You can't what?" she asked, cutting him off.

"I can't walk, damn it."

"Of course you can walk. Kangaroos have two legs and they can't walk—they hop. So learn to hop if that's what you want."

"You're being ridiculous."

"You'll walk if you want to walk. And I for one am going to see to it that you do. I won't have you staggering about on crutches or sitting like a lump in a wheelchair. There are devices. We'll have you fitted with one. It will take some getting used to, but eventually you'll be able to walk as normally as any other man."

"Almost as normally, you mean."

"All right, almost," she said angrily. "Face it, Marcus. You lost a part of your leg doing something you wanted to do. It was no one's fault but your own. Nothing will make that leg grow back, so you'd better get used to it. There are always alternatives for everything. A lousy short leg isn't the end of the world. I don't want a cripple for a husband, and I'm going to do everything I can to make sure I don't wind up with one."

She cuddled beside him. "Marcus, my love, together we can do anything we want. You can lean on me for a little while, but after that you're just going to have to lean on yourself. You can do it. I know you can."

"You always did give me the courage I never had."

"You've always had courage, I only reminded you that it is there inside you." She traced her fingertip across the fan of hair on his chest. "Just tell me one thing, Marcus."

"What's that?"

"That you love me."

He hugged her tight. "Of course I love you. I've never stopped loving you, really." He grinned. "I just got sidetracked for a while, that's all."

"Then you'll marry me?"

He fell silent, screwing shut his eyes. Amelia pushed herself up and stared at him. "Mark me well, Marcus," she warned. "You've had a sample of how good I can be in bed. But that's the last time you'll have me until after we're married. Now if you want to spend the rest of your life trying to find a substitute for me, then go ahead, but it will be a fruitless search. I was damned good, if I say so myself. Oh, just think of the beautiful babies we could have. Now that's something none of your French whores will be able to give you."

"Babies," he said with a sigh. "We always talked about wanting a big family. But—"

"But nothing. Don't for a minute think they are all going to be born with one-and-a-half legs."

He laughed in spite of himself, then grew serious again. "I don't want to be a burden to you, Amelia."

"The only time you were ever a burden to me, my friend, was when you were flapping around with those French floozies. I'm going to keep you so drained and weak and satisfied that the mere thought of another woman will make you physically ill. I'm going to buy one of those books on coital positions and memorize it. They say there are over a hundred and fifty different ones." She shrugged. "That only takes care of half a year. We'll just have to improvise for the rest of it."

"You're incorrigible."

"I'm hopelessly in love with you, Monsieur Nightsong. And now that you've deflowered me, you've got to do the right thing and make an honest woman of me."

"I really do love you, Amelia," he said, stroking her hair.

"And I love you, my dearest Marcus. I'd die if you ever left me again."

They kissed lovingly, their hearts pounding with happiness. Amelia felt him start to harden and reached for him.

"I think it's time for junior's feeding," she quipped.

He laughed as she lowered her head to his lap.

Neither of them was aware that Denise had come into the room. When she saw them on the chaise her eyes flashed. "What the hell is going on here?" she demanded.

Amelia's head shot up. She smiled and said, "Hello. You must be Denise."

The girl's anger didn't faze Amelia, who continued to smile. "I want to thank you for taking care of my husband for me."

"Husband?"

Denise glared at Marcus.

"Didn't Marcus tell you he had a wife?" She wagged a finger at Marcus. "That was very naughty of you, darling."

"Marcus?" Denise demanded. "Is it true? Are you married to this...this woman?"

Marcus lowered his head to hide his smile. "No, not really, Denise."

Amelia quickly said, "But we're as good as married. We've been engaged for years and years and when I came here I was a virgin. Now," she added, brazenly exposing her bloodied thighs, "I am a virgin no longer. Marcus will have to marry me if I am to have his child."

Denise fumed. "You are crazy. How did you get in here?"

"Madame Claire let me in. I told her I needed work, but then I found my beloved Marcus who is going to take care of me so that I never have to work again. Isn't that so, darling?"

Marcus grinned at her. "You really are crazy, you know that, don't you?"

"About you? Yes. Very crazy." She pecked his mouth. To Denise she said, "I'm taking Marcus away with me. Please show me where his things are so I can get him packed."

"Take him away? Where? Where are you going to take a cripple?"

Amelia's pleasant expression changed suddenly into such an ugly, menacing frown that Denise took a step backward.

"Don't you ever call him a cripple," Amelia warned as she got off the chaise and sprang toward Denise, her nails flashing. "I'll rip out your eyes and then your rotten heart if you so much as utter that word again."

"You can't take him anywhere," Denise said. "There is money owed to me for taking care of him."

"What money?"

"There was a man here. He said he would see that money was paid to me every month so long as I looked after Marcus."

"There isn't going to be any money paid to you by

anyone, Madame." She purposely said "Madame" instead of "Mademoiselle"—a stinging insult that infuriated Denise.

"Marcus," Denise said. "I have been very kind to you. I saw to everything. Do you owe me nothing for all I've done for you?"

Amelia stood between Marcus and Denise. "Whatever money is due you for past services, Denise, just name the amount and I will gladly pay it. But if for one minute you think that I intend leaving Marcus here, you are badly mistaken. And don't count on getting money every month from anyone. I'll see to it that you don't get another franc if you try to pressure Marcus to stay. I'm sure you were well paid for everything you did for him. Marcus is not a poor man, or at least he wasn't until he refused to accept money from the family who loves him."

Denise was astonished. "You could have had money and refused to take it, Marcus? You made Denise spend her money on you, knowing you had money of your own?"

"It wasn't like that, Denise," Marcus said. "I just didn't want anyone in my family to see me like this. I would have repaid you in time."

"Time? Look at me, Marcus. Look at my face, my body. Does Denise have time to squander on a cripple?"

Amelia flung herself at the prostitute. "I told you never to call him that." She raked her nails down the girl's cheek, drawing blood. Denise screamed and tried to fight her attacker off, but Amelia proved too strong. She easily pushed Denise against the wall and began pounding her.

The ruckus brought Madame Claire to the room. Turk towered behind her with his muscular arms folded across his chest. "What is the meaning of this?" Madame Clair shouted.

"I don't want any trouble, Madame," Amelia said. "I will tell you the truth. I came here under false pretenses. I had to find Marcus and could think of no other way. I am taking him out of here, so please don't try to stop us."

"Perhaps he does not wish to go with you, Mademoiselle."

Amelia turned to Marcus. She saw doubt and hesitation in his expression. "Do you want to come with me, Marcus?"

He lowered his head. "I don't know, Amelia." He looked around. "I'm safe and secure here. I don't have to see the pity in people's eyes when they look at me."

"Damn it, Marcus, didn't you just hear Denise call you a cripple...and more than once, too? They all pity you. They all want to be paid for hiding you away. Damn it," she swore again. "That is not the kind of life I want for you. I don't feel one bit sorry for you. You can be a whole man again, or you can stay hidden away up here on the top of a whorehouse. But when you become too costly or an embarrassment or too old, then where will you go? You don't believe for a second that they'll continue to take care of you." She flung some clothes at him. "Get dressed, Marcus. We're leaving." She whirled around, her eyes blazing. "And if any of you three think you can stop us, I would suggest you have second thoughts. I can cause a lot of trouble for you all, so kindly step aside and tell me where I can collect Marcus's things."

Denise pointed toward the adjoining room, where Amelia hastily packed Marcus's clothes and toiletries. When she came back into the sitting room, Denise was helping him on with his shirt.

"He can do that himself," Amelia ordered, shoving Denise away. To Marcus she said, "I'm going downstairs and get into my street clothes. I won't be long."

So far, so good, Amelia told herself as she started to put on her dress. And what happens when he tires of your ass, she started to wonder? She'd amuse him for a while, of course, but after that he'd have to amuse himself. This was the part of the therapy that would be difficult. Her sexual enticements could only be stretched so far. After that, it would be up to Marcus to heal himself.

She wasn't gone more than ten minutes, and when she came back upstairs she found Marcus sitting nervously in his wheelchair.

"No wheelchair," she ordered. "You'll have to manage on crutches. The chair makes you look too much like an invalid."

No one interfered with their slow progress down the stairs. Amelia both supported Marcus and lugged his heavy suitcase. Once they reached the street, Marcus turned and looked up at the third-floor window.

"Don't look back, darling. I want you only to look ahead."

"We can't go home, Amelia. I don't want the family to see me like this."

"Then we won't go home. I have a room at the Hotel Marjorie. It will serve our purposes until you decide what you want to do, where you want to live."

"I'd like to stay here in Paris for a while."

"Then that's settled. We stay in Paris."

"They say there's a war brewing."

"What of it? It can't be any more terrible than what you've been through these past months. You survived that, and you'll survive a war if there is one. We both will if necessary."

"You're quite a woman, Amelia. I never realized."

"Perhaps if I'd shown my true self a little sooner none of this would have happened."

He shook his head. "No, I would have driven in that race no matter what."

"You can still drive in races, darling. I'll never try to stop you."

He chuckled and looked down at the flapping pant leg. "You might not stop me, but that missing part of me will."

"Ridiculous. We'll have you fitted with one of those artificial things and you'll be as good as new once you get used to it." She clutched his arm and hugged him tightly. "Just don't let anything happen to that lovely big thing between your legs. I don't think I'd like an artificial one of those. A leg I can live with, even like, but I want your sex to be the real thing."

He kissed her. "I'll be careful. I promise."

Amelia hailed a passing taxi. When they were settled in the back seat, Amelia said, "You do intend marrying me?"

"Whenever you say."

She thought for a moment. "I think I'd like to wait until you can walk on your own. With a little work that shouldn't take too long. In the meantime, of course, despite what I said before, I have every intention of looking upon you as my husband. I'm willing to wait awhile for you to make an honest woman of me."

Marcus smiled and kissed her lovingly. "What will Mother say?"

"Lydia will wholeheartedly approve. I'm sure of that." They snuggled into each other's arms, totally unaware of the newsboy yelling and waving an "Extra" edition that revealed Germany's threat to declare war on Russia and France.

CHAPTER TWENTY-NINE

Though most of the country was sweltering in an August heat wave, San Francisco was comfortably cool. Dark clouds drifted across the afternoon sky, threatening rain. Lydia and Peter Haskings snuggled together on the couch, her head resting on his shoulder.

"Marcus and Amelia will soon be coming home," Lydia told him. "Marcus said in his letter that he's now able to run around like a hare."

"Good for Marcus."

"I wish they'd waited so we could have had the wedding here."

"We'll make them get married all over again when they get home. When do you think that will be?"

Lydia shrugged. "Marcus didn't say. He's all involved with building racing cars. I wrote and told him he should be doing that here in America." She sighed. "They'll come when they're ready." She laughed. "Amelia said that she's still trying to have a baby, but so far no luck. I told her in my letter that her luck might change if they tried placing the order here at home where they belong."

"Is Leon back in Hawaii?"

"He left yesterday morning. Marama is being extremely difficult. I suppose I can understand that. I know what it's like being separated from one's homeland and family." She rested her hand on his thigh. "Leon's determined to take the children away from her. He's consulted a lawyer over there to see what can be done legally."

"Speaking of which, the MacNair lawsuit has been officially dropped. Empress Cosmetics and MacNair Products are all yours now."

"Everything seems to have turned out all right. Still, I can't forget the look on little Lorrie's face when she made those terrible threats."

"She's just a child. Forget about her, Lydia."

"I only wish I could. I have the feeling that those threats weren't idle ones. That girl will cause trouble one day."

"We can worry about that day if and when it happens. In the meantime, my darling," he said, turning her face up to his, "when are you going to marry me? I'm becoming very impatient."

Lydia reached up and kissed him. "Yes, I think it is about time I set the date. How about September first."

"Do you mean it?" he said, beaming at her.

"Yes. I mean it most sincerely. I happen to be in love with you, Peter, in case you haven't noticed."

"I noticed, but I thought you still weren't sure you wanted to make it legal."

"I'm sure. I suppose with all my children away from me I'm beginning to realize that it's time for me to stop living my life for them and start doing what I want to do."

He kissed her. "You've made me very happy, Lydia."

"No happier than you've made me."

He thought for a moment. "The first of September? That doesn't give us much time to prepare."

"Let's not make any fuss, Peter. I think, in view of our ages, it should be a quiet affair. I'd like the children here, of course."

"I'll send them all cables tomorrow. Caroline will have time to get here from Los Angeles, but I don't know about Leon and Marcus." He kissed her again. "But I don't want to wait, Lydia. You might change your mind."

"No chance of that. I know that the right man has finally come into my life, and I'm not going to let you get away, Peter

Haskings." She started to get up. "I think I'll call Caroline now so she can make arrangements to take time off from her job."

"She's still working with Alice on that newspaper?"

"Yes, and she seems to be enjoying it. I know Susan and Sean will want us to spend the honeymoon down there. Caroline said their house is fantastic...a palace."

Lydia picked up the receiver and asked the operator to connect her with the Dillon residence in Hollywood. Susan answered the telephone.

"Susan? How are you, dear. It's Lydia."

"Lydia," Susan said anxiously. "I was just going to telephone you."

"You sound strange, darling. Is anything the matter?"

"It's Lorrie. She ran away last night. We haven't a clue as to where she went. I'm scared to death that she's run to that awful Michael Crane."

"Dear God," Lydia breathed. "Has she been in touch with him again?"

"We don't know. She's been acting very smug and remote for weeks now. They must have been corresponding somehow, but we've been keeping a close check on her mail and telephone calls. There was nothing the least bit suspicious. And then she just vanished. She left a note saying not to worry about her. Sean's furious, of course, as we all are. I just don't know what to do, Lydia."

"How perfectly dreadful, darling. But I suppose there's not much anyone can do. She'll show up when she's ready. At least you know she went on her own and not by force. She's entitled to find her own happiness wherever it is."

"I know, Lydia. But I'm so worried. She's just a child."

"She's a very grown-up young lady, Susan. She's going to be just fine, you'll see." She paused. "I'm not sure I should tell you why I called, what with you so upset about Lorrie."

"Why did you call?"

When Lydia announced her plans to marry Peter, Susan exclaimed with pleasure but couldn't promise to come up for the wedding in view of Lorrie's disappearance.

"I understand perfectly, Susan. Peter and I thought we'd come down after the ceremony."

"Please do, Lydia. I could certainly use your moral support right now."

When Lydia hung up she turned to Peter. "Lorrie's run off," she said. "They think she's gone away with Michael Crane."

"Good."

Lydia stared at him with surprise.

"The police have been keeping an eye on the girl, hoping she'd lead them to Crane. It looks as if their vigil is going to pay off. Lorrie will take them to Michael Crane, and that will be the end of that. I wouldn't worry about it, Lydia."

But the following day, August 3, 1914, Lydia had a new worry. Germany had declared war on France. And a day later, Great Britain declared war on Germany. She prayed that Marcus and Amelia would be able to get home safely.

Peter assured her that they would. "Nothing will ever trouble you again, Lydia," he vowed, kissing her tenderly. "I'll see to that."

"You're marrying into a very disorganized family, Peter."

"I like that idea. I've never had a family before. I hope I make a good father."

"You'll be perfect, darling. Absolutely perfect."

ABOUT THE AUTHOR

V. J. Banis is the critically acclaimed author ("the master's touch in storytelling...."—*Publishers Weekly*) of more than 200 published books and numerous short stories in a career spanning nearly a half century. A native of Ohio and a longtime Californian, he lives and writes now in West Virginia's beautiful Blue Ridge.

You can visit him at http://www.vjbanis.com

www.ingramcontent.com/pod-product-compliance
Lightning Source LLC
Chambersburg PA
CBHW050545260626
47157CB00002B/442